In One Year and Out the Other

A New Year's story collection from today's rising fiction stars!

KATHLEEN O'REILLY gives a real angel a hand in matchmaking for her earthbound ex-boyfriend in the heaven-sent tale "Halo, Goodbye" . . . **BETH KENDRICK** works out the agony of being dumped—and the ecstasy of looking toned in Marc Jacobs—in "The Bad Breakup Regime" . . . Can a New Year's smooch foretell what the year ahead will bring? **EILEEN RENDAHL** tempts fate in "Midnight Kiss" . . . The doctor-patient relationship gets a whole new twist when **TRACY McARDLE** examines the surprising revelations hidden behind closed doors in "Happily Never After" . . . **LIBBY STREET** ponders the morning after—and the pros and cons of finding a stranger in one's bed—in "The Luckiest People."

In One Year and Out the Other

A New Year's Story Collection

doWn tOwn press

NEW YORK   LONDON   TORONTO   SYDNEY

An *Original* Publication of POCKET BOOKS

 DOWNTOWN PRESS, published by Pocket Books
1230 Avenue of the Americas
New York, NY 10020

ISBN: 1-4165-0330-7

First Downtown Press trade paperback edition December 2004

10 9 8 7 6 5 4 3 2 1

DOWNTOWN PRESS and colophon are
trademarks of Simon & Schuster, Inc.

Manufactured in the United States of America.

For information regarding special discounts for bulk purchases,
please contact Simon & Schuster Special Sales at 1-800-456-6798
or business@simonandschuster.com

Contents

Contents

The Bad Breakup Regime

BETH KENDRICK

"I need pizza," Bill gasped, cresting at the top of his hundreth sit-up. "Pizza and a whole case of Sam Adams."

"You can't have *pizza*." I increased the pace of my treadmill, feigning horror at the mere suggestion of all those empty carbs and fat grams. Trying to banish the visions of Krispy Kremes dancing in my own head. "Pizza is not part of the new regime. Do you think *they're* sitting around, moping and eating pizza all day?"

"Moping, no. Pizza, yes." He gave up halfway through his hundred-and-first sit-up and collapsed back into the sweat-soaked gym mat. "They're probably scarfing down pepperoni with extra cheese right now. In bed."

And I had nothing to say to that, because he was probably

right. Together, Dan and Erika had become the embodiment of everything we couldn't have, couldn't do, couldn't be.

Before the breakup, Bill and I had known each other in a vague, friend-of-a-friend sort of way due to all the double dates we'd shared when he was with Erika and I was with Dan: dinner at Carmine's II, movies at the Westwood Mann, self-consciously ironic forays to the Hollywood Wax Museum. But not until last New Year's Eve, when Dan and Erika announced they were leaving us for each other, did we really bond.

In retrospect, the signs of impending relationship doom were all in place by Thanksgiving—Dan had started spending a lot of time "at work" and stopped wanting sex—but there are none so blind as starry-eyed girlfriends who will not see. I chalked it up to his stressful job and the chaos of the holidays. After all, he still called me "Sweetpea" and sometimes even brought me flowers for no reason. Guilt bouquets, I know now.

And Bill reported it was the same with Erika, except she used me as her alibi. She told him that she was hanging out with me on Friday and Saturday nights, that all her new lingerie and perfume had been purchased on our many nonexistent trips to the Beverly Center. He figured that girls' night out was a harmless way for her to work off all that extra energy she suddenly seemed to have and shrugged off his doubts. After all, she still called him "Honeybear" and got her forehead Botoxed in what she passed off as an effort to look even sexier for him.

We were fools. Chumps. The last to know and all those old chestnuts.

But we were in love.

So when Erika turned away from Bill at the New Year's Eve company party that she and I were required to attend every December and kissed Dan rather than her boyfriend . . . and Dan kissed her back with the intensity of Ralph Fiennes in *The English Patient* . . . and then they turned to us and explained that "they didn't want to start a new year living a lie" . . . well, it came as quite a shock. I'm told drinks were thrown in faces, although I've blocked out the details.

Luckily, my department manager was already drunk, so I still have my job. And so does Erika. But we've done an admirable job of avoiding each other since then; the unspoken rule is that she stays on the eleventh through twentieth floors of our office building, floors two through ten are mine. The lobby and the cafeteria are neutral territory, but I never see her there. She has her father's money and the love of my life—common decency dictates that she lunch at the bistro around the corner.

Erika had been my roommate at UCLA, where she slowly developed the habit of borrowing my stuff without asking. High heels, handbags, halter tops—we shared everything. I never really minded, as long as the items were returned in their original condition.

Well, this time I minded.

And Dan was not going to be returning, never mind in his original condition. "I know this hurts, but I think you always loved me more than I loved you. It's not fair to either of us." That's what he said in the breakup e-mail—yes, *e-mail*—he sent me after he packed up all his worldly belongings in the middle of the night and relocated to Erika's rent-controlled apartment in Santa Monica. Then he blocked my e-mail address on his account and my phone number on his caller ID so I couldn't respond with an appropriately scathing diatribe. Or stalk him. Or beg him to reconsider.

(Not, of course, that I ever tried to do any of those things. More than a few times per day.)

Dan moved on without a backward glance and in so doing, displaced Bill. Erika kicked him out and changed the locks even though both their names were on the lease, her main argument being: "My father owns this apartment complex." Bill, still in the first flush of post-breakup self-righteous rage, countered with "Then tell Daddy to put you up in another luxury suite, Princess," but that just got his clothes, baseball card collection, and golf clubs tossed out the window. His 1952 Topps Mickey Mantle was lost forever to the vagaries of rush-hour traffic on Ocean Avenue. It was hard to tell what he was most bitter about: losing Erika, losing Mickey, or losing rent control.

"Do you know what they're asking for a frickin' studio in Westwood these days?" he ranted when I ran into him two weeks later at my neighborhood Blockbuster.

I did know. Because now I had to pony up all the rent for the two-bedroom I used to share with Dan, who earned roughly double my salary.

So we opted for the obvious solution: moving him into my empty extra bedroom and transforming the apartment into a heartbreak recovery ward, complete with family-sized boxes of

Kleenex and a strict all-sweatpants-all-the-time policy. We shook hands and rented *Better Off Dead* to seal the deal.

By Groundhog Day, Bill and I had resigned ourselves to spending all our free weekends together, hunkered down in the living room with the shades drawn and the TV on, wads of used tissues dotting the carpet. None of our other friends could stand to hear any more about the breakup, but we weren't ready to let it go.

We tried to fill the holes in our hearts with pizza, pasta, and enough Girl Scout cookies to sustain an entire troop for a year. Blockbuster, a three-block walk from the apartment, was eventually deemed "too labor intensive." Why leave the apartment when we could order DVDs online? Our tastes in movies, though eclectic, tended toward the time-consuming and dramatic. Epic films, documentaries, and acclaimed television series—the longer, the better. Perhaps, we reasoned, healing and health would sneak up on us while we zoned out in our pj's. In that spirit we devoted February to viewing seasons 1–6 of *Sex and the City,* despite Bill's weak protests that overexposure to cosmopolitans and cute shoes would render him effeminate.

"It's official: I'm turning gay," he said glumly as we watched Carrie fling a bag of French fries across Mr. Big's kitchen. "I can feel it happening. I'm turning gay, and it doesn't even matter because without Erika, I've lost my will to date."

"You're not gay." I patted his shoulder and passed the Thin Mints. "You're a metrosexual."

"Whatever. After this, let's watch *Will & Grace* and plan my coming-out party."

• • •

The worst part (well, okay, not *the worst* part, but one of the most galling aspects of the whole affair) was that Erika had never been my obvious dating superior. She was not a willowy blonde with gravity-defying breasts about whom one would say, nodding sadly, "I always knew she would one day steal your soul mate." It's true that she'd been a little more sexually adventurous than I (her threesomes-while-in-college count stood at two; mine at zero), but other than that, we were pretty much comparable in the looks, career, and IQ departments. I could understand if Dan had left me for, say, Gisele Bunchden. I'd be bitter for a while, but then I'd resign myself to the fact than no mere assistant advertising executive could compete with a Brazilian supermodel and it was nothing personal. But the fact that we lived in Los Angeles, a city positively teeming with willowy blondes, and he dumped me for another size-8 brunette who got wicked PMS was a slap in the face.

Bill felt the same way about Dan. "I'm taller than he is and I make more money. He's not even good-looking. What the hell?"

"He *is* good-looking," I explained in between bites of my Tagalong. (Our version of Sunday morning brunch in the living room: cookies, doughnuts, chips and salsa.) "But in an unconventional, Alan Rickman sort of way."

He scratched his three-day-old stubble as he reached for the Doritos. "He'll never give her a foot rub every night after work like I did."

"No, he definitely will not." I shook my head, my unwashed

ponytail swishing against my cheek. "And she won't be able to handle his mother's constant criticism with the grace and diplomacy I did."

"Erika? Ha. No way."

We sat in silence for a moment, flailing in the quicksand of depression and burning envy.

"We were supposed to go to Paris for my birthday in April," I said.

"I was planning to propose to her on Valentine's Day. The entire sales staff at Tiffany knew my name, sports team preferences, and two months' salary to the penny."

"He used to make me heart-shaped pancakes on Saturday mornings and bring them to me in bed. Then he'd read me 'Dear Abby' and force me to have, like, a point-counterpoint debate about whatever issue Abby was covering." I paused. "Someone tacked a 'Dear Abby' column up on the bulletin board in the conference room last week, and when I saw it, I started to cry. I barely made it to the ladies' room before my boss saw me. Isn't that psychotic?"

"She used to make me take vanilla bubble baths with her. On Sunday nights. Our apartment had this gigantic bathtub in it, with all these candles around the rim."

"I remember."

He took off his glasses. "There's a store a block from my office that sells candles and perfume and whatever else it is you women slather all over your bodies in secret. It smells exactly like those vanilla bubble baths, and I hold my breath every time I walk by it so I don't have to think about them. Except, while I'm holding my breath, vanilla is all I can think about. Now, *that,* my friend, is psychotic."

Both of us grabbed our mimosas and quaffed deeply.

"But we'll show them." I brushed the cookie crumbs off the flannel pajama pants I'd been wearing since Friday afternoon, then hit Play on the remote. "They'll be sorry they ever left us."

"Yes." He licked the Doritos dust off his fingers and stroked the burgeoning paunch around his belly as we headed into our fourth straight hour of *The Sopranos.* "They'll be sorry."

Back in college, when we still fancied ourselves the *ne plus ultra* of postmodern feminism, Erika and I used to buy *Cosmopolitan* magazine on the sly, then take the quizzes together and discuss whether the guys we knew would really be turned on by "the butterfly position." And in one of the articles in one of those *Cosmo*s, a psychologist opined that dumpees often needed twice the length of the relationship to recover from the breakup. Which meant, in the case of Dan and myself, that I might be looking at two years of unremitting heartache. Bill's sentence: twenty months' hard time.

When I mentioned this to him in April (he had spent Easter morning devouring a package of marshmallow Peeps and wondering aloud if there was something wrong with both of us for not being able to move on), he blanched.

"Twenty months? Jesus, I hope not."

"I know! It's not fair! I already wasted enough of my life in love with him. Do I have to waste the rest of it trying to forget him?"

I liberated a Cadbury Creme Egg from the stash in the cupboard and flung myself onto the sofa.

"She's ruined me," he growled between mouthfuls of candy. "Ruined me! At first I thought I was turning gay, right? But no— it's worse. I'm now asexual."

"Wow. Asexual. That's pretty serious."

"Tell me about it. If there were any justice in this world, I'd be rebounding like Dennis Rodman. In fact, if this were a movie, you and I would be hooking up and starting a brave new life together."

"That's right." I nodded. "We'd realize that Dan and Erika weren't so great after all, and we'd slowly come to care for each other through a series of madcap hijinks."

"And then they'd realize that they'd thrown away the only thing that ever mattered in their lives . . . but it would be *too late.*" He took a minute to savor his cinematic vision. "Real life blows. And now, on top of everything else, I'm asexual."

"How can you be so sure?"

"The cute new hire in marketing asked me out last week."

"And what'd you say?"

He shook his head, his eyes narrowing to little slits. "I said no. She's hot, too. Blond, sexy, smart, confident. And she wanted to have drinks with me."

"You should have said yes," I told him.

"I know. I definitely should have said yes, but it's like . . ."

"I know."

"I am so sick of this. I hate thinking about her. I can't stand that I still love her."

We sat there in silence, thinking about the people we loved, who had escaped our needy clutches and started a new life together. That's the thing about being left—all you can do is peer down the path he left, wondering what became of him and why he went and how you failed him.

Less than a year ago, on the Fourth of July, Dan and I had gone down to Hermosa Beach to watch the fireworks over the ocean. We curled up together on a tiny beach towel, digging our toes into the cool, damp sand. He wrapped both arms around me and pulled me against his chest, pressing one of my hands between both of his while I smiled into the darkness. Something shifted between us that night; I felt totally loved and totally in love for the first time in my life.

"I could never ask for more than what we have right now, this second," he'd whispered into my ear.

And, as we watched explosions of color streak across the endless black horizon, I believed him. That promise of safety and solace kept me happy and blind until he kissed Erika on New Year's Eve and finally forced me to admit that my happiness had been a lie. I still didn't know when he stopped loving me. It might have been the day after his promise, it might have been months later. He might never have loved me.

Judging from his vacant expression, Bill was lost in a similar reverie of nostalgia.

"I'm very angry," I said.

"Then let's watch *Reservoir Dogs*. That's always good when you're mad."

• • •

Finally, somewhere around Flag Day, we realized that we had hit rock bottom and that, although we could grab a shovel and keep digging, we probably shouldn't.

This epiphany dawned at four o'clock on a Sunday afternoon, right in the middle of a Bugs Bunny marathon on the Cartoon Network. I was shuffling through some photos of my friend Kim's bachelorette party. This party had been held poolside at her sister's house, with much laying out and wearing of bikinis.

I was midway through a box of animal crackers when I came upon a close-up of my swimsuit-clad self from behind.

My heart stopped. When? *When* had my body become a pasty-white homage to cellulite? When had I become one of those women whom Dan was always deriding as "letting themselves go"? (By this point, I was starting to realize that perhaps he hadn't always behaved the way a soul mate ideally should.)

The photos jolted me out of my slack-jawed, glucose-induced trance long enough to seize the remote and click to the History Channel.

"Hey." Bill frowned at the sepia-toned World War II soldiers now marching across the screen. "I was watching that."

"No." I shook my head. "Listen to me. We have to stop this."

"Watching TV?"

"All of it. Watching junk on TV, putting junk into our bodies, feeding the depression. Look at me. *Look at me!*" I threw my arms out, the better to display my greasy hair, oily skin, and threadbare UCLA sweatshirt. "I've gained fifteen pounds, I haven't had my hair cut since last Christmas. I almost wore my bunny slippers to work yesterday by accident. I'm like the 'before' picture in a Prozac commercial."

"Well, what about me? I had to buy all new pants since my old ones don't fit anymore, my stock portfolio is tanking, and I don't even care. I'm getting a bald spot. A bald spot! Here!" He whipped around and pointed at the back of his head where, sure enough, I could see pale patches of skin peeking through.

"Look what they've done to us."

"No. We've done it to ourselves." He stuffed the remaining Thin Mints back into their box and trudged to the garbage to throw it away. "*They're* off having margaritas at El Cholo, probably taking your rightful trip to Paris, and here we are, turning into Cartman. It's got to stop. The new regime starts today."

The Bad Breakup Regime went like this: Eat well, go to the gym four times a week, start reading "real" books, and stop watching television except for programs on PBS, Court TV, the History Channel, and, in moments of extreme weakness, HBO.

We divided up the tasks according to ability. Bill, an accountant by training, worked up an exhaustive list of acceptable foods (e.g., carrots, tofu, poached fish, energy bars that taste like sawdust) and forbidden foods (e.g., sugar, salt, anything remotely appetizing). He even created an Excel spreadsheet to track our calorie intake and expenditure. Since I had the degree in English literature, I selected monthly reading assignments for our official Breakup Book Club (*The Great Gatsby* for July, *Great Expectations* for August, *The Bell Jar* for September, etc.). As exercise was equally loathsome to both of us, we went to the gym together to prevent lassitude and outright lies about attendance. Bill, who had slightly crooked front teeth, found an orthodontist and vowed to attain dental perfection once and for all. Twice a week we taped *Dr. Phil* and forced ourselves to watch it.

Come January we'd be cultured, articulate hardbodies. We chose role models to inspire us. (Me: Dorothy Parker trapped in the body of Rebecca Romijn; Bill: Will Rogers meets the Rock.)

Mental and physical health was right around the corner!

The regime took on a twist of revenge right around Halloween.

By then we had nearly regained our prebreakup physiques along with (for the most part) our sanity, which gave us the time and energy to contemplate the future beyond next week. One day, right after Dr. Phil had emphasized the importance of honesty with oneself and communication with others, we had a frank discussion about our progress.

"So." He kicked back on the sofa with his customary post-workout indulgence: low-fat frozen Tofutti. "How's it goin'?"

"Pretty well, actually." I was amazed at what a little more exercise and a lot less refined sugar had done for my outlook on life. "I'm feeling better. 'Dear Abby' doesn't reduce me to a mascara-smeared shell of a woman. Let's see . . . what else? I no longer have to give myself a big come-to-Jesus pep talk in order to shower or change out of my pajamas. And I think I look better."

"Definitely." He pretended to give me the once-over and an exaggerated wink.

"No, I'm serious. I'm almost back to my old weight, my

clothes fit right. A cute guy smiled at me in the parking garage yesterday, and I *smiled back*."

"Wow." He looked impressed. "Did you get his number?"

"Of course not. I don't actually *talk* to cute strangers in parking garages—that's serial-killer territory. But my point is, I didn't just tear up and start obsessing on how the only man for me is off gallivanting with my ex-best friend. I flirted back like a normal human."

"Without talking."

"Right. See, now, if I run into the same guy in the elevator or the Starbucks in the lobby, I'm all ready to go. And speaking of the ex-best friend, I haven't run into Erika at the office in . . . I don't know . . . at least three months." I frowned. "Which kind of bothers me, actually, because, as far as she knows, I'm still the unwashed, puffy-eyed loser who went to pieces after her stupid boyfriend dumped me."

He scoffed. "That is so *not* what happened."

"But I want *her* to see that, you know? She's already smug enough with her cushy digs by the beach and her vanilla bubble baths for two and her family's Scrooge McDuck vault full of cash."

"You want to talk smug, what about Dan? He's the one taking those bubble baths with her every week. Jackass," he sneered. "With his full head of hair and his pre-owned Lexus."

"But my muscle tone is a lot better than hers now. I could snap that girl like a twig. And pretty soon I'll even wear a smaller dress size. Ha! How you like me now?"

"I'm taking the Tiffany engagement ring fund and buying a car. A *new* one. It's gonna put his sorry little Lexus to shame."

"I actually read the entire front section of the newspaper this morning. I can intelligently discuss current events in the Middle East and the financial impact of the latest consumer spending reports."

"You know, I only read that *His Needs, Her Needs* book because you forced me, but it was actually pretty helpful. I'm all sensitive and shit now. I know that women want to be listened to. And to feel appreciated. And to be squired around in my brand-new luxury automobile."

"Listen to us. We're new and improved. We are great catches." I paused as a lightbulb popped on over my head. "We're too good for them now."

"That's right." He propped his feet up on the coffee table. "You know it. I know it."

But *they* didn't know it.

And that began to bother us more and more.

"I'm going to have to face them, you know. Both of them together. At the company party on New Year's Eve." My voice echoed off the high ceilings at the Los Angeles County Museum of Art.

"Hmm." Bill crossed his arms and rocked back on his heels, studying Rembrandt's *The Raising of Lazarus*.

"*'Hmm'*? I'm staring down the barrel of another New Year's Eve with my archenemies and that's all you have to say?"

"I'm thinking."

"About what? How I should get a new job before December thirty-first to spare myself the anguish and humiliation? I'm still single, not to mention extremely bitter, with no date in sight for the holidays because that cute parking lot guy never resurfaced. *Damn* him!"

But Bill had finished thinking. He turned away from the artwork with a diabolical glint in his eyes. "We should go together. You and me. To show them how well we're doing without them."

I opened my mouth to protest at the immaturity of this, then succumbed to the schadenfreude of the many comeuppance fantasies forming in my head. "Yes. To show them that we don't miss them."

"To show them that they missed their chances."

We stepped sideways to examine the next painting.

"He should know that I now have muscle definition in my triceps," I said. "Not to mention my thighs."

"She should know that I'm now the kind of guy who spends Saturdays at the museum. Voluntarily."

I rolled my eyes. "I'm not sure if I'd describe your attitude this morning as 'voluntary.' " He'd wanted to spend his day watching the Raiders game and organizing a football betting pool for his office. Only a long-winded spiel about how Erika loved museums and Dan had always refused to go, accompanied by a bribe of complimentary Lakers tickets I'd gotten from a client, had lured him into the cultural milieu.

"Were there any cattle prods involved? No. Totally voluntary.

You know me—I live for European portraiture." He sighed restlessly and checked his watch.

"Obviously."

"So we'll go together to the New Year's Eve thing," he said. "And we'll be great. We'll blow them away."

"Metaphorically, of course."

"They won't know what hit them."

"I'll buy a new dress."

"I'll get a new suit."

"We'll splurge and get our hair done at Fred Segal."

He paused. *"We* will?"

"Don't worry, you don't have to get your eyebrows waxed or your nails buffed. We'll just get the basic cut and color."

He blanched paler than Rembrandt's Lazarus at the mention of hair color. "For God's sake, woman, keep your voice down!"

"Oh, come on. You'd look great with a few blond accents around your forehead. My boss gets her highlights done there, and her hair looks phenomenal."

"Let's get one thing straight: I may be a metrosexual, I may even have watched *Sex and the City* for hours on end because I was suicidally depressed and unable to wrestle the remote away from you, but I ain't your spa buddy. I draw the line at highlights."

"Oh, come on, you're so repressed! It's a new millennium—men get highlights all the time! Look around you! Go to Skybar on any given night."

"The Euro-trash at Skybar. Yeah. I'm convinced now."

Not for the first time, I missed Erika as well as Dan. In one fell swoop last New Year's Eve, I'd lost both the boyfriend who held my hand and the girlfriend I'd gotten manicures with. "Aw, *man*. I never get to have any fun."

He progressed to the next painting. "You get highlights, I'll get a new car."

"Fine. Be that way." I planted both palms on the back of his shirt and pushed him toward the doorway. "Let's go see the Rodin gallery."

"Rodin? Now, *there's* a guy who probably waxed his eyebrows."

"Shut up, Bill."

I found The Dress the weekend before Thanksgiving when Bill and I braved the crowds at the Century City Shopping Center. Neither one of us had particularly wanted to go shopping, but then Sara, my coworker in the advertising department, had called to include me in an impromptu Friday night get-together.

I'd been enthusiastic when she first issued the invitation:

"Just a bunch of people from work having drinks and dessert at Killian's in Santa Monica."

Then I asked Bill if he'd like to come along and he shut me down faster than a hacker virus on a public PC.

"But why not? It'll be good for us to get out and socialize. And there'll be some cute single girls there. I bet you won't be feeling asexual when you see Sara. She looks like Brooke Burns. For real."

"Are *they* going to be there?"

"Well . . . Killian's *is* right down the street from Erika's apartment, and she *does* know Sara . . . but maybe they have other plans."

"We can't chance it." He held up a hand to curb my protests. "The New Year's Eve party is only six weeks away, and we still have a lot of work to do."

"Such as . . . ? "

"Such as get new clothes, new haircuts, and in my case, a new car."

"I see." I rolled my eyes. "Will I be borrowing jewels from Neil Lane and Harry Winston for the occasion?"

"If you think you can swing it, then sure, give old Harry a call."

I knew that he was right and that I was weakening only because I really wanted a mojito. (Which was verboten under the new regime, anyway.) "Why don't you just change your shirt and slap on some aftershave, and we'll just do the big showdown tonight at Killian's?"

He shook his head. "Do you want to have your first official post-breakup run-in with Dan and Erika looking mediocre when you could wait a few weeks and look incredible?"

"Excuse me. I look 'mediocre'?"

"Not *mediocre,* but . . ." He sighed over the voracity of the feminine ego. "You know what I mean. Wearing black pants and a tank top when Erika will pretty much be wearing the same thing. And Dan and I will both be wearing khakis and some standard-issue J. Crew shirt. And I still have two weeks until I lose the braces."

"Just keep your mouth closed when you smile! We still look good."

"We'll look better if we wait until New Year's Eve. That's always been the plan. Now is not the time to deviate from the plan." Ever the accountant.

I mulled this over after dinner while I struggled through four miles on the treadmill at L.A. Fitness. I could see the wisdom of his argument—we didn't want to blow our wad, so to speak, too early. Why settle for cute when you could look one-hundred percent, drop-dead, call-me-Gisele-and-put-me-on-the-catwalk gorgeous? If I waited until New Year's Eve, I'd be armed with a designer dress, professional hair and makeup jobs, and the icy hauteur that comes from knowing for a fact that you look ten times better than your rival. *That would show her.*

And Bill would be all tricked out in an Italian suit, flashing his now-perfect smile, dangling the keys to his new car. Still taller than Dan. *That would show him.*

Erika would be green with envy, and Dan . . . well even if he didn't want me back, he might finally realize what he had lost. Maybe he would leave a contrite message on my cell phone, begging forgiveness from the only woman who had really loved him with her entire heart and soul. Or picture my face next time he had sex with Erika.

By the time I collapsed on the floor mats to cool down, I had to admit Bill was right about this. Revenge was a dish best served cold, with a side of devastating good looks. So we flaked on Killian's and devoted our Friday night to scouring Bloomingdale's for outfits that would make them weep with regret.

It's not that we wanted them to be wretchedly unattractive or unhappy. We just wanted them to be slightly less attractive and happy than we were.

"Yep, that's it. That's the dress that's going to make Dan cry like Gwyneth Paltrow at the Oscars," Bill said the moment I stepped out of the dressing room in the very last dress I'd pulled from the rack.

It was black. It was slinky and low-cut. It showed off my new-found litheness to perfection. That was the good news.

The bad news: It was Marc Jacobs and cost as much as my share of the monthly rent.

"Do you really think so?" I tried to sound modest as I smoothed the silk chiffon over my hips, but I was secretly delighted. All those push-ups and cardboardlike energy bars had paid off. I was a new girlfriend's worst nightmare.

"You look like a Bond girl," he said. The highest compliment a man could bestow. "You're getting that dress."

"Well"—I frowned down at the price tag—"it's a little more than I was planning to spend."

"You can't put a price on looking like a Bond girl. Don't be insane. Cash register's over there." He pointed past the racks of coats and sweaters.

I checked the tag again, hoping that the decimal point would suddenly jump another space to the left. And I still had to pay for a hairstylist, shoes, makeup. . . .

"I have to think about it," I said sadly, turning back to the fitting rooms.

When I came out, he snatched the dress from my hands and

marched over to the line of harried holiday shoppers waiting to max out their credit cards. "You're getting this dress," he informed me. "I'll pay for it myself."

"You're not paying for it! I can't possibly—"

"Yes, you can. Don't worry—I'm really doing it more for me than for you. I *have* to see the looks on their faces when they see you in this. It'll be worth every penny," he gloated.

"You're not paying."

"I am so."

"I can't let you do this."

"Try and stop me." He whipped out his wallet. "I just got a raise."

"But what about your new car?"

His braces glinted when he grinned. "That's what we're doing tomorrow. And you're coming along in an advisory capacity."

"Oh no."

"Oh yes. *I* had to go to the museum, remember? Besides, I'd say a few hours of tire-kicking are worth . . ." He glanced down at the price tag and pretended to pass out.

"All right, all right," I relented. "I have my price, but I don't come cheap."

"Neither do top-of-the-line European roadsters."

"So which is sexier: an SUV or a convertible coupe?"

"Well . . ." I furrowed my brow and gave this question some thought while the dealership salesman with overly long sideburns glowered at me. He had tried to railroad Bill into a four-wheel drive behemoth suitable for military combat the moment we set foot in Prestige & Precision Luxury Cars, and he clearly didn't appreciate my interference. "I don't know."

I could see the salesman ("Steve," according to the embroidery on his polo shirt) taking my measure, trying to gauge my relationship to Bill. Was I the sister? The personal assistant? Or the bitingly critical and unimpressed girlfriend?

After scrutinizing my old jeans, flip-flops, and insouciant demeanor, he decided to take a chance on either sister or personal assistant. Turning back to Bill, he resumed his pitch. "The Range Rover is a babe magnet. You'll be fighting them off with a stick."

Bill shot me a look and began to toy with old Steve-o. "Really? Are you positive?"

"Swear to God, they love it. It's the Colin Farrell of utility vehicles. In fact"—he lowered his voice and adjusted the collar of his shirt—"Colin was in here last week, test-driving the floor model."

"Wow. Colin Farrell." Bill did his best impression of a starstruck tourist from Arkansas. "Well, if it's good enough for Colin . . ."

I couldn't keep a straight face any longer. "If I were you, I'd stay away from SUVs. They're a turnoff for the environmentally conscious babes, and you want to keep your options open."

He raised an eyebrow. "Environmentally conscious babes?"

"Yeah. Like Angelina Jolie, Cameron Diaz, Gwyneth Paltrow . . ."

"Okay, forget the SUV. The XK8 coupe, then?"

I wrinkled my nose at the snazzy convertible with leather seats and enough trunk space to accommodate a single box of waffles.

"Eh. It screams 'overprivileged youth' or 'midlife crisis,' neither of which applies to you."

He recoiled as if I'd slapped him. "Overprivileged youth? Midlife crisis? Really?"

Steve shot me a look that could freeze the Malibu coastline. "Oh, no, sir, quite the contrary! Just take a look at this state-of-the-art machine. This is the ultimate status car. This car lets people know you've *arrived.*"

I tilted my head, eyeballing the streamlined chrome. "Imagine this car tooling down the PCH. What's blaring out of the stereo speakers?"

Bill laughed. "Fifty Cent or Steely Dan."

"I rest my case. Cars like this make it look like you're compensating for something."

"Which I definitely am not," he informed Steve.

"You're successful, good-looking, confident," I said. "You don't need to overplay your hand."

He beamed, relishing this image of himself. "What about a sedan? Maybe a C-class in black?" He pointed to the fleet of Mercedes behind the BMWs.

"Very classy," I said. "I think James Bond would approve."

"James Bond drives a convertible," Steve said, every word dripping with acid.

And so finally, on December 31, after six months' deep depression and six months' preparation, it all came down to Bill and me (aka 007 and the Bond Girl) purring down San Vincente Boulevard in the Mercedes and Marc Jacobs.

We felt fabulous. We looked fabulous. We were locked, loaded, and ready to rumble.

Sort of.

"God, I'm nervous." I resisted the urge to wipe my sweating palms on the whisper-thin chiffon of my new dress.

"We could still stop for pizza," he offered. "Take a breather until you calm down."

"Oh, no, you don't." He had been pestering me to order a pizza since the onset of the new regime and hadn't let up for months. That's what he missed most about the old regime—thin crust and anchovies. I missed Milky Ways. We both missed beer. "The new-and-improved Bill doesn't eat pizza, remember?"

"But he *does* jones for it like a crazed heroin addict. This better be worth it, is all I have to say. They better be down on their hands and knees, begging us to take them back."

A horrible thought seeped into my head. "What if they don't even show?"

From the grim expression on his face, I could tell he'd considered that possibility. But when we stopped for a red light, he announced, in a voice of forced confidence, "They have to show. It's Erika's *job*."

"Yeah, but there are always a few people who manage to weasel out of attending. Maybe they're down with the flu. Maybe they decided to spend the holidays at her family's cabin in Snowmass. Maybe they decided to stay home and take one of their world-famous bubble baths." I took a deep breath and dug my freshly manicured nails into the soft leather seat. "Maybe we've spent the whole year psyching ourselves up for nothing."

"They'll be there," he insisted, downshifting as we approached the valet station. "I watched Dr. Phil. I went to the museum. They *have* to be there."

But the conversation kind of dried up after that.

The doorman opened the restaurant's massive glass doors and ushered us into a mob scene of clinking glasses, pounding salsa music, and illicit cigarette smoke.

"Okay." Bill straightened his silk tie as we surveyed the dimly lit throngs of my glammed-out, half-drunk coworkers. "Let's do this."

Both of us scanned the crowd, dreading but desperate for the moment we'd make contact with the old flames who'd sparked the new regime.

And then I saw her. Standing by the bar, stroking the back of a man in a shiny blue shirt, drinking what she always drank—Grey Goose and tonic.

It was Erika.

She was wearing the same Marc Jacobs dress as me.

And when she lifted her glass to her lips, I spied the huge diamond ring on her left hand.

"Oh, my God," Bill said.

"My sentiments exactly."

"Isn't that the same thing you're wearing?" He whistled long and low. "What are the fucking odds?"

But I wasn't listening to him anymore.

She had my dress and Dan's diamond ring. Hands down, no doubt about it—she had won.

I took a step back in my brand-new, bank-breaking Giuseppe Zanotti pumps, but before I could determine the quickest path of egress, she looked our way.

Our gazes locked under the spinning silver disco ball and I knew that if I retreated now, I'd go right back to spending Saturday nights cloaked in woe and ratty bathrobes and eating Oreos for breakfast. The listless sense of defeat would creep back into my heart. Well. The year 2004 might have been a wash, but I wasn't giving up 2005 so easily. She'd have to fight me for it.

And it looked as though it might come to that. She charged toward us. Bill inhaled sharply and froze in place.

"Be cool," I hissed at him. "Think about your new car out in the parking lot. You're James Bond, remember?"

"She doesn't know about the car," he hissed back. "We should have brought it inside with us."

"Well . . . just grab your Mercedes key chain and dangle it ostentatiously."

But he didn't have time. Erika was upon us, eyes flashing and arms akimbo.

"Look what the cat dragged in." She gave Bill a hard smile and leaned in toward his face, stopping just short of an air kiss. "I wasn't expecting to see you here."

He pulled back only slightly, a stalwart canary trying to stare down a grinning, sharp-fanged feline.

She ignored his expression of abject horror and finally deigned to acknowledge me. The smile vanished and her eyes narrowed as she took in my blond highlights, my newly slim frame, my Marc Jacobs frock. "Well, well, well. Nice dress."

"Yeah," I forced out. "You, too. What a . . . coincidence."

The smile blinked back on. "We always did like the same things, didn't we?" She let her gaze drift down to her left ring finger.

"So." My former best friend crossed her arms and arranged her features into what I recognized as her imitation of supreme ennui. "Are you two *together*, or what?"

"Oh. Well, no, we're just—"

"Because that would be just too funny! The four of us playing, like, romantic musical chairs!"

Bill backed off a few feet.

"You look"—I struggled for an appropriate word—"engaged."

"You noticed!" She practically gouged the diamond ring into my eye. "We're planning a June wedding at Shutters Hotel. Right on the ocean. Black tie, caviar, the works. I'm wearing Vera Wang—gorgeous Chantilly lace with a cathedral train—and Daddy says he may even be able to get Carly Simon to play the reception. I've hired Mindy Weiss to plan the whole thing, of course. . . ."

As she blathered on about the platinum-plated union that would spring from the two hearts broken on this occasion last year, I caught Bill's eye. He looked horrified.

"Hey." I cut short her rhapsody about Lily of the Valley boutonnieres. "Listen, is Dan around?"

"Oh, he's over at the bar, I think." She dug a pack of Marlboros and a lighter out of her black beaded evening bag. When had she started smoking? "Probably on the phone with his mother."

I frowned. "His mother?"

"Or should I say his *smother?* The woman who calls us three times a day 'just to check in' and invites herself along on our romantic getaways to Santa Barbara."

The initial shock wore off enough for me to register a few pertinent facts: Bill had fled to the bar, Erika was drunk, and the guy she had been stroking seductively at the bar wasn't Dan.

She pointed her cigarette at me. "Why didn't you tell me his mom was such a piece of work?"

Because I felt guilty for hating the insufferable old bat. Because I didn't want to acknowledge the cracks in our relationship. Because I thought Dan would change someday and stand up to her.

I just smiled sweetly. "Oh, she's not so bad."

She gaped at me. "She's a psycho bitch from hell. But, I mean, I'm *sure* he'll grow a pair and stand up to her after the wedding. It'll be different once we're married. Don't you think?" When she took another drag off the cigarette, I noticed new lines creasing the delicate skin around her eyes.

So this was what a year of living with Dan had done to her. I vaguely remembered feeling stressed and snappish when he was mine, but I had always chalked it up to my own unrealistic expectations. Relationships were tricky, after all, that's what everyone said. You had to work and work at them. Even with your soul mate.

"Erika . . ." But I had no idea what to say. Should I point out the flagrant tackiness of discussing her nuptials with me, given the circumstances? Should I ask her when she'd become so angry and tired? Should I warn her that even the Hope Diamond wouldn't compensate for a lifetime of Dan's mother?

The speech I'd mentally composed and revised for months about our amazing good fortune, how full my life was, and how happy Bill had been without her, never even occurred to me.

Because she had my soul mate and I'd had a narrow escape.

And here came Bill, back from the bar, with two glasses of champagne in hand and Dan trailing behind him.

Erika automatically reached out to accept one of the glasses, but he handed it to me and kept the other himself. We looked at each other in dismay and drank deeply.

Just a few months ago I would have sold my own grandmother to inspire the look on Dan's face. The man I'd given my whole heart to was staring at me like I was, well, Dorothy Parker trapped in the body of Rebecca Romijn. "Wow. You look . . ."

I tipped my head back and prepared to bask in the glow of some long overdue karmic payback.

But he never got around to selecting an adjective. Instead, he whipped around to Erika and said, in the dry tone that cut straight to the quick, "It's amazing how different this dress looks on her."

She puffed away on her cigarette and glared at him.

"You'd better get cracking if you want to get back in shape before the wedding. And how many times have I asked you not to smoke? It's against the law in here, anyway."

She tossed the smoldering butt at his feet, spun on her heel, and stalked back to the bar, where she resumed her hair-twirling, eye-batting conversation with the shiny-shirt guy.

Dan made a big show of ignoring this, focusing all his attention on Bill and me.

"What?" he said irritably when he saw the looks on our faces. "She's going to get lung cancer and die. It's for her own good."

I could see the silver glint of the Mercedes-Benz key chain in Bill's closed fist, but he didn't take the opportunity to flaunt it. He just took another sip of his champagne.

"So what's your story?" asked the man who'd vowed to cherish me forever. "Are you and Brooks Brothers here an item now?"

It was all coming back to me now: the constant sarcasm he liked to think of as his trademark. "East Coast humor," he'd called it (not that he'd ever lived east of Pasadena). Probably envisioning himself as a younger, hunkier Woody Allen without the nasty lawsuits and oedipal girlfriends.

I blinked a few times in rapid succession and tried to put together an appropriate response to this.

He motioned me aside. "Erika said you put on some weight, but you look thinner. Did you finally take my advice and stop with all those low-carb fad diets?"

I finally smiled. "So you . . . think I look good?"

"Thinner," he corrected. Then squinted and frowned. "I don't know about your hair, though. It's too blond."

And there you have it.

I excused myself and turned back to Bill, who finally asked the question that had been on my mind since Erika first started in on Vera Wang and Carly Simon:

"What time is it?"

I grabbed his wrist and checked his watch. "Just past eleven. What do you want to do?"

He shrugged. "We said we were going to stay here till midnight, reveling and rubbing our total health and happiness in their faces."

"That is what we said," I agreed.

But I looked at him and he looked at me, and we both knew that we didn't want to start another year overshadowed by the specter of Dan and Erika. Right there on the dance floor, blinded by confetti and the strobe lights reflecting off the silver disco ball, we overthrew the regime and reclaimed our independence.

"So . . . you wanna go grab a pizza, then?" he yelled over the pounding bass line.

"Sounds good." I started toward the glowing red Exit sign. "And you know what else sounds good?"

"A six-pack of Sam Adams?"

"You read my mind."

We ran out the door, buoyant and free, suddenly starving for the cool night air.

There was no line at the valet station, but since we had arrived at the party so late, the parking attendant had to sprint down the street, around the corner, and God only knows how many city blocks to retrieve Bill's car.

"He'll be back," I said, trying to sound reassuring. "I'm sure your baby is safely stowed in a secure location."

"Please. It's probably already stripped and sold for parts." He shook his head. "I might as well have left it running in Compton. This is the last time I trust another man with my valet key. The very last time!"

Someone behind us cleared her throat. "Um . . . I'm sorry, I don't mean to interrupt, but . . ."

We both whirled around to find Sara, the advertising world's answer to Brooke Burns, resplendent in a red satin minidress with a plunging neckline.

She smiled shyly at Bill, then turned to me. "Is this your purse? I found it on the back of the banquette where you were talking to Erika, so . . ."

"Oh. Yeah. That's mine." I stepped forward to claim the tiny black clutch. "Thanks."

"No problem." Her smile widened as she turned her focus back to Bill. "Hi. I'm Sara."

His eyes were the size of Frisbees. "I'm . . ."

"Bill," I supplied.

"Yes." He nodded, still staring. "Bill."

The parking attendant interrupted this little Hallmark moment by roaring up to the curb in a shiny Mercedes.

"Nice car," Sara said.

"Thanks." Then Bill did a double take. "Except that's not my car."

"It's not?" The valet emerging from the driver's side looked horrified.

"Nope." Bill pointed to the bodywork. "Mine's black. This is midnight blue."

I squinted through the darkness. "How is it that you can wear a brown and a gray sock together and not notice, yet you can discern the subtle differences between black and navy in the poorest lighting imaginable at eleven o'clock at night?"

He shrugged. "It's a y chromosome thing."

"I like guys who aren't too into their wardrobe," Sara murmured.

"How many brand-new C-classes can there be at this party?" I demanded. "If that's not your car, then whose . . ."

"Mine," came another voice behind us, this one deep and masculine.

It was the cute guy from the parking garage. No lie.

I flung myself in front of Bill and Sara and jutted out one hip, trying to appear both demure and provocative. "You're kidding."

"Nope." He held out a poorly marked valet claim ticket. "Good thing I decided to cut out early, huh?" He tilted his head and looked me in the eye. "Have we met?"

I started to blush. "I've seen you around."

"You're that girl from the parking garage at work, aren't you?"

"Uh . . ."

"I remember you. I said hello, and you ran away like I was some kind of serial killer."

"What can I say? I've been watching a lot of *Court TV* lately."

He laughed. "It's time we were formally introduced. I'm Kurt. I can provide a full set of fingerprints if you need to run a background check."

"I don't print on the first date," I assured him. Then I remembered that we weren't actually *on* a date.

Until now. "Listen." I cleared my throat and wished I'd tossed back a few more drinks to steel my nerve. "We were just going to find a low-key place to grab a pizza. If either of you is interested . . ."

Bill jumped on the bandwagon so fast, he nearly overturned it. "Yeah! Sara, you could ride with me and . . ."

"I'll lead the way to a great little dive I know on Third Street," Kurt finished. He stepped to the curb and opened the passenger door to the midnight-blue C-Class. "If I may . . ."

"You may." I body-checked the valet in my haste to clamber in.

Forty-five minutes later our cozy little quartet was pleasantly buzzed, counting down the final seconds of 2004 over pizza and beer.

While Sara chatted with the waitress, Bill motioned me in and muttered, "Remember how I said I'd turned asexual?"

"Mm-hmm." I closed my eyes and savored the fat-laden goodness of cheese, tomato sauce, and white flour.

"I'm back to being heterosexual. In fact, I'm pretty sure I felt something thaw out. Maybe it was my heart."

I opened my eyes and glanced at Sara's exposed cleavage. "Somehow I doubt it was your *heart.*"

"Shut up. I love her."

"Yes, but will Carly Simon play at your wedding?" And then I turned back to Kurt, who grinned and said, "One minute to midnight. I'd kiss you, but I don't want to scare you off again."

"Oh, I'm a whole new woman now. I like men with a hint of danger." I leaned in to meet him halfway.

And thus began Operation Over It.

*　*　*

BETH KENDRICK became a novelist "by accident" after completing her Ph.D. in psychology. Her first novel, *My Favorite Mistake,* was published in 2004 and her second, *Exes and Ohs,* will be released in April, 2005.

Beth lives in Arizona with two dogs and one major online shopping problem. You can visit her website at www.bethkendrick.com.

Resolved: A New Year's Resolution List

CARA LOCKWOOD

Resolution 128:
Make a shorter resolution list.

It was three weeks before New Year's, and Megan Hale's resolutions filled twelve typed, single-spaced pages.

They were divided into categories and subcategories; they had explanatory paragraphs, and in one case, a diagram.

And then, reading through the list, she realized that there weren't enough days in the year to possibly accomplish every last resolution. She had 528 of them.

Resolution 11:
Make better use of therapy sessions.

"Do you think five hundred and twenty-eight New Year's resolutions are excessive?" Megan asks her therapist, a woman in her late thirties, who often answers questions with questions.

"Do you think it is excessive for you?" her therapist asks.

"That's almost one and a half resolutions per day. I think it is excessive. What do you think it means that I have so many?"

"What do you think it means?"

"That I'm a mess?" Megan offers.

Megan's therapist, who does not acknowledge any self-deprecation by Megan, writes something in her notepad, then looks up from her paper.

"For next week, why don't you try picking out the ten resolutions that you think are the most important for your self-improvement," she says. "And then we can concentrate on those."

Resolution 43:
Learn to be more comfortable alone
(since most of your time is spent that way).

"What do you mean you're not going out?" says Megan's best friend, Lucy, who happens to be the sort of take-charge person that Megan aspires to be. Lucy decides things on whims, such as switching primary-care doctors regularly in order to maintain an even supply of antidepressants. "It is *New Year's Eve.*"

"My therapist says I'm never going to find anyone unless I'm comfortable with myself, first," Megan says. "Besides, you know how I feel about parties."

"Yes, yes, you're scared to death of meeting new people," Lucy says. "I know. Still, I don't think your therapist would approve of you hiding in your apartment on New Year's Eve. Not to mention, how often do I have to tell you that what you need is Xanax, not therapy?"

"Call me old-fashioned," Megan says. "I think maybe I should talk through my problems."

"I still think your problem is that you're just shy," Lucy says. "Besides, I think you have something to celebrate. How long have you been free of Mr. X?"

"Three months," Megan answers dutifully, like a recovering addict. Mr. X is her former boyfriend, the married one, who has two kids and a spacious house in the suburbs.

"I'd say that alone deserves some champagne," Lucy says. "Don't you?"

Since, at the very mention of his name, Megan feels the old, familiar urge to call his mobile phone, she does not feel like celebrating.

Resolution 2:
Do not sleep with married men.

It was never Megan's intention to be the Other Woman. Megan only wanted to be the Woman.

Not the Other One.

Other Women were deplorable and despicable. They were the ones always being portrayed on *Oprah* as the villains, the grainy photographs of women who ran off with their best friend's husband. They were always the ones who decline to be interviewed.

Besides, she didn't look like the Other Woman. She wore Gap sweaters and pants from Banana Republic, not fishnet stockings and crotchless panties. She didn't even own a thong. If presented with a garter belt and stockings, she'd have no idea how to put them on. Her sexiest pair of underwear, in fact, was made of simple black satin. She wore her dark hair in a bob, and simple, barely there makeup, and rarely wore a sweater with a neck lower than crew-cut.

Her whole life she'd only slept with five men. She could count them on one hand. It's just that the fifth one was married, and she's pretty sure that he counts for five thousand partners on the S&P Whore Index.

Resolution 301:
Only date men willing to be known
by their real names.

"You keep referring to him as Mr. X," her therapist says in session. "Why not use his real name?"

"He's still married and he has children and told me not to tell anyone his name because he feared losing his kids if his wife ever found out."

"Our sessions are completely confidential," Megan's therapist says. "You can say his name here."

"I don't know." Megan hesitates.

"By saying his name, it might help you get over him."

"That's what I'm afraid of."

Resolution 513:
Do not go out with people met in elevators.

Megan met Mr. X in an elevator at work. For nearly a year he was her Elevator Boyfriend, the cute guy she'd see in passing in the elevator some mornings and afternoons, the guy she was so terrified to talk to that she could barely even look at him directly without breaking out into a cold sweat. Of course, this happened to be the same reaction she had with every remotely attractive man she saw. She may never have learned his name except that one day, the elevator stopped completely, stuck somewhere between the seventh and eighth floors, with only Megan, her Elevator Boyfriend, and a UPS deliveryman.

"Doesn't that seem like fate to you?" Megan asked her therapist the morning she had first gone to see her, after her boss—finding her crying in the bathroom—suggested she take advantage of the free counseling sessions offered as part of the company health plan.

"Do you believe in fate?"

"Well, no—yes, sometimes," Megan said.

"Sometimes people use fate as an excuse to do what they were going to do anyway."

In the elevator, Mr. X had said, "Welcome to the seventh and a half floor of the Mertin-Flemmer building."

Immediately, Megan recognized this from her favorite movie, *Being John Malkovich*.

"And fifty other lines to get into a girl's pants," she'd said, which was the only line she could remember from the movie. It was probably the most forward thing she'd ever said to anyone, least of all a stranger. The boldness of it completely shocked her. Where had that come from?

The UPS man looked from one to the other of them, and after a beat or two, Mr. X started laughing.

"That's my favorite movie," he said.

And just like that, Megan fell in love.

Resolution 3:
Always check to see if a man has
a wedding ring before falling in love with him.

After she somehow found the will to break the long, protracted eye contact that they shared—the this-is-beyond-flirting-and-into-love-at-first-sight kind of eye contact, Megan happened to glance at his left hand, and there it was. The wedding ring. A slim platinum band.

"You're married," she'd said out loud.

"Technically, separated," he'd said.

Resolution 5:
Never date a man who uses the word *technically*.

If this had been one of her friends in the elevator with Mr. X, Megan would have said do not agree to lunch and do not give him your phone number. Because a man who is technically separated is still technically married. But Megan, who had been accused by her friend Lucy just last week of never taking *real* chances and of always *playing it safe* with love, decided that maybe she would just go for lunch.

Lunch, after all, wasn't sex. What was the harm in lunch?

Megan felt at ease with Mr. X right away—an ease that came from the sure knowledge that he was not Boyfriend Material, and therefore she didn't need to worry about whether her hair looked good, or she had smeared makeup, or that she was saying something dumb. She could relax and be *herself* for once, because there were not first-date jitters. Lunch with a married man— even a technically separated one—you see, was not a date. It was more like a *practice* date. No strings. No pressure. She already knew where this story was going to end—nowhere.

Resolution 12:
Remember that being shy is a condition,
not an excuse.

Megan has always been shy. She was born shy. Her father said, in fact, after she was born, she didn't cry for three whole days, which worried doctors, who thought she might have a problem with her lungs. It turns out, she could breathe fine. She just didn't like to put up a fuss. She was so quiet, in fact, that when she was four, her father once caught her finger in the back door of the family station wagon, and she didn't make a single sound.

Resolution 29:
Do not be afraid to talk about your feelings.

After four sessions, Megan's therapist diagnosed her with social anxiety, after Megan scored 52 of a total score of 68 on a social anxiety test, which put her as "very likely" to be suffering from social anxiety. Megan's social anxiety, her therapist said, explains Megan's fear of small talk, and the reason she has not met any new friends since age five.

Her therapist suggested, in the short term, that Megan start attending anxiety group meetings once a week. The group is made up of an assortment of people with varying degrees of functional anxiety. The worst cases, in Megan's opinion, are Ed, a self-admitted sex addict, and Charlene, a woman who sometimes locks herself in her own bathroom for days at a time.

"We are not here to judge. We're here to help," her therapist says, and the group repeats it in unison, all except for Megan, who is thinking, "But I am judging everyone else so they must be judging me."

Resolution 9:
Do not let your anxiety define who you are.

In group therapy, everyone takes turns discussing their anxieties in the first half of the session, and then in the last half of the session, one designated member of the group acts out an anxiety. Charlene's, for instance, is to be in public and hear someone laughing.

"I think they're laughing at me," Charlene says. "I know it's not right, but I can't help the way I feel."

"I once had an escort laugh at me," Ed the sex addict offers. Almost all of Ed's anxieties are related to the sex he feels compelled to have with prostitutes.

"I will validate that feeling," says Debra, the group's motherly figure, who uses more therapy-speak than Megan's therapist. "This is a safe space."

Group therapy is often referred to as a safe space, which implies to Megan that it ought to have padded walls and no sharp corners.

"Fruit loops" is what her dad would say about people who go to group therapy. But then again, Megan's dad, who worked for thirty-five years installing phone cables, also applies the term to a broad range of people, from the homeless man on the corner who talks to himself, to his neighbor who mows his lawn in circles rather than clean, straight lines.

"Megan? Do you have anything to add?" her therapist says.

Megan shakes her head no. She usually doesn't have anything to add, since her problems seem so small by comparison. She had never once considered, for instance, staying in her apartment for a full week, as Charlene once did.

Resolution 41:
Understand that just because all the single guys you meet are losers, it doesn't mean it's a good excuse to start dating the married ones.

Megan's boyfriend before Mr. X was a computer programmer named Lars (short for Larry), who never called when he said he would call. He was always promising to do something that he had no intention of doing—calling, going out, or driving her to the airport. It got so bad that Megan had taken to calling him Opposite Day Boy, since the reverse of everything he said was true. "I'll call tomorrow" meant he wasn't going to call. "I'll come over tonight" meant he would show up at her apartment the following morning around 5 a.m., after a night out of drinking with friends, looking for some drunken, booty-call sex.

Megan would not have tolerated Lars at all, except that she'd been boyfriendless for a record two years before him. She had begun to think that, at age thirty-one, perhaps she had turned the corner on boyfriends. Maybe it was all downhill from here. The pool was only getting smaller and smaller, and maybe there was someone even worse than Lars, like one of the regular guests on *Maury Povich*. At least Lars was smart and handsome. He could single-handedly beat a roomful of her friends at Trivial Pursuit, and he had such pretty blue eyes that they almost looked fake.

Still, the lying was getting ridiculous, and Megan knew she had to end things, and soon, but the thought of being thrown back into the shallow end of the dating pool had about as much appeal as a Brazilian bikini wax after a bad sunburn.

This changed at her company holiday party when she found Lars kissing and fondling one of her coworkers in the last stall of the women's restroom. He'd said, "This isn't what it looks like," and being that the opposite of everything he said was true, Megan knew that it was exactly what it looked like.

Resolution 67:
Remember that men who play games sometimes go to great lengths to look as if they aren't playing games.

The problem with Mr. X was that he was the exact opposite of Lars and all the bumbling single guys that Megan had dated, who seemed to have some sort of elaborate math equation in their heads for when to call, when to lie, and how long to keep you waiting. In other words, Mr. X did not play games. Megan decided this was probably because Mr. X was married, which meant that he had less time for games, and that he already knew how to treat a woman well enough to get her to agree to marry him in the first place.

When he said he would call, he called. He didn't forget to return her emails. Compared to Lars, he was a dream. And she told herself that it was all a platonic friendship—the lunches that had turned into a habit were simply a nice diversion. Sitting across the table from Mr. X was like eating lunch at the Art Institute. She could look but not touch. This, she thought, she could handle.

Besides, Mr. X made her feel at ease the way no man or, in fact, anyone had made her feel since she was five. It was an instant easiness in their friendship, such that Megan would often forget she'd only known him a short time.

She started telling him things she didn't tell anyone else. She talked about Lars, about her latest sexual drought, about how she feared she'd waited too long and that all the good guys were taken and she might have to face the real possibility that she would never get married.

And when he acted shocked that she'd said this and replied, "Any man would be lucky to be married to you," Megan felt her face grow warm, and the warmth traveled down her throat and into her lower belly.

Resolution 412:
Seek spiritual enlightenment.

Megan was convinced that all of her bad deeds (once the petty kind like ignoring panhandlers on the street and failing to donate money to the Easter Seals while using their address labels anyway) had been upgraded to Commandment Breakers. By her own calculations, she'd now broken Commandment Three (taking the Lord's name in vain), Four (breaking the Sabbath), Five (dishonoring parents for breaking Commandment Seven), and Seven (adultery).

Of course, Megan took some solace in the fact that adultery was number seven; it didn't even make it into the top five commandments.

Resolution 102:
Improve karma to avoid being reincarnated as Anna Nicole in your next life.

Megan decided that her usual means of improving her karma (letting people into her lane on the freeway and opening doors for the elderly) would no longer do her much good since she was now a Commandment Breaker. So, she decided to spend every Wednesday night tutoring underprivileged children.

Encouraged by her therapist, because the work involved strangers, Megan took on the project hoping that working with children would be easier than working with adults. Of course, what tutoring really amounted to was sitting for an hour across from a sixth-grader who knew more math than she did.

When Sandra, her student, whipped out a pre-algebra book, she knew she was going to be in trouble.

"What does the *X* mean?" Sandra asked.

"*X* is an unknown factor," Megan said. "You're supposed to figure out what *X* is."

"How do you do that?"

Megan wished she knew.

Resolution 66:
Despite the fact that you're thirty-one, do not overestimate your ability to be An Adult about things.

Megan's first real date with Mr. X involved salsa dancing and drinks the weekend his wife went out of town for a business trip and the children were visiting their grandparents in Florida.

They were sitting in Mr. X's car, outside Megan's apartment, when Mr. X admitted his short-lived separation with his wife was over and that he was living in the house again—naturally, sleeping in a separate room. For the sake of the children.

He then showed her pictures of his children. They had his big brown eyes.

"So you'll never leave them?" Megan asked him, feeling flushed from too many sangrias. "Or your wife?" This, of course, is what she had already gleaned from countless magazine articles and talk shows. Married men do not leave their wives. It's a fact carved in the dating Rosetta stone, right under the one that says, "If you go outdoors without makeup and in sweats, you'll invariably run into an ex-boyfriend."

"I don't think I can leave them," Mr. X said, sounding sad. Megan took this all in surprisingly calmly. After all, would she want to be with a man who would abandon his family? There was something perversely reassuring about that. If he didn't leave them, even if he'd fallen out of love with his wife, that was a level of unsurpassed commitment—a kind of commitment she'd never in a million years get from guys like Lars. And maybe if she had even half this level of commitment—just a small, part-time relationship with Mr. X, maybe this would even be better than having a whole relationship with Lars.

"If you want to never see me again, I'd understand," Mr. X said. "I probably can't offer you what you deserve, but I can't stop thinking about you and this connection we have."

And Megan, who found herself unable to stop staring at his lips, found her heart speed up at the word *connection.* That implied some hint of destiny, maybe, or of an unseen force that neither of them might be able to resist. It also implied that he had thought of her during times when they were apart, at least enough to formulate a theory about the two of them together: a connection.

But, Megan realized, Mr. X also was asking for sex. She wasn't completely mad with romantic hopes. She knew what he wanted.

And Megan decided, looking into Mr. X's deep brown eyes, that she was going to give it to him. She was, after all, tired of the one being cheated on. The one on the other side of the bathroom door from people like Lars. Why not her? Why couldn't she be a vixen for once? Do something bad? She was always the conservative one, the one who doubled the Three Date Rule, choosing Date Six as the one she preferred to have sex on. This is probably why she could count her sex partners on one hand. Few of the men she dated lasted past Date Four.

I'm An Adult, Megan told herself. I can handle this.

"So what you're saying is you want a fling? Just sex?" Megan asked him.

Taken aback, Mr. X blinked. He didn't say a word. Just looked at her. As if he was afraid of what she might say next, so he said nothing.

And Megan, who had never before even had a one-night stand or done anything so reckless as have sex just for the sake of sex, told herself that she could handle it. One night, probably. Two, at the most. She felt happy, giddy, even, at the thought of breaking her own rules, of being reckless.

"I'd be lying to you if I said I wasn't dying to touch you," Mr. X said.

His words made Megan's stomach jump. And she surprised even herself by saying, in a throaty, hoarse voice she didn't know she had, "Touch me then."

Resolution 519:
Repeat to self: I am worthy of love.

There's a man at tutoring who helps a boy across the room from where Megan is failing to teach Sandra pre-algebra. He reminds her of Mr. X in some ways. He has the same broad shoulders, the same thick neck. But otherwise, he's different. He has blond hair, while Mr. X had brown.

Even thinking about introducing herself to him makes her stomach seize up in knots and her breath come short and fast. Social anxiety, clearly, Megan thinks. She wonders, not for the first time, if being diagnosed with a condition is better or worse than not knowing something was "officially" wrong with her in the first place. While Sandra works on a problem quietly, Megan finds her eyes sliding to the spot where the man sits. She calls him Guy in Khakis, since that's almost exclusively what he wears.

"Do you like him or something?" Sandra asks Megan, catching her staring at him.

"What makes you say that?" Megan asks.

"You turn bright red every time you see him."

"I do?" Megan cries, dismayed, her hands going to her face. It's one of her ongoing fears. That she's bright red and doesn't know it.

"Gotcha," Sandra says. "You're not red. But now I know you like him for sure."

Resolution 120:
Don't be afraid to use the Law of Relativity
to inflate self-esteem.

Ed in group therapy is admitting that he has downgraded his sex addiction to simply oral sex. He calls it his Bill Clinton plan, and a few people in the group laugh at this. But Megan does not think it's funny. Megan keeps wondering why Ed always gets to talk about his addictions, when the group is supposed to analyze their anxieties.

During the Move Beyond Your Fear segment of group, the part of group therapy when a member practices overcoming a social phobia, Megan's therapist announces that Janice, a group member, will practice opening and shutting the door to the meeting room.

Janice is agoraphobic and mildly obsessive-compulsive and once missed her sister's wedding because she was afraid to open the church door in public. She had a fear that all eyes in the room would be on her.

In front of the entire group, Janice walks to the door of the meeting room and opens it and closes it ten times. When she's done, the group applauds.

Megan glances at her therapist and wonders, not for the first time, if her therapist is trying to show her that she's not as crazy as the people in group, or that she is.

Resolution 31:
Ignore your father's well-meant advice.

"How are the fruit loops?" Megan's dad asks her in one of her weekly calls to her parents' house. "Your mother told me about your therapy."

Megan's dad says *therapy* as if it were a curse word. Megan makes a mental note not to tell her mother anything again. She is forever spilling secrets. Megan's mother's loyalties have always been to her father first. They have one of those rare and loving relationships where Megan's mother agrees with everything her father says and will sometimes wait to hear her father's opinion before forming one of her own.

Megan felt sure that if her mother had to save either Megan's father or Megan from a burning building, she would save Megan's father first. And while Megan lay dying of smoke inhalation, her mother would say, "When you fall in love, you'll understand."

"They're not fruit loops," Megan says, even though she's not quite sure of this herself. "They're just people, Dad."

"Well, don't let them fill your head with a bunch of poppycock. Next, your mother will be telling me you've run off and joined the Scientologists."

"Dad, therapy is not a cult."

"You could've fooled me."

Resolution 502:
Do not assume friends will be understanding, or will even still be friends, after telling them about Mr. X.

"You are going out," Lucy says on the phone. "There's no reason for you to feel like you have to stay in. It'll be better if you get out."

Lucy grew up next door to Megan, and they used to play together in the blow-up pool on the lawn. Lucy makes friends easily, wherever she goes. At her wedding, she jokes, the guest list will be a thousand people long. Megan has trouble making new friends, but Lucy has always kept room for her in her friend roster. One of the benefits of friend seniority.

"Give me one good reason why I should go to one of those New Year's parties, pay one hundred dollars to get in, and then spend the night watching a bunch of happy couples sucking face at midnight," Megan says.

"We'll make it a girls' thing. Just you, me, and maybe Sarah."

"Sarah!" exclaims Megan. "Sarah hates me." Sarah, their mutual friend since kindergarten, has semihappily been married to Ben Bratt look-alike Luke Douglas for three years. Megan made the mistake of telling her about Mr. X after ingesting one too many margaritas. Sarah was harsh and swift in her judgment of the situation and has since barely spoken to Megan.

In fact, the stunningly brutal reactions of the first three people she told about Mr. X pretty much ensured she didn't tell anyone else about him. Each new reaction to her misdeed confirmed her greatest fear—that she was no longer a "good person who'd done something bad," she was crossing into the territory of being a flat-out bad person.

"And what about her husband?" Megan asks.

"He's got some business trip to New York, if you can believe it," Lucy says. "Sarah's solo for New Year's."

The idea of spending an uncomfortable evening avoiding the fact that Sarah so strongly disapproves of Megan's recent relationship decisions that even the breakup with Mr. X has not changed her cool distance does nothing to persuade Megan that a night out is what she needs.

"I'll think about it," Megan says. But what she really means is that she'll think about coming up with an excuse not to go.

Resolution 529:
Avoid holidays designed to make single people feel badly about themselves, such as New Year's Eve.

"How did you do on narrowing down your resolutions?" Megan's therapist asks in their private, one-on-one session.

"Not so good. I added five more."

"Why do you think you did that?"

"Do you know how they say that a child has an infinite capacity to learn? I think I have so many faults that I think I have an infinite capacity for self-improvement."

Resolution 42:
Every day, at least once a day, repeat to self that great, mind-blowing sex does not equal love.

Megan read her share of romance novels. The sort that describe in great detail all the intricacies of mind-blowing sex. Megan, while she had read about the kind of sex that was supposed to make you quiver, had technically not had *really* mind-blowing sex her whole life. She'd mostly just had Polite Sex. Gentle Sex. And Loving Sex.

Sweaty, Wake Up the Neighbors Sex only came when she started having sex with Mr. X.

In fact, she'd never, technically, it must be said, climaxed during the Polite, Gentle, or Loving Sex. She had come only during Gentle but Determined Foreplay and, a few times, during a

Loving Afterthought. But never during the act itself, and at times Megan had wondered if something was wrong with her.

But Mr. X had changed all that. Megan had guessed that part of what made the sex so good was its forbidden nature, but what Megan didn't understand until later was that the sex was so good because it had no future. There was no reason to be inhibited. She was convinced after a week she'd never see Mr. X again. So she didn't worry about the usual things like sucking in her stomach or trying to look sexy or being cautious about the sexual positions she felt put her assets at their weakest advantage. She turned herself over, wholly and without reservation, the way you might do after having a few drinks on a topless beach in a far-off country where you're sure that you'll never see any of the people around you again.

But then a week turned into a month, and a month into six, and it gave Megan time to think. She started thinking that maybe the mind-blowing sex *meant* something. Maybe, although she'd never in her life believed in soul mates, maybe, just maybe, there was something to the connection they had. The way, during sex, their bodies seemed to melt together in a heart-pounding, sweat-slicked knot, how she couldn't sometimes tell where she ended and he began, how they came together again and again, at once, in an endorphin-fueled rush.

Resolution 148:
Admit to yourself daily that you are an adrenaline junkie, and, possibly, a sex addict.

Mr. X called her twice a day. He emailed her constantly. He showered her with attention, bits and pieces of it that he could steal away from his family.

They might have been scraps, but they were heady and addictive scraps. This was probably the worst thing she'd ever done in her life, and it felt ridiculously good.

They had sex in cars, in elevators, hotel rooms, and her apartment. She gave him blow jobs in the backs of cabs, while he was driving, and once, in the office broom closet. He made her come in a million other ways—in the women's bathroom, on her desk late one night in the deserted office, in the back of a movie theater.

It was a heady, thrilling rush, like nothing she'd felt since her first sweaty groping in high school. And she didn't want it to stop. She'd never been The Vixen before, and she decided she liked it.

And while it seems obvious now, she never expected that the karmic price of having good sex would be falling in love.

Resolution 7:
You are in charge of your own destiny.
Never let someone else dictate your schedule.

And she couldn't get enough. Everything became about waiting for him to call, for him to write. Her life was an elaborate game of Red Light, Green Light.

Red Light: He can't come to meet her for drinks because his son has soccer practice.

Green Light: His wife is taking his son this time, and he has a couple of hours before he has to pick him up again.

Red Light: His wife wants him to fix the roof, so he can't come over.

Green Light: He and his wife are fighting about the roof, and he's leaving.

Red Light: He has to be with his kids and he can't have dinner.

Green Light: His business meeting was canceled; he can spend the whole afternoon with her.

Before long, Megan couldn't tell if she was addicted to Mr. X or the idea of waiting for him.

Resolution 10:
Prepare to have bad-parking karma the rest of your natural born life.

Megan circles the tutoring center for an elusive parking space. She doesn't find one. After looping around four times, she gives up and parks a block down on the street. On her way in the door, she sees Guy in Khakis, who is up ahead of her, holding open the door for one of the elderly tutors. He glances up and catches Megan's eye and gives her a half smile that reaches his eyes. Hurriedly, Megan looks away, and her eyes fall to his left hand, where she sees no wedding band.

"Hi," says Guy in Khakis.

As usual, when addressed by a stranger, Megan panics and stares at her shoes, then walks past him at a quick pace.

Resolution 89:
Work on strengthening core female friendships.
Or find new friends.

"Lucy told me that you think I'm mad at you or something," says Sarah, Megan's married friend, on the phone, catching Megan by surprise at work. The tone of Sarah's voice implies she is, indeed, mad.

"Why did Lucy say that?" Megan asks cautiously.

"She says you won't go out with us on New Year's because you think I'm mad at you." Sarah is blunt and to the point. She has been since age eleven, when she told Megan she really ought to look into shaving, since she was beginning to develop underarm hair.

"Well, *are* you mad at me?" Megan asks.

"Look, I don't agree with what you did, but, whatever," Sarah says dismissively. This is as close to a pardon as Sarah is willing to get.

Resolution 458:
Come to terms with that you may not ever be happy.

Megan once read an interview with Melanie Griffith, who met and fell in love with Antonio Banderas when they were both married to other people. She said that she and Antonio decided that even though it was going to hurt their spouses, they had to take a chance to be truly happy.

Megan, who could not imagine making a declaration like that, wondered if happiness was like a rare artifact. Only the determined and skilled will find it.

"What if you can't be happy unless someone else is unhappy?" Megan asks her therapist.

"You can't be in charge of someone else's happiness," her therapist says. "You can only really be responsible for your own. What will make you happy?"

"Someone else."

"Happiness comes from within," her therapist says, sounding like a fortune cookie.

"But what if I'm not capable of happiness?"

"We're all, to some degree, capable of happiness."

Resolution 199:
Do not dwell on the past.

Because Megan's mother adored Megan's father, they were a couple like none other Megan knew. Whereas most of her friends had mothers who were bitterly disillusioned with their husbands and had marriages in various states of decay, Megan's parents were always sneaking off on trips together, giggling behind closed doors, looking startled and springing apart if Megan came home early from school when she wasn't expected.

Megan found herself sometimes wishing her parents were like Lucy's, who had a bitter divorce when Lucy was nine. It was wrong, Megan knew, but she couldn't help it. Lucy became the central focus of everything. Custody battles, visitation rights, the back-and-forth art of gift one-upmanship as both parents tried to prove their love for Lucy with extravagant gifts.

Megan on the other hand felt as if her parents sometimes forgot she was even there at all.

Resolution 89:
Try not to judge others.

"I don't think I can do this," says Pam in group therapy. Pam has a fear of writing in public places. She is convinced that her fingers are too short and too fat and that people stare at them and make judgments. It's why she wears gloves most of the time, even in June.

"Go at your own pace, Pam," suggests Megan's therapist.

Pam is attempting to fill out a bank deposit slip while the group watches. Her hands are starting to twitch.

"We are not here to judge," says Megan's therapist. "Right, everyone?"

"We are not here to judge," says the group in unison. This is one of many group chants, including "You own your anxiety; your anxiety does not own you."

"I like your hands," Ed the sex addict tells Pam. "I think they're very feminine."

Pam blushes and smiles, then finishes filling out the deposit slip, which she holds above her head.

The group applauds.

Resolution 13:
Do not, under any circumstances, call Mr. X.

Mr. X had no social anxiety at all. He mingled at cocktail parties as if he were born to do it. He was the sort of person who knew the first name of the guy at his dry cleaner's and his favorite restaurant. He wouldn't let a taxicab driver take him anyplace without striking up a conversation with him.

Megan admired this. She, in fact, has a history of being attracted to extroverts. Outgoing people, after all, need a willing audience, and if there's one role she was designed to play, it is audience member.

Mr. X's outgoing nature, however, led to complications once they started seeing one another. She had to avoid public places, and she had to abide by a few of his rules.

Megan could only call Mr. X's mobile, and then, if he answered with "Hello," she knew he was in his wife's company and she'd have to make the conversation brief, while Mr. X pretended he was talking to one of his softball buddies.

If Mr. X answered "Hello, sexy," she knew she was in the clear, and she could talk to him at length. Of course, there were other rules. She was not to call after 9 p.m. any night of the week. Weekends were off-limits, as well as holidays, which he spent with his in-laws. And she could not call several times in one night, especially if his wife was there, for fear of rousing her suspicions.

And at times, when Megan sat alone in her apartment, the thought of Mr. X at home, cozy in bed with his wife, spooning, would drive Megan nearly insane. She would write him long, anguished letters that she'd crumple up and never let him read. She'd cry and curl up on her bed and wonder why, if Mr. X felt a tenth about her that she did about him, he couldn't manage to leave his family.

And then Megan would sometimes think maybe she was a masochist, that the only sort of relationship that could make her happy was one that drove her insanely jealous, one that opened her up to tiny hurts every day. Since every night he turned away from her to go back to his wife.

But then, during a stolen hour, Mr. X would tell her how much more beautiful she was than his wife, how much more sexual she was, how she was simply *more*.

He would whisper, "I've never felt this way before," in her ear as he held her close. He filled her with reckless hope by saying, "I think we were meant to be together," and, "I wish I could live my life with you." She filed these sweet words away and would bring them out again when she started to have doubts, when she wondered if he really loved her. And though she knew it was dangerous, she let herself dream.

And then she told herself to be patient.

One day he would come to her.

Resolution 304:
Stop saying "I'm smarter than this"
every five seconds.

"How did you feel about Mr. X's children?" Megan's therapist asks in their private session.

It should have bothered Megan that he had children, but it didn't. When she heard him talk about them, so lovingly and so profoundly, she realized that he was aeons ahead of the guys she'd dated in the past, who couldn't manage to commit to a brand of toothpaste, much less the possibility of having offspring. And instead of making him less attractive, the children made him more attractive. He became like some sort of Super Dad: sensitive, nurturing, and with a deep and seemingly endless capacity to love.

"I knew that he would never leave his wife because of the children," Megan says. "And this was okay with me. I reminded myself of this often."

"Did it help you control your expectations?"

"I didn't really want him to leave his family. I mean, if he left them to be with me, then he'd grow to hate me, wouldn't he? His wife would turn his children against him, and eventually I'd start distrusting him, wouldn't I? Thinking he was having an affair? In the movies, these things work out, but in reality, I knew it wouldn't."

"Do you think maybe you were looking for a complete family? Maybe dating a married man helped you feel like you were dating a family and not just a person?"

Megan thinks about this. "Maybe." Megan sighs. "I still wanted a happy ending, though."

"And what ending would that be?"

"Maybe that his wife runs off with another man and I'm there to comfort him?" Megan says, partly joking and partly serious.

Megan's therapist is silent, as she usually is when she's judging something Megan has done, but doesn't want to add to the guilt spiral she has already diagnosed.

When the silence goes on a beat longer than Megan feels comfortable with, she says, "I used to think I was smarter than this."

Resolution 401:
Make more of an effort to meet new people.

"Tell me about Guy in Khakis," Lucy says at Cosi's, their favorite sandwich shop. "Any new news?"

"He smiled at me the other day," Megan says.

"That's a start. See? You see that there are so many other options out there for you? You don't need Mr. X."

"A smile hardly counts as a relationship. Besides, it was probably just reflexive."

Lucy sighs and looks to the ceiling. "Sarah's going to join us for lunch," Lucy says suddenly.

"What do you mean?"

"She wants to prove to you that she isn't mad."

Resolution 212:
Resist carbs in all their evil forms.

"You've always been shy, but I don't think that's a good reason for therapy," Sarah says, arriving in time to hear the tail end of one of Megan's group-therapy stories.

"It's not just about being shy," Megan says.

"Well, I'd rather shoot myself than tell a bunch of strangers my problems," Sarah announces.

It's moments like these when Megan really thinks she should work on being able to make new friends.

"Are you on a diet?" Sarah demands, watching Megan pick at her salad.

"Yes," Megan admits.

"I hope it's not that anticarb thing," Sarah says. "That's supposed to be terrible for you."

Megan shrugs. "Well, short of stomach surgery, I have to do something, or else I'm just going to keep marching up in dress sizes." Megan doesn't add that while she was dating Mr. X, she was stunningly thin: the combination of being so in love she couldn't eat, and that she was having so much sweaty, calorie-burning sex that every muscle in her body felt sore.

"You're fine," Sarah says dismissively. Sarah can eat anything, in any quantity, and never gain weight. She's a perpetual size 6.

"I'm going to go get more iced tea," Lucy says, jumping up. This is her way of leaving them alone so that they can work out their differences.

Megan and Sarah fall into a small silence.

"So," Sarah says. "I have one question for you, and then we can drop it."

"Drop what?"

"You know what." Sarah's talking about Mr. X.

Megan steels herself. "Yes?"

"What did he say about Mrs. X?"

Resolution 50:
Remember that even though a man says he's no longer in love with his wife, it doesn't mean that he's ready to leave her.

What didn't Mr. X say about Mrs. X? Megan thinks. She wanted to know everything, and he told her everything. How she'd lost interest in sex after her second child was born. How she started insisting that the lights be off during sex. How she had never, even in the early days, been willing to swallow. How she didn't like to receive oral sex, and how over time their sex life had just disintegrated to a bimonthly union of obligation.

How now he sees how different they are: She likes to go out, he likes to stay in; she wants to travel, he wants to save up money for retirement; she doesn't read newspapers and doesn't care about politics; he's a news junkie. They have nothing to talk about anymore, he says, except the children.

"What do you mean, what did he say?" Megan asks cautiously.

"Did he talk about her at all, that's what I want to know," Sarah says.

"Yes, a lot."

"And didn't that make you feel bad? I mean, *I* could have been Mrs. X."

"You aren't anything like Mrs. X." Megan doubted that Sarah had such severe hormonal mood swings that she'd throw a toaster at her husband, as Mrs. X once did.

"What did he say about her?" Sarah persists.

"He complained—a lot. But, he stayed with her in the end, so I don't think it much matters what he said. I'm sure most of it was lies. You can't really trust a man who cheats on his wife, you know."

Megan, proud that she'd actually absorbed something she'd learned in therapy, gives Sarah a weak smile.

Sarah bites her lower lip. "I think Luke is cheating on me," she says, then starts to cry.

Resolution 99:
Use powers of deduction for good, not evil.

Having been the Other Woman gave Megan a unique perspective into cheating situations. She knew, for example, that they were never as black-and-white as presented on *Oprah*, and that seldom did someone really deserve to wear a red *A* for Adulterer.

You don't, for instance, need to punish Other Women; the relationships they're in are punishment enough. The constant jealousy, the hurt of always coming in second, the seemingly endless parade of personal slights (not being able to properly celebrate her birthday since it fell on a Saturday; the flush of anger when Megan once attempted to hold Mr. X's hand in public; going a full two weeks over Christmas without hearing from him once; his admission that he still has sex with his wife, and while it isn't good sex, it's still passable, even at times enjoyable).

For a time, Megan even envied Mr. X's wife. She could exist in ignorant bliss of what was really happening. She could pretend that everything was fine. Megan was the one who lay awake nights wondering if Mr. X was even, at that moment, in the arms of his wife. Or worse, that he thought of her not as someone to love, but as a problem to fix. Maybe, at this moment, he was standing in front of his mirror practicing his breakup speech.

And the alternative wasn't much better. If Mr. X showed up on her doorstep with his packed bags, she wasn't sure she would really want to take him in. Would she want to live with the knowledge that he would probably, eventually, tire of her too?

Resolution 301:
Do not pass judgment on others, even if they are all too willing to pass judgment on you.

"What makes you think Luke is cheating?" Megan asks, alarmed.

"I caught him online," Sarah says. "He was in an adult chat room."

Megan exhaled. "That's nothing. That's just basically porn." Megan sighs. "It doesn't mean anything."

"He was watching a woman masturbate!" Sarah exclaims.

"Watching, not touching."

"Dr. Phil says that's one step away from cheating."

"He's probably not cheating." Megan fails to add that if he were getting some *in person,* he probably wouldn't resort to risky online camera flings.

"How can I find out for sure?"

Megan sighs. "What, am I the infidelity expert now?"

Sarah doesn't say anything.

"Check his mobile-phone bill." Megan sighs. "And his ATM records."

Resolution 209:
Resolve the following question: If a good person does bad things, does that make her a bad person?

"You should feel good about helping a friend," Megan's therapist says. "You're taking a bad personal experience and using it to help others. Doesn't that make you feel good?"

"It makes me feel like I'm a big raging whore," Megan says.

"What did we say about labeling? Labeling doesn't help anyone. And most often, you're the one putting on the labels. Not other people."

"I used to think I was a good person," Megan says.

"Good and bad are relative terms."

Resolution 190:
Read *All I Really Need to Know I Learned in Kindergarten.*

"Why don't you write him a note or something?" asks Sandra, Megan's student in tutoring, as she catches Megan staring at Guy in Khakis. This is what Megan usually does when she likes someone, she stares at him, trying to work up the nerve to say something to him.

"Why a note?"

Sandra shrugs. "That's what we do. Or you could send him a text message—that is, if you know his cell phone number."

"What should I write?"

"Ask him if he wants to go with you—duh."

Resolution 95:
Be more open to group therapy.

"You've been very quiet these past few sessions," Megan's therapist tells Megan in group. "Is there something you want to share with the group?"

Megan looks around at all the eager and friendly faces. "I don't know what to say."

"Whatever you feel like talking about. You're in a safe space," Megan's therapist says. A few of the others in group nod their heads.

"I miss my ex-boyfriend," Megan says. "And I fear that I won't ever meet anyone new."

More people nod. They are so encouraging that Megan decides to take an extra step.

"Our relationship was wrong. He was married. But I think I liked the fact that our relationship was secret."

"I think everyone can relate to not wanting their personal affairs public," Megan's therapist says.

"It's a common symptom of social anxiety," adds Charlene.

Megan feels relief, and for the first time, acceptance.

Resolution 523:
No matter how obvious it is that the cup is half-empty, tell yourself it is half-full.

Talking about Mr. X makes Megan feel relief and yet, at the same time, the urgent need to call him. She hasn't felt this strongly about contacting Mr. X since the weeks after their split, when just about anything would make her want to call Mr. X—a Charlie Kaufman movie on cable, walking by the same restaurants they visited (always the dark ones in out-of-the-way places), seeing a couple in a movie theater kissing (as they had done in the back rows of so many dark, nearly empty theaters). In fact, just standing in her office elevator made her so sad, she started taking the stairs, even though her office was on the twenty-sixth floor.

Megan reminded herself how much better off she was without Mr. X. Look at all the freedom she had. She'd never again have to be on call, ready to drop all her plans and lie to her friends—all to be available, at a moment's notice, should Mr. X find himself free.

She never had to worry about whether she was seen with him; listen to him talk about how guilty he felt about lying to his family; or see him flinch when she touched him in public. She was now free to wear perfume and sweet-smelling lotions without having to worry about the scents as evidence, rubbing off on his clothes.

And when he was running late, as he did on occasion, she'd never again start to wonder if Mr. X had been in a car accident and died. And then start to panic, because if he did die, she might not find out for days.

She was free of his oppressive love, which kept her off-limits to the truly eligible men, the sort that could offer her a real future.

She was free, she reminded herself every day. But free to do what exactly? Be alone?

Resolution 337:
At least once, try to party like it's 1999.

"I think we've made a lot of progress today," Megan's therapist says in group. "Now, Megan, it's your turn to confront a fear. What would you like to do?"

"I want to practice meeting new people," she says. "I do terrible at parties."

"I hate small talk," Amy admits. Amy has a fear of strangers.

She once ran away from a man who asked her directions. "Just what are you supposed to say? I never know."

"That's why I prefer escorts," says Ed. "You can't talk to most people the way you talk to call girls. With them, it's easy. You just tell them what you want, and they tell you how much it will cost. With strangers at a party, you've got to worry about their feelings."

Megan stares at Ed. She can't get the image out of her head of him negotiating the cost of a blow job on the street corner.

"Let's stick to the topic at hand," Megan's therapist says. She smiles at Megan. "What would you say at a party, Charlene?"

"I've never been to a party," Charlene says.

"Not even a birthday party? As a kid?" Ed asks her.

"I am allergic to flour, so cake makes me break out in hives," Charlene says.

"That's the saddest story I ever heard," Ed says.

"I think working on being comfortable in a party setting would be beneficial to everyone. Why don't we plan on having a mock party at session?"

Resolution 577:
Do not always share everything with friends, and that includes therapy sessions.

"You're going to have a mock party with a roomful of social degenerates and you won't go out with your best friends in the whole world?" Lucy exclaims, offended.

"That's not fair. This is treatment, not a choice," Megan says.

"Are you sure you don't want to try some of my Xanax?"

Resolution 167:
Say hello to a stranger.

"I'm sorry, did you drop this?" Guy in Khakis says to Megan during her last tutoring session before New Year's Eve. The tables are nearly empty; it's technically during the students' winter break, but some of the students, especially Sandra, who fears she might be held back for the third time for sixth grade, have come to a special tutoring session.

Megan freezes, as she does when strangers say things to her. She's been known to take a long time to answer a question as simple as "What time is it?" She'll stare at her watch in a panic, desperately trying to remember how to tell time, as if the stranger were conducting a pop quiz and grading her on her ability to read the hands on her watch.

"Uh," Megan stutters, at a complete loss at what to say.

"It's probably someone else's," says Guy in Khakis. There's an awkward silence while Guy in Khakis weighs his options between finding something else to say or leaving.

"Hey, mister," says Sandra, Megan's student, just as Megan is certain Guy in Khakis is going to walk away. "Do you know how to find for X?"

"Uh, sure," he says, looking at Megan.

"Well, sit down then, 'cause we need help," Sandra says.

Sandra winks at Megan.

Megan gives her a look. Sandra just smiles and blinks her eyes innocently at Guy in Khakis.

He looks down at the textbook and pulls up an empty chair next to Megan. He's so close to her that she can smell his after-shave.

"The key to these things is always doing the same thing to both sides," Guy in Khakis says. "You have to have balance first, then you can find for X."

Resolution 39:
Stop worrying so much.

The day of the mock party in group, there are festive streamers hung up on the walls, along with a folding card table and a bowl of nonalcoholic punch. The group's usual circle of chairs have been removed entirely.

Ed and Charlene are hovering uneasily by the punch bowl. The rest of the group are scattered throughout the room. Most of them shift constantly, as if trying to find a stance or pose that doesn't feel too forced.

Megan's therapist begins directing them as if they're all planes and she's an air traffic controller.

"Charlene and Dennis," she calls. "I want you two in a conversation. Christi and Pauline, you two, and Megan and Ed. Yes, you two."

"Should we try the practice conversation?" Ed asks Megan.

He's referring to a "mock" conversation Charlene and Megan's therapist demonstrated in front of group two weeks ago. It went something like:

Person A: Hello. How are you?

Person B: Fine. How are you?

Person A: Fine. Nice party, isn't it?

Person B: It is a nice party.

Person A: How do you know the host?

Person B: The host is my uncle.

Megan doesn't have an uncle, so she's not sure this mock conversation would really work for her.

"Nice party, isn't it?" Ed asks Megan now.

"Um, it is a nice party," Megan says.

"Can I offer you some punch?" Ed asks, moving on to Mock Conversation #3, even though they are nowhere near the punch bowl.

"Yes," Megan says.

Ed doesn't move.

"Are you going to get the punch?" Megan asks.

"I thought it was just an exercise," Ed says.

Resolution 4:
Be extravigilant about birth control, especially during an illicit affair.

During the mock party, while Ed practiced his small-talk scripts, Megan thought of what would happen if she brought up the

Big Talk, the one she had had with Mr. X, right before they'd broken up.

It went something like:

Megan: My period is a week late.

Mr. X: . . .

Megan: Aren't you going to say something?

Mr. X: . . .

Megan: Please say something.

Mr. X: What do you want me to say? "Thank you for ruining my life"?

Resolution 331:
Do not underestimate a jerk's ability to be a jerk.

Three weeks went by without Mr. X calling. Nearly a month went by, and nothing. This after he used to call two or three times a day, as if always wanting to know exactly what she was doing.

Megan's period came and went. Mr. X never called.

Megan left him a message on his cell phone, telling him she wasn't pregnant. He still didn't call.

She saw him, after work one day, in the lobby of their building. She almost said hello, but before she could, she saw Mrs. X come through the revolving doors, wearing her Kate Spade shoes, carrying a matching bag, two of his children in tow.

He hugged his children, bringing the girl up on his shoulders, and he smiled down into his wife's face and absently brushed her hair out of her eyes. Megan recognized the gesture. He'd done the same thing to her a million times.

Then, he looked up and saw her.

His eyes clouded. With panic? With scorn? She couldn't tell. Then he looked away.

Resolution 397:
Watch "What Not to Wear" on the off chance you leave your apartment for an occasion other than work.

"Is that what you're wearing?" Lucy asks Megan, picking her up at eight o'clock New Year's Eve, for an outrageously expensive party at the Intercontinental Hotel.

Megan is wearing a safe outfit of black pants, a black cashmere sweater, and flats. Lucy, on the other hand, is wearing a miniskirt made of red sequins, stiletto heels, and a black halter top.

"I don't want to go," Megan says.

"What have you been going to group for, except to help you be more socially confident? I see I'm going to have to do a fashion intervention."

Lucy raids Megan's closet, and they don't leave her apartment until Megan is properly attired in a 1950s-style strapless cocktail dress and heels.

"Better," Lucy says.

Resolution 151:
Be less selfish.

When Lucy and Megan make it to the Intercontinental, Sarah is already there, sitting at the bar.

They order a round of drinks and Sarah says, "I hired a detective to follow Luke around."

Lucy and Megan look at each other and then at Sarah.

"He wasn't cheating after all," Sarah sighs. "I overreacted."

Resolution 19:
No matter how tempting, do not blame the wife.

Megan wanted to blame Mrs. X.

After all, how is it fair that Mrs. X could abuse Mr. X—throw coffee cups at him and curse him—and still, despite it all, be a better companion than she is?

And why is it fair that even when Mr. X said mean things about his wife, if Megan even said so much as "She's being ridiculous" he would come to her defense? And because she had no one to confide in, not really, her resentment of Mrs. X just grew and grew, a big black oil slick of dislike inside her, a frightening dark combination of emotions.

She had what Megan didn't: Mr. X.

But watching her friend Sarah, Megan reconsiders. All the excuses in her head, the ones that were propping her up, making her feel justified in sleeping with Mr. X—that you can't pick whom you fall in love with, that Mrs. X is a tyrant, that she, herself, might be having an affair—melt away.

"I'm glad he didn't cheat," Megan tells Sarah.

"Me too," she says.

Resolution 229:
Circulate more at parties.

"Excuse me," Megan tells Lucy and Sarah. "I'm going to the bathroom."

On her way, she collides straight into Guy in Khakis from tutoring. Except he isn't wearing khakis, he's wearing black tuxedo pants and a simple white shirt.

"You," Megan says without thinking.

Guy in Khakis (now Tuxedo Pants) takes a look at Megan. "And you," he says, a smile playing around his lips.

"What are you doing at this terrifically overpriced party?" Guy in Tuxedo Pants asks.

Megan freezes temporarily, the parts of her brain in charge of conversation stunned. Then she thinks of Ed and the mock party.

"It's a long story," Megan says.

"How about you tell me over a glass of champagne?" Guy in Tuxedo Pants says.

Resolution 200:
Flirt with handsome strangers.

"I hate New Year's," Guy in Tuxedo Pants says.

"Me too," Megan agrees.

"I think it's a Hallmark conspiracy. That whole finding-someone-to-kiss-at-midnight thing. Hallmark is trying to chip away at our self-esteem so we become so vulnerable that we feel the urge to collect Precious Moments figurines."

Megan laughs. "You're funny," she says, and smiles.

"That's what all my ex-girlfriends tell me." Guy in Tuxedo Pants winks. "So, about this kissing-at-midnight thing. Want to make a pact?"

"What kind of pact?"

"Well, if you don't have a boyfriend or girlfriend or anybody to kiss, how about me?"

"You?" Megan asks, surprised by the offer.

"Don't say no, or else I'm going to have to run out and buy a Precious Moments figurine just to get over the rejection, and I'm pretty sure no Hallmarks are open at this hour."

Megan laughs. "OK."

"You'd kiss me? You really would?" Guy in Tuxedo Pants asks, surprised. "Score!" he shouts, and puts two hands in the air. This makes Megan laugh again.

Resolution 601:
Change mobile phone number to
avoid calls from Mr. X.

Megan's mobile phone vibrates.

And without even looking at the caller ID, she already knows who it is. Mr. X. Who else would be calling on New Year's Eve? Not her parents, who always go to bed before ten-thirty, even on major holidays.

"I'm sorry, it's my phone," she tells Guy in Tuxedo Pants as she reaches into her clutch to get the phone.

"I miss you. I need to see you" comes the familiar voice of Mr. X. "Can you meet me? In a half hour?"

Resolution 499:
Take responsibility for the addiction.

Megan feels her heart start to speed up. And instantly she knows even though she should say no, even though every ounce of pride she has tells her to hang up on him, she can't.

She feels herself being pulled, as if on strings, toward him, and she knows before she speaks what she will do.

"Where?" she asks him.

Resolution 30:
Do not look to the past for happiness.

She meets Mr. X in the parking garage of their old office, the site of a number of their clandestine rendezvous, and her heart is beating quickly, so quickly, and her mind is moving at light speed through different scenarios. *He's going to tell me he loves me,* she thinks. *He's going to tell me it's all been a horrible mistake. He'll have his bags packed. He'll be waiting for me to take him in. He'll put his arms around me and tell me he loves me.*

Mr. X is wearing sweatpants and a baseball cap, and he gives Megan a sheepish smile. "I told my wife I was going out to get some milk."

It takes a moment for Megan to absorb this. *I told my wife I was going out to get some milk.* It implies he'll be returning to her, and soon. Megan glances uncertainly from his car to him. He has no bags. He doesn't plan to leave.

"What do you want?" Megan asks him in a voice harsher than she intended.

"To see you," he says simply. "I know you deserve someone better than me. I know you deserve someone who can love you fully. Someone who won't be there just part-time for you."

Megan nods and looks down at her shoes. She feels the pull of him, the electric energy that still exists between them.

He doesn't love her more, she thinks. He is just bored. Trapped with his family for a whole week, nothing to do but think of what he doesn't have.

"Aren't you even going to hug me?" he asks, opening his arms.

She imagines stepping into them, kissing him. The starting again of Red Light, Green Light, the thrilling sex, the series of slights and disappointments, the end at which he breaks her heart again. She realizes she came hoping he would talk her into something foolish.

"I shouldn't have come," Megan says to her shoes.

Megan doesn't say good-bye. She simply gets into her car and shuts the door. Mr. X says, "Wait."

But Megan is tired of waiting. Waiting for him to call. Waiting for him to leave his wife. Waiting for him to fall in love with her. She is done waiting.

She feels a light switch flip in her heart. This, she thinks, is it.

"Good-bye, Daniel," Megan says, turning on her ignition and putting her car into drive.

And driving home, Megan doesn't cry. Or even feel sad.

She feels as if a weight has lifted, a heavy, flat stone she's been carrying on her back for months, gone. This, she thinks, must be what a clean slate feels like.

In her car, the DJ on the radio wishes her a happy New Year.

Resolution 615:
Find a new therapist.

"I'm leaving this field," Megan's therapist informs her in the last five minutes of their latest session. "I'm changing careers. I'm going to law school."

"But . . . you can't do that," Megan says, her heart speeding up as it does when someone is breaking up with her. How long had her therapist been keeping this secret? Days? Weeks? Months?

"Megan, you've made a lot of progress."

"That isn't true," Megan whines. She doesn't feel any more ready to tackle the world today than she did the day before. Her resolution list, after all, has grown to nearly 610 in just the last week alone, and it was already two days into the New Year.

"You only have one more session left of group," her therapist points out. "I think you're ready to be released into the wild."

"I don't feel ready."

"You are ready." Megan's therapist smiles.

"I'm not. I haven't even told you Mr. X's name."

"What's his name?"

"Daniel Starks."

"See? You wouldn't have been able to do that a month ago."

"I still don't feel cured."

"It's not about a cure. It's about making peace with yourself."

Megan imagines a scene from the Israeli-Palestinian peace talks: her new self promising not to car-bomb her old self in exchange for a place to live.

"I'll be around next week if you want one more session with me."

Megan is silent.

"If you want to continue counseling, I can recommend some good people," her therapist says, sounding like any number of Megan's matchmaking friends who try to set her up on blind dates. "But if you want my opinion, you've reached a good place."

"What about my resolution list?"

"I think you ought to tear it up. You really don't need it. You're going to be fine."

Resolution 21:
Do the math.

At tutoring, there is no sign of Guy in Khakis. Megan feels disappointed, and partly responsible. After all, she had ditched him on New Year's.

"I still think he likes you," says Sandra as she completes her math homework.

"I don't know about that."

"Didn't he come to your party?"

"How did you know about that?" Megan asks.

"Well, I did tell him where you were going. I overheard you talking to one of your friends, and I thought you could use a little help in the romance department."

"I can't believe you did that."

"Well, I finished my math homework first." Sandra smiles.

Resolution 56:
Seize the day. Whatever that means.

In the stairwell, leaving tutoring, Megan runs into Guy in Khakis.

"There's Cinderella," Guy in Khakis says.

"Cinderella?"

"Isn't that what you call a beautiful girl who disappears before the clock strikes midnight?"

"I'm sorry. My friend . . ."

"That's OK," Guy in Khakis says. "You don't need to explain."

"But I want to explain."

"In that case, maybe we should grab a drink?"

Resolution 614:
Get to know a stranger.

"I had an affair with a married man," Megan blurts, almost before she's even taken a half sip of her drink.

Guy in Khakis doesn't even blink. "For how long?"

"Nearly a year." Megan looks down at her champagne glass. "I just felt like you should know that about me."

"I see. Well, we all make mistakes. If love made us do rational things, they wouldn't call it love, would they? It would be something else entirely, like *logic.*"

Megan gives him a smile.

"So, I think you owe me a kiss," he says.

"I do?"

"You promised on New Year's Eve."

"But that was for when the ball drops."

"Would you feel better if I reenacted it for you?"

"Maybe."

"OK. Ten. Nine. Eight. Seven. Six . . ."

"You're crazy."

"That's what my therapist tells me. Five. Four. Three. Two . . ."

"One," they both say at the same time.

Then, Guy in Khakis bends down and kisses Megan sweetly on the lips. It's the sweetness of the kiss that makes Megan's heart start beating a little faster.

"I'm sorry, what did you say your name was?" he says as he pulls away.

"I didn't, I'm Megan."

"I'm Tom."

They shake hands, and looking into his face, Megan sees a future full of possibility and second chances.

Resolution 150:
Be open to change.

"My name is Megan and this is my last session," Megan says, standing up and speaking before the group. "I want to thank everyone for all their help, I learned a lot about myself."

"We'll miss you, Megan," the group says in unison.

Then, everyone applauds.

Resolution 659:
Tear up your list of resolutions.

The next morning Megan picks up her heavy stack of resolutions. They are the size of a novel.

She sits down and reads through them, one by one.

Lose weight. Love more. Appreciate every day a little more than the last. Avoid complicated relationships. Strengthen friendships. Learn to trust self more. Improve self-esteem.

The more she reads them, the more she hears the nagging quality of them, the merciless tone of disappointment. Maybe she should just follow one simple resolution: *Do the best I can.* Maybe the key to self-improvement isn't to tackle the problem all at once, like eating a foot-long sub in one bite. Maybe it's better just to start with a nibble and work your way in from there.

She looks at the stack of papers, then starts tearing up the resolution list, one page at a time.

CARA LOCKWOOD was born in Dallas, earned her bachelor's degree in English from the University of Pennsylvania in 1995, and then moved back to Austin to spend her formative years working as a newspaper journalist. She married shortly thereafter and moved with her husband to the frigid tundra of Chicago, where she currently pines for sunshine and Tex Mex.

Her first two books, *I Do (But I Don't)* and *Pink Slip Party,* have been published by Downtown Press.

The Future of Sex

MEGAN McANDREW

 If life imitates art, the waning year 2002 had resembled for Agatha a certain puzzlingly popular TV show about women looking for sex in New York City. Except that Agatha had not been looking for sex. Agatha had been looking for a husband—an academic distinction perhaps, as neither sex nor husbands were to be found in the world of food styling where she made a living. What *were* to be found were nice gay men who urged Agatha to try internet dating, which Agatha duly tried, launching herself into cyberspace via an arch profile that trimmed ten pounds off her frame and confessed to a fondness for red nail polish. It turned out, however, that the Web was haunted by the same lost souls she had already met at wine-tasting class, Metropolitan Museum lectures on Byzantine art, and even, though she wasn't

Jewish, the Thursday-night singles' mixer at Temple Beth Sholom on the Upper West Side: conflicted, dissatisfied harborers of unfinished manuscripts and dusty saxophone cases, clinging to the last dregs of youth with the desperation of the damned, blanching like virgins at the word *commitment* even as middle age beckoned like Hamlet's ghost.

All the same, Agatha had submitted to the indignities of urban mating with the resigned but still hopeful feeling of the battleworn, for Agatha had a higher purpose: Agatha was going to get pregnant. She was forty-two. She was financially secure. Her mother had died two years ago of breast cancer, increasing the odds that the same fate awaited Agatha. She wanted to leave something behind besides pictures of profiteroles. She wanted a baby. And a husband. Or so she had at first told herself, for having been raised by a narcissistic, petulant, chronically attention-seeking single mother, Agatha was convinced that children were better off with two parents.

And so she had reentered the dating waters and made the mistake of being frank (except for the ten pounds), for it turned out that, in her two-year hiatus, men hadn't evolved any more than possums. Agatha knew she would not be considered a prize: She liked to eat and looked it; she had no patience for ineptitude; she suspected she was fussy. The average balding lawyer, on the other hand (she didn't even bother anymore with artists and musicians), remained bafflingly innocent of the kind of self-knowledge that Agatha considered a sign of adulthood. Convinced of his eminent desirability, he sallied into restaurants with the strut of a conqueror, made mendacious claims as to the thread count of his sheets, and, in what Agatha considered to be truly staggering hubris, listed his desired age range for a mate as twenty-five to twenty-eight.

Agatha had not specified an age range. She had clicked *yes* to *want children* and affirmed an interest in marriage. To the coy *in my bedroom you'll find,* she had replied *a bed.* All of which had netted her two dates in four months, until, for the sake of experiment, she had posted a photograph of herself in a red satin negligee, reinstated the ten pounds, alluded to a predilection for Brazilian bikini waxings, and professed an interest in men over fifty, thereby opening the floodgates to every sexual degenerate this side of the Hudson.

After a particularly dispiriting date with a commercial real estate broker, who had made her pay for condoms only to abscond the next morning with the box, Agatha had her epiphany: Maybe she didn't need a husband after all. If the only reason to get married was to have a baby, maybe she could just skip the married part. A husband, assuming she could snare one, would only get in the way. He would make demands and boss her around. He would mess up the bathroom. He would insist on idiotic names like Ashley or Vanessa (in her heart Agatha knew she would have a girl), then have a midlife crisis and vanish. She would end up like her mother. This thought, more than anything else, galvanized her.

She first approached her friend Max. Max was gay (all her male friends were gay), but being plump and bald, was not as promiscuous as he would have liked to be. Agatha worried about the baldness—it wasn't as if her own genetic material were anything to write home about—but Max was witty and brilliant and English and had gone to Princeton. He loved Nancy Mitford. He would make a wonderful father for a girl, buying her pretty dresses and taking her to the ballet. In fact, after a performance of the *Nutcracker,* which she and Max attended every year, Agatha had raised the subject.

"Why me?" Max had cried in alarm. "I don't even like children!"

"You'd never have to see her," Agatha had wheedled, her heart sinking as visions of croquet parties and country estates dissolved like fairy dust in the air. Trying to get pregnant after forty was enough of an indignity that, surely, one shouldn't be reduced to begging as well.

"Really, Agatha, have you no family values?"

She tried Hugo next and did not fare much better ("I'd love to, darling, in theory, but I mean, how would we . . . ? " His nose twitched distastefully, as if he'd just smelled a herring), and when Howard, frankly her last choice, invoked similar reservations, she gave up in disgust. She considered deceit—a judiciously timed internet date followed by a one-night stand—but New York bachelors weren't that stupid. They insisted on condoms, even if you were on the pill. The idea of poking holes through the wrapper with a pin, which Agatha briefly entertained, was farcical, though her interest *was* piqued by a cautionary notice in a pack of ultrathin, lubricated Durex about the latex-dissolving properties of Vaseline.

When her friend Marcie suggested a sperm donor, Agatha was horrified. They were sitting in Agatha's neighborhood pâtisserie, of which she was a frequent and valued patron—she had even considered asking the pâtissier, whose buttery glance had lingered more than once in her cleavage as she'd selected an éclair, but it seemed like the kind of thing a Frenchman might balk at— and Marcie, her mouth full of fat-free blueberry muffin, had exclaimed vehemently, "Who needs them, this is the twenty-first century! Technology, not the penis, is your ally!" Marcie had recently read a book called *The Future of Sex,* which made grim (depending on your point of view) predictions about the imminent obsolescence of the male sex, most of whose useful functions, according to the author, a professor of gender studies at the University of California at Santa Cruz, could be performed more efficiently by computerized robots. "Their days are numbered," Marcie went on. "Pretty soon they'll be reduced to the status of sex slaves—and that's just the cute ones. Reproductive services will be entrusted to a scrupulously screened elite, whose semen will be kept frozen in banks."

As if this idea held particular appeal, Marcie bit enthusiastically into her muffin. Agatha sank her fork into her napoleon, releasing a blob of pastry cream onto her plate. Visions of rubber mats and turkey basters rose in her mind. She felt vaguely ill.

"Do you know how many calories that thing has?" Marcie said, pointing at the collapsed napoleon.

"As many as your cardboard muffin. François had to put twice as much sugar in it to make it edible. Anyway, if I'm just going to end up hooked up like a cow to a mechanical inseminator, who cares how fat I get?"

"You might still want to get laid occasionally."

"I'm tired of getting laid," Agatha said, though this wasn't true. Agatha *liked* getting laid, it was the process of getting laid that she found disheartening. She wished she could just pick up men in bars, but ever since the smoking ban, New York bars had acquired the curiously sanitized feel of airport lounges.

"Whatever," Marcie said. "The problem with you is that you're too sentimental. Look at it this way: The most scrofulous sex maniac can post his profile with impunity on any dating site. Your average sperm bank, on the other hand, is harder to get into than Harvard. You should at least check it out."

Agatha had to concede that Marcie had a point. It was reproduction she was after, not seduction. She returned to the Web. She typed *Sperm Donors* in Google and, once she had weeded out the smut, found herself with a surprisingly long list of legitimate-sounding firms that catered to the fertility-challenged. Marcie was right: The criteria employed by the more reputable sperm banks to screen donors were more stringent than those for acceptance to the Ivy League. Applicants had to undergo a complete physical and blood count and full urinalysis, were tested for every genetic disease on earth, were measured for sperm motility, and had to submit exhaustive personal and medical histories, as well as often quite soulful handwritten essays explaining their motivation for wishing to impregnate strangers:

The thought of bringing someone so much happiness fills me with joy.

I just want to help out.

It makes me feel closer to God. Agatha wasn't so sure about that one.

The more she read, the more Agatha was entranced: no sign here of dyspeptic lawyers or writers manqué, nary a middle-aged lothario with wandering eyes. . . . Instead, page after page of frisky Ganymedes (most banks wouldn't even consider anyone over thirty-five), the dew still clinging to their lips, many with poignantly esoteric interests like chess and medieval history, and none of whom seemed to be an inch under six foot one. How could she have even considered Max, not to mention Howard, when for $600 she could obtain two vials of sperm at the Minnesota Cryobank (Minnesota appealed to her, with its open prairies and well-intentioned Scandinavian liberals) from Donor 587, a brown-haired, green-eyed fencer who read Chaucer and cooked his own meals!

How sweet they all sounded: the poetry writers and aspiring sculptors, untainted yet by failure, the bakers and gardeners, the six-foot-three, blond English major of German and Irish ancestry with excellent semen parameters and post-freeze-thaw motility, who liked to take long walks alone in the woods and wrote, in adorably childlike handwriting, *I know you'll be a good mother.* . . . Oh, Agatha wanted them all!

But she had to make a choice. She picked five candidates and called the Minnesota Cryobank, where, in exchange for her credit card number, she was informed she would receive via FedEx complete twenty-six-page profiles, including SAT scores, shoe size, and favorite color, as well as childhood photographs and a candid audio interview. Then Agatha called her ob-gyn. This, she told Dr. Zhang, would be her New Year's present to herself: a baby, on her own terms, with none of the mess and fuss of marriage. Dr. Zhang agreed that Agatha had hit upon a sensible solution, and unless you got into the more technologically complex scenarios, which she didn't think they needed to contemplate just yet, the procedure was remarkably simple. Once Agatha had selected a donor, his sperm, which had been frozen upon harvesting (Agatha had to repress a giggle here) at two hundred degrees below zero, would be packed in liquid nitrogen and shipped directly to Dr. Zhang's office. All they needed to discuss was the manner in which Agatha wished to be impregnated, for there were several options, all more or less ghoulish, though every one more dignified, when you thought about it, than tarting yourself up for a balding lawyer on a low-carb diet. As it happened, someone had just canceled an appointment and Dr. Zhang had an opening on December 31 at two-thirty—her very last, before she departed for Vail. Would Agatha be able to come in?

Agatha made the appointment. That evening, she opened a bottle of Barolo and a box of Belgian chocolates and settled down to select her donor. She was torn between 587 (the green-eyed fencer) and 913, a left-handed Russian-literature major of wiry build (a consideration) who described himself as honest, kind, and generous, but whose handwriting was sloppy. An earlier favorite, 719, was sold out through October, which information made Agatha slightly nervous. In the end she settled on 587, the Chaucer-loving fencer, who had written in his essay, *I wouldn't worry too much about my personal details. My childhood will have little bearing on how your child turns out. Most of us survive our parents.* It was exactly the way Agatha felt.

Apart from her appointment with Dr. Zhang, Agatha had made no plans for New Year's Eve. The blizzard that had been forecast was bound to put a damper on public revelry, and besides, Agatha hadn't celebrated New Year's Eve since 1996, when she had attended a party thrown by Marcie, only to spend the night consoling her when the man she had earmarked for her personal consumption had left early with a twenty-two-year-old. The present circumstances, however, clearly warranted a celebration. After her appointment, Agatha planned to swing by La Maison du Chocolat on Madison Avenue, where they did a nice boxed assortment, and then pick up a bottle of champagne, which she intended to drink by herself. For her supper, she would order a slab of foie gras from Chez Jacques, her favorite bistro, and maybe a dozen oysters. You only lived once. The snow was already falling in fat, swirling flakes when she emerged from the subway. With a spring in her step, Agatha turned onto Sixty-seventh Street and stopped in front of the town house with Dr. Zhang's office. She was about to press the buzzer when a loud voice behind her made her turn around. A few steps away, a man, who must have just come out of the building next door, was shouting into a cell phone. This in itself was not a remarkable sight in New York City, except that the man, who was wearing a pristine Barbour jacket that pegged him as neither an Englishman nor a hunter, was shouting in Italian. Agatha paused. There was something familiar about this man, who now cried, with anguished exasperation, *"Ma non è possible!* I *must* be in Rome tomorrow!"

Agatha narrowed her eyes. There was something about his

voice—but, no, it couldn't be. . . . And then the Italian, who must have sensed her gaze upon him, looked straight at her, and Agatha gasped. She hadn't seen him in over twenty years, and he'd been wearing rather less then, but there was no doubt about it: Standing before her on this unremarkable stretch of East Sixty-seventh Street, his face contorted with irritation, was Massimo Rinaldi, the greatest—the only—love of her life, whose flight to Rome, Agatha gathered from his outraged imprecations, had been canceled because of the blizzard.

Massimo, however, did not appear to have recognized her. Having glanced at her for a second and found no reason to linger, he had gone back to his tirade, his irritation, Agatha suspected, only exacerbated by the discovery of her plainness, though she had dressed and made up with care for her appointment, Dr. Zhang being flawlessly chic and thin in the maddening way of Chinese women. Anyway, it probably wasn't even Massimo. New York was full of Eurotrash at this time of year, cluttering up the aisles of Bloomingdale's and looking helpless in the subway. You could hardly tell them apart. Somewhat mollified by this thought, not to mention secretly pleased that this rude European would have a hell of a time finding a hotel room on New Year's Eve, Agatha was about to press Dr. Zhang's buzzer again when another shout erupted behind her. Once more, she turned around. Massimo's—she knew he wasn't Massimo of course, though he did look an awful lot like him—Massimo's cell phone must have died, for he was shaking it at the sky and would undoubtedly have hurled it into the nearby trash bin had he not felt Agatha's gaze upon him again. His voice suddenly all unctuous and charming, he called out, "Excuse me, signora, my battery seems to have run out—could I perhaps borrow your cell phone?"

Agatha couldn't believe the nerve of this man. She was about to suggest that he find a pay phone when a confused look came over the Italian's handsome face. He hesitated. He stared. "Agata?" he uttered incredulously, breaking into a smile so beatific that poor Agatha thought her knees might buckle. How well she knew that smile—she had once, unbelievably, provoked it.

"Agata?" he repeated, coming closer.

Instinctively, Agatha's hand flew to her head. Why, why, why had she worn a hat? Most people looked dumb in hats, but Agatha looked ridiculous. She'd only worn one because she felt a head cold coming on. Massimo, however, was already upon her. "Agata? Is it really you?"

"Yes, it's me," Agatha croaked. At least she'd put on lipstick. Dr. Zhang always wore lipstick, usually red, and interesting shoes. Agatha too favored interesting and expensive shoes, but had put on galoshes today in deference to the weather. Her eyes flew in a panic to her feet. Massimo was wearing beautiful Italian loafers that would get ruined in the snow. Now his hands were on her shoulders and he was kissing her cheeks. His hair brushed against her skin, the scent of his aftershave filled her nostrils. Agatha felt faint.

"What on earth," he said, "are you doing here?"

Agatha thought the same might well be asked of him.

She had been seventeen the summer Massimo moved in with

the Werthers. The Werthers lived next door and had boys—loutish thugs who belched and played football, except for Duncan, who was gay, though his parents had no clue, and who dreamed of Italy. It was Duncan's desperate desire to visit that country (and get away from Stamford, Connecticut) that had prompted the Werthers to sign up for an international summer exchange program. Duncan felt terrible about subjecting a cultured European to the wasteland of Stamford, but saw no other way to get to Italy and had made Agatha promise that she would look out for this Massimo, whose own family would be hosting Duncan in Rome. It was a complete mystery to Duncan why a Roman boy would want to spend the summer in Connecticut, though Agatha had suggested that, being from a major European capital, he might find American suburbia exotic. Besides, no one was forcing him to come.

No one could have predicted, either, that the Werthers' houseguest would look like a Roman god. The first time Agatha saw Massimo, she had gulped for air. He wore a leather motorcycle jacket (in summer!), had masses of tousled black curls, and extravagantly fringed bedroom eyes that, in a certain light, looked as violet as Liz Taylor's. The Werther boys having instantly pronounced him a fag, it was left to Agatha to make Massimo feel welcome, a responsibility that might have proved overwhelming had it not been for one fact: Agatha—unpopular, overweight Agatha, who spent her summers at the library—possessed one thing that Massimo lacked: a driver's license.

He'd been there for a week, so achingly beautiful and foreign that she hadn't had the nerve to approach him, until one day, as she drove to the library, she saw him walking by and slowed down to offer him a ride. He was on his way into town, where, he charmingly explained in his halting, accented English, he hoped to shop for clothes. Clearly, no one had explained to him that downtown Stamford was miles away, not to mention hardly worth driving, let alone walking, to. Agatha took him to the mall. He asked about the beach, and she drove him there too and came back for him, for her pale skin flared like a beacon in the sun. On the beach he wore a tiny black bathing suit that cradled his genitals like a palm, and once, Agatha caught a bunch of the local boxer-shorted swains sniggering, though Massimo seemed oblivious to their derision. Pretty soon he was coming over every day to get a ride somewhere, or play chess or just watch TV. She heated frozen pizzas for him, thinking they might make him feel at home. His English wasn't really good enough for conversation so they sat mostly in silence, smiling at each other. He was lonely at the Werthers', who tiptoed around him as if warily circling an extraterrestrial. He wanted to visit New York City. Agatha hesitated. She kept thinking of that bathing suit, of the strange turmoil it produced within her, the feverish dreams that woke her at night. Maybe they could go together. They would have to take the train, she couldn't drive that far.

After that first trip to New York, Massimo seduced her. Even today, twenty-six years later, Agatha felt dizzy just thinking about it. They had gone to the Metropolitan Museum (he liked art!) and then walked down Fifth Avenue, where Massimo had shopped with an intense concentration Agatha had thought only possible in girls. They had returned to Stamford in the evening, and he'd come back to her house. Her mother, who suffered from crippling migraines induced, Agatha was sure, by the excessive consumption of white-wine spritzers, had already gone to bed. When, as she was getting them sodas in the kitchen, he'd come up behind her and kissed the back of her neck, Agatha had thought it was some kind of joke. But then he'd wrapped himself around her and started caressing her arms, and then her breasts, and he'd turned her around and slowly, luxuriantly kissed her, and she'd made a sound like a cat, which had mortified her, but had seemed only to inflame him all the more. After he'd hoisted her onto the kitchen counter and unbuttoned her shirt, he'd weighed her awful, heavy breasts in his hands and suckled her like a child. That was when he'd called her beautiful, *bella, bellissima,* so taking her breath away that she'd slid off the counter and ripped frantically at his belt buckle, ending up on the linoleum, where he'd made love to her with the passionate ardor that only the young can muster, crying ecstatically *Dio mio!* as he came. It was the most romantic thing that had ever happened to her. The next day she went to Planned Parenthood and got a prescription for the pill.

And now he stood before her, in front of Dr. Zhang's town house, where she, Agatha, turned bright red, something that happened all too frequently with her coloration. Massimo smiled as if he actually expected an answer. What, indeed, was she doing there? "I—" she started. "I'm just dropping something off."

"Amazing," Massimo marveled. He looked different. His curls, now tinged with silver, were elegantly cropped, though longer than an American might have worn them. The motorcycle jacket was gone. He looked like the successful businessman he had undoubtedly become, but his voice was the same, though his English much improved, and he still had the same delighted smile that had wrenched Agatha's heart. Agatha said nothing. She gaped. She thought of running away. Then Massimo did something that completely threw her off-balance. He reached over and tugged at her hat, releasing her hair. "Ah," he said happily, and Agatha's eyes, to her horror, filled with tears.

He had loved her red hair, stroking and braiding it for hours, burying his face in its depths until she could feel his breath on her scalp. She hadn't known boys could be sensual. Her few experiences of lust had been furtive and brutish, gropings in dark corners by boys who were ashamed to want her. Massimo didn't seem to know shame. He reveled in her, gloried in her flesh. Even her embarrassing orange thatch sent him into ecstasies. He would position himself between her thighs (those fat, marbled thighs she so hated) as she lay back, like a princess in her bower, and with tongue and playful fingers tease her until she nearly wept with pleasure. He said the flesh down there was as pink as a seashell, her labia like little roses. Agatha, like Rosalind, knew you couldn't die of love, but she had thought she might.

"You are crying!"

How desolate he sounded. A few years later she'd traveled to Rome, and she'd understood something that had bedeviled her, how someone as beautiful as Massimo could actually have been nice too. It turned out all Italians were nice, it was part of their nature. They smiled with genuine warmth and were always kissing and touching each other and gesturing expressively with their hands. No one, on that first trip, had kissed or touched Agatha, though the night clerk at her hotel had winked at her several times, but just by watching she too had partaken of the generous sensuality that hung over this wonderful country like a golden haze. When her career took off and, though naturally inclined to thrift, she found herself with disposable income, she began to take her vacations there, staying in nice hotels on Capri or the Amalfi coast, sipping a Campari on the piazza in the evening, occasionally satisfying herself with a waiter or a bellboy, for her look appealed to the lower classes. In New York, construction workers smiled as she walked by, as did the nice ex-convicts who swept the streets in her neighborhood.

She had to pull herself together. As Massimo gazed at her with perplexed concern, she sniffed loudly, certain her nose was bright red, her eyes pink and smeared with wet mascara. "It's nothing," she said. "I've had a long day." To reassure him, she smiled.

Massimo's brow instantly cleared. She remembered that this too, his incapacity for misery, had amazed her. He broke again into his dazzling smile. Then he said, "I must call my wife."

His wife. Of course he would have a wife. He was beautiful and, Agatha now recalled, rich. He'd been sent to America to improve his English, which he would need one day to run the family business, something to do with cars, or was it cheese? Though he'd confessed to Agatha that, in his heart, all he really wanted to do was drive motorcycles. She fished her cell phone out of her bag and handed it to him. It probably cost a fortune to call Europe. But already he was chattering in Italian, waving his free hand around. Dr. Zhang would be wondering where she was.

"*Sì . . . Sì . . . Ma non lo so!*" He was getting impatient. His wife would be annoyed. Undoubtedly she was beautiful too, and imperious. She wouldn't like having to change her plans. Agatha found the idea of this irritated Roman wife mysteriously appealing. She smiled sweetly as Massimo handed her back the phone.

"I must find a hotel." He sounded a little disappointed.

"You can stay with me." Agatha told herself afterward that it had just come out, though in fact she had known all along that she would offer, just as she had known the moment she saw him that she was going to miss her appointment with Dr. Zhang.

Again the ecstatic smile. "No, no, you must have plans."

Plans? Agatha was momentarily confused. Could he possibly have guessed—but, no, he meant New Year's Eve plans, of course. Massimo would have had plans. Scenes from Fellini films unfurled in her mind: a glamorous party, champagne, the beautiful wife in a black cocktail dress . . . Except that, if things had gone according to plan, he would have spent the night on an airplane, crossing the Atlantic.

"My wife is angry," he explained. "I was supposed to be home yesterday, but first they delayed the flight from Atlanta, and . . ." He made a little shrug.

"What were you doing in Atlanta?" Agatha asked curiously.

"I was attending a food show. We sell a lot of cheese there." He broke into his dazzling smile again, crinkling the skin around his impossibly blue eyes. "And now, I find you!"

"Yes," Agatha said, beaming back, though beaming did not come naturally to her. In fact, she had to quash a sentiment that came much more naturally, that it was a bit outrageous, really, to just expect good things to happen to you. Didn't he know that life was a vale of tears? "And I don't have plans, as it happens. I was going to catch up on some work," she added, thinking that this might make her sound interestingly severe, as opposed to alone and dateless on New Year's Eve, unless you counted Dr. Zhang.

A puzzled look came over Massimo's face. "Work?"

"Yes."

"What kind of work do you do?"

"I'm a food stylist."

Massimo beamed. "Aaah, you are a cook!"

"Well, I don't really cook, I make food look good for magazines. By the time I'm finished, it's usually inedible."

A look of blank incomprehension crossed Massimo's handsome face, and Agatha recalled that irony hadn't been his forte, that he, truth be told, hadn't been very bright, which she had at the time thought might have explained his interest in her. Not that it had mattered to her how smart he was. Agatha was smart enough for two, and Massimo cared even less. All he had wanted to do that long, humid summer was buy clothes and have sex with Agatha, endlessly, on the kitchen floor, and in the den, and once, even, thrillingly, in the Werthers' garage amid the bikes and lawn-mowing equipment, for, as it turned out, Massimo had a secret vice: he liked fat girls, fat redheads especially. In his fantasies, he was engulfed in pale flesh, kneaded it like dough, rode it like waves to unfathomable ecstasies. Agatha shivered. Then she experienced a moment of irritation. Oh, God, she thought, he'll expect me to cook for him! For Agatha hated to cook, considered it tedious drudgery, took all her meals out, in the excellent restaurants that festooned her neighborhood, where dishes were properly plated and sauced, served and removed by waiters. Agatha *liked* being waited on and favored formal establishments where the staff didn't act like your friends. She was a consumer, a *gourmand,* not a laborer, and she hated messing up her kitchen, which had once been photographed for *Saveur* magazine, though she'd never as much as boiled an egg in it.

"I will take you out to dinner," Massimo said.

"Oh," Agatha demurred, "we'll never get a reservation," until she remembered the snow, now falling in earnest, and she added, "Well, maybe we can go somewhere local."

In her apartment, she poured them glasses of wine, which she kept in a well-stocked, temperature-controlled storage cupboard, and put out a dish of Marcona almonds, and another of plump, glossy Sicilian olives. Agatha liked to have little treats around, to pamper herself with indulgences. She saw no reason to deny herself life's small pleasures just because she was alone, as so many women seemed to, subsisting on stringy salads and fat-free yogurt. Massimo sat in her favorite chair, by the fireplace, his eyes traveling appraisingly around the room. She remembered that he'd liked beautiful things, and there were many in her home, for Agatha, though she had grown up in a suburban box, possessed the aesthetic instincts of a Medici. Normally (as if anything about this evening were normal) she would have chosen a French or Italian restaurant, but an obscure, atavistic impulse told her that it would be best to stay in. In the end, she had suggested

Chinese takeout, figuring, correctly, that Massimo would find it exotic. Having made him comfortable, she had slipped away to the bathroom, where she had dusted herself with the finest film of shimmering powder and glossed her lips. She was glad that she'd dressed up for Dr. Zhang, her violet cashmere wrap bringing out the green in her eyes, the white of her skin, for Agatha had lovely skin, pale and smooth as an egg, so delicate that, at pressure points, it was almost translucent, the capillaries beneath reminiscent of the veining on a particularly fine piece of porcelain.

"I always wondered what happened to you," Massimo said when she returned, his eyes suggesting that he appreciated her efforts.

Agatha was going to answer, "Right," in the snarky tone she would normally adopt around Max or Hugo, but to her surprise, she found that she wasn't bitter. Massimo had been a mirage, a fluke. She hadn't expected to ever hear from him again. A realist already at seventeen, she had known he would go back to Rome and resume a life that had nothing to do with her, riding his motorcycle around fountains, getting indifferent grades, blithely accepting the world's goodwill. It was as if two members of different species had briefly collided, only to be flung again out of each other's orbit. She sipped her wine, a more than decent Bordeaux, and said, "As you can see, I've done quite well." It wasn't what she'd planned to say, but once it was out, it hit her with the gentle force of a pleasant revelation. She *had* done well. The room they sat in reflected this, from the framed botanical prints on the walls to the plump, down-filled sofas and Chinese vases, rotund and lambent in the lamplight. It was the room of a woman who liked her comforts and took them.

"You are not married," Massimo observed.

"No. And you?" She laughed in a *silly me* way, made her voice sound slightly pitying. "Oh, but of course . . ." Recumbent on her silken couch, for she had stretched out and kicked off her shoes, she saw herself through his eyes and a memory welled within her, of the power she had once held over him.

"Tell me about her," she said pleasantly. She had no interest, of course, in his wife, did not need him to describe her, for she was surely as banal in her own way as any Betty in Omaha, but something in the observance of these proprieties curiously aroused her, something she wanted to drag out and bask in, like a cat with a string.

A proprietary pride came into his voice. "We have three children: Leopoldina, Fabrizzio, and Chiara."

So the wife didn't even rate a mention. . . . But, no, he was just being discreet. Europeans didn't discuss their wives with former lovers, unlike Americans, who whined and moped and blubbered in therapy, tormented by their ids. Agatha loathed the idea of therapy. She didn't *want* to know herself any better and certainly didn't want anyone else to. That kind of knowledge, she knew in her bones, only led to disappointment. More and more of late, she felt that she had been born not only in the wrong country, but in the wrong century. She would have been at home in seventeenth-century Holland. At the Vermeer show at the Met, she had been almost achingly drawn to the lucent, orderly interiors of Delft, had pictured herself inhabiting one, taking her place among the heavy, richly clothed women she so resembled, gorging daily on cream and cake, opening lazy thighs at night to strangers—for Agatha found the idea of arranged marriage profoundly appealing. She wondered now if that was what had drawn her to Massimo, the pull of an older, more mannerly world. If she'd lived at the time of Vermeer, she would have had her first child at sixteen, her last at thirty, and instead here she was, long past the natural age for reproduction, devoured by a biological imperative that both fascinated and horrified her, for even as Agatha wanted a baby, the thought of it vaguely sickened her.

"Do you have pictures?" she asked.

Massimo produced a snapshot from his wallet. It showed three perfectly groomed children ranging in age from about twelve to five, dressed for some formal occasion, the girls in crinolined dresses and the boy in tailored shorts, a long-necked woman of aristocratic appearance poised behind them, her hands resting on the boy's shoulders. Agatha was transfixed. She saw, with lapidary clarity, these children, could practically smell the cologne in their hair. The picture had obviously been taken in their living room, which was gracious and elegant, not abandoned to domestic squalor in the defeated way of so many American homes. These were exactly, in fact, the children Agatha would have wanted, and there, sitting before her, his hand reaching for the almonds, was their sire, who had once desired her with such passionate intensity that he had sunk his teeth into the flesh of her buttocks; who had released inside her, with profligate abandon, teeming rivers of semen that had trickled down her thighs and dried to a film on her skin before being scrubbed away in the shower, lost forever. Then the intercom buzzed.

"Ah," Massimo exclaimed. "Our dinner!"

Agatha was suddenly overcome with such an unendurable sense of waste that the idea of hot-and-sour soup seemed an obscenity. This must have been reflected in her expression, for having hesitated for a second, uncertain perhaps as to the protocol attending the delivery of Chinese food, Massimo jumped up and reached for his wallet, saying, "Allow me," as he hurried to the door. Agatha's eyes fixed on his ass. As she watched its muscular lobes moving under the wool flannel, she was visited by a moment of preternatural clarity. Ever since she'd hatched the plan of getting impregnated by a stranger in Minnesota, she'd kept scrupulous track of her monthly cycles, charting them in a special notebook which she kept by her bed. Right now, she straddled the middle, hungrily fecund. She could almost feel her womb slackening, waiting to be filled, and the thought made her want to growl like a dog. Instead, she fanned her toes, which were painted blood red, and which she'd noticed Massimo glance at several times throughout the evening, perhaps wishing to suck on them as he had once done so many years ago. A lazy smile formed on her lips as he returned with the bag of takeout and the air filled with the cloying smell of gluey sauces and overcooked shrimp. He was obviously starving. Agatha too felt ravenous.

"Why don't we just eat here?" she said, motioning to the coffee table. Massimo set the bag down. He seemed a little out of his element suddenly, a little shy. He still had that sweetness of not-too-bright boys, that eagerness to please, though it was tempered now with the confidence of success. And there was something else too: She sensed he'd learned cruelty. Suddenly she wondered if they shouldn't dispense with the awful meal. She could just go over and unzip his pants, pull out his cock, close her lips around it. She'd tried this with the last man she'd gone out with, quite horrifying him. How she hated the false pageantry of dating, the cheap sentiment, the Hallmark tawdriness. In her fantasies, she was fucked by strangers in hotel rooms, took orders, pleaded for more.

"On the floor?"

"On the floor."

A look of suppressed excitement appeared in Massimo's eyes. Agatha bet his wife didn't let him eat on the floor. She looked as if she ran a tight ship, putting out just enough to keep him on his toes. Agatha removed the containers from the bag and arranged them on the tabletop. She'd ordered cold noodles in sesame sauce, chili shrimp, fried pork dumplings. Trash food, awash in salt and oil. Food for polluting yourself.

"I think we'll have champagne, no?" she said when she'd shaken out of the bag the last little packet of duck sauce, and she turned on her heels and, swinging her haunches like a street-walker, went into the kitchen. She could feel his eyes burning into her back.

It had been so long since she'd felt the pull of a man's desire that Agatha was disoriented. She rested her hands on the counter. As her skin came into contact with the cool marble, calm re-turned, and with it clarity: This was no time for sentiment. What she had felt for Massimo twenty-five years ago could not be relived. She had lost the ability to suspend disbelief. Whatever niceness and sweetness she'd possessed had long been stamped out by tedium and disappointment, by pettiness, by watching her mother die. There, in the next room, was opportunity in its most naked form, to be treated accordingly and without fuss. If Agatha could make a plate of *boef bourguignon* look concupiscent enough to grace the cover of a magazine, then she could maintain, long enough for him to impregnate her, the tenuous web of memory and illusion in which Massimo was currently suspended.

This of course would involve deceit, for, just as Agatha knew that she could have Massimo for one night, she was equally sure that he would run like a rabbit if he found out what she was really up to. Calculation, however, came naturally to her. If you weren't one of the lucky few, like Massimo, to whom things were freely and constantly offered, then you grabbed what you could get, using the means at your disposal. And Agatha didn't want Massimo. He was already married to the kind of woman men like him invariably married, and he wasn't going to give her up for a fat American food stylist. He would fuck her, yes, that she was sure of, but he would ask about contraception, he wasn't an idiot. Well, except that he wasn't too bright either. When she told him she was on the pill, as she intended to do, it wouldn't occur to him not to believe her. Agatha felt a twinge of guilt about this because she liked Massimo, but she wasn't going to let that interfere with her project. While his sperm motility was undoubtedly no match for that of 587 in Minnesota, he was at least living and breathing and here before her. It surprised Agatha, who thought of herself as quite cold-blooded, how much this meant to her. Just as it surprised her that, as she spooned out the slippery noodles and shrimp and tried to teach Massimo how to use chopsticks, she felt as giddy as a teenager.

"This is impossible," Massimo said, laughing, flailing his chopsticks around, catching air.

Agatha picked up a shrimp and conveyed it to her mouth. "Like this." She demonstrated and expertly grasped an asparagus. She thought of offering him a fork, but then thought better of it. Though the slight awkwardness that had hovered between them had been dispelled by the business of eating, it seemed best to keep him on edge. Finally, triumphantly, Massimo succeeded in grasping a few strands of noodle, only to have them slither onto his shirtfront halfway to his mouth.

"I'll get a sponge," Agatha said. She jumped up and went back to the kitchen. She liked moving before him, feeling his eyes on her. She felt lithe and voluptuous, elastic, like a belly dancer or a harem girl, another occupation Agatha felt she would have been well suited to, swathed in filmy veils, a fat jewel winking in her navel. In her mind, she had already selected, and discarded, several items from her lingerie drawer, where they nestled in pastel puffs among lavender sachets. Agatha loved buying lingerie, the tartier the better, though she favored the expensive French stuff. In particular she loved corsets, with their intimations of restraint and abandon. Later she would slip away and change, dab perfume behind her ears, truss herself up like a whore. She wondered if Massimo went to whores; it was perfectly acceptable in Europe. It certainly made sense to Agatha, seemed no different from the urge to gorge on Chinese takeout or fried pork rinds, another dark craving to which she occasionally succumbed. If Agatha were a man, she would definitely avail herself of the services of prostitutes. Both food and sex in America had become so drearily hygienic, it made a girl yearn to be defiled. Once, during that long, hot summer, Massimo had torn her underpants in his eagerness. As she ran the sponge under the tap, Agatha thought of him ripping off the violet corset she had settled on, with its frilly, matching *cache-sexe,* and was quite overcome. She squeezed out the sponge, then pulled open the cutlery drawer and got Massimo a fork.

When she handed it to him, he looked ineffably grateful.

"I am very hungry," he confessed. He speared a shrimp and chewed it rapidly, smearing a bit of oil on his chin.

"Of course you are." Agatha was thinking that his wife probably didn't feed him properly. Except for cleaning ladies and *salumeria* owners, most of the women she'd seen in Rome looked anorexic. Where all that pasta went was a mystery. "Stop for a second," she said. She moved the container aside and kneeled before him. Carefully, for the fabric was fine, she dabbed at his shirtfront with the sponge. His eyes, she knew, had sunk to her cleavage.

"You'll have to take it off," she said. "I will launder it for you." With plump, delicate fingers (Agatha took exquisite care of her extremities) she undid the buttons, her hand grazing the wiry hair on his chest. The cadence of his breath altered. Agatha took note of this, but the sight of his gold medallion caused her own breath to catch; the all-forgiving Madonna, who he had believed as a teenager, with a placid faith completely outlandish to Protestant Agatha, watched over him and protected him from all harm. She had an almost physical memory at that moment of the way the small disk had felt against her cheek, the metal warmed by his skin.

With a groan, he grabbed at her. Agatha slipped out of his grasp and rose, his soiled shirt in her hand. Without it, he looked younger, more helpless. He'd kept himself trim, playing tennis probably, or golf. Agatha felt as ancient as time. She felt like Demeter, like Circe, like Hera, the great conniver. No one had expected the goddesses to have pure hearts.

"Please," he gasped.

"Wait," Agatha said, though her own heart hammered. "Finish your dinner," she instructed over her shoulder. She vanished down the hallway to her bedroom, where she closed the door and, her step once again steady, went to her underwear drawer. She pulled out the violet corset, the ruched garter-belt trimmed with rosebuds, the frilled panties—Agatha hated thongs, thought they made women look like Sumo wrestlers—then she opened her stocking drawer and found a silk pair the color of ivory with little bows at the ankles. She removed her clothes and folded them and, with fastidious care, trussed and snapped herself into the hourglass shape prized by Victorian gentlemen, finishing off with a filmy peignoir before easing her small feet into feather-trimmed mules that fluttered as she walked. Then she went into the bathroom and brushed her hair.

When she emerged, Massimo had laid waste to the shrimp and dumplings and most of the asparagus, leaving only cold noodles, slick with peanutty grease, and the eggplant in garlic sauce, which had obviously not appealed to him. At the sight of her, he scrambled to his feet, uttering a strangled *"Porca Madonna!"*

Agatha made a clucking sound. "Poor baby," she murmured. The sofa blocked the way between them, and registering the wild look in his eyes, and the bulge in his pants, she thought for a second that he might leap over the furniture. "All in good time," she said, nimbly circling the sofa, for despite her girth, Agatha was surprisingly light on her feet. She arranged herself among the cushions and drew up one leg, so that the peignoir fell aside with practiced abandon.

"Do you want me?" she asked.

"Dio mio!" Massimo gasped, and he leapt over the coffee table, sending cardboard containers flying. He ripped at his belt and sent that flying too, yanking his pants to his knees before falling upon her. His hands kneaded frantically at her breasts, tugged at her garter, tore at her underpants. *"Puttana,"* he moaned, and with a rough shove, he turned her over and mounted her, entering her with such a violent thrust that Agatha had to steady herself against the armrest. He fucked her with no regard for her pleasure and came quickly and desperately, with a strangled shout, and as he did, Agatha willed herself into total receptivity. She pictured an egg, a great pulsing yolk, particles colliding, membranes welling and separating, she pictured blood vessels and capillaries, viscous fluids, wet, warm canals. She pictured all these things, filled her mind with them, and was visited by an illumination: Marcie was wrong about the future of sex. Sex in the future would be no different from sex today, or sex in the four-

teenth century, or in Vermeer's time in Delft, in those luminous rooms that stank of chamber pots. Babies were born of lust, not calculation. The earth—New York, Cairo, Brazzaville, even Stamford, Connecticut—teemed with the products of one-night stands and ripped condoms, of drunken fucks and bad judgment and worse luck, and somehow—and this was the miracle—the species hobbled along. Tonight, Agatha joined the ranks of these hapless propagators. The thought filled her with a wide and arching joy.

Massimo collapsed on top of her. Like a seal rolling underwater, Agatha turned, the better to hold his seed inside her. She felt like a great, slushing vessel, a pot, a ship in the night. Gently, she cradled him. He must have been tired from all his traveling, the cheese show, his demanding wife, his maybe not-so-perfect children, because he fell almost instantly asleep. Squashed against her breast, his mouth made little bubbling sounds. He began to snore. Agatha looked down at him and marveled at the miracle of life. A warm trickle descended her thigh, and she thought of 587's gelid semen, frozen in its metal canister. One day her daughter would ask where she had come from, and she would tell her about this night, about how she had loved Massimo at seventeen, though she'd barely known him, and he had magically reappeared on New Year's Eve to make her a child. In its way, it was as perfect a love story as any.

＊　＊　＊

MEGAN McANDREW'S first novel *Going Topless* (also available from Downtown Press) was hailed by *Newsday* as "masterful . . . Like [Diane] Johnson, McAndrew has a wry, comic voice and a sharp eye for the minutiae of cultural signifiers." McAndrew grew up in France, Spain, and Belgium, and is a graduate of Brown University and the Yale School of Management. She lives in New York City with her thirteen-year-old son and is at work on her second novel.

Happily Never After

TRACY McARDLE

 I never intended to spend New Year's Eve in Beverly Hills with my gynecologist, much less involve him in the final demise of my relationship or promise to get his screenplay read by an influential producer named Bum-Chin, but by midnight that's the place I was in. Like most unexpected and quick affairs of the heart, it wasn't what you think.

I hate going to the gynecologist. That's fairly obvious; most women welcome the appointment with about as much enthusiasm as bra shopping or choosing a Mother's Day card that can't possibly be misinterpreted. Both tasks are excruciatingly time-consuming and filled with anxiety and self-doubt. Both must be seen to at least once a year, and both, if performed inadequately, can lead to disaster. I have a special fear of a pelvic exam, a truly gut-wrenching dread of each visit. This is because nothing has ever been wrong. Therefore, it's only a matter of time. Plus, I was raised Catholic, and now, at thirty-five, with my sexual conquests heading well into the double digits, I'm just waiting for the hand of God to surprise me with a second uterus, unexpected twins, a missing fallopian tube, or a nasty case of . . . something.

I hate writing *Dr. appt.—3:30* in my day planner. I hate telling the president of worldwide marketing at the movie studio whose advertising campaign I'm working on that I'll be late tomorrow, due to a doctor's appointment. I loathe driving through Beverly Hills, searching in vain for free parking, knowing that I will soon have to enter Cedars-Sinai, the Saks of Western medicine. I resent having to endure the sight of nurses in playful scrubs (bunnies, turtles) wheeling bandaged, sad patients on cold gurneys. I detest the tense musings about the weather in the elevator. Silence, silence, Muzak, then someone with a Botoxed forehead, on cue: "Sure is a hot one today." Unlike Hollywood Boulevard or the *Tonight* show green room, the elevator at Cedars-Sinai is an irony-free zone.

"What's the big deal?" asked Tim, my sexy but noncommittal British boyfriend, on December 21, the morning of my yearly exam. He was trolling through *American Cinematographer,* engrossed with the photos. "Everyone hates going to the doctor, Jules." Tim's face is really skinny, with huge cheekbones, like a starving Abercrombie model. He looked at me through his floppy black hair and sleepy, mocking grin. This grin, while often maddening, weakens me like a double shot of tequila. It's had that effect since the day he dropped off the rough cut of the B thriller *Game of Chicken* at my editing shop three years ago and stayed all night.

"Not everyone," I protested, busying myself with various jams and half an English muffin. "You don't mind going to the doctor."

Tim looked up from his article. "That's 'cause I'm still excited about someone paying for my health insurance. Hell, now that I'm not coughing up three hundred bucks a month, going to the doctor's a bloody *treat*." Tim only recently made it into the Directors Guild after months of his life disappeared while shooting second unit on *Baby Be Mine*. Now he has top-notch health coverage and goes to the doctor when he has a pimple, just to stick it to Aetna and put his name in front of the Guild frequently.

"You know, you're lucky to enjoy the benefits of preventative medicine," Tim the Privilege Police scolded, tossing the $4.95 magazine on the counter. This was not the first time he'd used that tone—half-listening, half-amused, mildly condescending, intended to be comforting but not. Perhaps you've heard that tone from your boyfriend. Perhaps it made you too want to rip out his goatee, hair by hair.

Tim sauntered sleepily to the stove and poured a cup of strong Peruvian blend from our French press, the device with which artistic people make coffee. He moved close to me and pressed his hands behind him into the counter so that his white elbows poked out at a weird angle. His boxers hung off him like a rock star. "It's just a checkup, luv, everything will be fine," he purred in a husky morning voice. Suddenly he grabbed my thigh and pinched hard. "Horse bite!" he yelped, but I didn't giggle as usual when I slapped his hand away.

"Someone has her grouchy knickers on today," he teased, and I glared. He retreated to the fridge, which was covered with holiday greetings: standard happy-family photos of friends and their beautiful children and pets posing in winter wonderlands, and a few holiday party invitations, addressed to Jules and Tim. No last names. We were just Jules and Tim. Three years now of being three syllables. Nothing more. Nothing less. Which was fine with Tim, who was twenty-nine. Not so fine for those over thirty-five with a uterus. But he was sweet and fun, energetic and interesting—or at least, that's how I used to feel. These days it felt as if we were roommates. I kept hoping it would pass, kept pretending it would work itself out. It had for Demi and Ashton. Why not us? Tick tock.

"Are we going to Pete's for New Year's or what?" Tim asked the contents of the refrigerator, changing the subject, which he often did abruptly when his little tricks to elevate my mood didn't work. Pete was Pete Horn, successful producer, Hollywood Hills homeowner, and single-female magnet. Pete had dropped out of UCLA and lied his way into the CAA mailroom agent-trainee program, got his boss fired, and became a partner by the age of twenty-five. Then he started his own firm and became a manager and, because he couldn't act, decided that the only way to feed his ego sufficiently was to produce. Every year he had a legendary New Year's Eve party, a who's who of Hollywood agents, managers, producers, and directors. Only cool or ironic actors were invited. Johnny Depp, Christopher Walken, Lili Taylor. Odd couples were often discovered in compromising situations in the pool house after midnight. Pete's parties were huge, expensive, endless, and extravagant but they weren't really fun for me because Tim spent the entire evening networking. Last year he kissed Heidi Klum at midnight instead of me. "She was standing right there all alone, it would have been rude not to!" he'd argued. "Spare me," I'd snapped, storming home in four-inch heels down Coldwater Canyon.

"Sure, we always go to Pete's, we booked our London tickets around Pete's, let's go to Pete's," I said blankly, my mind already laid out flat on the gynecologist's examining table, my fears deep in the stirrups. I inevitably had my annual exam around the holidays because I always put it off until the last possible moment of the year.

Tim sighed an exasperated, freshly weary sigh. "Everything will be fine, Jules. Cheer up, one fanny-poker visit, five more days of the white-collar sweatshop, and it's vacation!" This is how Tim referred to my work as head creative at the marketing agency where I toiled making movie posters, TV commercials, and radio scripts so that the studios could sell B movies to unsuspecting audiences. Tim liked to joke that my job was basically calculating how to most effectively steal $8 from as many American consumers as I could every weekend. This always got a laugh at dinner parties. What I never pointed out but knew to be true was that when part of that $8 went to Tim someday for directing a fat slice of Tinseltown trash, it wouldn't be stealing. It would be . . . work.

Tim headed for the shower. "You get on, luv, I'll do the washing up. Lots of luck." He winked and went off to spend thirty minutes wasting hot water. I glanced at the clock, cringing, and swilled the rest of my caffeine. No putting it off any longer.

As women know and men can only guess, the gynecologist is not fun. What's interesting is the nature of the exchange. You, the patient, lie naked and exposed as a man who is not your husband, boyfriend, or even someone you know well probes your womanhood with cold steel instruments and nasty plastic devices, while making small talk, humming, or in one case, pitching a movie idea about his childhood idol, Hannibal the Great.

Dr. Jimmy Hackman was a nice man, but he was odd. He'd graduated from Harvard Medical School, married, settled in Brentwood, and steadily built a clientele of thin, rich, successful women who worked in entertainment companies or had husbands who owned them. Now in his late forties, he was boyish—taut and fit, with half a head of strawberry-blond hair like Ron Howard's once was. He was cheerful and always, always, a little too clean. His forehead shone as if he'd just been removed from the dishwasher. I suppose in a doctor this detail should have been comforting, but somehow it wasn't. I wondered what his wife was like, or how she felt about his obsession with Hannibal the Great. The photos in his office, however, were of the two children. The largest piece of art was, of course, a portrait of Hannibal the Great crossing some passage on an elephant, valiantly leading his men to—what? Somewhere, I don't know. The movie hasn't come out yet.

When he finished his pitch that day, Dr. Hackman told me

(his hand still firmly in utero) that his life-size bust of Hannibal was his most prized possession. It scared his kids. "Wow," I had mumbled, legs aloft.

At Cedars I got off the elevator on the eighth floor and headed down the bright, garland-draped hallway, which always reminds me of the spooky one that Dorothy must travel before getting her assignment from the Wizard. Two hugely pregnant yet somehow thin women emerged from the office just as I was heading in.

"Well, hi there, Julie," chirped Bess, Dr. Hackman's receptionist. Bess was plump and had brassy blond hair and bright pink lipstick that were both sadly dated, as if she'd arrived in Beverly Hills on the same bus as Marilyn Monroe and had lost track of the passage of time. But she was comforting in the same odd, unnamable way that Dr. Hackman wasn't, so I welcomed her. Today Bess was wearing a ceramic Santa pin that a grandchild had clearly made. For a moment I was lost in its construction, the crystalline plastic in red and green, the black-beaded eyes, the red felt cap. Little fingers had painstakingly crafted these details out of unconditional love and a raging urge to please.

"I thought we were never going to see you again!"

"Sorry, it's just my schedule," I muttered, embarrassed to be known at the doctor's office as The Canceler.

"Examining room four, honey." She waddled behind her counter, which displayed a variety of Christmas decorations and New Year's party favors, and shooed me on ahead. "You know what to do." Bess disappeared behind a mound of papers, and I closed myself into the cleanest, brightest, most cheery torture chamber you've ever seen.

The Beverly Hills gynecologist. It's not the same level of existential weirdness brought on by, say, the Burbank bikini waxer or the Santa Monica facialist, people who frame certificates authorizing them to rip out your pubic hair and squeeze your blackheads, respectively. But it's weird. Especially during the holidays, when cheerful Christmas carols accompany every moment of the experience.

The examining room is designed to be void of any sexuality whatsoever. Sitting half-naked under fluorescent lights while staring at a coldly clinical chart of the female reproductive system, you go to a different place altogether: *I am woman, hear me whimper.* As with sex, the activity that brought you here, what's significant is not the act itself but the anticipation. It's The Wait. You sit and you wait, stare alternately at the scale (I dare not get on), the diplomas (this man is certified to jiggle my breasts and put his hand and other objects inside me,) your chart (all embarrassingly personal details, I wonder if he thinks I'm a slut) . . . and you feel the weight of Eve's guilt upon your shoulders. That's what the wait for the doctor is about: Your Sexual History and Its Consequences. Stationed on pink tissue in the interrogation room, you wait for Judgment to breeze in as Bing Crosby dreams of a white Christmas.

Do colored condoms work as well? Should I have taken two pills when we changed time zones? If only I hadn't gotten so drunk. If I were accidentally pregnant, would I tell Tim right away?

Just as I donned my paper johnny, my cell phone buzzed. I hobbled to the dressing closet in bare feet and dug the phone out of my bag: ROBIN@WORK. I let out a small smile and hit a button. "What?"

"Are you *there* . . . with *him?*" my friend Robin asked in a mock horror voice before playing a recording of Vincent Price cackling on the *Thriller* track. Robin Sherman was a successful but lovably silly Executive Vice President of Production for Squab Films. Squab was the vanity production label of gigantically successful producer Ned Bunkin, who had a well-documented nickname, due to an unfortunately severe dimple beneath his lower lip. Yes, Bum-Chin. Bum-Chin was tough but fair, driven and crazy, madly rich and impossible. Of all the aspiring D-girls in Hollywood, only Robin had successfully ridden out the brutal job to a full partnership. There were two reasons for this: Robin was unstoppable, and Bum-Chin actually appreciated good movies. Robin and I had grown up together in Hollywood, starting at the desks of a horribly mean and successful producer and a horribly mean and successful publicist, respectively. Robin loved Vincent Price and it was a favorite trick of hers to ask my assistant for my voice mail and leave Vincent's trail of hideous laughter for minutes on end. The only thing I didn't like about Robin was that she asked me weekly when Tim was going to marry me and how long I was going to live with him "in late-thirties limbo," a malaise she had coined after noticing several of her friends carrying aging eggs in similar situations—living with Men Who Weren't Ready. Robin rooted out these issues like a truffle-sniffing pig (her favorite metaphor) and forced me to acknowledge them, as frequently as possible. What are best friends for?

"Did he say you have two weeks to live?"

"You're a shit." I was still smiling, though.

"Did Tim go with you?" she asked, and I could hear her clacking through emails.

"Are you kidding?" I snorted.

"Right, no need to be reminded of your reproductive capabilities," she quipped.

"Rob, don't," I said testily.

"Sorry," she said quickly. "When you headed to England?"

"Day after Christmas," I grumbled. We never went to Cleveland for Christmas, where my family was. It was always London. "Going to Pete's?" she asked, and I was grateful for the comfort of our shorthand.

"Course."

"All right, see ya then. I'm off to Montana with Bum-Chin tomorrow." For Robin it was a term of endearment. After all, he respectfully called her The Shermanator. I put the phone away and sat down hard on the padded table.

Dr. Hackman swung through the door in all his freshly scrubbed and clean-shaven Beverly Hills Gay Manliness. Only he's not gay, but I pretend he's gay because he's my gynecologist. My palms were sweaty and so, unfortunately, was my ass, which was sticking to the table in a most unpleasant manner.

"How are we doing?" Dr. Hackman chimed, full of Beverly Hills doctor teeth, large hands, and thinning hair.

"Um, fine, I guess, but the new pill is making me fat."

"No, it isn't." He smiled and I wanted to hug him. Then he finished, "Water gain should only be a couple of pounds, and it typically isn't noticeable. Your weight gain is probably due to something else." He opened my chart. "Mid-thirties now . . . could be your metabolism." He glanced at my ample womanliness (in another city I would be *voluptuous*). I sat silently steaming, wrapped in folds of tissue like an oversize gift from Fred Segal.

Dr. Hackman smiled crisply, like the Stepford gynecologist. "Any problems?" he sang while snapping on the gloves.

Weight gain and resulting low self-esteem. Anxiety over my eggs dying daily and Tim not addressing it. Looming spinsterhood, excessive caffeine, hormone-related mood swings, that lone black hair sprouting from my left nipple, a constant urge to pee, sexually transmitted diseases he may have missed during my last ten exams, lack of intimacy with Tim and resulting orneriness, inability to maintain lasting or meaningful relationships . . . probably due to weight gain and resulting low self-esteem . . .

"Nope," I said.

"How about your libido—still having trouble with that? Is the new pill helping?" Suddenly I regretted the confession of my last visit. I'd hoped for a biological answer to the problem. Of course, I should have been talking to Tim or a shrink, not my gynecologist.

"No trouble," I lied.

"Great. Let's do it." Then he assumed the position. "Scoot up now, Julie . . . more . . . more . . . ," until my crotch was just as close to his face as either of us wanted it to be. He clicked on his headlamp, an obvious excess. I imagined it with its own windshield wiper and fog dimmer lights. "Alrighty, let's see what we've got." And he stared. "Jingle Bell Rock" droned through the ceiling. This has to be the weirdest moment of the whole exam, when I pretend to look at the ceiling so I don't have to look at him looking in me. I hid behind my tissue fortress and thought about the latest ad layout for the studio's Academy campaign, featuring Mel Gibson. There were two shots, each with Mel looking equally forlorn, but in one he looked especially pensive. We'd been calling this one "the furrowed brow" shot, and it had tested well with older, more conservative audiences, the ones most demographically similar to the Academy members whom we needed to vote for Mel. Meanwhile, Dr. Hackman discussed the merits and drawbacks of a competing studio's marketing campaign, something about SpongeBob SquarePants and over-branding.

Then without warning he furrowed his brow just like Mel Gibson, as if he saw something that had no business being in there. A long moment passed, then his brow unfurrowed and a proud smile formed. "Hmm . . . looking good." And I wondered absurdly, *Is this a compliment?* Should I say, *Thanks?*

"There's just one thing," Dr. Hackman said casually, loudly, tossing the gloves into the scary red biomedical-waste container, and the words were like another personal invasion. What one thing?! Somewhere, Vincent Price cackled.

"What?!"

"It's not terribly serious, Julie, don't be alarmed," he said quickly. I swallowed and tried to count to ten as I felt my blood pressure rise and my head swell with heat. Dr. Hackman spun back on his stool.

"There may be some . . . abnormal cells . . . on your cervix." My mouth opened but nothing came out. "I can't be sure until the cytology report comes back from the lab, but we may need to take a closer look and perhaps have the affected area . . . removed . . . that's all." He smiled cheerfully, stood up, and prepared to leave me feeling sullied and alone in my johnny.

"What?!" I repeated, and Bess appeared in the doorway. Madonna's version of "Santa Baby" piped into the room. She'd had her baby at this hospital, I thought. There was nothing wrong with *her* cervix. Unfair.

"Actually, you're in luck." Dr. Hackman beamed as though he had not just told me that I might require more unwelcome vaginal action. "We can probably get you in before the New Year." Then, to Bess, as though I weren't in the room, "Possibly some atypical cells. Schedule a colposcopy in the next few weeks to rule out dysplasia, and let's get the Pap back this week."

"But—" I squeaked. Dr. Hackman swiveled his head toward me and smiled tightly. A common Hollywood smile. A "this meeting is over" smile.

"Try not to worry," he explained patiently on his way out. "Atypical cells are fairly common—the important thing is to detect them early, and that's just what we're doing. A colposcopy will let us take a closer look, and if the cells have dysplasia, we'll remove them."

"How?" I choked.

Dr. Hackman remained at the door, smiling. "Well, there's a few possibilities. One is called a LEEP procedure and it's done right here. Fairly routine. Bess can give you some literature so you can get up to speed and know what to expect. But let's not worry until we see the pathology report." *Up to speed?* Pathology report? My heart sank into my ankles. They both left, and I contemplated escaping through the window. Instead I dressed, zombie-like, plagued in silent doom.

"We'll call you when the results are in, and to confirm the appointment," chirped Bess back at the reception desk as she wrote my name with a star next to it in the slot on December 31. As she wrote, the Santa pin jiggled on her collar, its tiny plastic pupils bobbing in their eye sockets. Mocking me. Bess darkened the star with her pen.

"What does the star mean?" I asked carefully, imagining it was a code for terminally ill patients that the office should be extra-nice to.

"Don't worry, Julie. We'll know more when we get the Pap back, but plan on keeping this appointment. That way, we're covered!" She beamed happily and filled out an appointment card with the date and time and thrust it toward me with a green holiday Hershey's kiss and a handful of pamphlets. "We'll put you in on the thirty-first at four forty-five—look, you're the last appointment of the year!"

As I escorted myself numbly to the door, I had no idea that dysplasia was a scary word that translated to "pre-cancerous cells on my cervix." I found that out later at about 4 a.m. when I was surfing gynecology websites in full panic mode, Tim on the floor beside me after I'd made him come home early from the set of *Slice of Death*. He read Bess's pamphlets as I printed articles.

"Says here it's a relatively common procedure that loads of

women have," he mumbled in that slightly condescending, trying-to-be-empathetic tone.

"You don't get it!" I cried unreasonably. "Precancerous cells on your cervix can lead to *problems*. This might affect our ability to get pregnant!" Of course, I had no idea if this was actually true, but it sounded convincing. He shot me a look as though I'd suddenly turned into someone else. "Jules . . ."

"What, Tim?" I challenged neutrally, but his face said, *We're not having this conversation again now, are we?* The conversation about him preferring Jules-and-Tim the way we were. Me wanting to be Mr. and Mrs. Jules and Tim and possibly baby or two. Lots more syllables in my version.

"Cup o' tea, luv?" Tim asked me wearily, quietly, putting his hand on my shoulder and exiting the room. Rather than consider for the tenth time breaking up with him and moving on, as usual I chose the easier route of resenting him and plotting to change his mind. I read the printouts:

Moderate cervical dysplasia can progressively worsen without management with colposcopy-assisted surgeries. . . . During the LEEP (Loop Electrosurgical Excision Procedure), the abnormal cells on the surface of the cervix are removed with the help of a thin wire loop that is attached to an electrosurgical generator. A painless electrical current cuts away affected tissue.

Merry Christmas!

While we were in London, I checked the messages four times a day, Tim rolling his eyes with each call as the pounds, euros, and dollars clicked by. I'd made him promise not to tell his family about my "condition" and pretended that my incessant dialing had to do with Mel Gibson's approvals for the Academy-campaign radio ads (*Over forty top film critics agree!* as Mel roared in the background about duty and honor). Details of my job always seemed to impress Tim's family, originally sheep farmers from Leeds who'd accidentally become real estate moguls.

"Now tell us, Julia dear, why does it cost a bloody fortune to go to the pictures?" his grandmother would demand sweetly, and I'd feel solely responsible for the glut of low American culture polluting the other continents. The Christmas dinner passed as usual: gallons of sherry, doddering relatives, stale carols. Tim gave me a spa gift certificate and a beautiful Baume & Mercier watch, gifts that, in my state, only reminded me of the sound of my biological clock and an urgent need to relax. I gave him Final Cut Pro for our home office.

On December 27 at 9:47 p.m. while picking at fish and chips at Soho House, the slick gathering place of the London film industry, I heard Bess's message, cheerfully confirming my worst fears through thousands of miles of cellular technology. Even though I was expecting them, the words sliced through my stomach like a shot of acid: *We have your results. The Pap indicated moderate to severe dysplasia. We're all set for the LEEP procedure on the thirty-first. Inpatient surgery.* I retired my fork in a pile of tartar sauce and went to the window to replay the message. Tim shot me a look, concerned, then continued mesmerizing Kate Winslet with his stories from the set of *Slice of Death*. Bess's voice continued, "Don't hesitate to call if you have any questions, Julie. I feel terrible leaving you a voice mail, but, well, you insisted! Hope you're having a nice holiday."

Yes, my cervix and I are enjoying our last Christmas together, thank you very much.

"Bad news?" asked Tim in a voice of fake concern, as Kate Winslet widened her already enormous eyes.

"No, just work stuff." Kate smiled genuinely. I lied easily to actors, it came with the territory. As I sat back down, pale as a London native, Tim squeezed my hand affectionately as if to say, *Thank you for not ruining this for me with your bizarre and irritating hypochondria.* Soho House was festive; Christmas songs played and an old fireplace roasted real chestnuts with real fire. It made me miss L.A.

"Want to see the cutest picture of my son?" Kate Winslet suddenly asked me, fishing through a giant, shapeless sack that seemed rather unfashionable for a star like her. She hauled out a small photo album and proudly displayed the dog-eared page of her year-old son in a giant pumpkin costume. He was round and fearless, cute but noble, and his eyes held the confidence of a thousand princes before him and the adoration for a million mothers. He was beautiful, and I felt my heart leap at the sight of him. What could Kate Winslet be thinking, sitting here listening to Tim instead of being at home with that gorgeous little creature?

Kate Winslet could not have known that I suspected I had female cancer and would never have a son of my own to stuff into an orange velour outfit, especially if I waited for Tim to marry me, much less impregnate me, and so she was rather puzzled when I burst into tears and excused myself to the ladies'. Tim didn't speak to me the rest of the night, and when Kate awkwardly took her leave to attend a holiday party that we weren't invited to, he glared at me, his hollow cheeks puffing air like an angry, emaciated hamster. "Fucking hell, Jules" was all he said as we climbed into a taxi that wasn't taking us to a fabulous party.

A visit to Hampton Court Castle, seeing the crown jewels, and riding the double-decker bus did nothing to bridge the distance between Tim and me that Kate Winslet's son had inadvertently created. There really is nothing like a pending gynecological procedure to deflate holiday cheer. Plus, it was obvious now that the joy of planning for children together had escaped Tim, who liked to "live in the moment and not be chained to a schedule." This was, of course, one of the things that made me fall for him in the first place. Stupid girl.

"I can't believe you've taken an appointment for New Year's Eve," he complained again on our last night in London. He'd spent the day in used-record shops and I'd spent it sipping tea and inhaling scones while on the phone with Robin, soaking up the restless boredom of a big holiday. Days once spent in pleasant idleness with family: eating, walking, reminiscing. Maybe a leisurely drive to see a piece of land that someone had read about. A quick trip to 7-Eleven for more butter. That's what we'd do in Cleveland if we were there, I thought. Instead our days, the postholiday groove of a struggling couple, were empty with filling time and spending money. Tim called it freedom. Now we were alone together in a cheap curry joint.

"What do you want me to do, Tim? If I cancel now, they won't be able to see me for another three weeks. By then my cervix might fall off!"

"Sweetheart, nobody's cervix is going to fall off," he replied in that tone, a little more pedantic than usual. He always got that way when we spent time in London. I battled for control as the waiter put down plates of steaming, multicolored food. This had been a sexless holiday, and the tension between us held a resentful hunger: *I want sex but not with you, you insensitive jerk/uptight freak.*

"It just doesn't seem to be the most entertaining way to spend the evening, that's all I'm suggesting," he continued, slumping into his chicken vindaloo.

"If you're worried about missing Pete's, don't. I'll be home by six. Or you could just go by yourself. I'm sure there'll be someone to kiss."

Tim sighed, blowing a forelock of disheveled hair from his face. "We don't have to go, Jules. It's not the end of the world, it's only New Year's Eve." His tone implied strongly that I was ruining all his fun. We finished the meal in silence. The plane ride home wasn't much different.

That I was not the only woman in the world to have dysplasia did nothing to calm my nerves about the procedure to treat it. The bottom line is that part of the cervix has to be removed. Not a big deal; you lose a little bit of your cervix every time you get a Pap test, bed a well-endowed lad, or in female-hysteria legend, fall from a horse. During the LEEP they cauterize a piece of it off—

and in case you're wondering, yes, *cauterize* is a euphemism for *burn.*

I arrived at Dr. Hackman's early on December 31, still jet-lagged and swollen from a week of too many pints and no exercise. I wore a new Irish woolen sweater Mom had sent, a Christmas gift. Hardly necessary in Los Angeles, but I cherished the sense of family warmth it seemed to represent. I felt protected wearing it, like a child wrapped up against the world and my unmet expectations of it.

"Well, there she is!" said Bess, beaming, in the exact spot I'd left her two weeks earlier.

I gulped. "Let's get this over with." I smiled weakly. I'd told Tim I'd meet him at home by six-thirty. We were going to the party at eight—fashionably late, but not so late there wouldn't still be tables of free, expensive food for dinner.

"Right down to business, that's our Julie!"

I nodded and followed her into an examining room, this one larger than the last. I sat down on a cold steel stool and took a breath. The room had been prepped. Fresh paper stretched across the table, stirrups raised and waiting. Tools of the trade lay on the counter. They looked creepily similar to the bright New Year's Eve party favors in the lobby.

"Dr. Hackman will be right in to review the procedure for today," Bess said, and whooshed out efficiently. I listened to the din outside, patients bustling out; nurses and receptionists departing. Pregnant, preserved women called out "Happy New Year!" to the staff on their way out. Another doctor said, "Goodnight, Jimmy, Happy New Year," and I heard Dr. Hackman bid him goodnight in return. Carols still played on the stereo system. I imagined the collection of holiday Hershey's Kisses was almost empty now, a few unwanted silver ones resting tiredly in the bowl amid tiny chocolate crumbs. I changed into a johnny, turned my cell phone off, and took up a stiff position sitting on the table. Four-forty exactly.

Dr. Hackman opened the door with an uncharacteristic lack of energy. "Well, hi there," he said wearily and almost—quietly. He was still meticulously neat but something was missing, something was—deflated about him. I forgot for a moment to be terrified. The whole time he was explaining the LEEP procedure, I was wondering what had happened to him, to his zest, his zip, his joie de vivre. I'd always assumed that examining healthy vaginas and detecting bad ones made him happy; clearly it was his life's calling. His hobby was Hannibal the Great, and he had a wife and two kids. The End. But now something was wrong. Some bit of untidy humanity was escaping from him like an untucked shirt or a loose shoelace or a stray heroin track on an otherwise pristine forearm. I didn't want to know if my doctor had emotions. I preferred him to be odd, clinical and capable.

". . . so I don't think it will take more than forty minutes, if we're lucky, and you should be just fine. Some slight discomfort, perhaps, but we'll numb the area." He was finishing a speech he'd probably given a thousand times, like a cop reading the Miranda rights, as Bess worked frantically around him, prepping still more things, turning on instruments, laying out fresh gloves, turning the blinds just so. I waited patiently for him to finish, then as Bess pumped the blood-pressure cuff around my arm, I said, with as much dignity as I could muster, "I really think you ought to give me a Valium for this."

Dr. Hackman looked surprised, and Bess took pause on my arm. "Oh, now, I don't think that's going to be necessary." Bossy know-it-all that he was. He wriggled into his gloves.

I stiffened. "Well, ah, I'm a little tense and, ah, I—"

"Just try to relax," cooed Bess helpfully, gently pushing me back on the table, but it wasn't helpful. The more I looked around the room, the tools, the instruments, and thought about the procedure, the more I wanted to flee the building.

"Okay, scoot back now. Now forward a bit—"

"I just think this would be easier for all of us if I had some Valium. I really do."

"I can't give you Valium now; we're about to begin," Dr. Hackman replied irritably. "You should have told me before." He edged closer on his stool. Bess looked on sternly, then wheeled an instrument that looked like a thin version of the *Lost in Space* robot toward my legs.

"Well, okay," I said, panicking slightly. Dr. Hackman moved toward me, aiming the speculum like a weapon. "If you could just tell me what's happening, um, so I know in advance, that would help," I stammered, heart racing. Dr. Hackman looked mystified, as if he couldn't possibly understand what the big deal was about burning my cervix off.

"Now I'm going to turn on the ventilation machine," said Bess in a tone usually reserved for five-year-olds.

"Why?" I asked.

"To offset the odor," she said calmly. Now they were insulting my personal hygiene? What fresh hell was this? "What odor?!" I demanded.

"Burning flesh," she said matter-of-factly. And so we began, me longing for Valium, Bess and Dr. Hackman wanting the procedure to be over so they could get home to their New Year's Eves with people who had married and produced offspring with them. I tried not to squirm as the device went in and the tools did their job. The pain was specific and insistent. It hurt in a personal, big way. Imagine someone seizing the most vulnerable core of your being with giant tweezers—and poking it repeatedly with a lit jousting stick. I'll leave it at that. Before long I was inching up the back of the table, away from the doctor and his instruments, while simultaneously trying to make it seem as if I weren't, like a naughty puppy. Dr. Hackman practically chased me up the table. "Steady now, easy," he said, and I thought of Robert Redford in *The Horse Whisperer.*

As I was wincing and (pardon this nasty word coming up) *clenching,* Dr. Hackman paused. He'd been patient with my squirming, but now he threw up his hands and complained wearily, "You're making this really difficult. I can't work like this." It was about him.

"Sorry," I mumbled, wondering when it had gotten so weird.

"You're going to have to relax or we just can't do this, Julie," Dr. Hackman said firmly, waving an instrument in exasperation. Now his brows were really furrowed.

"I *asked* you for the Valium," I said helplessly. I glanced at the clock: 5:32.

"Well, if you want, we can reschedule and you can come back with a Valium prescription," Dr. Hackman said, and Bess sighed disapprovingly. I propped myself up onto my elbows. "If I leave now, believe me, I'm not coming back."

"You know, this is *not a big deal,*" Dr. Hackman argued.

Easy for him to say. I felt relatively certain that no matter what gynecological skills he had, however sympathetic he was, whatever celebrity vaginas he'd entered, he simply had no idea what it felt like to have your cervix burned off on New Year's Eve. "Well, if you could just warn me what is going to happen before it happens, it would help," I repeated.

"All right, so you want to proceed?" he asked patiently.

I shifted in the stirrups. "Let's do it."

"Try to think of something else," he pleaded. "You're so fixated on this, you really are making it harder than it has to be."

I tried thinking about Heidi Klum. Then Mel Gibson. Then my new sweater. Then Robin and Bum-Chin, reading scripts in Montana. Each thought lasted only a moment. And then I saw it again. Kate Winslet's little baby, in his bright orange outfit. I pictured them on Halloween, at a friend's party. I pictured them taking a walk to Big Ben and riding on a big bus. Reading *Goodnight Moon* together. I pictured them at school, under a Christmas tree. His bright, trusting face and her huge, vivid eyes, taking him in. I wondered at the end if any of my eggs that Dr. Hackman might accidentally be taking could possibly have contained the recipe for a being as lively and wonderful and full of promise as the Orange Pumpkin Boy.

Five fifty-nine p.m.

Then it was over. The machine clicked off. Bess exited the room. It was dark outside. "Well, I've never worked this late on New Year's Eve before," said Dr. Hackman mildly, calmer now. He put a hand on my knee. "You okay, Julie? We didn't lose you there did we?" The skin on his large, white hand was soft and cold, like leftover meat loaf.

"No, I'm okay," I lied, feeling queasy and a little as if I'd been on a boat for a week with horrible cramps. I was aware of a vague relief—it was over. But the last thing I felt like doing was going home to Tim.

"I'm sorry you were so uncomfortable. But the good news is we got it. We were lucky, that's what preventative medicine is all about." He sighed, glancing for a moment at the diplomas on his wall.

"You sound like my boyfriend," I groaned, and I heard Dr. Hackman give a slight chuckle.

"Well, that's good—I guess." When I said nothing in reply, Dr. Hackman asked innocently, "Is he the one?" in an almost normal tone.

I leaned forward, trying to sit up, but a million heavy bubbles of vertigo rose to the top of my head and weighted me back down with a plop. "He's British," I slurred, and Dr. Hackman laughed again, louder and more naturally.

"Hey, you look a little green," he said, vaulting from the stool to fetch a paper cup and fill it with cold water. Outside, dusk was falling and the air had assumed the anticipatory, controlled glee of a holiday evening. I let my head drop back on the pillow and sank into the table. Dr. Hackman handed me the water and I drank greedily.

"So he's British, eh? Bad teeth?"

"Bad ambition. Bad case of . . . American ambition." Had I said that? To my gynecologist? Something about the procedure had unleashed the honesty beast. Dr. Hackman looked at me in a new way, with understanding and . . . pity. For a moment our eyes met—mine black from my runny mascara, his bright yet full of fatigue and . . . resignation?

Just as one of us was about to break the odd spell, Bess's head appeared in the doorway, blond and somewhat antsy. She sensed an unfamiliar connection between us and must instantly have assumed it was inappropriate because she retreated, cleared her throat, and chirped, "How're we doing?" more to the room than to either of us, as if she might have to rescue him from a malpractice lawsuit or worse, my freakishness.

"Aside from being a little green and having a British boyfriend, she's just fine," Dr. Hackman replied, bustling with the blinds. I tried to nod and smile, but I felt hot all over and a little faint. Bess clearly had somewhere to be, had hors d'oeuvres to heat, sparkly stockings to squeeze into, and grown children to greet. I tried to imagine going home and enduring the ceremony of getting ready for New Year's, and the idea filled me with nausea. Tim was probably home pacing, not wanting to miss a second of Pete's party. I hadn't even planned an outfit, a situation that guaranteed we'd be late.

"I should go," I mumbled, glancing at the breast self-examination poster and squishing into the pillow. A new, dull pain was starting, and I was suddenly hit with the sense that this must be what labor felt like. Sort of. I shuddered, and Dr. Hackman moved over to the johnny closet and took out a fleece blanket and covered me.

"You're not ready yet. Why don't you rest here for a few minutes?" he suggested. "I'll be back in a few minutes to check on you." Before I could protest, he and Bess closed the door and I heard them talking in soft tones. Keys jangled. *Happy New Year*s were exchanged. A door opened and closed and I heard the familiar elevator.

Six fifty-eight p.m.

How time does fly when you're not having fun. I heard Dr. Hackman's practiced steps take him back to his office. A computer sang its trademark tone greeting. *I really should stop being a baby and get up now,* I thought, but I felt exhausted. I closed my eyes and breathed deeply, imagining Pete, Tim, Robin and Bum-Chin, Heidi Klum, and of course Kate Winslet . . . and suddenly she and Mel Gibson were starring in my latest poster, with the movie's tagline just over their heads: *You Ought to Give Me a Valium for This!* Everyone at the studio's marketing meeting, the next scene of the dream, loved my new TV spot, which featured Tim chasing half-eaten Hershey's Kisses across London Bridge with a large camera. The waiter from the curry place was his soundman.

Seven forty-nine p.m.

There was a knock at the door, and I bolted up. Shit. Shit shit shit. I felt awful, as though there had been a keg party in my uterus and there were still people who needed to go home. My head ached, I was thirsty, and my mouth tasted like yesterday. I looked at the clock on the wall. Shit shit shit. Oh, shit. Tim was going to kill me.

"Julie? Are you okay? Are you awake?" Dr. Hackman's voice was concerned but relaxed. I heard a television. It was a movie, an old one, you could tell by the music and the pace of the conversation.

"Yes, I mean, I'm okay. I fell asleep."

"Okay if I come in?"

"Sure." It wasn't like he'd never seen me in a johnny before. I pulled the blanket around me.

"Looks like we lost track of time a bit, eh? How are you feeling?" His eyes were warm, concerned, tired, and falling into what must have been the expression he wore when he got home at night. I wondered if he'd called his wife.

"Okay, a little weak to be honest." I sighed and tried to fix my hair, which I could tell looked as if I'd just had sex. A cruel irony.

"You look a little pale. I'm going to just take your stats." He walked over quickly, professionally, and before I could protest, I had a blood-pressure cuff closing around my biceps. God, I hate that thing. I hate how it makes you feel your own blood straining against your skin, a grim reminder that your brief life is contained in one vulnerable rhythm.

"Got mellow plans for tonight, I hope?" he asked, knowing I couldn't answer with the thermometer in my mouth. I shook my head. "A party then? New Year's Eve again, can you believe it? We always order in. Chinese. From Chin Chin." Doctors must practice these strange conversations they know they are going to be having with themselves during these awkward moments.

"I'm sorry to hold you up, Julie, but I do think you need to be still a bit longer," he said, looking into my eyes with an annoying bright light. He glanced at the clock: 8:01.

A voice in my brain, somewhere in the foggy crevices, said, *I really should call Tim to let him know I'm okay. Why am I not calling him? I could get up right now and—*

"It's a dumb party anyway," I said quietly.

"Aren't they all," he agreed, then added, "We'd always just end up fighting on New Year's Eve. Something about it brings out the worst in a couple I think."

"You and your wife?" I asked plainly. Here I was on New Year's Eve, half naked, still woozy from surgery, talking to my gynecologist about his holiday fights with his wife.

"Yes. We fought at every party I think." He laughed weakly, lost in some thought from another time. "I guess that's why we stay in now."

"Jeez, she must be worried about you by now," I said suddenly. "I feel bad making you miss your holiday. I'm really sorry. I just—I don't know why I can't seem to get it together—"

"It's no problem," he said quickly, and in such a way that I instantly knew he'd rather be here any day than home with his wife. "I couldn't have let you drive yourself home in the state you're in, and I had paperwork, so it wasn't wasted time." He flashed a polite smile, rubbed his eyes, and glanced out the window. Cars were stacking up on La Cienega, neon was snaking through the Strip. The city was coming alive in its lazy, horizontal way. "The kids are asleep by now anyway."

I looked at him as if for an explanation. Then there was that moment, between two people, when something might be said, but isn't. Something might connect, take hold somewhere in the other person's brain, waiting for a gate to open, a light to signal, a carpet to unfurl, saying, yes, come in, come across, step inside, oh, you won't believe how long I've wanted someone—anyone— to just come inside for a moment. Just a moment. Will it be you? And as I looked into Dr. Hackman's eyes, I saw it there, sensed the controlled pain, understood the potential of his anguish, whatever it was. I opened my eyes a little wider, leaned forward, and willed him to say something. Instead he vaulted toward the opposite end of the room, washed his hands briskly at the sink, and said, "Do you feel up to getting dressed?"

I wondered how many times a day he washed his hands. A lot. I stared at his back and decided I couldn't let the moment just pass. We spend every minute of every day holding. Holding things in, holding shit out. Holding it together, holding ourselves away from the ones we wish most would take us in. It was the end of the year, a piece of my cervix was gone, and I was with the wrong man. And I was blaming him, instead of myself, which was wrong.

"Why aren't you in trouble with your wife for missing New Year's?"

He turned his head slowly toward me and didn't look at all surprised. He waited a moment before speaking as he dried his hands thoroughly on a paper towel.

"I haven't missed it—still have four hours to go," he tried cheerfully, smiling tightly, but this is L.A., I fool people for a living, and I called him on it.

"I have to leave my boyfriend," I said suddenly. "He's fun and sexy and smart—well, okay, he's not that smart but he's kind, mostly—but he's shallow. He wants money and power and a three-picture deal and a nicer house and a skinnier girlfriend and all the things everyone here wants. That's okay, it's what he wants. There are so many things he wants. But he doesn't want to marry me."

Dr. Hackman looked at me with a new face. Loose, relaxed, compassionate. As if someone had unplugged him. "Well, that's a relief. I wondered when you were going to realize that."

I looked at him in horror. "At least it explains your lack of sex drive," he continued. "I know you were worried about that." He sounded warm, confidential, and—gay?

"You knew?! Why didn't you tell me it was because I was with the wrong guy? I thought something was biologically wrong with me!" I cried.

"I'm not that kind of doctor." He shrugged. "There was nothing physically wrong with you. It's not that uncommon, you know. Great girl, big dreams, wrong guy, ticking clock . . ." This last bit was too much. I cried stupidly, black tears running down my face like liquid tar. "Sorry," he said quickly, handing me a handkerchief from nowhere. "I hate that expression too.

"Listen," he said. "Lots of people are too tired and restless to have sex. It's the millennial age now, you know, we don't even need sex anymore. Technically." He laughed pitifully, a little too deeply. It was clearly a release.

"You must see it all the time," I replied, encouraging the conversation.

"What?"

"People wanting to blame their lack of sex drive on something physical that's easier to define. Less scary to understand."

"You're pretty perceptive."

"I'm not the only one." The words hung there, sharp and pointed. The drawbridge was down, the welcome mat dusted off after years of storage.

"Look Julie, are you going to your party or not?" It was a friendly tone, an inviting one, as if he were tempting me to cut class and go to the beach.

"No. I'm not. I never wanted to go in the first place."

He didn't seem surprised, just stood there, leaning against the sink, looking sort of amused and sort of like he might want to confess something of his own but wasn't sure yet if I could be trusted, the girl who begged for Valium. "Because of Tim."

"Yes, because of Tim," I answered. "And Kate Winslet's baby." When his face changed to an expression of concern again, I had to laugh. Suddenly I felt horribly, desperately lonely.

"I guess you don't have to explain that if you don't want to." He smiled.

"It'll take all night," I sighed.

Dr. Hackman took a moment, then his eyebrows shot up.

"Okay, Julie MacDonald, you're on. But I think you should get dressed." He swooped into the changing corner, grabbed my clothes, and handed them to me. My Beverly Hills gynecologist outfit—Mom's Christmas sweater, artificially faded, overpriced jeans, and Ugg boots. He smiled sheepishly as he left me there, and the room became a different place, suddenly textured but soft and inviting, a place you could sink your teeth into and taste a bit of human truth. I dressed slowly and smoothed my hair.

Eight-forty p.m.

"It's not like she misses me. She has the kids. And I have my work." It sounded as if he'd said it before, to himself—many times. Dr. Hackman took another sip of water and watched Bette Davis and Joan Crawford writhe on the sand in the final scene of *What Ever Happened to Baby Jane?* "Besides, we haven't been close in years."

We were in his office now, which had a comfortable couch and a television with a built-in DVD player on the cherry credenza. His desk was stacked high but neatly with folders, articles, messages, a medical catalog, and a few signs of his children—a badly painted paperweight, a family photo on a ski slope, a newsletter from Crossroads School.

"To be honest, we were never close." Then he opened his desk drawer, pulled out a pack of Marlboro Lights and an antique silver lighter, and lit one perfectly cylindrical symbol of death. For a moment I thought I was hallucinating. My female plumbing growled for narcotics. "You don't. Smoke?" I asked incredulously.

"Tragedies and holidays," he answered without missing a beat.

"Or both?"

"Today, both. Holidays *are* tragedies." He stared at me through the cloud of fumes and suddenly looked like a different person. Someone ancient and tired. "I'm gay." The words hung in the space between us like visible molecules from a cartoon about how air works.

"Oh," I replied. Maybe, I thought to myself, I should have gone to Pete's party.

"That's what I said," he breathed. "When I found out." He exhaled with a deep satisfaction.

"When was that?"

"Years ago. His name was Billy. William actually." He looked wistful, then disgusted. "I'm with the wrong person. Just like you."

The moment that followed was like the wait for thunder after you catch a flash of lightning in a summer storm. What would come next, and how big would it be? I still felt woozy, sore, defeated by the surgery, but this was a conversation I wanted to hear.

"Well, that's a relief," I finally said dramatically. "I was wondering when you were going to realize that—at least it explains your lack of sex drive."

His laugh was deep and real, reaching into empty, cavernous places in his soul, a you-got-me laugh. "You're not bad, Julie MacDonald. Not bad at all." I took a cigarette from him and we smoked contentedly in silence.

"Smoky Treats," I sighed, hauling deeply at the old taste. I hadn't had a cigarette in years, and it felt absolutely forbidden, akin to screwing someone else's husband in the restroom at work. Deliciously unthinkable.

"Excuse me?"

"That's what we called them years ago. Smoky Treats. My girlfriend Robin and I, when we'd go outside, out of our bosses' view. At the time it seemed like the only way to deal with having horrible jobs." It seemed a lifetime ago that I was young enough to hide my smoking from anyone.

"You *Hollywood* people and your *horrible jobs*. Try being a resident in ER," he scoffed affectionately, and I had to give him that. He sucked on the cigarette hungrily. "I used to go behind the bleachers to smoke with girls in high school. But"—he exhaled the smoke toward the ceiling—"I could never figure out what to do once we got there, so we'd end up talking. I did most of the listening actually. I became 'the Nice Guy.' " He smiled broadly.

"The curse of the brotherly label."

"Exactly. Then, naturally no girls wanted to go out with me— thank God—and I just listened to their guy problems. I became the nerdy guy who took care of the girls. It was very educational. Prepared me for being the perfect husband."

"And the perfect gynecologist," I said helpfully, shifting on the couch and looking at his diplomas.

He flicked the ash off his cigarette and looked at the ceiling, pursing his lips in thought. "I've never told anyone," he said quietly, looking right into me. "I've no idea why I just told you." His eyes were sad now, and his skin had a slight sheen that seemed not so clean anymore. He looked more like a person now instead of an idea—vulnerable, real. A flash of youth passed over his face like a sudden ray of light. Who might he have been? "But it sure feels good to say it," he allowed quietly. "Not that it matters anymore. I've learned to live with it."

"What about William?" I asked carefully, taking a long haul off my cigarette. The toxins seared my lungs, and my throat burned. My uterus hurt, my heart ached, and both ideas repulsed me.

"Never saw him again. A one-night stand, one night in medical school after cadaver lab."

"Now that's sexy."

Suddenly he put his cigarette out and stood up, a flash of fear on his face. "Why am I telling you this? Good God, you're my patient, you've just had surgery, it's New Year's Eve . . ." He looked exasperated, defeated. He wrinkled his face in scorn and said, "I'm so sorry."

He didn't seem to know what to do, looking helpless, standing there under his diplomas and awards and in front of his wife and children, his entire life a fraud. I stood up, reached out to him, and felt the blood in my head move like an elevator. I sat back down quickly, instantly feverish and light-headed. "Whoa."

He rushed over and caught me just as I was about to hit the floor. "Julie? Julie? Are you all right?" In a moment I was on the couch, my feet propped up and a pillow under my head. "Mmm-hmmm," I managed. "That's quite a lot for a girl to take in one night," I mumbled, and he laughed, an easy, relaxed sound, and in a moment I was sleeping again.

Eight-fifty-nine p.m.

The loud knocking jolted me awake as though a woodpecker were boring into my head for insects it was never going to find. I saw a blur in white and realized that Dr. Hackman was headed for the front lobby, where the sound was coming from. I heard him open the door, almost feeling his confusion—who could be knocking now? Then I head a terrible, unwelcome sound. A familiar sound. Tim's voice. Panic and guilt rose in waves to my chest, my heart pounding my head back to reality.

"I'm looking for a patient, mate, Julie MacDonald? Is she here?" The voice was anxious, demanding yet polite, but not, I deduced, fearful. It was not a voice that was worried about me, where I was, what might have happened. It was a voice that needed to get to Pete's party. I could smell Tim's preparty-preparation pheromones floating wayward from the reception area—soap, hair product, toothpaste (all natural, of course, from Wild Oats on Wilshire, where I once saw Ben Affleck buying a shot of wheatgrass).

"Is she *here?*" my boyfriend repeated. "She was supposed to be home hours ago, and, ah, I'm a bit worried." There was a strange pause and I heard the television. The New Year's movie marathon was still going on.

"I'm sorry, who are you?" I heard Dr. Hackman inquire politely from a professional distance, and I realized that even in this bizarre circumstance he was respecting patient confidentiality. "I'm Tim, her—em, roommate. She was supposed to be home half-six and now—"

Dr. Hackman replied in a tone that I hadn't heard him use before. "Oh, *Tim.* Her *roommate?*" It sounded like a biting accusation and I smiled inside. My gay gynecological knight in shining armor.

"Yeah. What time did she leave?"

"Well, Tim, since you're her *roommate,* and not family, I'm afraid I can't reveal any of the patient's personal information."

There was an awkward silence, which seemed to last years. Then I heard Tim say, "Are you . . . *smoking?"* His tone was so revolted he may as well have asked Dr. Hackman if he were playing with himself.

Finally I couldn't stand it and I called out, "Tim, it's okay. I'm in here."

Tim strode through the lobby, into the office, and stopped in his tracks as though someone had shot him. He stared at me, lying on the couch, full ashtray on my stomach—where I'd left it before dozing off—fully clothed except for shoes, my feet propped up, the TV on, and—what's *this?*—an open bottle of Johnnie Walker Black on Dr. Hackman's desk. Tim took a moment to take it all in. His face reddened, and his eyes scrunched in defensive confusion.

"Jules, you might explain—"

"I'm sorry, Tim, I should have called," I said quickly, and a sound escaped from Tim's mouth, a noise like a confused whale might make. Dr. Hackman remained behind Tim, who was staring at every detail in the office as though to make sure what he was seeing was real. His eyes rested for a moment on the portrait of Hannibal the Great.

"Julie. What the fuck."

"Tim, please—"

"I'm at home frantic, wondering where in God's name you are, leaving you messages, and the whole time you're in here, *partying* with, with"—he gave a hateful backward glance toward Dr. Hackman, who had by now extinguished his cigarette—"your . . . *fanny* poker?" Dr. Hackman raised his eyebrows like a confused young boy. "No wonder you're so *terrified* of coming here!" Todd spat sarcastically, and I could see he was . . . hurt.

"Tim," I breathed. "This isn't how it looks," I said calmly, but I was trembling. None of this was Tim's fault. He didn't irritate me anymore. I just wanted him to stop not understanding me.

"And how is it? Jules?" he asked quietly, a vein on his forehead pulsing angrily.

"I think you should leave now," offered Dr. Hackman.

Tim whirled on him. "Excuse me, Doc, but my fucking girlfriend is lying on your couch, she's three hours late for a very fucking important party, and you—should shut—up." Tim said the last three words emphatically with a finger jabbing into my gynecologist's chest.

"Now she's your girlfriend?" asked Dr. Hackman in a mocking tone.

We were all silent as the seconds passed. It occurred to me then that Tim looked ridiculous. He was wearing baggy green leather pants, a black Versace blouse, and a rodeo champion's belt buckle. Kenneth Cole loafers topped off the ensemble. But they were orange. He thought he looked cool. Suddenly I was content that he didn't want to marry me or have cute children who could be stuffed into pumpkin outfits. He was selfish, shallow, not someone who'd feel like staying home and nursing my weary uterus instead of trolling the latest schmooza-palooza in his trendy borrowed duds. Still, he wasn't really a bad person, just a bad boyfriend, and I did owe him an explanation. I hadn't planned this, but the time had inexplicably slipped away into the gynecological New Year's Eve matrix.

"Tim, I—"

"Why didn't you *call?!*" he barked, his face a mass of redness, his neck bulging with freshly worked-out and fat-free tendons. I had never seen him so unhinged, and it wasn't sexy. His normally hollow cheeks were puffy.

"I didn't feel well. I needed to lie down, and Dr. Hackman—"

"You look fine to me."

"I'm feeling better now." I was speaking plainly, as if I didn't have the strength or desire to be witty, mean, or sarcastic, a rare occasion. A new version of me had emerged following my surgery. Like Scrooge on Christmas Day, I had a whole new outlook after waking up in my gynecologist's office on New Year's Eve. Suddenly I felt bad for Tim. He had tried to understand me, had tried to make me happy. It was my fault for not admitting sooner it would never have worked out. We were too different, I asked too much, and let's face it, he was just too skinny.

"Right. Well." Tim stamped an orange loafer and I heard Dr. Hackman let out a little sigh. I took a deep breath. It occurred to me that Tim was waiting for me to get up. I settled deeper into the couch. He stiffened.

"Are you fucking coming or not?!"

"No. I'm not, and the doctor's right. You need to go." I stared at Tim. He looked incredulous, then saddened, then irritated. I saw him make a quick calculation in his mind. He checked his watch. "Fine. You two have a grand old time." But he stood there, testing me. The movie was over and the credits were rolling. Dr. Hackman moved toward his desk and poured what I assumed to be his second glass of Scotch. The bottle must have come out when I was sleeping. The liquid glubbing into the glass was the only sound in the room.

"Drink before you go?" offered Dr. Hackman, sitting down again calmly in his chair. Their eyes met, and Tim seemed to relinquish some of his anger, resigned to the assumption that his live-in hypochondriac girlfriend was having an affair with her fanny poker.

"No thanks." Tim gave one last look of confusion toward me. "Bloody hell," he muttered, and strode out.

"Tim," I called after him. He whirled.

"I'm sorry. I really am."

Nine thirty-seven p.m.

"I don't know what to say," I said evenly. Dr. Hackman sipped the liquor and looked over the glass at me. I sat up.

"I'm sorry," he offered in response. "Please excuse me for saying so, Julie, but I think you're better off without him."

"Easy for you to say. You're happily married." I smiled wickedly and Dr. Hackman grinned and shook his head. "What are you going to do now?"

"Why, you kicking me out?" It occurred to me that Tim and I were over and I didn't feel like going home. Ever again.

"No. But if we're staying here, I need to make a call." He

shifted uncomfortably and glanced at the photos on his desk, then he opened a drawer in his desk and pulled out a script. He held it a moment, then tossed it to me on the couch. "You could spend some time reading this if you're tired of Joan and Bette," he said a little meekly. I looked at the title. *Hannibal the Great*.

"Your Hannibal script!" I tittered. "You really wrote one!" I opened the first page excitedly.

"Try not to laugh," he pleaded in an openly gay voice. "I'll be next door, pretending to complete some paperwork."

I watched him walk out of the room, tall, straight, and thin as a piece of uncooked linguine. He turned at the doorway, his face a complex montage of fatigue, hope, and peace. "Chinese or pizza?"

"Pizza. Always."

"I was hoping you'd say that," he said gratefully, and headed for the phone.

Ten fifty-five p.m.

I gave Dr. Hackman my notes and he gave me another horse-pill-size ibuprofen. He had forbidden me to have any alcohol, as he was still my doctor and I had just undergone a surgical procedure. This time he was on the couch and I was at his desk, rocking in the large leather chair.

"I really think it's good, and I'm not just saying that 'cause I need a place to stay." I laughed.

"Really?" he asked eagerly.

"Yeah. Painstakingly researched. Great character, great detail—incredible detail, actually. How many books have you read about this guy?"

"Lost count," he said, lighting a cigarette. "When your life's a sham, you'd better have hobbies."

I offered him a small smile, unsure of how to respond.

"You have any?" he asked me.

"What?"

"Hobbies," he said obviously.

"Yeah. Projecting." The tears started, and though I willed them back into their cave, they resisted forcefully until the pain of controlling them became too much.

"Tell me about Kate Winslet," he said gently.

"Oh, that." I snuffled embarrassingly, snot and drool forming on my upper lip. I laughed a hideous fake snort. "It's so pathetic. *I'm* so pathetic. It doesn't matter now."

"Go on," he coaxed, pouring another Scotch, but this time he offered it to me. "Just a little," he warned, and I took it.

"It's just, we were in London for Christmas to see Tim's family, and we're out at this trendy bar and he's chatting up Kate Winslet, 'cause, you know, clearly she could be useful."

"He's an actor?"

"Director," I said, balancing the glass and swallowing a gulp of the Scotch, which tasted like smoke and fire and sorrow. I rushed on, "So she had these photos of her son, and he was this perfect, cute little child, and there she was sitting with us instead of being home with him, and it made me really resent Tim. Him wasting her time like that, when she could have been home with her son, when he doesn't even care about having a son." I stared into the glass and took another taste. The flavors danced on my tongue and settled, paving a road of ease for the next swallow.

"That's his prerogative, isn't it?" he said, but it was not a question. He leaned forward with his hands folded into each other. He sighed forcefully with a sincerity that caught me off guard. "You're not married, he's interested in his career, not children. And you've stayed with him, trying to change his mind. Telepathically. For three years."

"Three and a half," I answered tightly. An eternity passed as I controlled my blubbering, realizing how very right Dr. Hackman was, Robin was, anyone in my life who cared about me enough to ask *what* exactly Jules and Tim were *doing*. Then I said it. Years of denial in four small words: "I waited too long."

"It's not too late, Julie," Dr. Hackman said earnestly. "You'll meet someone else, someone more appropriate for you than Tim. I'm sure," he said evenly.

I stared at him. "How?"

"How do you think I got this script written? Persistence. Persistence is the key to life, Julie."

"Dr. Hackman, I—"

"Oh, for God's sake, call me James." He laughed and stood up.

"I thought it was *Jimmy,*" I joked weakly. Clearly he'd been dubbed that boyish nickname against every gay fiber of his will.

"Thanks." He rolled his eyes. "How nice *not* to be Jimmy, if only for the magic of this New Year's Eve. Now let's crack that bottle of Dom I've got here somewhere."

"Dom? You've got a bottle of Dom in your office?" I sat up and wiped my face. No more crying.

"Patient gift," he said excitedly, opening the cabinets above his desk with a flourish. "Location is everything you know. You wouldn't believe the things I get from patients and patients' husbands. Last year someone gave me a five-thousand-dollar gift certificate to Barneys." He laughed, and then his face fell as his eyes met mine. "There are some perks," he added a little sadly.

"You really ought to do something with that script. You have talent. And the studios are dying for historical epics, you know."

"I thought everyone hated *Troy?*" His face was young again, his eyes sparkling but relaxed.

"They never hate Brad Pitt," I declared. "They hated *Alexander.*"

"That Colin Farrell's a dirty little mick, isn't he?" he said devilishly.

"I'd do him in a second."

"So would I." And then another moment, open, easy.

"You know, it's not too late for you either," I told him suddenly. "Lots of people have"—I searched for the words—"mid-life . . . transitions." Dr. Hackman looked at me and laughed softly. "I mean it. It's not too late. . . ."

He touched my chin in a paternal way and met my gaze. His kindness was palpable, like a warm breeze, or the smell of fresh roasted chicken. "I have a brother, you know," he said. "He's straight. Art director. Successful. Nice."

"I have a powerful friend. Works for a big producer. Gets good scripts made into great movies." We stared at each other for a moment, smiling inside and out.

"Happy New Year, Julie."

"Get the Dom," I commanded. And he did.

TRACY McARDLE spent twelve years in entertainment publicity in New York and Los Angeles. She now resides in Carlisle, Massachusetts, where she happily cares for one horse, one goat, one dog, one man, and her cat Little. Her writing has appeared in *Premiere Magazine* and *The Boston Globe,* and her first novel will be published by Downtown Press in September, 2005. She is currently at work on her second novel.

Halo, Goodbye

KATHLEEN O'REILLY

New Year's Eve used to be my favorite holiday—the operative words being *used to be.* My first kiss came on New Year's Eve. New Year's Eve was the first time that Jeff whispered, "I love you" in my ear. My first marriage proposal was *supposed* to be on New Year's Eve. Unfortunately, a bad thing happened on the way to the engagement.

I died.

I know what you're thinking: "Ewwww, she's a dead person." Well, shame on you. You shouldn't judge until you've met a real live dead person. We're not all freaky.

My name is Madelyn Arbrewster, late of New York City. Current address: #37 Saint Peter Place, and my town house here is *sooo* much nicer than the East Village studio that I subsisted in.

My new place has lots of space with a really nice music collection as an added bonus. The Beatles (John and George, live from Saint Paul's Pavilion), two of the Brothers Gibb, Jimi Hendrix, and Jeff Buckley. Even better, most are autographed.

Sounds perfect, idyllic, divine, right? Yeah, I know. And heaven is more than just great music. Before I died, I had heard all the imagery: A place with clouds and little angels that glide around with harps and halos. Let me be the first to correct the mis-stereotype. In actuality, it's a huge metropolis with Starbucks on every corner (all free), eternal 90 percent off sales, and twenty-nine hour days. At first the clock thing really confused me. Why twenty-nine hours? Why not, for instance, forty-two? But after a few months I began to understand that *five* extra hours was the perfect amount. Not enough time to cram in *another* project for the day, but just enough to have a quality goof-off experience.

Yup, heaven is truly a great place, and I mean, I'd be a total wuss if I had complaints, wouldn't I? So I don't complain.

It's been almost two years since D-Day (New Year's Eve is in three days), and I've made a few friends since I've been here. Oscar is probably the person I trust the most. Sadly, he still has death issues. I'm a supportive friend and try to help him, but tell me this: If Freud can't help him, why do I think that I can? It's these sort of conundrums that keep me busy in eternity.

Oscar shows up every morning for his daily rant, so at 10:45, when the doorbell rings (church bells, v. grandiose), it doesn't take divine intervention to know who's behind Door Number One.

"You get your assignment yet?" he says. "This is *bleep*ed."

Then he gets his snarly face, which signals the onset of acute rage. (There are no high-blood pressure issues here—HELLO? Dead already.) "I hate it when they *bleep*ing do that!"

Oh, yeah. I forgot to mention the one little drawback. There's a serious Big Brother thing going on here. The Angels of the Fourth Celestial Order decreed a *long* time ago that there would be no swearing in heaven, because the Big Guy would take offense. Ergo, as what happens in decrees, swearing was outlawed. It's only the spoken stuff, though. Big Brother hasn't gotten as far as actual thought censorship, so most of us don't have an issue with this. Oscar has issues with everything.

However, I am well adjusted, calm, and even-tempered. I smile nicely at him, with just a hint of moral superiority, and remain silent.

He crosses his arms across his chest, and because he knows what I'm doing (and best of all, he knows I'm right), he takes a deep breath and forces the calm to move in. Oh, Oscar's nice enough to look at, with dark hair and dark eyes (a Puerto Rican–Scottish mix, which explains lots of his personality quirks), but he's also heaven's leading candidate for irredeemable man. There are women who might be willing to dream the impossible dream, but my feet are planted firmly on the, uh . . . ground. I had never been friends with a guy on earth, but in heaven it seemed to work out. One day at a time, that's my new motto.

"Did you get your notice yet?" he asks, looking a little friendlier.

Much better. See how nicely it goes when we follow the rules?

173

"Not yet," I answer, although I wonder what's taking so long. Everybody gets a couple of years to adjust to their new way of life, and then we get thrown tasks. An assignment of some sort: counseling, gardening, music appreciation, or needlework (and yes, the projects actually get finished up here. I was the world's best procrastinator when I was alive. Not anymore. No, siree! I've got all the time in the world).

When you get the assignment, it's sorta the angels' way of stamping you *Team Player*. Since Oscar now has his assignment, and I do not, I'm thinking there's a big flaw in the system. However, "God only knows" is more than an expression up here, it's a way of life. Besides, secretly I think I've figured it out. I think my assignment is to help Oscar deal with his anger. I had five sisters; I've dealt with the worst in human nature. To me, Oscar should be a walk in the park.

"What're you supposed to do?" I ask, more than a little curious.

"They want me to *bleep*ing set up some woman for New Year's Eve. Tell me how the *bleep* I'm supposed to do that from up here? For two years I've been twiddling my thumbs, waiting for something to do. Something important, something monumental, something to justify my death, and now I get this??? They want me to play *bleep*ing Cupid! Can you *stop that?*"

"It's the rules, Oscar. Live with it, sport." However, in deference to his hellish temper, I adjust the music selection on my stereo so that Miles "Choke a White Man" Davis is playing. I think Miles solves many problems. I spent the first three months after my death listening to "Blue in Green," and eventually I found much tranquility.

As the strains of soothing music wash over the room, he collapses on the couch. I take a seat in my counselor chair (it's actually a Barcalounger, but I take my roles seriously). "You don't know that your assignment's not important. I mean, what if you're destined to bring about world peace? Who is she? A UN delegate or something?" I ask, trying to be helpful and thinking that a bowl of dark chocolate truffle ice cream would be nice and helpful, too. And, Holy Ben & Jerry's, there it is! (Neat trick, aye? Heaven.)

"Christine D'Amore," he says, and then poofs up a cup of ambrosia.

"Porn queen?" I mutter between bites. Just FYI, you can actually scarf cold stuff very quickly up here with no icky brain freeze.

Oscar shakes his head. "Says in her bio she's a publicist."

"Do you know who you're supposed to set her up with?" I ask, being the kind, considerate, "Doctor Is In"-type friend. Told you I was good serious about this.

"Martin Coleburn," says Oscar, checking his parchment.

Coleburn? What a coincidence. "Not on Thirteenth Street," I say, still wearing my perky, heaven-smile.

"Yeah." Oscar looks at me, all weird-like. "How did you know?"

How did I know? See, Martin Jeff Coleburn (don't ever call him Martin—it's a family name) was my fiancé, the boy I decided to marry when we rode the crosstown bus home together from the Dylan Thomas School of Advanced Environmental Studies and I dropped my Walkman in the seat behind me. It broke and then, miracle of all techno-miracles, he fixed it with a rubber band. Together we rode the C train and ripped CDs (not at the same time). My own metropolitan love story.

Sadly, I still love Jeff and miss him lots (mostly late at night when the ambrosia wears off, and you're all alone in your bed for your required twelve hours of sleep), and I wonder how my Jeff is holding up. He was really broken-up when I died. Matter of fact, I was, too. Death by subway is never pretty.

"Jeff's first name is Martin," I say, but I'm still thinking this is a huge misunderstanding. Actually, it's impossible. Jeff would never do that to me. Not in a million years. And it's only been two. The whole thing's completely inconceivable. I scarf down the last scoop of the ice cream, and then promptly poof up another one.

"Oh, sorry, kid," he says, his dark eyes full of pity. "But people move on. Even boyfriends."

"He's more than my boyfriend. He's my fiancé," I say, and pause dramatically, waiting for trumpets to flourish.

Silence.

Nada.

Zip.

I repeat the magical words, just in case God missed the cue. These are words I've said to myself so many times (I died before I could say them to an actual living person). I've been practicing up here, late at night, when nobody but Big Brother could hear me, but it's not the same.

Oscar looks at me with counselor-type eyes. "You didn't tell me that you were engaged."

"Well, it wasn't *exactly* official. Besides, it's personal, you know?"

"Do you want to talk about it?" he says.

"I just did," I answer, not sure what he expects me to say.

"So he was your fiancé, huh?"

Was. God, I hate that word. Have you ever analyzed the meaning of *was?* Was. Was. Was, was, was. Nothing *is* anymore, only *was.*

I smile at Oscar like everything's fine, because after all, I'm in heaven. "Let's not talk about this anymore. Turn on the TV, okay? What's his channel?" I ask, pretending I don't have it memorized. Look at me, I'm smiling. See Madelyn smile.

"7341837."

I click on the remote to Jeff-TV. Now you're saying, "Uh, Madelyn, don't think there's a Jeff-TV. Diving right off the deep end, aren't we?" Uh, no. Everybody on earth has their own channel, and we up here get to watch what you're doing. Did you ever get that feeling that somebody was watching you? Well, I'll let you in on a secret. You were right. So when you think nobody saw you run that red light at midnight—think again—J. Edgar is keeping files.

I should tell you that from up here people-watching is a lot more boring than it sounds. Although when I first died, I did it a lot. I'd watch my family: Mom, Dad, and four of the absolute bitchiest sisters in the world (actually, only Miriam, Mary, and Meggie are truly of the devil; Maggie is really nice). And then I'd watch Jeff. And sometimes, when twenty-nine hours was five hours too many, I would sit there watching the crowds at Macy's and practice my spiel. See, when I was alive, I worked in the visitor information booth. "Hello, welcome to Macy's. I'm Madelyn. How may I help you today?"

It was very sad and pathetic and eventually I realized that it was time for me to find something else to do. Currently I'm still looking.

Anyway, Oscar and I, we sit there and watch. There's Jeff, sitting at his desk (he's a loan officer for Chase Manhattan), playing with the desk-bowling set that I gave him for Christmas two years before I died. Previously I thought that he kept it to humor me, but I've watched him play for a good two years now; I think he actually likes it.

When he looks up, the God-Cam zooms in on his face and I study it closely. Are there any lines of sadness marring the olive skin of his forehead? *No.* Telltale circles to indicate sleepless nights? *None.* Little unhappy apostrophes hovering around the mouth? *Missing.*

In fact, that looks like a smile hovering on the edge of his mouth. People who aren't familiar with Jeff's emotional-concealment abilities might think so, but I know better. I've known Jeff all my life, at least from high school on. Nobody knows him like I do. (Favorite color: bright green. Best CD: *Ritual de lo Habitual.* Band you'd camp out for three days to see live: Queen.) Nobody can ever know him like I do.

When I look up, I can see my own face in the glass of the screen, a ghost of the woman I used to be.

Frown lines? *Check*. Circles under the eyes. *Check*. Unhappy apostrophes. *Check*.

God, I look like crap.

Tell me what's wrong with this picture? I'm in heaven. Why are there unhappy people in heaven? Heaven should have no unhappy people; that's why they call it *heaven*. Hell is where the people are not happy.

I click off the TV and my image of happy-Jeff. I can't watch this; I refuse to believe he could fall in love with someone else.

And of course immediately I ask, "What's her channel?" falling into the age-old ploy of tormenting myself with the other woman (okay, other woman-to-be). I hope she's fat and ugly with bad pores (Jeff used to really love my skin).

Oscar, who if he were smarter would stop me on my path to self-flagellation, checks the parchment again. "83720."

I change over and up zooms an image of Christine D'Amore. My unhappy apostrophes sink lower in the side of my mouth. "He'll never go for her, look at that cleavage. Fake boobs. He hates 'em."

Oscar tries to hide the fact that he is checking out Christine's Barbie-boobs. I give him points for trying, but I still hit him. "Stop it."

Mr. Man, who probably dated strippers in a past life, tries not to look like he's been busted. "This can't be healthy for you. You should go talk to somebody. A shrink or something."

I am in no mood for patronizing psychobabble, so I smirk back, completely nondivinish. "Screw you, Oscar."

"Excuse me! She said 'screw you,' doesn't that count, you *bleep*heads?" he says, and then makes a big deal out of looking for secret listening devices.

Those who don't know Oscar as well as I do might consider this rude, but this is Oscar's way of cheering me up, which I think is very un-Oscar of him. Yeah, I know the relationship is weird, but the most high-maintenance people truly do make the best friends.

Sadly, I realize that the high-maintenance shoe is now on the other foot. My foot. "I'm sorry. That was mean and I know you're trying to be nice, in your own unique way, but . . ." I stop, transfixed by the screen. She's gorgeous. How can Jeff *not* want her? I sink into my couch and torment myself further. "Do you think she looks like a bitch?"

Oscar has learned his lesson and doesn't hesitate before responding. "Absolutely."

"And fugly, too, don't you think?" I ask, mainly because I want to test out this new and improved Oscar. Just how far will he go?

Neatly he dodges the question, "You shouldn't do this to yourself. Get out of the house. Mark Twain is speaking at the Olympus Theater, should be fun." He takes in my apathetic stare, stands up, and starts pacing around the room, his hands stuck in his pockets. "Look, it's obvious that this is a bad idea. . . . You shouldn't be involved."

"NO!"

"I don't think this is healthy, Madelyn. Go see the Angels of the Seventh Order, you know, like you're always trying to get me to do." He looked pleased that he thought of this, and I realize that I *have* been making progress and didn't even know it.

But the Angels of the Seventh Order? The *last* thing I want is more Life Therapy. (Imagine yourself in a quiet place. Tranquil. The water is flowing . . .)

I crank up Miles even louder.

Then I look at Oscar, a woman completely in control. "Of course I have to help you. You can't handle this Cupid stuff all by yourself, you said so yourself. Tell me what you know. I want to hear all the details. Don't leave anything out."

He stays silent and stubborn, still needing to be convinced.

I laugh. "Oh, please. It's been two years. Of course I'm over him. It's time, you know? Now. Details." I smile at him encouragingly. "Please?"

Oscar sighs, knowing I'm unstoppable. "He's going to run into her on the Eighth Avenue local during rush hour."

I smother my heart attack. Not the C line. That's our train.

"She thinks he's cute and will kick her bag under his seat—" The slut.

"—then he's going to ask for her phone number."

I begin to study Christine in earnest. "I don't think he will. She's really not his type, and the old-kick-the-bag-under-the seat is just so obvious."

I don't mention that I met Jeff that way. But he was younger then, less wise in the ways of women. Oscar's got too many problems of his own for me to dump on him. I'm supposed to help him, not screw him up anymore. Besides, I've got things to do, people to see, lives to interfere in, and I'm not about to listen to more lectures from Oscar.

"You should go; it's six hours to rush hour. And more important, it's time for *Crossing Over*." To Oscar, those are magic words. He is wildly obsessed with the spiritual world. A psychic predicted that he would save the life of a little old lady who was in the path of the M100 bus. He saved the little old lady, but died in the process. He's blamed the psychic ever sense. Told you he had death issues.

He glances toward the door, temptation in his eyes, and then he looks back at me. "I don't think. You won't do anything stupid, will you?"

"Oh, yeah," I scoff. "Come on, we're in heaven. What the heck can you do up here? You worry too much," I said, which was a complete lie because Oscar isn't a worrier by nature, but I needed him out of there. And fast. I checked the clock. "Isn't *Crossing Over* coming on in about ten minutes?"

"It's being preempted for *The World's Great Unsolved Mysteries*."

Unsolved Mysteries is our own little version of Reality TV up here. Very popular, although not usually Oscar's style. "Who's on?" I ask, diverting Oscar from my ulterior motives, all while still trying to figure out what Jeff could possibly see in her (once you got past the platinum-blond hair, the breasts, and the teeth). I don't think he'll go for her. Really I don't.

"Nicole Simpson. They're really hyping the whole 'who killed Nicole' thing."

"Go on," I say, waving my hand carelessly in the air. In fact, I even power off the television. Still he hesitates. "Go," I say, "get outta here."

Finally he nods and walks out the door.

After he's gone and I'm safety alone, I page through the electronic flyers until I find the one that I had bookmarked.

Have you recently widowed your man? Wanting to cement yourself in your life partner's life for all eternity? Join the Ladies of the Black Hat Society for an afternoon your dearly left-behind won't soon forget.

Perfect. Absolutely perfect.

The meetings were set in the Dorothy Parker Auditorium. I had walked by it a million times, but never dared pass through the hallowed walls.

It's a huge place; the main hall is filled with women, of all colors, sizes (although perfectly shaped—heaven-perk, no fatties unless you opt for it, and *no* one opts for it). And everyone is wearing a black hat. There are black marabou feathers, black sequined flapper hats, even a few black burkas. I put a hand on my now conspicuously bare head.

Instantly a uniformed woman appears, black hat in hand. "You must be one of the newly dead," she whispers as she thrusts it in my hands.

"Actually, it's been almost two years," I say, rather loudly (but I do jam the black trucker cap—ICK!—on my head).

"Denial for all eternity," she says, shaking her head before pointing to a seat near the front—dead center, of course.

I eye the bodies that I'll need to plow through to get there. "Don't you have one in the back?"

She starts to laugh, a high cackling voice. Heads turned. I am shamed. I use the trucker cap for cover and make my way to the front.

"Madelyn Arbrewster?" comes a voice from the front.

Uh, I'm in the middle of sitting down, thank you very much. "Here," I answer, casting an apologetic look to the poor woman who has my butt in her face. Damned auditoriums are too small.

"No, Madelyn, we know you're here. We're ready to hear your story. It's Black Hat Protocol."

I sit down in the first available seat.

"We can skip right over that. My story is boring. A real yawner," I say, as loud as possible.

The camera zooms in on my face and suddenly I'm on the Jumbotron. The voice booms on: "My husband used to tell me that the only thing I have to fear is fear itself. You're among friends. Speak."

And yes, for the record, it is possible to be publicly humiliated in heaven. "Do I have to do this?"

"We all do, dear. It's part of the grief process."

Okay, fine. I take a deep breath. "I was engaged to be married. . . ."

The crowds *ah's* together.

"How long?"

"Well, *technically* we weren't engaged yet. But we nearly were—"

"No, how long since you died?"

"Two years."

"He's thinking of moving on?"

I nod, and the woman next to me whispers, "The cad!"

"He's really very nice," I whisper back, needing to defend the man I would've married.

"Oh, they're all nice until you die. Then you might as well be yesterday's *Post*, as much attention as they pay to you."

"Has he found someone new?" asks the woman up front (who I have decided looks suspiciously like Eleanor Roosevelt).

"No," I answer back.

"Then there's still time. Don't worry, dear," she says, and then pounds with her gavel. "So let's get back to business. We've all met Madelyn, and now I'd like to introduce our speaker today, Helen, who will tell us the importance of the tender memory and how to keep the fires of passion burning forever."

There is polite applause, while a Grecian-clad Helen comes forward to the podium and nods graciously. She taps the mike.

"Is this on?"

The crowd titters.

"Hello, ladies. Today we're here to talk about fidelity. We're loud. We're proud. We're dead. But how does your civil union hold up when death breaks you apart? Will he stay true to memory or is your dearly nondeparted thinking of parking his chariot in some other country?"

The black hats start to bob in concert, and the murmurs begin.

"Yeah, sister."

"Amen to that."

Helen pulls the microphone free and starts to walk around the stage. "A face can launch a thousand ships, but what good does that do you up here? It takes brains to keep your man faithful after death. And a commitment on your part. A commitment which, for some of you, may last another fifty, sixty, or seventy years if your man's in good health. So ask yourself, is he worth the trouble? Let's face it, there are a lot of great men up here in heaven. How do you know *he's* the one?"

Lots of heads nodding and thoughtful looks.

"So tell me, is he worth the trouble?"

"YES!"

Helen smiles and then a checklist appears on the Jumbotron. "Then it's time for action. Here are what I like to call Helen's Hints for Happier Post-Death Relationships. Step One: Subtle Reminders. Does he have a favorite oil—"

Eleanor whispers to Helen.

"—oh, sorry, perfume, that he adores?"

Jeff liked Eternity by Calvin Klein.

"Use it sparingly, discreetly. At night spray his pillow with just hint. After all, you don't want him smelling like a Macedonian whorehouse."

"Step Two: Night Whispers. When he's asleep, this is your time to be most lethal. Whisper in his ear, telling him how much you miss him. A ghost-breath in the ear, and he'll be pulling out the bronze likenesses of you and putting them next to his bed—back where they belong."

I didn't remember if Jeff still had our picture on his bedside or not. I made a mental note to myself to check.

"The last step, our ultimate weapon in the fight to keep our man for all eternity, is pure self-preservation. You must be the harsh critic of *every single woman* who ever enters his life. Are her eyes crooked? Are her shoulders stooped from the strain of manual labor? You're the only one who can pull the blinders from his eyes."

I look around at the sea of desperate women who haven't let go. Is that me, too? Is love supposed to last for all eternity, or is that another urban myth, right up there with alligators living in the New York sewers?

But then I look at the women on the stage, the thousands of women around me, and realize that we can't all be wrong. Right?

I begin scribbling notes like mad. I could tell Jeff that Christine has hooters that are tougher than titanium. But why should I *have* to tell him about the faults of the other women in his life? He should see them on his own. All women should fall short when compared to the glory of Madelyn. If I were his true love, he would be faithful forever.

For a moment I sit and contemplate the injustice of two people separated by death. But what if (aagh . . . uck . . . ick) Christine is his destiny, and I was just roadkill on his path to true love?

Do I want to stay in this relationship (such as it is) enough to stoop to the level of desperation that is permeating this room? Of course I do, but I can't. Not while there's life still in this body.

Ignoring all the hacked-off coughs and glares, I get up to go. Before I can make it to the safety of the door, the usher stops me. "You shouldn't leave. We're here to help."

I clutch at my gut. "Stomach problems. Must . . . leave."

She's not buying it for a minute. "Can't cut it, can you?"

"I don't need this," I answer.

"Everybody says that their first time, but then you see a new toothbrush next to his, and it's not so easy anymore. You'll be back."

I just give her a little half smile that says "not on your life," and then walk off, the very image of a woman who has confidence in the love of her man.

Sorta.

By the time rush hour hits New York, I'm back at the town house high in the heavens, dark chocolate truffle ice cream in the bowl, and life-size Jeff heading for the C train. It's time. Oscar shows up and sits down, quirking an eyebrow at the ice cream. "Three bowls in one day? You told me you're okay. You're not, are you?"

"Look, ice cream is much better for you than all that ambrosia you've been slamming down," I say, simply because it's much easier to deal with Oscar when he's angry than when he feels sorry for me. I can't stand pity.

"That's *bleep*" he snaps, the pity gone, but I don't feel as satisfied as I should.

Then I notice that Jeff is heading down into the Chambers Street station, and my eyes lock on to the screen.

"He reads *The Wall Street Journal?*" asks Oscar.

I shake my head. "Nah. He never reads it. It's just to impress the guys at work."

We watch as the train pulls in, and Jeff sits in the seat next to the door. Immediately he pulls out the paper and starts to read.

I begin to wonder if I ever really knew Jeff. Perhaps he's a serial killer, too, and I never knew that about him, either. No, no, no, I'm jumping to rash conclusions. "You know, he's probably matured since I've died. The paper gives him some respite from the overload of emotional—" I stop speaking when I look at Oscar's face.

Oscar points. "There she is. Geez, she must have poured . . ." he starts, and then winces. "Sorry. Look, I'm a guy, you know. I'm not dead. Okay, technically, I am, but I still have eyes in my head, and you know me, I'm not Mr. Sensitive. And that dress . . ." he finishes, almost apologetically.

"It's Chanel," I mutter under my breath, because I could never afford Chanel on my salary, but at birth, Chanel-recognition is burned into the female psyche, smacked right in there between neurosis and denial.

I crank up the volume of my stereo because I'm afraid that when they meet there will be trumpets, and flourishes, and all that cool stuff that wasn't there for us, and I'm not sure I want to hear it.

And then Jeff and Christine are sitting across from each other. He looks up from his paper and freezes.

"Christine?"

He knows her? I look over at Oscar. "You didn't say he knew her. Why didn't you tell me that?"

Oscar gets an "I didn't do it" look on his face. "I didn't know. The angels didn't tell me."

(FYI: Angels can really be pesky little devils if you're not careful. The expression "angel of mercy" was "angel of *no* mercy" in its original incantation. And that's a note that you'll never find in the dictionary.)

"Do I know you?" Christine asks, and I personally think she's being a little uppity. I mean, Jeff's cute. Come on, now.

Jeff smiles and I remember all over again how perfect he is. *Was.* "From the bank. You came in the other day."

Recognition flashes. "Ah. Yeah, sorry. I try and block the money troubles out of my mind."

I snicker. Yeah, that's me, too. Well, not quite. Now I don't have any money troubles anymore. YAY! (Of course, if I'd known I was going to bite the big one, I probably would have charged that BCBG sundress and matching sandals at Macy's.)

They keep talking and I notice how her foot is kicking on the straps of her bag (Prada, the whore). Slowly, inch by inch, the bag is scooching it's big bag weight across the ick of the subway car floor. Jeff—who is not watching her feet—is oblivious.

"Run now, run while you can," I whisper to the TV screen.

"You shouldn't be watching this," says Oscar.

Damn. I forgot about the audience. "I was talking to the shady character in the corner. I think he's going for the bag, but the security cop is watching the whole thing. He's going to get busted if he goes for it." It's all a complete untruth but hopefully Oscar won't catch on.

"I think you should consider therapy. All this rage can't be healthy," says Oscar, sipping on his ambrosia, and just my luck, he's sharp enough to catch on.

"How many glasses of that are you drinking a day now?"

"Deny it all you want, but I know—"

Jeff starts to talk: "—New Year's Eve?"

WAIT! I missed that!

I point my finger at the screen and rewind.

"What are you doing on New Year's Eve?" Jeff is saying.

"He's asking her out!" I yell, and immediately jump up, because I'm trapped, trapped in heaven. So why am I freaking? Am I freaking? I'm not freaking. Of course I'm not freaking. She's hot, she's gorgeous, ergo, she's already got plans. Heck, I bet she's got plans for the next decade.

"Me and Dick are staying at home."

Ha! Told you. (Dick? Who dates a guy named Dick?)

"Your boyfriend?" Jeff asks, too polite to ask why the heck she's dating a man named Dick.

"Dick Clark."

Shit, shit, shit.

"Want to do something?" Jeff says, putting *The Wall Street Journal* aside, moving to serious and—oh, God—more meaningful endeavors.

"OF COURSE SHE WANTS TO DO SOMETHING. YOU ARE A DOOFUS!" I yell at the man I was planning to marry. It seems appropriate.

Oscar gets up and reaches for the Power button on the television.

"DON'T TOUCH THAT DIAL!"

Obediently Oscar sits. "This is wrong. This is so wrong. I can't believe I'm sitting here. I'm worthless as a friend, aren't I? Maybe this is God's way of paying me back for all those times I was crappy to women. I don't know."

I flash a smile in his direction. "Stop worrying. I'm fine." Then I calmly put my hands in my lap and I concentrate on something else.

For instance, the pillows I quilted two months ago. Oh, God, they are SHIT!

No, no, I can do this. I am a mature, sensible dead woman. I can watch as the man I love moves forward with his life.

"I'd love to go out," Christine says to Jeff.

And how did I know that's what she would say? Possibly because although Jeff is not the world's greatest hottie, he's handsome and has a smile that can melt even the most steely inhibitions. Christine is a mere woman. She can't resist him, any more than I could. And worst of all, she's alive.

"Madelyn, stop. You have to start over," says Oscar to me, taking a respite from his psychic-murder thoughts to show compassion for his currently high-maintenance friend. Truly, I think he's moving on, and I feel a little warmth that I was able to help.

Christine crosses her legs, Jeff's gaze razors in on them, and my warmth is gone; instead my fingers itch for another bowl of dark chocolate truffle. It is very hard to restrain myself from poofing up another one, but I do. "I'm dead. We don't move on."

"Why not?"

"Have you?" I ask, which is a rhetorical question, because Oscar is still fixated on murdering Madam Psychic in the parlor with the crystal ball and we both know it. I am not contemplating nondivine felonies, merely the man who holds my heart.

He rubs two fingers into his forehead like he's dodging a bad hangover. It's all that ambrosia he drinks; I know it. "The *bleep* needs to learn she can't jack people around like that."

"They'll kick you out of here if you don't watch the attitude."

"Heaven sucks."

I'm ready to deny it, but as I sit here on my couch, watching my ex-fiancé make moves on a woman who is so much better looking than I was (am), I realize that heaven is not quite the idyllic vacation spot that people would have you think.

There are people up here who lived a full life on Earth, or even better, passed away after a lengthy illness. These are the lucky ones. They got to apologize for spilling Diet Coke on that great silk blazer that they swore they wouldn't borrow. They got to say goodbye to their parents. They got to arrange a quick deathbed ceremony so that the love of their life is cemented to them for all eternity—by something other than seven absolutely perfect (yet ephemeral) memories of New Year's Eve.

They say life isn't fair. Well, it's a helluva lot fairer than death.

"Why do we have feelings up here?" I ask him, because it seems to me, heaven would be a much easier place if we didn't have emotions.

"Without sorrow, there is not joy. Without anger, there is no peace."

My eyes cut over to make sure I'm not suddenly sitting next to Gandhi. Okay, not Gandhi. "Did you make that up?"

"No, they teach it in my anger-management class. There's a

grief-management class, too. Marie Antoinette is leading the session this time."

That's it. I just can't handle it anymore, so I turn off the television, ready to scream. Later I'll sneak a peek when the coast is clear; right now I don't want my only friend to see a woman on the verge of a nervous breakdown. At this moment I'm eternally grateful for my four sisters because I spent twenty-seven years hiding my feelings; I am the master of all things quashed. I smile at him, my heaven-smile. "Maybe it *is* time to move on."

"Go to one of the dating services."

"You've been out on any dates since you died?"

Oscar shakes his head. "I'm too busy."

Oh, puh-lease. "You have all the time in eternity."

"So do you," he says, shooting me one of those "holier than thou" looks that I'm intimately familiar with (mainly in my mirror).

"Are you going to give me a lecture?"

He shakes his head like I'm a foregone conclusion, and then he gets up. "Call me if you need me." Then he's gone.

So . . . here I am, three days to New Year's Eve, and I'm alone. In heaven.

Instantly another pint of ice cream appears. And cupcakes (better than Magnolia Bakery, truly). I walk over to the stereo and put on Orgasmatron, which suits my mood *so* much better than Miles.

Unable to resist, I turn on the TV and watch as Christine is coloring her hair. You would think she would go to one of the chic-chic places in Chelsea to get it done, but no, she's sitting in her tiny bathroom, towel on head, the egg timer set to precisely 25 minutes. Slowly the minutes tick away. Hair coloring is a tricky business; so many things that could go wrong.

So many things . . .

So . . . many . . . things.

I began to smile. This woman doesn't deserve Jeff. I mean, who is she? She's obviously financially irresponsible, dressing in Chanel and then taking out a bank loan. What's that about? I could see Chapter 11 in Jeff's future, if he wasn't careful. If he didn't have his own personal guardian angel watching over him. . . .

It took only a second to move the dial on the timer back about—oh, 15 minutes. Am I feeling guilt? Do pigs fly (heaven note: even up here, pigs do not fly)?

Another thirty minutes go by before Christine unveils her new look, her hair now a glorious green hue. Very conveniently, it was Jeff's favorite shade. Then she looks into the mirror and I smile to myself, waiting for the shriek of horror.

Wow, she screams much louder than I ever could and I dust my hands, feeling completely satisfied. If I hadn't interfered, where would Jeff be? Probably panhandling outside of Trump Tower with the rest of Gotham's poor, that's where.

However, my moment of satisfaction is short-lived because Christine starts to cry. And it's not those graceful little tears that well up in the corner of the eyes. Oh, no, these are big honkers, and she's wailing her lungs out. Remember that guilt I wasn't feeling before? Okay, maybe it's there. Just a little. She cries harder. The guilt magnifies.

She hammers a fist at her mirror. "This isn't fair."

"No, it's not," I snap back.

Nervously she looks around her tiny bathroom, never considering the possibility that the dead love of Jeff's life is hovering nearby. But then she shrugs her shoulders, the green locks just brushing her shoulders. "He'll probably invent some excuse, a family emergency, or leaking pipes, and I'll never see him again because I LOOK LIKE A FREAK!"

Okay, she's not a pretty sight, I concur, but Jeff's an upright guy. He's not going to dodge out on a date, no matter how green her hair is. *"He wouldn't do that,"* I tell her.

"He's a guy isn't he? Of course he would. Do you know how long I've waited to meet someone nice, someone normal?"

"Too long?" I ask, because I know just what's she's feeling here. Dating in New York is the pits. Supermodels and rich guys, oh, yeah, they've got it made, but the rest of us? Forget it.

"Three years. It's been three shitty years."

"You'll find somebody new," I tell her in my soothing voice.

"I already did," she says, completely unsoothed, and then she collapses on the toilet and starts to cry, the voice from the Great Beyond conveniently forgotten.

I start to sniff while she sobs her heart out. She's not supposed to be nice. She's a bitch. I know she's a bitch because she's too great-looking to be nice. Somewhere buried deep inside my soul, my heart starts to crack in two, just as if it were still there. God, I can't stand this. Even the second cupcake doesn't help. So I turn to Jeff's channel, watching him walk the streets alone, pulling his overcoat close. The night is cold and dry and he looks so far away.

Overhead I know there are stars twinkling in the heavens, but when the city lights up, the heavens are obliterated.

My mother used to say that when it rains, someone in heaven is crying, but tonight the skies on Earth are cloud-free.

My mother was wrong.

I, Cruella De Vil, wake up the next morning, determined to do something productive with the rest of my life (or at least the next three days before the New Year) rather than messing up people's hair. After considering all the infinite (no lie) possibilities, I go to see the karaoke at Heaven's Gate, a little place I like to haunt. Last week they had Elvis, but he always sells out in like two seconds and fire regulations prohibit overcrowding. This week, it's Kurt Cobain, and the tickets are easier (most of his target demographics are still alive), but after two encore performances of "The Man Who Sold the World," the magic just doesn't seem to work.

Music was part of Jeff's world, and by extension, it became part of mine. But now I'm thinking it might not actually be part of me. With Jeff, I was the party goddess, always ready to go someplace new, even if my feet were killing me, the noise gave me a headache, and I didn't want to miss *The Daily Show* (love Jon Stewart, sorry he's not dead). Lately, I've just wanted to stay at home, eat, watch a little TV, eat, and shop.

Maybe Oscar's right (although I'll never tell him that). Maybe I should start looking for somebody new. After all, with the New Year just around the corner, I should start a new New Year's Eve tradition. Something involving my new life would be nice.

That's it; I'm going to do it. So I wing my way to Easy Street where the Angels of the Ninth Order run their matchmaking service. It's a little like Friendster, only tons more sophisticated.

A big golden sign hangs outside with two halos intertwined. This has gotta be the place. I take a deep breath (sorta), and remember that I'm dead, so, therefore, have nothing to fear.

When I get inside, it's like being in Macy's again. There are people everywhere. Counters with salespeople, and flowers. Lots and lots of flowers. I am charmed.

An angel comes up to me, smiling. "Hello, welcome to Soul-Mates. My name is Anael. How may I help you today?"

I look around at the milling crowds of dead people and realize there are a *lot* of lonely people in heaven. "This is my first time here."

He takes me under his wing and gives me the grand tour. "We're very proud of our success rate. It usually only takes one visit."

But there are so many people here. Everywhere you turn, you bump into a body. I hesitate, and Anael jumps before I can say no. "What do you say? Take a risk."

Okay, so he's a lot pushy, but maybe that's a good thing. Maybe I need to be pushed. So I let him lead me into this barren waiting room where he puts little electrodes on my head. "Is this necessary?" I ask.

"You can do it by hand if you like, but just zapping your brain takes a lot of the headache out of the paperwork."

"Fine," I say and sit down, but I'm thinking that being single in heaven is a real pain in the ass, metaphorically speaking, of course.

There's a slight buzz (like when they take dental X-rays), and then he smiles. "All done." The printer starts to whirr and three reams of parchment spew forth.

My eyes glaze over at the list of names. I'm looking at the entire population of the Western Hemisphere, and possibly China, too. "Are these all eligible men?"

"Men and women," he says primly.

Uh-oh. This is going to be tricky. Angels get funky about sexual orientation (they're asexual, but they try and deny it). "I like men," I say with an apologetic smile.

An apologetic smile doesn't cut it with this little cherub. "We don't care."

Time to move on and build a bridge. I smile my "that's okay" smile and ask what's next.

"Next is the connection process, where you'll see all the connections between you and each candidate."

"Connections? What do you mean connections?"

"People you have in common. They'll be laid out in a Venn diagram for your viewing convenience."

A diagram? A gazillion names? Everything seems so clinical. Where is all the spontaneity? All the uncertainty of falling in love? It's like being trapped in some bad scientific research project for *Cosmo*. But I need this. Something, anything, to kick me forward. And if it's a love connection by the angels, then so be it.

Anael leads me into a room that is full of holographic images of men and women, all standing around aimlessly, rather like Madame Tussaud's, only with ordinary (albeit, dead) people.

When I walk up to one guy, he starts to talk (which is a little freaky, but I recover nicely). "Hi, my name is Jonathan Spagnola, but I know you through your six-grade classmate, Ashley Masterson, who dated Jacob Meyerson, who dumped Teresa McGuirk in 1989, who went to St. Cecilia's with my brother, Phil, who still blames himself for my death."

"How is Ashley?" I ask, but I realize he isn't listening to me. No one listens to me. (Growing up, I was used to it, but I had assumed heaven would be different. WRONG.)

Anael is joined by a cadre of angels, who watch the whole interchange, and look so pleased with themselves, like they're doing me some wonderful service. "Who looks good?" asks one.

"Let me think," I stall as I wander through the Hall of Single People. Over in the corner I notice a dark-haired guy who is alone, and he looks a little grumbly. Ah, another disgruntled dead person. So I walk up to him.

"Who are you?" I ask.

"I have no desire to be here," he answers back.

Instantly I am fascinated. "I'm Madelyn," I say, not that he can hear me, but I think it'd be rude to ignore him.

The angels descend upon my choice. "Are you sure? He dresses a little frumpy," one says, pointing to the frilly white sleeves that dangle over the man's hands.

"I like frumpy dressers," say I, who have been known to dress frumpily on occasion myself.

Another angel joins in on the chorus of disapproval. "He writes poetry, too. Don't you want a manly man?"

This is my choice; this is supposed to be my life. Now they're just starting to piss me off, so I fix the little devils with my best bitch look. (FYI: I was never a bitch, even while alive. However, my sister, Miriam, is the world's biggest prima donna, so I've learned the part.) "Look, this is supposed to be a matchmaking service. Now, get over here and do your *bleep*ing jobs."

Everyone looks shocked. Miriam's bitch-look always works.

"You don't need to get all sassy. You want him, we'll set you up, but don't say we didn't warn you."

"What's his name?" I ask, fascinated by the man's dark, tortured gaze, which looks vaguely familiar.

"George Byron."

The poet? That George Byron? "*The* Lord Byron?" I manage to stammer. Now, I'm not a big lit-type, but I do remember this one from eighth-grade English.

The littlest angel bobs his halo. "But we don't call him that up here. Just George."

Okay, so maybe heaven is starting to look up. How many women on present-day Earth get to go out with the world's most romantic man? Is it practical? No. Is it petty? Yes. Am I loving this? You bet your ass. I give Anael my happiest heaven-smile. "I'll take him."

When I get home, I accidentally turn on the TV, to accidentally watch Jeff go home on the C train. It's New Year's Eve Eve and I'm wondering (hoping?) that he'll see Christine's hair and freak.

Then she steps on the platform and I can't help but admire the repairs. It's a little blonder than before, but it looks fabulous with her coloring.

"You did a great job with the color. It looks better than ever, honest," I whisper.

"Thank you," she answers back automatically, and then stops, shaking her head. The train pulls into the station, and before I realize it, there's a suit heading for the seat across from Jeff.

Christine steps in the car, her eyes meet Jeff's, and then she shrugs one of those little helpless "maybe-another-time" gestures. The suit takes another step toward the seat, and Jeff looks indecisive (he's confrontationally challenged). It's really no wonder Oscar got this assignment, because if there was ever a case for divine intervention, this is it.

"CAN'T YOU SEE THAT SEAT IS TAKEN?" I yell to the suit. Probably one of those corrupt Wall Street types. He looks around, and then shakes me off. Definitely corrupt.

However, I am not deterred; I worked at Macy's. I shove him into a side seat next to a young kid of indeterminate sex with iPod buds in his ears. The suit looks startled.

"Mind your manners, next time, huh?" I whisper to him and then watch as Christine sits across from Jeff. They share a secret smile and I realize what I've done. Now I'm the third wheel. All the reasons that I don't like her come crashing down around me. First and foremost, she's not dead.

Within ten minutes they're discussing the weather (cold, but no snow in the forecast), football (Jets in the playoffs? Ha, I may be in heaven, but that'd take more than a miracle), and the special year-end edition of *The Wall Street Journal* (who is this man, and what has he done to my fiancé?). I don't want to like her, I don't want to admire a woman who is two cup-sizes bigger than me, with better shoes than I ever dreamed of, and who also carries a Prada bag. But she seems nice.

Are the angels really right?

No way; those little buggers couldn't hit the side of the Empire State Building if they tried.

In fact, this could be a big plan to educate Jeff on how much he still loves me. Perhaps Jeff will commit suicide and join me in heaven after realizing his life can't go on without me. That's pathetic, isn't it? Yeah, I know it is, but *this is so not fair.*

There should be a silver lining in this cloud, but for the life of me, I can't find it. Oh, wait. There is something.

Tonight I have a blind date with Byron.

Yeah, top that, Christine.

At ten minutes to seven Mercury arrives with an engraved invitation from Byron:

Madelyn, my heart so dear, I count the hours till you're near. A mere touch of hands, a stirring sigh, another glimpse before I die. Earthly Delights at 9 p.m. I am desirous of your oh so magnificent company.

I'm touched. Sue me. Earthly Delights is a retro place that's designed to look like an old speakeasy. For a first date it's not bad. The generational gap is pretty serious. He's all "thee," "thou," "thy." And I'm like: "Whatever," but we're happening. He's a fascinating guy, with a taste for ambrosia that makes Oscar look like a saint. Things go downhill from there.

After two glasses of the stuff, he wants to talk about my death (he's a really *dark* guy), and then starts in on *all* the women in his life. You know these kind of guys, right? The braggarts? Well, he's like the king.

After his third glass, his eyes start to get a little fuzzy. "My darling beauty, to have you snatched away in midnight's gloom. The bloom of roses on your cheeks, your bosom heaving with the breath of love."

He gets this smile, and starts to shoot me the "hey, baby" look, like he's God's gift to women. Now, first of all, guys didn't shoot me "hey, baby" looks when I was alive, except when they were "hey, baby" drunk. Second, there's absolutely no way that this guy would ever go out with me again. He's a scammer. Oh, yeah, you can dress 'em up in nineteenth-century cravats . . . but they're still scammers.

Eventually I get up to go to the ladies' room and don't come back (there are actually no public facilities up here—it's the whole dead thing—but George is too drunk to know that he's been punk'd).

I walk home, opting not to fly. The unhurried speed suits my blue mood, and I shuffle along the gold-paved streets, past the rows of shining shops where everything is available in endless supply.

Why can't I be happy up here? What's wrong with me?

Heck, I just had a date with one of the world's greatest poets. Honestly, it was a horrendous date, but I can still be impressed. In heaven I can date musicians, politicians, statisticians, and any style of -ician I could ever imagine. You'd think with two hundred gazillion trillion fish in the sea, I'd be able to find *one*.

You'd think.

As I walk along, the most haunting song starts to play, echoing off the cobblestones, spilling down from the clouds, until I am surrounded. Eventually it's too difficult to walk, so I stop and lean against the nearest lamppost, listening to the magical sax.

The noises disappear and it's nuclear quiet. Like I'm the only person alive. I've always been a "lemons from lemonade" person. I always tried to see the positive in things, but I fail to understand how my being dead is anything more than fucked.

"Are you okay?"

I look up and wipe my eyes.

There's a man standing in front of me. Not a poet, or a musician. Sorta average. Like me (except he's got a Hell's Angels tattoo on his arm, which is curiously out of place on such normalcy). "I'm fine," I answer.

"Derek Bernstein," he says, holding out a hand, his smile a shade nervous.

"Madelyn Arbrewster," I answer, taking his hand and shaking it. It's still so quiet, but there's a definite hum in the air. Anticipation, liveliness, and the little queasies that I get in the pit of my stomach.

"Been dead long?" he asks (which is pretty much the heaven equivalent of "what's your sign?").

I give him a surreptitious once-over. Happy green eyes, a crooked smile, and a tiny cleft in his chin. "A couple of years. You?"

"About that."

There's a long silence, and my mind races to think of something clever to say. And just like normal, I'm drawing a blank. Here I am, face-to-face with an Opportunity. Maybe it's not true love, but I'll never know unless I try. I think it's time to try.

"You didn't die on New Year's Eve, too, did you?" I ask, because I don't believe in coincidence.

He nods. "But it's not as strange as its sounds. Lots of people die between Christmas and the New Year. Just that time of year. Accidents, the cold weather, even suicides."

I nod (completely goofy, but that's okay). "Do you have plans for New Year's Eve?"

"I was going to watch Dick Clark."

"Did he die?" I say, shocked, horrified, but immediately thinking that this would put a huge damper on Christine and Jeff's romantic evening. Morbid, yet practical. That's me.

Derek shakes his head. "No. But they're having a pay-per-view at the Coliseum."

"Could we go together, you think?" I ask, and there's that hint of nervousness in my voice that I used to hate. *Used to* being the operative words. Now I kinda like it because it's just like when I was alive.

"Sure."

We trade addresses and he flies away. I start to walk home, but this time I'm smiling

. . .

New Year's Eve comes before I realize (actually, that's a lie because I've been counting the hours—all thirty-three of them—with a weird mixture of anticipation and dread). Due to the time zone differences, I get to watch Jeff go off to meet Christine, and still make it to the Coliseum before the ball drops.

I sit down, watching until I see Jeff taking the subway to Christine's apartment, then I flip over to her channel to make sure she's not entertaining some other guy in there, or is really a terrorist or something awful. But no, she's standing in front of her mirror wearing a red dress that looks great. I spy a green one in her closet that I know he would flip over.

"The green one is better," I whisper, almost to myself

She stares in the mirror and then frowns. "Do you really think so?"

"Trust me, huh?" I tell her. Before I know it, she's got on the green dress, and if I do say so myself, it looks smashing.

"You hurt him, you die," I say conversationally.

She looks around the room. "Who *are* you?"

Now, what can I say to that? I swallow hard. *"I'm your guardian angel. You know, doing all that guardian angel stuff. By the way, be careful tonight. New Year's Eve is really dangerous . . . and watch the buses, they're murder."*

She smiles to herself, and I can't believe she bought it, but okay, she's not me.

About 10:00 EST, Oscar comes over, still determined to fulfill his mission (I gotta say, he hasn't done crap, but he thinks he has, and what, you think I'm going to cause trouble?).

"You got plans for tonight?" I ask, because I want him to know that I do.

"No. New Year's Eve is highly overrated. It was only good for getting laid."

"Oh, I bet you were a charmer with the ladies when you were still breathing."

He shrugs. "I held my own. What about you? You're going to watch Jeff all night? I should stay here. You know, make sure you don't do something bad, like blow up the world, or something."

He looks concerned, which is very sweet, but blowing up the world is not on my agenda. *"I* have a date in exactly 5 hours and 37 minutes," I say, wearing my heaven-smile. "And I think I'm getting a manicure and facial before I leave."

"Then why are you still here? You're lying to me, aren't you?" he says, looking so proud of himself for figuring it out.

"No, I think it's time to move on," I say, only partly a lie this time.

"You went to grief-management?"

I shake my head. "Nope. Met a guy."

He gives me a considering look. "I though Jeff was the one."

The One. Why do we limit ourselves to only one love? What happens when fate intervenes? Are you damned to live all eternity all alone? These are the questions you really don't ponder until you're dead. "When I was alive, he was. Now we're at different places and I need to accept that."

I hear footsteps at Christine's door.

Oh, God. No, I can do this. I can really do this.

"Holy *bleep*. This new guy, who is he? Casanova?" Oscar says, lapsing into the same surly Oscar I know and love.

"No, he's just an ordinary, average dead guy," I answer, then sneak a glance at the television to get one long, last look at Jeff. I'll never forget him. Never forget the way he made me feel like I was the only one. We did have something perfect, but why can't you have perfect more than once?

Christine buzzes him up and I watch for just a few more minutes. But that's enough. I don't want to watch his hello. I only want to say my goodbye.

Tonight is New Year's Eve, and I think I'm going to start a new tradition. Unfortunately, I've still don't know what it is.

But you know what? I've got all eternity to figure it out.

KATHLEEN O'REILLY has done nothing extraordinary in comparison to other author bios. She is not a former CIA agent, nor has she ever been president of the United States (nor slept with him, either). She graduated from Texas A&M in 1987, which her parents do consider extraordinary and has been married for fourteen years, but not to Mick Jagger, nor to Justin Timberlake. No, she merely lives with her husband and two kids in New York, and not even Manhattan, just your typical suburb. Her first trade paperback, *The Diva's Guide to Selling Your Soul,* will come out in April 2005 from Downtown Press. Due to the mundaneness in her life, she has chosen to write fiction, which seems best, all things considered.

Midnight Kiss

EILEEN RENDAHL

 I first suspected that my midnight kiss on New Year's Eve possessed prophetical powers the year I went out with Brad Layton. I had lusted after Brad in my heart (and other body parts) for several months. He was easily the blondest boy I had ever seen. From three rows behind him in Intro to Psychology, I could see the fluorescent lights glinting off his shining locks. Outside, his head became a blinding beacon in the Arizona sunshine. His shoulders were broad. His eyes were blue. Even with his unfortunate tendency to occasionally call me "dude," I found him irresistible. I couldn't figure out why his girlfriends kept dumping him.

Then he kissed me at midnight on New Year's Eve.

It was, without a doubt, the most slobbery, vile, disgusting kiss I have ever received. He was like a human water fountain. I was wet down past my chin. My velvet top was half-soaked and had to be dry-cleaned. Then that spring, Phoenix experienced a bizarre and anomalous El Niño year. We were beset by torrential rains and flash floods.

That's what got me thinking. Was there a connection between the kiss I received at midnight and what the following year might bring? As I looked back through my life, I found plenty of other examples including, but not limited to:

- the year I kissed Doreen O'Farrell's ex-boyfriend at midnight just to (and I quote) "burn her butt," and she developed a hemorrhoid less than a month later.
- the year that my midnight kiss was an awkward affair of clinked teeth and bumped noses, and I ended up breaking my leg, needing stitches, and having two car accidents over the next twelve months.
- the year that John Peterson kissed me in the dark of his parents' basement with all the sweetness any fifteen-year-old boy could muster, and I ended up getting three cavities.

Gives you a touch of the heebie-jeebies, doesn't it? It's enough to make you stay home on what my alcoholic friends refer to as Amateur Night, isn't it?

Yet here I was, driving down Carefree Highway along the northern edge of Phoenix and Scottsdale to my friend Amanda's new Suburban Wonder Home, on my way to a party, and crossing my fingers that I'd meet someone fabulous to kiss at midnight. I didn't expect it to be like the movies, with fireworks bursting over our heads as the handsome leading man took me in his strong arms and pressed his lips to mine. I just wanted it to mean something. I wanted it to be special. I wanted there to be a distinct absence of drool.

I have had some good New Year's Eves. My first New Year's Eve with Jeremy had been great. We'd bar-hopped along Mill Avenue in Tempe and then walked back to my condo. I'd had enough to drink to make my head whirl, but not enough to make the room spin—the perfect New Year's tightwire to walk. Jeremy had had just enough to make him silly and sweet and serious all at the same time.

That was the night I fell in love with him and I stayed that way for the whole year (See! See!). Unfortunately, that was three years ago.

As I pulled into Amanda's driveway, I double-checked the house number before I rang the bell. She and Tim had moved into this house four months ago, and I'd been out here at least eight times. But since it looked exactly like the house on its left and exactly like the house on its right, on at least three of those eight times, I'd rung her neighbor's doorbell instead of hers.

All the houses in Amanda's neighborhood were covered with pinkish stucco. Amanda claimed that theirs was Desert Rose. The neighbor on the left was supposed to be Wimple Gray; the neighbor on the right was supposedly Navajo Beige. They were all sort of pinky brown. Amanda also claimed that the subdivision had four different floor plans. As near as I could tell, everyone in the immediate vicinity of Amanda's house had chosen the same one.

I rang the bell, and Amanda darted her head out. "Oh, good,

Mikayla. You're here and you parked in the driveway. We can get three more in there, and then we'll only have five or six on the street."

I looked at her, not comprehending. "Okaayyy."

"The Homeowners' Association Parking Nazis will probably be policing tonight."

"What?"

"The CC&Rs say that you can't have more than seven cars on the street for an event unless you get special parking permission from the board. That means you have to go to the board meeting before your event. The board only meets once a month, and who can plan a party that far in advance, I ask you?"

Since I have trouble planning what I'm going to wear the next day, I understood her point. "What will they do if you have too many cars?"

"Oh, Bud Lawlor from down the street will call Tim and ask him to move the cars. If we don't move them within an hour or so, we'll get fined."

"Fined money?" I was aghast.

"Of course, money. The Homeowners' Association is not going to take their fees in sexual favors."

Okay. That hadn't occurred to me, either. I'd met Bud Lawlor one of the times I was out here, and I wasn't sure what horrified me more: the thought of Amanda servicing an old man with a bad comb-over or having to pay money because she had too many people parked on the street in front of her house, a house for which she and Tim had paid a lot of money. There was no good option. "They wouldn't really fine you, would they?"

"Listen, last week Tim left the basketball hoop out two nights in a row, and we got an official letter of reprimand. It's in our permanent file."

"For a basketball hoop? This sounds like high school."

"Yeah, except we're talking hundreds of dollars instead of time in detention. The basketball hoop pales in the face of the river-rock debacle." Amanda shook her head. "Not only is there an official letter of reprimand and a two-hundred-dollar fine, but we had to take out all the river rock that was the wrong color and put in a whole bunch more that was just two shades pinker."

"I never thought I'd say this, but high school was better."

Amanda rolled her eyes. "Tell me about it. What's in the suitcase?" she asked, eyeing the bag I trailed behind me.

"Clothes."

"Are you moving in?"

I know it was excessive, but Amanda had told me that the dress for the evening would be "smart casual." I had no idea what "smart casual" was. I would have known better what to bring if she told me to dress "stupid sloppy" or "idiot formal." "I couldn't decide what to wear, so I brought some stuff. I thought you could help me decide."

"Let's put it in my bedroom and then we're off to the kitchen. Gretchen's already here," she told me with a head shake that indicated her impatience at my inability to make any decision—including what to wear—without examining the pros, cons, and possible outcomes. I realize it seems hard to put that all in a simple head shake, but Amanda and I have known each other for fourteen of our thirty-two years, and we take a lot of verbal shortcuts.

I trotted after her through the house. "Who else is coming?"

"People. Some from my work. Some from Tim's. Some from the neighborhood. Why?"

"Just curious," I said, trying to seem nonchalant.

"You're not starting the kiss business again, are you?"

I opened my eyes wide, hoping I seemed surprised. "I don't know what you're talking about."

"Look, Mikayla, El Niño is a disruption of the ocean-atmosphere system in the Tropical Pacific having important consequences for weather and climate around the globe. It has nothing to do with whom you kissed at midnight in any given year or how slobbery his kiss was. Get over yourself."

I dumped my suitcase in her room (and by room, I mean Master Bedroom Suite with a bathroom bigger than my living room that contained a huge whirlpool tub and separate shower, along with enough floor space to hold a yoga class) and made my way through what seemed like miles of highly polished saltillo-tile hallways to the kitchen with my container of homemade salsa. Gretchen stopped filling tiny little pie shells with an unidentified filling to throw her arms around me. "Mikayla! It's so good to see you."

We hadn't seen each other in a while. Gretchen was up for tenure this year at the University, and every spare minute seemed to be spent pursuing that little slice of job-heaven security. It didn't leave a lot of time for late-night girlfriend gab sessions or long girlie lunches. "It's good to see you, too," I said. "You look great."

She did look great. She'd lost some weight. Either that or she was now buying her pleated pants two sizes too big instead of just one size too big. Either way, they hung on her athletic build. Her hair had grown out a little, and even though it could have used a trim, the longer style suited her better than the tight little middle-aged bob she'd been wearing for years. If you haven't guessed, fashion is simply not Gretchen's bag. She's awesome with rocks, though.

"So do you," she said, smiling and pushing my hair back behind my ears for me. "Are you okay?"

"Of course I'm okay," I said, shaking my hair back out again. "Why wouldn't I be okay?"

She shrugged. "The breakup. And I know how you are about New Year's."

Jeremy and I broke up right before Thanksgiving. Don't go all weepy about me spending the holidays alone; I hate them all anyway. Starting with Halloween, it's nothing but two sugar-and-fat-filled hectic months with no time to work out. New Year's is the first glimmer of hope that I'll ever make it back into my skinny jeans.

Maybe that's what I like about it. New Year's is about turning the corner, putting the past behind you, and moving on. Every faux pas, every bad outfit, every unwise hair highlight, every career misstep and gaffe can now be left behind. Maybe it won't be like it never happened, but you can resolve to put it behind you.

Besides, having my boyfriend dump me allowed me to sit in the corner and sullenly drink wine at my aunt's annual Thanksgiving dinner, which, to be honest, I would have done anyway, but would have gotten hassled for it. I was also able to duck having to sing the blessing over the candles at my mother's latke fest on the first night of Hanukkah and didn't have to go to Jeremy's grandmother's house on Christmas. I should have a boyfriend break up with me right before the holidays every year. In many ways, it actually improved my life.

It was sad to think that the demise of a three-year relationship was that easily counterbalanced, but maybe that was just one more hint that I'd spent two more years in it than I probably should have. He was just so cute, though! So blond. So broad-shouldered.

Amanda clapped her hands. "Ladies, we have work to do. Gretchen, you finish the tomato-basil tarts. The miniature quiches are defrosting. Mikayla, the cracker bread is over there. There's smoked turkey, cream cheese, and cranberry sauce in the refrigerator to make pinwheels. I'll start the crab-and-artichoke canapés."

"And I brought the herring!" Gretchen said.

Amanda and I simultaneously said, "Why?"

Gretchen's brows drew down and her wide open face clouded. "For good luck. It's a tradition. You're supposed to eat herring on New Year's Eve."

"Says who?" says I.

The brows went down farther. They were going to merge into a unibrow if I upset her any more. "My mother and my grandmother."

"Yeah, well, my mother says it's illegal to drive barefoot, and my grandmother wears knee-hi hose under dresses. I'm not buying it. It's easier to drive when you're not worried about scuffing your heels, and if you ever catch me wearing knee-his under my dresses, you're permitted to euthanize me." A thought occurred to me. "Maybe it was an ancient form of birth control. You know, your breath smells so bad after eating herring at midnight that no boy will want to touch you."

Amanda gave me a hug. "I've missed you, sweetie. I never laugh as much as I do when I'm with you. Now, make the sandwiches, will you?"

I pulled the turkey, cream cheese, and cranberry sauce from Amanda's absurdly clean and tidy refrigerator. I can't keep a fridge that clean and I don't have a husband and a kid to take care of. Speaking of which, I wondered where Amanda's two-year-old son was. "Where is Cody, anyway?"

"Tim's taking him over to his parents for the night. What are grandparents for, anyway?"

"Clearly for babysitting on nights when it's impossible to get a babysitter." I started reading the directions on the cracker bread label.

"Though only with major begging." Amanda looked up from picking shells out of the crabmeat. "What are you doing?"

"I'm reading the directions." I held the sheet up.

Gretchen turned around from her tarts. "They're sandwiches. What directions could there be?"

"I won't know until I've read them, will I? Maybe there's something special you do to the bread before you roll it or some specific order you're supposed to layer stuff."

They both turned back to their own projects on the granite-top counters. "If she'd been that conscientious when we were in college, she wouldn't have flunked astronomy the first time around," Gretchen told Amanda.

Amanda snorted.

"Yeah, well, then I wouldn't have met you, would I?" Gretchen had been my tutor. I am somewhat math-impaired. Astronomy had sounded like a great idea until I'd found out that it was related to physics and not to the fact that I'm a Gemini. I'm thirty-two and I still don't get what a logarithm is, and please don't even start with sine waves.

The doorbell rang. I looked up at the clock. It was seven. The party didn't start until eight. "You getting something delivered?"

Between Amanda's salary as an anesthesiologist and Tim's salary as a lawyer, not only could they afford the Suburban Wonder Home in North Scottsdale along with the fancy SUV, but they could also spring to have stuff catered or flowers brought in.

Amanda shook her head. "No. Would you get it? I'm covered with fish." She held up her crabmeat-covered hands.

I headed for the door, wondering who it would be. Why was I nervous? It's not like I had to worry about running into Jeremy or any of his friends at Amanda's. Our friends had never mixed well—starting with the time his friend Mike threw my friend Siobhan (and, yes, you have to spell it that way) into the pool while she was fully dressed. She found out that her mascara was not truly waterproof and the keyless entry for her car never worked quite right again. In short, she didn't find it anywhere near as amusing as they did. Not that Jeremy's friends even noticed, overgrown frat boys that they are. Which is pretty much what ruined our second New Year's Eve together.

We'd thrown a party. We'd invited his friends and mine. Big mistake. Big *big* mistake.

Let's start with the fact that his friend Kevin spilled his bong all over the carpet in my second bedroom, the one I use as my study and guest room. The one where my *parents* stay when they come to visit.

I don't smoke dope. I'm not saying I never experimented with it. I won't even give you a Clintonesque "I-did-not-inhale" (and for the record, oral sex does, too, count). I did go to college, after all, and maybe I would be more tolerant if I liked it better, but it makes me both stupid and paranoid, which, I must say, is a very soul-crushing combo.

Anyway, not only did Kevin bring and partake of an illegal substance in my home without my permission, he made a mess with it that I can still catch an occasional whiff of during monsoon season.

I'd given Jeremy a tense kiss at midnight before running off to stop his friend George from peeing off my balcony. The whole next year had been one extended headlong rush to avert disasters and clean up the ones I couldn't stop.

Well, back to the present—and the chance for a neater New Year.

I opened Amanda's door. A really cute guy—tall, blond, broad-shouldered, completely my type—was on the other side, holding a bottle of wine. It was like I just won Mystery Date and I didn't even remember spinning the dial.

He thrust the bottle of wine at me. "This is Amanda Silver's house, right? I'm in the right place, aren't I?"

I stared at the bottle. Not a bad Cabernet. I stared at him. Not a bad kiss prospect. "It is, but the party doesn't start until eight." Then I froze. What if he was an acquaintance with the extraordinary bad timing to show up right before the big party? "You are here for the party, aren't you?"

He ran one hand through his longish hair. "A full hour early? Man, that's really not like me. I could have sworn she said seven."

I didn't know quite what to do, so I took the bottle. "Do you want to come in?" I asked at the same time he said, "Maybe I should go."

"Don't be silly. Come in. We're in the kitchen." I took his coat and hung it in Amanda's front closet (which could probably house several college students comfortably) and ushered him toward where we could hear Amanda and Gretchen laughing.

I walked along behind him, frankly admiring the view and how it was encased in a pair of vaguely military-styled khaki pants and a plain black long-sleeved shirt stretched across a lovely broad back. It suddenly occurred to me that Amanda must have invited him for me. He was totally my type. Tall and fair. Very California Surfer Dude-ish. Amanda must have deliberately told him the wrong time to get him there early so we could be all coupled up before the party started. Amanda is simply the best friend ever.

"Amanda," I trilled in my best charming girlie voice. "Uh . . . someone . . . I mean, your friend is here." Damn. I hadn't even gotten his name. I already had us in a midnight lip-lock, and I didn't even know what I should murmur lovingly in his ear. So much for being slick on the social scene.

Amanda turned from her crabmeat. "Max! What are you doing here?"

He went all pink under the just-enough beard stubble on his

cheeks. How adorable was that? "You invited me, Amanda. Remember? At work?"

Now Amanda blushed. "Of course I did. I didn't mean that. It's just that you're, uh, a little early." Amanda's voice rose on the last word as if it was a question.

Max went pinker. "I thought you said seven."

"Well, no matter," Amanda said, straightening a little. "You can whip the cream for the Irish coffees. Mikayla, get Max an apron so he doesn't end up looking like a Dairyland Jackson Pollock."

In uncomfortable social situations, I tend to try to ingratiate myself. Gretchen goes completely silent and withdrawn. Amanda falls back on her own particular strength: bossing people around. I went to the hook behind the door where I'd earlier scored the pretty apron with the rosemary on front that says "HERBS" across my chest. I don't know who Herb is, but he apparently has claim to my breasts when I'm cooking at Amanda's. I pulled the only apron left there now off the hook. "Uh, Amanda, only the ass apron is left."

Amanda's maiden name was Butz. Feminist feelings aside, no one could really blame her for leaping at the opportunity to change her last name to Silver when she married Tim. For the record, I did suggest she hyphenate and become Amanda Silver-Butz, but that suggestion was received with such a ferocious scowl that Gretchen told me to knock it off. It wasn't until Amanda received her first set of monogrammed towels as a wedding gift that she realized that the initials of her new name, Amanda Susan Silver, spelled out the word *ass*.

Basically, she'd changed her driver's license, her social security number, her credit cards, and her checking account just to go from being a Butz to being an A.S.S.

"The ass apron?" Max asked.

I displayed it for him.

He looked down sadly. "I kind of deserve it for showing up early," he said.

I like a man who admits it when he's wrong and is willing to take his punishment. At least, I think I do. I've never actually spent any time with a man like that, so I guess I don't really know. It's not like Jeremy ever . . .

Oh, God. How many times had I thought about Jeremy in the past hour? Maybe I wasn't as over him as I'd thought. I turned and gave Max my brightest "fun girl" smile.

Amanda put a last sprig of parsley by the poached salmon. "There. All done." She looked over the dishes, ticking something off on her fingers as she looked at the table. Tim had come back from dumping Cody on his parents and rescued Max from spending the entire evening in the kitchen wearing the ass apron. Max had been funny and cute. Sort of inept with the hand mixer, but quite adept with the bruschetta and definitely relieved to escape to the den and watch Top Ten shows with Tim until everyone else got there.

Turns out he's a physician's assistant at the Outpatient Surgical Center where Amanda works as an anesthesiologist, and he likes snowboarding, red wine, and Led Zeppelin. Definitely dream-date material.

"There's plenty of food," I assured Amanda.

"I know," she said, still counting. "I'm trying to figure out how many I can eat of each thing. I banked a lot of points this week, but with the booze it might not be enough. I don't want to exceed my Flex Points."

"Your what?" Gretchen asked.

"Flex Points. From Weight Watchers." Amanda scribbled something down on a notepad.

"Why are you on Weight Watchers?" I asked. I'm not saying that Amanda is skinny; she's not. But she's not fat, either. She's normal.

She looked up from her notepad calculations. "I think because my level of self-loathing finally exceeded my appetite. I've finally realized that I exist on some dialectic continuum between the two all the time. By the time I hit 145 pounds, the self-loathing takes over and dominates the appetite. By the time I hit 135 pounds, my appetite exceeds my self-hatred and I start to eat again."

Gretchen nodded as if she understood. I felt like I'd been hit with the "duh" stick again. In case you haven't guessed, Gretchen and Amanda are a lot smarter than me. I'm never quite sure why we're friends since they always seem to be three and sometimes four steps ahead of me. Yet, here we are, a good ten years after Amanda and I got our bachelor's degrees together (Gretchen is a couple years older than us), still hanging out together. Apparently, I make them laugh. Unfortunately, I sometimes suspect that it's at me and not with me.

It did seem as if lately, however, I was finally starting to catch up. My art history degree had left me unprepared for being much more than an overeducated secretary at Madewell Avionics, and not a very good one at that. I was making some money, more than Gretchen and Amanda were making in graduate school and medical school. Then they'd graduated and zoomed past me like rocket ships headed for distant galaxies, while I was just a satellite orbiting the earth. When Gretchen got her Ph.D., I'd moved up to administrative assistant. By the time Amanda finished her residency, I'd managed to do the corporate ladder dance up to human resource and training assistant.

This past October, a few short weeks before Jeremy dumped me, I'd been promoted to human resources manager with an assistant of my own.

And I was pretty sure I knew exactly what Amanda meant with her self-hatred/appetite dialectic continuum. There's that point when your favorite skirt starts looking like someone's filled it with cottage cheese and suddenly chocolate isn't quite as appealing as it used to be. Then, one day when you can actually wear the stretchy capris you unwisely bought when you thought the weight loss from the stomach flu would be permanent, a margarita with chips and salsa becomes irresistible. Bam! You're back to cottage cheese in no time flat.

"You'll feel better once we're all dolled up," I said. "Let's go change."

"Change into what?" Gretchen started to pick up a crabmeat canapé.

Amanda slapped her hand away. "Our party clothes," she answered in a tone that indicated all too clearly what she thought of Gretchen's question.

"We're supposed to have party clothes?" Gretchen looked to me for backup. She didn't get any.

"Party clothes," I confirmed.

"But you said the dress was 'smart casual,' " Gretchen wailed.

"It is," Amanda said.

"Then this is fine, right?" Gretchen gestured at her pleated droopy khaki pants and light blue cotton top. "I mean, I'm smart and this is casual, right?"

"Wrong," Amanda and I said in unison. Then we each grabbed one of her arms and marched her down the hall toward Amanda's giant bedroom.

"Thanks for Max, by the way," I said to Amanda behind Gretchen's back.

"You're welcome, but I'm not sure for what."

Modesty? Humility? Not Amanda-like at all. "For the fix-up. He's perfect."

"Fix-up? Max?" She grabbed a pair of black pants and a halter top from her huge closet and thrust them at Gretchen. "Put these on. I can't wear them anymore, anyway."

"What's wrong with Max?" I asked.

"First of all, he's practically a Jeremy clone," Gretchen piped up.

After seeing Amanda put on a leather miniskirt, boots, and a blouse so sheer you could see her bra underneath it, I changed into a pair of snapdragon jeans with a satin lace-up front and my creamy beige off-the-shoulder sweater. "So I have a type. What's wrong with that?"

Amanda rolled her eyes. "What's wrong with it is that they

never work out. You're constantly falling for big blond jock types and then acting all surprised when they act like big blond jocks."

"I really think it's time you got over your Christopher Atkins infatuation," Gretchen said.

I blushed. So what if I'd had a *Blue Lagoon* poster in my bedroom until I was twenty?

"How's this?" Gretchen asked.

We turned and looked at her. The pants fit great. The problem was her posture. She stood with her legs spread and her hands jammed into her pockets, her shoulders rolled slightly forward as if she was getting ready to duck a punch.

"It's a party," Amanda said. "Not a prizefight."

"What?" Gretchen picked at the design on the front of the halter top. "What is this for, anyway?"

"For us to know that you shouldn't be wearing that," I said. I pulled a skirt and top that I'd worn to my cousin Holly's wedding out of my suitcase. "Try these." There was no way she could stand with her legs apart in a skirt that was cut that straight.

Gretchen started stripping down again.

"Do you call that a bra?" Amanda asked her.

"What else would I call it?" Gretchen asked back, her blue eyes wide after glancing down at her chest.

"A waste of cotton. What support can that thing give you? It doesn't even have an underwire."

"I don't need an underwire."

"We're over thirty now. Trust me, you need an underwire. Gravity's coming for you just like it's coming for everyone else."

Amanda burrowed in a drawer and threw something at Gretchen. "Put on this Wonderbra."

"So what are your resolutions this year?" I asked, rifling through Amanda's giant selection of lipsticks. Amanda picks lip color the way I sample candies at See's. She takes at least one of everything home and then zeroes in on her favorites for repeats. I usually have a daytime color (something sort of natural in a pink-ish tone) and a nighttime color (something sort of red without being too brassy). Of course, maybe if I spent more on lip color and less on chocolate, I'd be the one with the husband and the baby and the fancy house in the suburbs.

"I'm not doing resolutions this year," Amanda said firmly. "I'm doing affirmations."

I looked at Gretchen and lifted my eyebrows. Affirmations? What New Age crap was that? But Gretchen barely glanced at me; she was too busy rearranging her boobs within the confines of the Wonderbra. I thought she had them, then one of them jumped out the center. "I'm not doing resolutions, either," Gretchen announced, shoving the boob back into submission. "I'm doing goals."

"Fine," I said, feeling more than a little exasperated. "What affirmations and goals are we doing?"

Amanda composed herself in front of the mirror, stared directly into her own eyes, and said, "I take charge of my own life. My eyes see clearly the world around me. I am a spark of divine love."

Gretchen pulled a list from her purse. "One, get tenure. Two, exercise more. Three, adopt a baby."

Amanda and I dropped our lipsticks.

"Stop frowning like that," Gretchen said calmly. "You're making anticlines on your foreheads."

"You can't drop a bomb like that and walk away," Amanda argued.

"How is it a bomb? And who's walking anywhere?" Gretchen argued back.

"What's an anticline?" I asked.

"A fold with strata sloping downward on both sides from a common crest." Gretchen sketched a shape in the air.

"And that's on my forehead?" I peered into the mirror. "Do you think I need botox?"

"Mikayla!" Amanda snapped.

Gretchen sighed. "Look. I'm thirty-four years old. I'm not dating anyone. There's no one even on the horizon. Truth is, I haven't even been out on a date in more than eighteen months."

I felt bad. Picking up social cues, particularly romantic ones, was not Gretchen's strong point. I had usually been there to give her a little shove when some poor guy was trying desperately to make a pass at her, and she thought he was completely fascinated by her discussion of groundwater problems in dairy farming.

"You might meet someone tonight," I said, still staring at my forehead in the mirror. If I needed botox at thirty-two, what would I need by the time I was forty-two? A complete face-lift? Would I end up looking like Joan Rivers? Or simply as if I were Asian? Would that be all bad?

"Even if I met someone tonight, there might not be time," Gretchen went on. "Let's say I did meet someone tonight. Maybe we'd date for a year before we'd decide to get married. That would make me thirty-five. Then there's a year for wedding planning and all that. Then maybe a year or so to be married before I get pregnant and bam! I'm thirty-eight, my eggs are old, and my chances of getting pregnant have dropped exponentially."

I was stunned. I hadn't even heard my biological clock tick yet, and Gretchen's alarm had already gone off.

"Thirty-eight is not too old to have a baby. Lots of women wait that long and have no problem," Amanda said, putting on eyeliner.

"Lots of women wait that long and find out the door is shut before they even got a chance to knock on it," Gretchen said.

"Or be knocked up by it," I added.

"Mikayla!" Gretchen and Amanda said in unison.

"You're overthinking this," Amanda told Gretchen. "Like that's a surprise," she said in an aside to me.

"Easy for you to say," Gretchen shot back with uncharacteristic sharpness. "You've already got the husband, the house, and the kid, along with the great job. I love my job. In another few months I'll probably be able to buy my own house. I'm just saying I'd like there to be a nursery in it."

Gretchen pulled the top over her head and straightened it into place. My jaw dropped.

I'd never seen Gretchen look like this. Maybe because I'd never seen Gretchen dressed like this. When she was forced to get dressed up, she favored skirts with gathered waists (the ones our mothers told us "hid" tummies, but actually create them on everyone) or large flowered sacks.

But now, in my tight little skirt and top and with a little help from Amanda's Wonderbra, Gretchen was all sleek curves. She looked like a dangerous section of road. The low-cut skirt skimmed her slim hips. The top stopped an inch or two above the waistband, and while it wasn't precisely low-cut itself, with the Wonderbra, it did display a fair amount of cleavage.

"If that outfit doesn't get you knocked up, I don't know what will." Amanda leaned back against the bathroom counter to take in the full glory of Gretchen all glammed up.

"I c-c-can't wear this," Gretchen stammered, staring at herself in the mirror.

"Not with those eyebrows you can't," Amanda said. Her fingers reached for a pair of tweezers. "Mikayla, go get some ice cubes."

"How do you feel?" Amanda asked Gretchen, standing behind her in the mirror.

"Like your big Barbie doll." It was impossible to miss the trace of resentment in Gretchen's voice.

"You look a little Barbie-ish, too," I said. With all the curves, she did have that impossibly wasp-waisted fashion-doll look. Though with the sprinkle of freckles she had across her nose, I pegged her to be a little more Skipperish than completely Barbie.

We heard the distant sound of the doorbell for the third or fourth time. Amanda raised her head. "We'd probably better get out there."

She'd sleeked her hair back into a low ponytail that made her eyes look huge and her cheekbones high. "You look fabulous," I said.

"Do I?" she asked with a trace of a tremble in her voice.

I was surprised. Amanda is nothing if not confident. All the time. About everything. "Of course you do."

"I don't know." She smoothed her hands over her hips. "I've got five pounds of baby weight that just won't seem to come off."

"If you do, they're all in your chest. Tim must be happy."

She gave me a rueful little smile. "You'd think so, wouldn't you?"

We'd just gotten out the door when Amanda dragged me back into her bedroom and shut the door behind us as Gretchen rejoined the party. "I need to talk to you about something. I need you to make me a promise," Amanda said.

She looked so serious. I knew instantly that whatever she was going to ask was very important to her. I also knew just as quickly that I would do whatever she asked. Even if it was icky or involved body fluids. I took her hands in mine. "Of course. What is it?"

Keeping her eyes on me, Amanda opened her closet and pulled an Easy Spirit shoe box from the shelf. "I want you to promise me that if something should happen to me and Tim, that the second you hear about it, you'll race here and destroy the contents of this shoe box."

What was she, a spy? An embezzler? Did Amanda have a secret identity? "Is this a joke?"

"No. It's not a joke. It's a porn box."

Apparently Amanda *did* have a secret identity. "A what?"

"A porn box. You know, some homemade stuff. Of me. And Tim. Together. Naked."

I shoved my fingers in my ears and started chanting "I can't hear you" over and over.

Amanda pulled my fingers out of my ears. "Grow up, Mikayla. Where do you think Cody came from?"

"I know where Cody came from. I just don't want to think about pictures of his conception."

Amanda waved her hand. "There aren't any pictures of that night in here. Get serious."

"You're making official arrangements to have your porn box destroyed in case of your untimely demise, and you're telling *me* to get serious? Besides, what's with all the 'in case something happens to me' talk? Has your mother been sending you articles again?" Amanda's mother was famous in our dorm for sending the best brownies at finals time and newspaper clippings of various stupid ways to die. The former were chocolate with chocolate chips. The latter ran the gamut from the young man who peed on the third rail of the El train in Chicago and electrocuted himself, to the young woman who discovered her hitherto unknown peanut allergy by going into anaphylactic shock at a Thai restaurant, to the frat boy who drank too much and developed a nosebleed in his sleep and drowned in his own blood.

"Of course she's still sending them, but now they're about babies dying instead of college students. But that's not what this is about. Tim and I made out our will last week."

"Your will? You guys have a will?"

"Of course we have a will. We have a child. And a house. And two cars. And life insurance. And a porn box. Come to think of it, maybe two porn boxes." Amanda pulled another box off the shelf and glanced inside it. "Yeah. This one, too, okay? So everything's all set for us to crash our oversize SUV on the 101 and die in a fiery inferno except for the disposal of the porn boxes, and I'm trying to take care of that right now."

"Fine. I'll destroy the porn boxes."

"Without looking inside?"

"Without looking inside. I swear."

Amanda hugged me. "I knew I could count on you."

We left her bedroom and launched ourselves into the party. It was hopping already; I hadn't noticed how many times the door-bell had rung while we were getting dressed. Amanda floated off to hug people I didn't know. I headed off in search of champagne and Max. I had a kiss to arrange, after all!

The champagne was easy to find. Amanda had bought the stuff by the case from Costco. Max proved to be somewhat more elu-sive. I couldn't figure out how a guy that tall could disappear into a crowd that easily, but I hadn't really expected the crowd to be this dense. Amanda and Tim must have invited everyone they knew.

A quick glance out the front door confirmed that we were al-ready in parking trouble. Maybe Bud Lawlor would be too drunk to notice. Maybe pigs would sprout wings and fly. Tonight, noth-ing was out of the question. After all, Gretchen had allowed us to put mascara on her.

The champagne bottle on the table was empty. An unopened one stood in the ice bucket. I twisted the foil off and then began to wrestle with the cork.

"Can I help?"

I turned. Definitely not Max. If anything, he was an anti-Max.

We were eye level. Granted, I was wearing heels and I'm not exactly short, but still, this guy was no giant. His black hair was cut short and a little spiky, and while he was wearing a shirt with actual buttons on it, he clearly hadn't ironed it. One pocket of his faded blue jeans wasn't completely tucked in, and the cuffs were frayed in places. Not artful places. Just frayed. Compared to Max's very stylish outfit (in fact, now that I thought about it—hadn't I seen that exact outfit on *Queer Eye for the Straight Guy?* I think it was the skater guy with the Italian girlfriend), he seemed rather rumpled. Still, he did have thumbs. I handed him the champagne bottle. "Thanks."

"I've found it's often to my advantage to facilitate beautiful women's access to alcohol." The cork popped.

I held out my glass. "And do cheesy lines often work to your advantage, as well?"

He smiled. No, more like smirked. "Often enough that it surprises even me." He filled my glass, set down the bottle, and then held out his hand. "Riley Montoya."

I shook it. "Mikayla Weiss."

"And how are you connected to the Perfect Couple, Ms. Weiss?" Riley asked, leaning against the wall.

I snorted. Amanda and Tim really were the Perfect Couple. Perfect house. Perfect jobs. Perfect child. Perfect. Perfect. Perfect. You couldn't even dislike them, because they were so nice. "Amanda and I went to ASU together. And you?"

"I met Tim when I was covering a city council meeting."

"Covering?"

"I'm a reporter. Sort of."

"Do you sort of report or do you only sort of have that job?"

He smiled. "A little of both. My father owns a local paper up here. According to him, I'm learning the ropes from the ground up. According to me, I'm putting in my time."

"Are you talking about *The Chaparral Press?* That's you?"

He nodded.

"I don't suppose you're the brilliant writer who reported on the fisticuffs between those two women from the travel agency and the diner, are you?"

"I am indeed that very reporter. Brilliant, you say? Why, Ms. Weiss, you get more and more beautiful every second."

"Seriously, any reporter who would be willing to call a winner in an altercation like that has some serious journalistic chops, as far as I'm concerned." I tapped my glass against his in a salute and took a sip.

"Not hard to do when one of the women is still carrying around a hunk of hair that she pulled from the other one's head."

"Yes, but didn't you feel the other woman had a moral edge? I mean, if the first one had actually been watching her child instead of letting her play pranks in the diner, Woman B would never have had the paring knife with her when she went to the bathroom, because she wouldn't have had to be jimmying the locks on the stalls." I mirrored his stance against the wall.

One corner of his mouth drew up. "Ah, but regardless of her original intent, Woman B still ran after a nine-year-old girl while brandishing a weapon. What mother wouldn't fly into a protective rage at the sight of a three-hundred-pound fry cook chasing her little darling around with a knife?"

"A mother who knew her kid was a brat?" I felt the corners of my own mouth draw up. Then suddenly I was wondering what it would feel like to have our lips pressed together. What would a kiss from Riley Montoya be like? More important, what would a kiss from Riley Montoya mean? Maybe I'd have a wisecracking intellectual year. That wouldn't totally suck.

"Don't you suspect that there's an inverse relationship between knowledge of one's offspring's brattiness and the actual level of brattiness? Based on my experience with two nephews and a niece, there's probably some constant like pi in the equation," Riley said.

"Oooh. Maybe it'll be like the golden section, and it will actually be a spiral that produces telemarketers who don't signal lane changes at the other end." I smiled.

Gretchen came streaking by, darting glances over her shoulder as she hurried toward the kitchen. A tall guy with glasses trotted after her with a goofy look on his face.

I was about to follow, really I was, but Riley refilled my glass with champagne and asked, "The Pixies versus the Smiths?" and in the two seconds it took for me to say, "Well, duh, the Pixies," I kind of forgot.

I know Gretchen darted through at least twice more as we established that Riley preferred Ernest Hemingway to F. Scott Fitzgerald and Sean Connery over Roger Moore and Pierce Brosnan, and that I felt that the cancellation of *Wonderfalls* while *Reba* continued year after year probably signaled the beginning of the Apocalypse.

Things went on like this until Amanda grabbed me by the forearm and pulled me into the other room.

"Keep an eye on things, will you? I'm going to go change," Amanda said, tears in her eyes.

"Why? You look fabulous."

"Not as fabulous as her." Amanda pointed over my left shoulder with her chin. I turned. A leggy brunette was standing next to Tim wearing—you guessed it—a leather miniskirt, boots, and a blouse so sheer you could see her bra underneath it. While we watched, the brunette flicked her hair, threw her head back, and laughed, all without ever taking her hand off Tim's arm. By the time I had turned back around, Amanda had disappeared.

I whirled around, trying to figure out how she could have left so quickly and finally managed to spot Max. I was about to go over and see if I could solidify my plans for an excellent midnight kiss when Riley tapped me on the shoulder. "Hey, Mikayla. I have to go. Believe it or not, I have to work tomorrow. I'm covering the big New Year's Day parade."

I desperately wanted to turn and see which direction Max was heading in, but I didn't want to turn away from Riley. It had been a while since anyone "got me." Strangely enough, the human resources department at a large aviation firm was simply not a good place to expect people to get jokes based on art movements or really anything besides sex and bathroom humor. It felt good to have someone who got my jokes and matched them with his own. I stuck out my hand. "It was nice to meet you."

He took my hand, but didn't let it go. He looked down at his shoes for a moment. "It was really nice to meet you. I was hoping . . . I mean, kind of wondering . . ."

"Oh, my God!" I exclaimed. I had just spotted Bud Lawlor cruising through the party throng like a hairless cruise missile in search of a Homeowner target—the parked cars.

Riley dropped my hand. "Wow. I don't think I've been shot down that fast or with that much horror since I asked Missy Semple to dance at the eighth-grade Spring Fling."

"No!" I exclaimed, even more horrified now. "It wasn't you."

"Please. We haven't known each other long enough for the it's-not-you-it's-me speech." He started to back away.

"No, no, no. It's not either of us." I grabbed Riley's shoulder and whirled him around. I pointed out Bud Lawlor, nudging through the crowd like a shark through a kelp bed. "Do you know who that is?"

"Sure. That's Bud Lawlor, head henchman for one of the most restrictive and exacting Homeowners' Associations in the Valley. Everybody up here knows him."

"Well, he's not here for the poached salmon, Riley."

Riley's eyes narrowed. "What's he got on 'em?"

"I think it's a parking violation. Apparently there was a basketball-hoop violation just last weekend and something about rocks that were the wrong color."

"He's scented blood, then." Riley clenched his jaw. "What do you want me to do?"

"Can you keep him busy for a few minutes? Distract him long enough for me to warn Amanda and Tim."

Riley glanced around. "Where are they, anyway?"

"Amanda went to change her clothes. I don't know where Tim went." He had disappeared. I hoped not off to some dark corner with the leggy brunette. *Please* not to a dark corner with the leggy brunette.

Gretchen came streaking by again, this time with tears in her eyes. She took off like a rabbit down the hall toward Amanda's bedroom. I called to her, but she apparently didn't hear.

"So how are you going to distract him?" I asked Riley.

Riley chuckled. "I'll bring up the proposed mini-storage place at Dynamite and Pima roads. That'll get him going for a while."

Riley headed off toward Bud. I grabbed a bottle of champagne and darted off to Amanda's room. Gretchen had already ripped the shirt off over her head and one comb from the side of her head as well. "I don't like this. They all keep touching me."

"Who keeps touching you?"

"Them. Men. Those guys out there. Their hands. They're everywhere. It's icky." She slithered out of the skirt. "Where are my khakis? I want my khakis back."

I held them out to her. "They're touching you? How?"

"In an icky way, aren't you listening? That space between where that top ends and the skirt starts. They keep putting their hand there, and all that's there is me."

"They're putting their hands on your back?"

"For God's sake, Mikayla, yes. I don't have time to draw you a diagram. Try to keep up."

I whirled around, sure I'd heard a funny noise from behind me. There wasn't anything there. "Did you hear that?"

"Hear what?"

"That noise? Kind of a squeaky chirp?"

Gretchen rolled her eyes. "No, Mikayla, I did not hear a squeaky noise. Perhaps because I'm more terrified about hearing male footsteps coming up behind me to fondle the small of my back in public without my permission."

"Were they really fondling? Because if they were, that's usually a good prelude to that whole making babies thing."

Gretchen lifted her hands in a gesture of confusion. "I don't know. I thought the first guy was really into me—I mean, the real me, Gretchen me—then he started with the touching. That's the problem—with this stupid outfit, how can I tell? I just know their hands land right on my skin and won't leave. No matter which way I move, the hands come with me." This time Gretchen's head whipped around after she wiggled out of the skirt. "Was that the noise? That little peep thing?"

I nodded. "Do you think they were coming on to you?"

"No. Maybe. I'm not sure." She threw Amanda's Wonderbra at me and snatched her own worthless piece of breast-covering cotton back. "The hands on my back made it so I couldn't think straight."

This time the noise definitely came from the closet. I put my finger to my lips and tiptoed to the sliding door. Gretchen pulled her blue top back over her head and slunk up behind me. The transformation really was amazing. I didn't think anyone would even recognize that she was the same person. I waved her away. I wanted her to keep talking to distract whoever it was in the closet from my approach. Typical Gretchen, she missed all my hints entirely. I shook my head and shoved the closet door back.

Amanda was huddled on the floor of her gigantic closet, rocking herself and quietly crying.

Gretchen and I kneeled beside her. "Amanda, what's wrong, honey? What are you doing here?"

She sniffed and took a swipe at her eyes. "Trying to catch Tim with whoever he's having an affair with. I figured he'd bring whoever it was in here." Amanda took the champagne bottle from me and took a big swallow. "He won't touch me outside of the bedroom anymore. Actually, he'll barely touch me in here, either."

"Is that why you think he's having an affair? Because he won't touch you?"

Amanda nodded, clearly miserable. "Two months ago I skipped my period, and I realized I didn't even have to worry about being pregnant because we hadn't had sex for the entire month."

"I'm so sorry, honey." I sat back on my heels.

"I figure he must be getting it somewhere. Men have needs, right?" She looked up at me, her tear-streaked face so sad that tears welled up in my own eyes.

"Women have needs, too." Gretchen plopped down on her behind and leaned back against the wall.

Amanda gave a little smile. "Tell me about it. I've started buying rechargeable batteries for my vibrator."

"You have a vibrator?" I asked.

"You don't?" Gretchen asked.

"You do, too?" I felt like my eyebrows might crawl all the way to my hairline, which is really high.

"Did you not hear that part about not having a date for eighteen months?" Gretchen reminded me.

Great. Not only were they smarter than I was, they were sexually more advanced, as well.

"There could be other reasons, Amanda," Gretchen said. "Maybe he's having some dysfunction. You know, like Mike Ditka and Bob Dole."

"Tim is not impotent," Amanda said. "That is not the problem."

"Then what is?"

"Don't you think I wish I knew? I've tried everything. I've lost weight. I've bought lingerie. I've made sure to ask about his work. I've given him time to himself." She grabbed the champagne bottle from me and knocked back a healthy swig. "Nothing seems to make any difference. Nothing. The apron is right: I am an ass."

"No, you're not," I protested.

"Nothing works out the way I plan it," she wailed. "I try to stop being a Butz and end up being an ass instead. I try to get a great home, and all I get is hours and hours of swabbing tile floors with a stinky string mop. I spend years in school to become a doctor—a doctor, mind you!—so that I can have a fabulous career, and I wind up doing nothing but endless knee arthroscopies, D&Cs, and fistula removals."

"What's a fistula?"

"You don't want to know," Gretchen told me.

"We used to be the kind of couple who had a porn box. We used to do it everywhere. On the kitchen counters. On the dining room table. One time I squatted down to take a video out of the VCR, and we ended up doing it on the living room floor. Now we don't even do it on Saturday night. We *always* did it on Saturday night."

We heard the door to Amanda's bedroom open. "Ssshhhhh," Amanda whispered.

"Where you goin', Tim?" we heard a slurry male voice ask.

Tim's voice replied, "I'm trying to find Amanda."

"Oh, man, are you ever whipped!" the first voice said.

Tim replied, "Whatever."

"Seriously, dude. There's plenty of other action right out there in your living room. If Amanda snoozes, she's loses."

"Take a hike, Oscar."

The bedroom door shut again.

Gretchen kicked Amanda. "Go talk to him," she whispered.

"Hush," Amanda whispered back.

"He's looking for you," I whispered.

"I know that," Amanda hissed. "I'm hiding from him, remember?"

"Not from him," Gretchen said. "More to ambush him. That's different, I think."

The mirrored door to the closet slid open, and Tim stood silhouetted by the bright bathroom lights behind him. "Amanda? Gretchen? Mikayla? What are you guys doing in here?"

While I sought for a reasonable explanation for why we were huddled on the closet floor, drinking champagne directly from the bottle, Gretchen piped up, "Amanda thinks you're having an affair. We're hiding in here, hoping to catch you with your floozy."

"Gretchen!" I said, smacking my forehead with the palm of

my hand. Had she no sense of discretion? On the other hand, it did explain what we were doing in the closet in an admirably succinct manner.

"My what?" Tim asked.

"Who uses the word *floozy* anymore?" I asked.

"Did you understand what I meant?" Gretchen asked me.

"Yes."

"Then it was a perfectly good word choice, wasn't it?"

"It's just such an old-fashioned word."

"I know, but *slut* seemed harsh considering we don't even know the woman."

"What woman?" Tim yelled.

We all looked up at him again. "The one you're having an affair with," Gretchen explained in a patient tone that I bet she used on bewildered freshmen.

"What affair?" he yelled a little louder.

I would have laughed, but he looked really mad. "The one you're having with the floozy," I said.

Tim looked at Amanda. "Why do you think I'm having an affair?" he asked, his voice deadly quiet.

Amanda just looked back at him, her lower lip quivering and tears welling up in her dark eyes.

"Amanda thinks you're having an affair because you won't have sex with her," Gretchen explained. It was like she was an intra-marital interpreter.

Tim shook his head. "I won't have sex with her? That's what she thinks? That I'm not willing?"

"Pretty much," Gretchen confirmed with a head nod.

"Am I the one who won't let their spouse see them naked? Am I the one who is always talking about how tired I am? Am I the one who obsessively mops the floor instead of coming to bed?" Tim's voice grew louder with each question until he shouted, "Am I the one who leaps out of bed at five in the morning to run like a hamster on the treadmill, instead of cuddling with my spouse in the few spare moments either of us have each day? NO, I AM NOT THAT PERSON. AM I, AMANDA?"

We all shrank bank against the cedar wall.

"AM I, AMANDA?"

"You're always asleep when I come to bed," Amanda said in a quiet, accusing voice.

Tim unclenched his jaw just long enough to say, "I work sixty- to eighty-hour workweeks, plus I'm trying to stay in shape, plus I try to spend some time each day with Cody. I am exhausted. There isn't a hard-on in the world that would keep me awake while you mop the damn tile." He crossed his arms over his chest. Tim's face was really red. Redder even than when we floated down the Salt River last May and he insisted that he didn't need any sunscreen. "And I think it's mighty convenient that you never come to bed unless you're sure I'm already snoring."

Amanda drew back against the wall. "I'm just trying to keep the tile nice and shiny like it's supposed to be."

"I don't care about the tile, Amanda. You can knock the whole damn floor out if you want to." Tim took a step forward. "What about the morning thing? We used to do it in the morning all the time. Now you're gone before I can even shut off the alarm."

"It's the only time I have to work out. I'm trying to lose the last of the baby weight." One tear trickled down Amanda's cheek. "I thought you might find me attractive again if I wasn't so fat."

Tim sank down on the floor. "Amanda, you're not fat. You had a baby. Our baby. I think you're beautiful."

"You do?" Amanda sniffled.

"I do." Tim reached for her and pulled her to him.

Gretchen and I smiled at each other over their heads, and I gestured to the door of the closet with a jerk of my head. We both started sliding toward the door, slowly and carefully, so as not to disturb Tim and Amanda.

I took both Gretchen's hands in mine. "Gretchen, we have a mission."

"We do?"

I've always loved how serious Gretchen's eyes can be. They're the most amazing pale blue and they can go absolutely like slate when she's focused on a task. Right now they were positively flinty.

"We do. We have to keep the Homeowners' Association guy away from Tim and Amanda until we can either change how all the cars are parked, or he gives up and goes away."

"What will happen if we don't?"

"He'll ruin Tim and Amanda's evening—and I think they've had a hard enough time already." Plus, the whole Homeowners' Association thing just galled me. Deep in my heart, I'm an anarchist. Well, as long as nobody trashes anything of mine.

"I'm on it. What should I do?"

"We have to repark all the cars so there's no more than seven on the street."

"This isn't like the time you convinced me that we had to dance around in the rain in our underwear, is it?"

"Not even close. We're talking serious business here."

"Good, because I don't have time for another bout with walking pneumonia." Gretchen and I hit the party and started begging for car keys and parking assistance. I'd gotten the keys to an electric blue Ford Explorer, a merlot Miata, and a silver Toyota Prius. Gretchen was working the other side of the room, and it looked as if she'd gotten herself some help. The tall guy with glasses who had chased her to the kitchen earlier in the evening and called her name as soon as she'd walked into the room and now was circling side by side with her. I was surprised he even recognized her.

Then there he was. Bud Lawlor. Association muscle moving in on my party. I plotted a course to intercept him. "Hi, Bud. I'm Mikayla. Amanda's friend. We met once before."

His gaze flicked over me, dismissing me as a non–mortgage-paying loser, before going back to scan the crowd. "I'm looking for Amanda and Tim. Have you seen them?"

"Not for a few minutes. Can I help you with something?"

"No." He shook his head. "It's something I need to discuss with them. Right away."

"Have you tried the kitchen?" I said with a big bright smile.

"Just came from there," he growled, circumnavigating me.

"Mikayla, there you are!" Max emerged from the crowd, stopping me in my tracks before I could follow Bud. "I was looking for you. I couldn't find you anywhere."

Lord, he was cute. And he'd been looking for me. "I'm sorry. I was in the closet with Gretchen and Amanda."

Max started to back up. He held his hands up in front of him. I could swear he blushed again. "I'm sorry. I must have misunderstood."

Huh? What was he talking about? "Misunderstood what?"

"Back in the kitchen. I thought we had, you know, kind of a connection. I was hoping I could get your number. I'm really sorry."

Sorry? What was he talking about? "I did, too. What changed?"

"Well, if you were in the closet and you just came out tonight, and I like foisted myself on you . . . well, I'd feel terrible. I'm not usually that insensitive. I never would have guessed about Amanda. She seems totally hetero."

Oh, my God. He thought I'd just told him we were gay. "No. No. When I said we were in the closet, I meant literally. Physically. In the closet in Amanda's bedroom, talking. *Only* talking. No girl-on-girl action."

"Oh. Well, that's different. I guess."

If it was different, why did he still have that weird look on his face?

He looked at me for a couple more moments and then finally blurted out, "So why exactly were you in the closet?"

I smiled up at him and threaded my arm through his. "Now, that actually is more difficult to explain, but I could try next week over coffee."

He smiled back. "That sounds like a plan. Listen, I've got to go. I've got another party to get to."

"Good!" I said, thinking that was one less car to move.

His brow creased. "Excuse me?"

"I meant good for you." I did an inner eye roll. I had to stop letting my interior monologue go exterior without editing.

So no kiss there, but I did get his number and a request to call him. Not bad.

Max had barely walked away when Riley came up on my other side.

"Mikayla, do you drive a red Mustang?"

"Mmm-hmm."

Riley held out his hands. "Keys, please. I need to move your car forward to make more room."

"They're in my purse in Amanda's room. I'll go get them." Riley followed me as we went down the hallway.

We heard them as soon as we walked in the door to the bedroom.

"Oh, yes, there," I heard Amanda moan through the closet doors. "I love it when you touch me there."

Tim groaned. "I love it when you love it. Oh, baby."

I didn't need a manual to know what was going on behind the closet door. Neither did Riley. Neither did Bud Lawlor, who had apparently arrived before us and was peeking through the closet doors. I grabbed my purse from the bed, fished out my keys, handed them to Riley, and then shoved him out the bedroom door before exclaiming loudly in by best indignant Scarlett O'Hara voice, "Mr. Lawlor, what on earth are you doing?"

Bud Lawlor jumped back from the closet. A guilty flush stained his cheeks, accenting what seemed to be a slight line of drool trickling down his chin. "L-l-looking for Amanda and Tim," he stammered.

I crossed my arms across my chest. "Sounds like you found them."

"Mikayla?" Amanda's voice sounded small and tiny inside the closet. "Is that you? Who else is there?"

"Yes, Amanda," I called. "I'm here with Bud Lawlor. Or maybe I should call him Tom Lawlor. Peeping Tom Lawlor."

Apparently, Mr. Lawlor felt it prudent to leave the party at this point. He rushed past me making strange strangling noises in the back of his throat.

Amanda and Tim emerged from the closet, clothes in disarray and hair becomingly mussed. "He was watching?" Amanda made a face. "Ewww."

"Would he have seen much?" I asked.

Both Tim and Amanda went beet red. Amanda said, "Let's just put it this way. Yippee-yi-oh-ki-yay."

Understanding dawned over me and I started to giggle as we headed back down the hallway. "Maybe you should ask Bud to get rid of the porn box, since he's already seen it all," I suggested. Amanda punched me in the arm.

Gretchen met us as we came into the living room and handed me my car keys. "I think we did it. I think we're down to seven cars on the street."

And about ten people in the living room. The party had

really cleared out. There was no sign of Riley or Max. Or Bud Lawlor.

"What happened to Bud?" Tim asked.

Gretchen shrugged. "He came streaking through here like the hounds from hell were on his heels, threw open the door, and ran out."

"Ten . . . Nine . . ." The countdown started.

"Mikayla!" Gretchen said. "It's midnight. And you're only with us!"

"Seven . . . Six . . ." The chant went on.

"There are no boys to kiss," Gretchen said.

"Four . . . Three . . ."

"Only us," Amanda said.

"One . . ."

Everyone started yelling. Horns tooted. Hands clapped. Amanda kissed me on one cheek while Gretchen kissed me on the other. I laughed. Then Tim grabbed Amanda and suddenly Tall Goofy Glasses Guy was tapping Gretchen on the shoulder, and there I was. Alone. At midnight.

An hour or so later, after doing a scavenger hunt throughout Amanda's house for half-empty champagne glasses and partially eaten hors d'oeuvres, I got into my Mustang to head home. For the first time in more than seventeen years, I hadn't gotten my midnight kiss.

I frowned. That wasn't really true. I had gotten midnight kisses—just not from a guy. I'd gotten them from Gretchen and Amanda.

Maybe those kisses would bring a different kind of New Year for me, one filled with warmth and love, laughter and support. That wouldn't totally suck. I flipped through my CDs until I found the Pixies and slid the disc into the player.

Still, I was a little bummed about Riley. Our banter had been short-lived, but I'd liked it, a lot. I thought he had, too. My dating instincts must be rusty after being out of circulation for a couple years. I backed out of the driveway and headed down the road.

Just as the Pixies launched into "Here Comes Your Man," I noticed a white paper rectangle on my dashboard. A business card. I pulled to the side of the road and flipped the map light on to read it. Riley's business card, with a scrawled "Call Me" on the back of it.

I smiled and tucked it in my pocket next to Max's card. Maybe not so rusty, after all. Maybe not such a bad year ahead, either.

EILEEN RENDAHL used to live in a Suburban Wonder Home in North Scottsdale and deeply regrets all basketball hoop violations and river rock infractions. Her first novel, *Do Me, Do My Roots,* was published by Downtown Press in April, 2004.

How to Start the New Year Like a Guy

PAMELA REDMOND SATRAN

STEP 1—
At 7:45 p.m. on New Year's Eve,
ask significant other what you're doing tonight.

Lily Cunningham sat pretending to read *People* magazine, holding her breath and waiting for Bobby to say something. It was nearly eight on New Year's Eve, but he had not yet made any mention of the holiday. Usually by this time he'd have asked her what they were doing to celebrate, expecting her to have their social agenda mapped out. Usually, well before this time, she'd have *told* him what they were doing. She would have laid out his tux, sent him to the store with a shopping list, *something*.

But not this year. This year, Lily swore that she was not, no matter how close to the wire they got, going to be the one to make the plans for New Year's Eve. She was always the one who made the plans, not only for New Year's Eve, but for every other fucking holiday, and she had had it. And this year, with the birth of their second child, with Lily cutting back her work hours and finding that every single job at home save taking out the garbage had fallen on her shoulders, she had been driven over the edge.

For Christmas, she was the one trolling the mall and panic-ordering from Toys "R" Us while Bobby watched football and ambled out on Christmas Eve to get her a pair of earrings, pretty but nearly exactly the same as the earrings he had bought her last year, the only gift he felt responsible for buying.

On Thanksgiving, she took the entire week off from work to prepare for the onslaught of his family. She made up cots, she shopped, she cooked, she set the table. He bought beer and played football when he wasn't watching it.

It was like this for all the lesser holidays too, even for his mother's birthday, when she chose the all-important sappy card and shipped the gift; even for her own birthday, when she made the restaurant reservations and specified what he should buy her, down to the model number, having learned the first year of their marriage that if she didn't do this, he might bring her home a set of cheap pots and pans or forget the occasion altogether.

She'd tried asking him to change, she'd tried getting mad, she'd tried not getting mad and just doing it herself. None of it had worked.

So this year, in the few minutes she had to catch her breath between the Thanksgiving onslaught and the Christmas crunch, she'd made her resolution. She'd even discussed it with her best friend, Sarah, who'd given it the official girlfriend seal of approval. Starting with the turn of the New Year, instead of playing the dutiful but pissed-off little woman, she was going to simply take life like a guy.

Which was not as easy as it looked. Glancing at the clock, then out of the corner of her eye at Bobby, hopping up to check on Nate, absorbed in his Pokémon cards, and on Simon, already sprawled in his crib, she was having trouble letting the evening keep ticking toward midnight. Turning over her social life to her husband, it seemed, was tantamount to hurling herself into the void. Was he just going to keep sitting here passively watching a *Seinfeld* rerun? Did he even realize it was New Year's Eve?

"So," she said finally, unable to contain herself any longer, but still trying to keep her voice casual, guylike, "what's up tonight?"

He turned his surprised eyes to her. This was fun, she had to admit, throwing him off guard like this. She even felt an unexpected little jolt of attraction, staring back into his wide dark eyes, at his big, handsome, clueless face.

Maybe this would work. Maybe she'd be able to turn things around, and they could get back to the way things were at the beginning.

"I don't know," he said. "Didn't you work something out?"

She shrugged, oh so unconcerned.

"Nah," she said. "I figured you'd take care of it."

His brow creased. She could sense his brain spinning. Was I supposed to do something and forgot? Could I possibly have made a mistake here?

"I didn't do anything wrong," he finally said, his usual conclusion.

And went back to watching Elaine debate whether her date was sponge-worthy.

Lily stood there gazing at the back of Bobby's head, flummoxed. This wasn't the way it was supposed to go. He was supposed to rise to the occasion, scramble to make plans so they'd have something to do for New Year's Eve, letting her emerge triumphant, mission accomplished.

Well, she couldn't back down now.

"*I* certainly didn't do anything wrong," she said, walking out of the room.

What now? She thought of saying she was going to go out and have a couple of drinks with the guys, but then she thought, What guys? What drinks? She looked in at Nate, happily shuffling his deck and talking to himself. Better not go there—she couldn't make it through a sentence of hearing about Pokémon without feeling her eyes cross. She definitely was not about to wake the baby.

She went and lay down on their bed, trying to think of what to do next.

After a few minutes, when *Seinfeld* was over, Bobby came in and stood over her.

"What are you doing?" he asked.

What would a guy be doing?

"Thinking about sex?" she said, but it came out like a question, with the uncertain intonation of a teenage girl.

He burst out laughing.

"I could help you do more than think," he said, trying to nudge his way into bed beside her.

"No!" she yelped, scrambling to her feet and out of range of his grasp.

Oooops, that was certainly not very guylike.

"It's New Year's Eve," she informed him, already breaking her resolution though it wasn't even close to midnight. "We've got to get ready to go out."

"Where are we going?"

"I don't know." She shrugged, remembering her role.

"We could just stay here," he said. "Get Nate to sleep, crack open a bottle of champagne, climb into bed, and have a private party." He waggled his eyebrows.

Of course: Why hadn't she thought of this? Left to his own devices, Bobby and most men she knew would choose to ring in the New Year with sex.

But she wasn't a *real* guy, just a woman trying to turn the tables.

"We can go to the Delmans' party," she said. The Delmans, who lived down the street, always threw a big blowout New Year's Eve bash to which they invited the entire neighborhood. While they usually opted in favor of a smaller dinner party or night on the town, Lily figured the Delmans' annual bash was a good fallback if Bobby didn't come up with anything better. And of course, she had asked Ryan from next door to babysit, figuring Bobby would never have been able to find a sitter at the last minute even if it occurred to him to try.

"Okay," he said. Then he narrowed his eyes. "What do I have to wear?"

If he'd headed for the shower without asking her and changed into something nice, she would have done the same. But now that she'd started, however haltingly, down this path, she wanted to stick to it.

She shrugged and sniffed her own underarm the way Bobby did when he was trying to decide whether he needed to change clothes, trying not to giggle. "I'm just going like this."

"Cool!" he said, brightening. "I'll go see whether we have any bad bottles of wine to bring along."

STEP 2—
When clock strikes midnight,
kiss nearest available member of opposite sex.

Midnight took her by surprise. One minute she was talking to Karen O'Connor about which first-grade teacher to request for next year, and the next she heard the voices of everyone gathered around the TV, chanting, "Ten . . . nine . . . eight . . ."

In panic, she scanned the room for Bobby. She hadn't seen him for hours, not since he'd started discussing the Green Bay Packers with Ed Delman and she'd figured she'd better run before she got trapped listening to an analysis of Brett Favre's passing game. She hadn't even missed him until now, as she watched all the other people in the room reach for their spouses for the first kiss of the New Year.

She and Bobby had been a couple for seven years. They'd spent every one of those seven New Year's Eves together, had kissed each other at every stroke of midnight. This year, as determined as Lily felt to turn things around in their marriage, she still wanted him to be the first one she kissed, felt almost superstitious at the idea she might not be able to find him before he exchanged a peck on the lips with whoever was standing next to him.

Oh, good, there he was, over by the bar. Thank God. Lord knew they had enough hurdles to get over to repair their relationship without tempting the fates.

But then, as she started across the room toward him, she saw something that turned her to stone in her tracks. There was Bobby, leaning down, kissing—not a peck, but a long, deep kiss—Marietta Finnegan-Freed, the tiny, dark-haired piano teacher from down the street, aka the Chihuahua Woman.

Lily was the one who called Marietta the Chihuahua Woman. She'd coined that name when she'd started teasing Bobby about having a crush on Marietta, whom he seemed to flirt with at every neighborhood party. Marietta was barely five feet tall and weighed probably ninety pounds; she wore tight pants that she must buy in the little girls' department. True, Lily was threatened: She felt so pale and enormous—white and gushy—next to the sharp and minuscule Marietta. But it was also true that, if you wanted to cast her in the worst possible light, Marietta *did* resemble a Chihuahua.

A Chihuahua down whose throat, Lily now saw with horror, Bobby seemed to be thrusting his tongue.

Rage leaping to her heart, Lily lurched toward Bobby and bumped directly into that new guy—Don? Dan?—who'd moved into the old Markson place.

"Excuse me," she said, looking beyond him to where Bobby's hand was inching up Marietta's narrow torso.

"Uh, Nate's mom, right?" Don/Dan said.

She focused on him. He couldn't have looked more different from Bobby: short where Bobby was tall, slim and compact where Bobby was hulking, still muscular but tending toward fat from his nightly three beers and bowl of chocolate ice cream. Don/Dan had reddish hair as opposed to Bobby's dark curls, an incongruously heavy beard on his narrow, eager-looking face, whereas the skin on Bobby's broad, placid face was smooth. Don/Dan could not, in other words, have been less Lily's type.

Lily looked across the room at Bobby, whose fingers were edging across the border toward Chihuahua Woman's lemon-sized breasts. Bobby didn't seem to have any trouble getting attracted to someone who was the opposite type from his spouse.

"Call me Lily," she said, laying a hand on Don/Dan's shoulder.

"Well, happy New Year," he said, moving in to peck her on the cheek.

At that moment, she saw Bobby come up for air from his kiss with Marietta and look straight through the crowd at her. Raising her eyebrows to let Bobby know she'd seen him, Lily swiveled her head so that Don/Dan's lips connected directly with hers. She had to bend down a little bit to kiss him, which felt weird after all those years of standing on her toes to kiss Bobby. The whole thing felt odd; she'd never expected to kiss any man who wasn't her husband seriously on the lips again in her lifetime, especially not some stranger she didn't even think was hot. But if she closed her eyes, she stopped thinking about what he looked like, and after just a second's hesitation, Don/Dan got into the kiss with great energy, moving his muscular little lips all around and battering her mouth with his tongue.

It wasn't quite as bad as it should have been, Lily reflected, especially when she saw through her slitted eyelid that Bobby was watching dumbfounded from across the room. She jammed her eyes shut and, flinging her arms around Don/Dan, kissed him with all she had, working as hard as she could to conjure and cling to a mental image of Jude Law.

She imagined Bobby striding toward her. Imagined him reaching out, squeezing her elbow, sweeping her into the passionate kiss that was rightfully hers.

Don/Dan's kiss, on the other hand, was getting awfully aggressive. And that beard was beginning to chafe against her chin.

She pulled away and looked around wildly for Bobby, who seemed to have gone missing again. Don/Dan's lips moved in the air the way Simon's did when she pulled her nipple away before he was ready to stop nursing. It took her a moment to locate Marietta, who was standing alone, looking toward the archway into the kitchen. Lily followed Marietta's gaze. Sure enough, there was Bobby, talking now to Lily's own best friend, Sarah Maclean, tall and blond and broad-shouldered, an editor at a women's magazine whose clothes and haircut always looked a little bit chicer than everybody else's.

And then Lily was flabbergasted to see him kiss Sarah happy New Year's too, although Sarah's husband, Steve, was standing only two feet away. A little more chastely than he'd kissed Marietta, but still.

STEP 3—
Kiss as many members of opposite sex as possible, while you can get away with it.

Leaving Don/Dan still working his lips like a beached sunfish, Lily moved in the direction of her husband, unsure what she was going to do—after she punched him in the gut.

The man was a total lech! Lily couldn't remember doing this any other New Year's Eve, but then again, they didn't usually go to such a big, anything-goes party. Lily had never realized that, given the opportunity, Bobby would be such a voracious kisser.

And then Sarah broke off her kiss with Bobby, turned directly toward Lily, and flashed her a big smile and a wink. Sarah knew all about Lily's resolution to become more guylike and approved wholeheartedly. Her wink seemed to signal that the games had already begun. Which made Lily stop and consider.

Maybe Bobby's behavior wasn't such a big deal after all.

Maybe, come to think of it, this New Year's Eve kissing-without-borders presented an important opportunity for Lily. If she was going to be more like a man, she should be a more promiscuous kisser herself! Less possessive! More flirtatious!

If Lily was totally honest, she had crushes on some men in town the same way Bobby lusted after Marietta. In fact, there across the room was that adorable Alex Rosen, tall and lean, dark and handsome and soft-spoken, ex-semipro-basketball player and noted watercolorist, with an actual painting in the Whitney Museum. He ferried the kids to and from school while his wife, Jill, who worked her Wall Street job into every conversation the way other people did their Harvard degree, hoofed into the city every day. Between parties and occasional sightings at kindergarten functions, Lily usually forgot that Alex Rosen existed. But then every time she did see him, she felt a strange lightness dangerously close to her groin.

She felt it now, in fact, as she moved toward him.

"Hi, Alex," she said.

He tipped his head down toward her, ever courtly, and smiled in his sweet way.

"Happy New Year," she said.

Then she stood on her toes and craned her neck up toward him and kissed him squarely on the lips. It was not the kind of assertive, tongue-plunging kiss she'd endured with Don/Dan or witnessed between Bobby and Marietta, but a solid yet soft, equal-opportunity meeting of the mouths, the kind of kiss that made her curious to know more.

He lingered above her, still smiling, and she kept looking up at him, smiling back, their faces a little too close.

And then another impulse rose up in her, one more powerful than the urge to kiss him.

"I have to tell you, Alex," she said, feeling the kind of rush she imagined she might feel if she were about to jump out of an airplane, "that I've always thought you were the cutest, sexiest dad at kindergarten."

He raised his eyebrows. "Wow," he said. "We should get together for lunch sometime. I make a mean tuna sandwich."

Lunch. At his place. Alone.

Just as she felt her face begin to burn at the vision of Alex

Rosen lowering his endless length onto her naked body, stretched out across sheets that another woman had washed—or was washing the sheets something Alex did too, along with the school run?—she felt Bobby's hand on her elbow.

"Come on, honey," he said in her ear. "Let's get out of here."

STEP 4—
As soon after midnight as possible, have sex.

How much had Bobby heard? What exactly had he seen?

As soon as they were outside the Delmans', she tried to talk to him about it, but before she managed to utter one coherent word, his mouth was over hers and he was kissing her in a way he hadn't since before Nate was born. Since *way* before Nate was born. He was kissing her, in fact, exactly as he'd been kissing Marietta. And Lily found that the sight of Bobby kissing all those other women, the memory of her own extramarital kissing, even her shame at having blurted her feelings to Alex, all seemed to fuel the fire that was roaring up unexpectedly from down below.

"I couldn't find you at midnight," he panted into her ear.

"You were busy with Chihuahua Woman," she whispered back.

He chuckled softly. "You seemed pretty busy yourself."

"I was jealous," she confessed, despite her best intentions to play it cool. "I know you have a crush on her."

"I have a crush on you," he said, his fingers, still warm from the crowded room, edging under her sweater.

"She's so skinny," Lily said, sucking in her breath at the mental image of her own midsection, still wobbly from her pregnancy with Simon.

"You're so beautiful," David said, beginning to kiss her again.

God, she couldn't even remember feeling this excited about him, about anybody. She wrapped her arms around his neck and rubbed herself against him. She could feel how hard he was even through their bulky winter clothes. An image flashed through her mind of the two of them in the bushes, doing it right there outside the Delmans' party. If it weren't so freezing, she might even make it happen.

But then the door burst open, shining the light and noise of the party over them like the beam of a policeman's flashlight. Lily grabbed Bobby's hand and, heart hammering, yanked him out of the spotlight and down the path. Giggling, they scrambled along the icy sidewalk, slipping as they went, until they reached the shadows in front of their own house. Where they began kissing again.

No wonder, she thought, high school had been one long haze of horniness. So many nights had been spent exactly like this: making out with random boys at a party, walking home with the one you really had a crush on, followed by more purposeful kissing in the dark outside her house, always with the danger of being seen at any minute, always yearning toward more but stopping short of real fulfillment.

There was no reason to stop now, though. Bobby was her husband.

"Let's go inside," she whispered.

"No," he said. "I have a better idea."

Enveloping her with his arms, he nudged her toward the driveway, pulling something out of his pocket and aiming it toward the minivan. The van's lights flickered and the beep sounded that signaled the unlocking of the doors. Another press of the button and the van's back door slid soundlessly open.

"You've got to be kidding," she said.

"No, I'm not," he said huskily. "Don't you feel like a kid?"

"But we're not kids," Lily pointed out. "It's freezing in there. And our nice warm bed is right upstairs."

"I'll warm this up for you," Bobby said. "Come on, baby. Humor me here for a minute. If you hate it, we'll stop."

Lily hesitated. All the excitement she'd felt a minute earlier had drained out of her. All she wanted was to go up to her bed and, at this point, go to sleep.

But Bobby's eyes were shining with an enthusiasm normally evidenced only when he was doing something like setting up his boyhood train set under the Christmas tree.

"Please," he said, sounding a little too much like Nate.

"Ten minutes," she said.

"Awwwwww. You've got to give me more time than that."

"I'll give you ten minutes. And then if I still want to go in, we go in."

"Okay," said Bobby. "Deal."

They climbed into the van, as if for a trip to the mall, and he started the engine, cranking up the heater full blast. Then he leaned across the front gearshift and kissed her.

"Bobby," she said. "We can't just sit right here."

As if to underscore her point, they saw the Delmans' front door open down the street and a knot of partygoers spill out into the night. From all those houses away, even with the car doors closed and the engine running, Lily could hear Sarah's raucous laughter.

"People will see us sitting here with the exhaust pouring out of the tailpipe. They'll think we're having a fight."

Bobby seemed to think for a minute. "Should I pull into the garage?"

"Great idea," Lily said sarcastically. "I can see the headlines now: 'Married Lovers Gassed in Suicide Pact.' Let's just go inside."

"I still have seven minutes," Bobby said with grim determination, throwing the car into reverse.

Lily fastened her seat belt as he headed up the hill, where the houses got bigger and farther apart. Then he turned off onto the road that switchbacked through the woods up to where the country club, the one they could never in a million years afford to join, sat on a grassy promontory overlooking the city.

"Warmer?" he said, reaching for her hand as he drove.

She had to admit, it was downright toasty in here now.

"Where are we going?" she asked.

"I know a place." He grinned.

Bobby had grown up around here and knew all the shortcuts, the secret paths through the woods and the gaps in the fences where you could sneak through someone's yard.

"A place you used to bring your girlfriends?"

"A place I've always dreamed of bringing you," he said.

Oh, he was good, he was very good, when he wanted to be, which he hadn't, not for a long time, with her.

But isn't that what had inspired her to want to try this "act like a guy" stuff? The desire to make him act differently toward her? True, this hadn't exactly been what she'd had in mind. She'd been hoping to inspire him to behave more like—well, more like a girl. To be more thoughtful, more considerate, to play a more active role in doing things with the kids and around the house.

Bobby's strength had never been in the domestic arts, however, she had to admit now, as he pulled the car into an opening that was almost hidden beneath the trees. She'd fallen in love with him, she reflected as his fingers slid once again under her sweater, because he resembled not so much Martha Stewart as Bruce Willis.

"You are so beautiful," he said.

"Mmmmm." She'd done her share of parking in high school too, often fumbling in one seat while another couple occupied the other. Now they were alone, though.

As if reading her mind, Bobby said, "Let's climb in back."

Lily looked dubiously behind her.

"Come on, baby," he pleaded.

Obviously trying to set an example, he scrambled over the console, maneuvering past the two car seats strapped in the individual second-row seats, landing on the bench seat way in the back.

"Come on," Bobby repeated, grinning and patting the seat of the van.

Lily kept staring at him. How would a guy get out of this situation? No guy had ever been *in* this situation.

"I'll give you a dollar," he said.

She couldn't help it; she smiled.

"What do I have to do for the dollar?"

"Kiss me."

"That's it?"

"That's it."

"You promise?"

"Promise."

Still grinning, she climbed into the back, feeling a plastic toy crack beneath her foot, and plopped down beside Bobby, planting a kiss on his cheek.

"There," she said. "Where's my dollar?"

He reached into the pocket of his jeans and drew out a crumpled bill, a five.

"Do you have change?" he deadpanned.

"I don't have any money."

"Then you'll have to do something else to earn the other four dollars."

"I'll give you four more kisses."

"Oh, no. You'll have to do more than that."

They'd never been the kind of couple—did this kind of couple really exist?—who played sexy games and dressed up in strange costumes to spark up their love life. In fact, their entire relationship, from the beginning, had been predicated on getting married and having children. They'd talked about baby names on their second date, gotten engaged after three months, married in a year, were parents by their second Christmas together. There had been no time to pretend.

"Well," Lily said now, unzipping her jacket, "I'll let you look at my breasts."

"At your tits," Bobby corrected her, "and for five dollars, you have to let me do more than look."

She pretended to consider. "All right," she said finally. "But I'm not taking any clothes off."

She pulled up her sweater, unhooked her bra and pulled that up too. She had so much material bunched up around her neck that she couldn't see her breasts herself. But she could see Bobby gazing appreciatively at them. Then he reached up and ran his hand across one nipple, which made her breast tingle as if in anticipation of nursing. She was easing Simon onto the bottle now and normally only nursed him in the evening and again in the morning. But her breasts were confused by this unexpected stimulation.

She yanked down her sweater, not wanting to spurt milk onto her husband.

"You don't get to touch for five dollars," she told him.

"What about," he said, reaching into his pocket again, "for twenty dollars? What do I get for twenty?"

She thought about that. She realized she was excited again, even more excited than she'd been outside the house.

"For twenty," she said, "I'll take off my pants."

He groaned—for real this time, she could tell.

"Do I get to have sex with you for twenty?"

"Oh, no," she said, unzipping her jeans and beginning to edge them down. "Sex is going to cost you a lot more than twenty."

"How much?"

"A thousand," she said, trying to keep from bursting out laughing. "No. Ten thousand."

He smiled. "Do you take credit cards?"

"No," she said, pulling the jeans along with her panties down to her knees, then slipping them off over her boots. "You can pay me later."

Bobby half-stood as if to make room for her to lie on the seat, but she stopped him.

"Stay right there," she commanded. "For that kind of money, you don't have to do anything but relax."

She pulled down his fly herself, straddled his lap, and eased herself onto him, moving up and down in a way that was thrilling, almost too exciting to bear.

"Jesus," Bobby said, cupping her bottom with his hands. "You are the sexiest girl alive."

"Sexier than Chihuahua Woman?" Lily panted.

"What?"

But suddenly Lily's breath was rising too precipitously in her throat for her to speak and her eyelids fluttered closed. Something about having him at her mercy like this, about controlling him and at the same time letting go of all the normal strictures—feeling confined to their bedroom, trying to be quiet so they wouldn't wake the kids—ratcheted up her excitement precipitously and then sent it hurtling over the edge. Usually, when they were making love, she was fully aware of him, of the bed around them, of the temperature of the air and the sounds outside the window and of the chores that would need to be tackled the next morning. But now, she couldn't focus on anything beyond her own body, beyond her surging pleasure.

"Oh," she heard herself cry. "Oh oh oh oh oh oh oh."

And then the only thing she was aware of was her orgasm, powerful and consuming.

The next thing she felt was him shifting beneath her, followed by the realization that she had drifted off, her mouth pressed against his neck, and that she was drooling all over him, her saliva drenching both his collar and her own cheek.

"Oh, God," she said. "I'm sorry. Wow. That was amazing. I must have . . ."

But her thoughts were interrupted by the dawning knowledge that he was still pressing against her down below—that for him, the party was not yet over. As if to prove it, he once again began moving inside her.

"Whoa," she cried. "Hold on there, cowboy."

He looked stricken. "But I haven't . . . ," he began. "I mean I didn't . . ."

She wiggled away from him. "That was it for me," she said, feeling, even as she said it, so exhausted that she could curl up and go to sleep right there on the backseat. "I'm sorry, Bobby. I've got to get home."

His mouth was hanging open and he seemed to be still trying to formulate a rebuttal, but she wriggled her jeans up over her hips and buttoned the waistband, yawning widely.

"But I'm not finished," he said finally, his big, handsome face totally bereft.

If she'd engineered this impasse to cap her quest to be more like a guy, she would never have been able to keep from breaking into giggles, their roles were so thoroughly reversed, and Bobby seemed so undone at finding himself in the unsatisfied position she'd been in countless times during their marriage. On the rare occasions when Bobby had been the one left behind, she'd always forced herself to keep going till he finished too.

But this time, she was so tired and uncomfortable—the word *spent* flitted across her mind—that soldiering on for Bobby's sake was out of the question.

"Sorry," she mumbled, straightening her clothes one final time and making her way to the front of the van, curling into the big, cushiony passenger seat. "Things are changing around here."

Bobby might have said something like "I'll say," but she wasn't really listening. She felt herself dozing off, and the only sound that penetrated her brain was her own contented little snore.

STEP 5—
Sleep through kids' middle-of-the-night cries and morning demands for breakfast to wake refreshed and confident about greeting the whole new year.

When Lily opened her eyes on the morning of January 1, she immediately felt as if the world were a brand-new place.

First, the sun was streaming full bore through the window be-side her bed. It had been more than five years, since right before Nate was born, since she'd woken up this late in the morning, with the sun this high in the sky. She yawned and stretched, feel-ing as if she might have been sleeping for days.

It took a moment for her to hear the boys' voices, along with Bobby's, filtering up from downstairs. They were in the kitchen, she could tell. A cupboard door slammed, a pot clattered to the floor, followed by a beat of silence, and then Simon's high-pitched wails.

The sound of the baby's screams sent the milk flooding to her nipples. She hadn't nursed him last night and so now her breasts were ready to work double time. Leaping out of bed, she raced to the stairs, prepared to rush down and feed Simon to ease both their pains.

But when she reached the landing, something unexpected happened. Something that stopped her in her tracks.

Simon stopped crying. She heard Bobby say something sooth-ing to him, and then Nate's giggle. The kitchen CD player came to life with the sound of the boys' favorite Raffi song. Bobby loathed Raffi—he was always trying, unsuccessfully, to educate his little sons to the appeal of ancient Grateful Dead tunes— but now Lily listened incredulously as she heard her husband start to sing along. Simon squealed with delight and Nate began singing too.

As quietly as she could, Lily tiptoed backward through the hallway to her bedroom. She was awake now, she had no desire to go back to sleep, but she might as well take a few moments for herself, while the boys were so happily occupied downstairs. She could take a leisurely shower, dry her hair without a child swinging from her leg, think for once about what she was going to wear.

Pulling her nightgown over her head and stepping out of her underwear, Lily caught sight of herself in the full-length mirror on her closet door. She had gotten into the habit, through her two pregnancies and their disastrous physical aftermath, of averting her eyes from her own naked image, preferring not to take in the sight of her swollen breasts, her sagging stomach, of all that cellulite and extra skin that seemed to exist only to depress her.

But now she did a double take. When she wasn't looking, all the stretched-out bits seemed to have sprung back into shape. She turned to the side, then looked back over her shoulder for the rear view. Amazing. She hadn't even been dieting, not consciously, and the weight seemed to have fallen off her.

Breathless, she moved into the bathroom and pulled out the scale she'd shoved behind the hamper in the sixth month of her pregnancy with Simon, nearly a year ago—not that she'd been able to forget for even one minute that it was lurking in its hiding place, taunting her. Now, judging from the way she looked in the mirror, she weighed less than she had *before* she'd got pregnant with Simon, before she'd got pregnant with Nate!

She stepped on the scale and waited for the magic number to appear. And then stood there staring. And staring. According to this scale, she weighed exactly what she had the last time she'd stepped on it. When she was six months pregnant. Far more than she'd ever weighed nonpregnant in her entire life. Oh my God—

if this was true, she was going to start this year on a diet that was going to have to stretch to next Thanksgiving.

Moving quickly as if the mirror might morph in her absence, she once again confronted the reflection of her naked body. There must be rolls of fat, whole cities of cellulite there, she hadn't noticed first time around. But no. Once again, without even trying to suck in her stomach, without tightening her butt or holding her breath, she looked slim, buff, nothing short of fantastic.

She raced back to the scale. Maybe she'd stepped on too fast. Or too slow. Maybe the fumes from the hamper had screwed with the scale's innards and it needed a few minutes to breathe before it could register an accurate weight. Maybe it was mad at her for stashing it back there all this time and was punishing her by refusing to budge from its last, inflated weight.

Apparently not. The scale showed exactly the same high number as it had last time. Lily even jumped up and down a few times to try to shake some sense into it, but the needle kept settling back to the same weight.

The mirror must be off. There was only one way to tell for sure.

She marched back to her closet, but instead of stopping at the mirror, she opened the door and retrieved her narrowest, skinniest jeans, the ones she kept on the back shelf as a token of hope. Someday, she always vowed to herself, I will fit in those jeans again. So far, she hadn't even gotten close. And she was still wearing the loose clothes she'd worn since Simon was born, not wanting to demoralize herself further by finding that her old things still didn't fit.

She stepped into the jeans. She pulled them up. Without even tugging, she buttoned the waist. The zipper zipped up with nary a snag.

It was a miracle. She stepped back and surveyed herself in the mirror again. She looked fantastic. She *felt* fantastic, her heart lighter even than her body. Maybe all the lifting of the baby and pushing of the stroller and chasing after two children had simply buffed up her muscles to the point that she was sleeker, if not actually lighter? Or maybe, after the triumph of last night, she was merely looking at herself through a man's eyes, noticing everything that was right instead of the tiny imperfections?

Whatever. The real point was that there would be no dieting, not this year. She was perfect the way she was. Heading triumphantly back to the bathroom, she took the scale and dumped it in the garbage.

STEP 6—
Spend rest of day thoroughly indulging self.
Do not, under any circumstances, feel guilty.

"The game?" Lily said. "What game?"

"It's New Year's Day, Lily," said Bobby, a smile playing at the edges of his lips. "Football."

"Oh," said Lily, wrinkling her brow. Football. She loathed

football. No way on earth was she spending today or any other day watching football.

Yet this introduced a quandary in her plan to act more like a man. Men liked to watch football. And on big holidays, even men who didn't like to watch football watched football. She'd be betraying her new spiritual gender if she didn't go along.

"Who's playing?" she asked, though she wasn't even sure why. Mightn't there be some celebrity football players? Celebrity football players with wives sitting in the stands wearing interesting outfits?

Bobby looked at her as if she'd asked him who was president. "It's the Rose Bowl," he said. "Wisconsin's in it this year. Our alma mater."

Nate cried, "Badgers!" and took off running in a circle around the kitchen, pumping his fists in the air. From his walker, baby Simon chortled and tried to follow his big brother.

"Come on, love," said Bobby, rubbing a hand over her hip. All morning, from the time he'd got up with the kids on his own through his cooking of breakfast and his cleaning of the kitchen, he'd been so sweet to her. Maybe he thought she wasn't going to make him pay her the $10,000. "It will be fun."

"I don't know," Lily said.

"We're going to Lenny's," Bobby said. "There'll be brats, beer . . ."

That clinched it. As much as Lily hated football, she hated Lenny, Bobby's overaged frat-boy buddy, even more.

"I think I'll skip it," she said. She was about to plead with him to take the boys on his own, promising to straighten up the house and get dinner ready in return, when she had an inspiration.

"I have to work," she explained.

"Work?" Bobby looked confused.

Lily tried to force her brain into a higher gear. Her part-time job editing copy at the newspaper did not usually involve bringing work home. In fact, that was one thing she'd always claimed to Bobby she liked about it: She went to the newsroom, she fixed up stories that went directly into the next day's paper, and when she left her job, it was over. In the office, she left her mothering responsibilities behind, and when she was home with the kids, she didn't have to worry about bosses or deadlines.

"There's that job Sarah told me about at the magazine," she said to Bobby now. "I was thinking I might apply for it, see what happened. But I have to read a bunch of back issues first."

She hadn't even been seriously considering applying for the magazine job, but now that it was out of her mouth, she thought, Why not? Nate would be in school full-time in the fall, the excellent sitter she already had for Simon was open to taking on more hours. It was over five years since she'd scaled back her career; maybe it was time to nudge it forward again.

"Oh," said Bobby, surprise in his eyes. "Okay. But we haven't talked about this, have we?"

He looked nervous, as if he thought they might have discussed the subject and he'd forgotten—a notion that was entirely in the realm of possibility.

"Sure we have," Lily said, deciding to run with it. "You claimed that anything I wanted was okay with you."

Which had been, more or less, what Bobby had said when she'd been debating five years ago whether to keep working full-time or cut back or quit altogether.

Bobby looked confused. "I don't remember saying that."

"Really?" said Lily. "Isn't that what you think?"

"Yeah. I guess."

"Good. So this works out perfectly. I'll get this work done while you and the boys go and have your fun."

This was the kind of thing that Bobby said to her all the time. Of course, being with the kids *was* fun. But it was also a good amount of work. She enjoyed watching him struggle in his own web, until the only thing he could do was gather up the boys and head over to Lenny's to watch the game.

Free. Alone in her house, with nothing to do. Or nothing real, anyway.

This was an unspeakable luxury. The only time she had home alone anymore was when they were getting ready for some high-pressure event—a visit from Bobby's mother, for instance—and Bobby took the boys out to run errands while she raced around cleaning and putting the house in order. Never did she have even an hour, even ten minutes, at home on her own with time and space to put her feet up and read and watch television and dream.

She found one of the magazines she'd told Bobby she was going to study. She lay back on the couch and opened it.

And immediately got absorbed in a story about a toddler undergoing heart surgery.

Well, this was a kind of studying, wasn't it? If she was seriously going to apply for an editor's job at this magazine, it was essential that she actually read the articles, not just skim the pages. After the surgery piece, she read a guide to reorganizing your closet, which inspired her to go upstairs and actually take a crack at reorganizing hers. As long as she was up there sifting through her clothes all by herself, she thought she'd play the new Beyoncé CD, the one she'd bought herself when she was Christmas shopping and feeling old and out of it. And as long as she was playing the new CD, she might as well crank it up full blast and dance around the bedroom, singing and doing all the hand motions the way Beyoncé did in the video Lily had seen on MTV when Simon was still waking her in the middle of the night to nurse. As she danced, she started trying on all the clothes in the closet, delighted as the pile of clothes that were too big grew higher than those that were too small.

Dimly, she heard the phone ring and danced over toward it, wearing a strapless, pink number she was able to zip herself into for the first time in years, pausing only to turn down the volume on the CD player. She fully expected it to be Bobby, telling her the game was going into overtime (yes!) or asking her to go over to Lenny's to pick up the boys.

Instead, she heard Sarah's voice on the line.

"So," her friend said, "where did you guys go after the party last night?"

"We didn't go anywhere," Lily said, feeling a blush rise to her cheeks.

"We walked by your house after you left," Sarah said. "We were thinking if it looked like you were still up, we'd stop in for a drink. But your car was gone."

"Oh," Lily said. "Bobby was probably taking the sitter home."

"You told me Ryan was sitting," Sarah said. "Ryan lives next door to you."

Lily loved living in a small town with a tight community of other moms. But the downside was that it sometimes seemed as if nothing were private. Everybody knew each other's husband's salary, how many times a week the other couples had sex, how much they'd paid for their house, and how difficult their kids were to toilet train.

And Sarah was the person whom Lily told even those things she didn't want anyone else to know. How worried she was when Bobby almost lost his job. How fervently she disliked Bobby's mother. How much she fantasized about that hunky guy who mowed their lawn.

But she didn't want to tell her about last night.

Instead, she did what Bobby would do when confronted with an issue he didn't want to discuss: She changed the subject, taking the offensive.

"That was pretty weird last night," she said, "watching you making out with my husband."

Now that she'd said it, she realized it *had* been weird.

"I was wishing him happy New Year," Sarah said. "Just like you were doing with Dan. Or Don. That goofy new guy."

"Yeah, but you're not married to Dan. Or maybe it is Don."

"You can kiss Steve," said Sarah, naming her own husband. "Any New Year's Eve."

"I'll keep that in mind next year," said Lily drily.

"So how's the 'act more like a man' resolution going?"

"Fine," Lily said. Although she'd been discussing the idea with Sarah for weeks, she suddenly found herself reluctant to say anything more.

"Fine?" shrieked Sarah. "I hope you don't think I'm going to be satisfied with *fine*. I expect all the juicy details!"

Lily was about to say something to deflect Sarah's attention when, from outside, she heard the slam of a car door, and then the sound of Bobby's key in the lock. Wildly, she looked around the room at the mess, down at the pink dress she was still wearing.

"I've got to run," said Lily.

"Let's get together tomorrow," Sarah said. "I want to hear all about what's been going on."

From the hallway below, Lily heard the boys' voices. Then Bobby called her name.

"No," said Lily, panicking.

"No?" said Sarah. "What do you mean, no?"

Nate's feet thundered up the stairs, followed by Bobby's heavier tread. "Lily?"

"I'll see you at yoga," Lily said, slamming down the phone at the same moment that Bobby and the boys appeared in the bedroom doorway.

She watched as Bobby took in the litter of clothes on the floor, Lily's dancing dress, her hand still resting atop the phone.

"I thought you were supposed to be working," he said.

STEP 7—
Rationalize, rationalize, rationalize.

Lily was seized by a paroxysm of guilt so sudden and intense she actually visualized flinging herself at Bobby's feet and begging his forgiveness. I'll listen to a play-by-play account of the entire football game, she thought. I'll promise to take care of the boys every Sunday until Valentine's Day. I'll give him a *blow job*.

But then she thought, Get a grip, woman. What exactly did I do that was so terrible? Inflate the importance of my magazine reading, maybe. Tell a little white fib to get out of going to a stupid Rose Bowl party. Nothing any self-respecting male wouldn't do in a reverse situation—without feeling even a millisecond's guilt.

"I finished my work," she said, "and I thought I'd do some reorganizing, so you wouldn't have to do it when you got home."

Bobby scrunched up his face. "What are you talking about? Why would I have had to reorganize your closet when I got home?"

Pretend you didn't hear him, Lily told herself. Most guys have that kind of selective hearing.

"I thought you'd want to relax," she said.

With that, he handed her the baby, who immediately burst into tears and made a dive for Lily's breast, sinking his new teeth into her pink dress.

"One second, sweetheart," Lily said, trying to hand Simon back to Bobby. "Let Mommy get into more comfortable clothes."

"Oh, no, you don't," Bobby said, backing away. "I had them all afternoon."

"I just have to change out of this dress. And get dinner started."

Bobby reluctantly accepted his squirming little boy and Lily ducked into the closet to change into sweatpants and a T-shirt, pulling the door shut behind her. The sight of her bare breasts might inflame both Simon *and* Bobby, she was afraid, for different reasons. She came out of the closet and skirted around them, making a beeline for the phone. Bobby stood there holding the baby and watching her, openmouthed, as she dialed the number of Mr. Dino's pizza and ordered a large pie.

"I thought you were starting dinner," he said when she hung up.

"Pizza *is* dinner," Lily said calmly, taking Simon from Bobby's arms and settling back onto the bed to feed her child, who greedily pulled at her breast. Act like a man, indeed, Lily thought as she relaxed against the pillows and gave herself over to her hungry baby. Who am I kidding?

She closed her eyes and let her head sink into the down and didn't realize she'd been dozing until the doorbell rang announcing the pizza's arrival. Baby Simon had fallen asleep at the breast, and she gently, very gently, carried him into his room and eased him into his crib before heading downstairs to eat. Bobby and Nate were sitting on stools at the kitchen counter—a big-boy treat for Nate—silently munching the pizza.

"Good?" Lily asked, lifting a slice from the box for herself.

Nate nodded enthusiastically—Lily guessed he had not eaten

anything more substantial than chips all afternoon, and Bobby hadn't noticed—but Bobby just shrugged and set down his half-eaten piece.

"I figured you'd have dinner ready for us," he said.

"I figured you wouldn't be hungry after Lenny's."

"That was lunch," said Bobby.

"Today is a holiday for women too."

She and Bobby glared at each other, until she noticed Nate was staring at them with a worried look on his face, his pizza suspended near his mouth.

Bobby jerked his chin in her direction. "You seem different."

"It's a new year," Lily said lightly, not meeting Bobby's eye. "Time for changes."

"Working full-time? Leaving me alone with the kids all day while you try on clothes? Pizza for dinner every night?"

Nate had begun nibbling again, but was still watching his parents with anxious eyes.

Lily smiled at Nate to reassure him but leaned close to Bobby and whispered in his ear, so only he could hear, "I can't wait to get you in bed and finish what I started last night."

STEP 8—
Resolve that from now on, you'll be proud to be yourself.

They lay in bed, the lights off, the house silent, Lily's arms around Bobby and Bobby's head resting on her shoulder.

"I'm sorry," he said. "I just can't."

"That's all right."

Though, to her surprise, it really wasn't all right. Despite the sexual fireworks of the night before, Lily found she wanted Bobby again. *Really* wanted Bobby again.

But Bobby needed to talk. They'd tucked Nate into bed, waited until they were sure he was asleep, taken off their clothes, and slipped naked between their own sheets. Bobby had started talking about what had happened that day, what had happened the night before, and she'd listened until impatience overtook her, four minutes into his discussion, when she'd tried kissing away his words. But he kept nudging her away and launching into his soliloquy again.

She wasn't really listening to him, he claimed. Didn't really care about his feelings. He felt that she wasn't really *there* for him. Oh, sure, she wanted his body. But did she really want *him?*

Of *course* she wanted him, she soothed. She was *crazy* about him! He was so smart, so funny, so much more than just a penis to her!

Relax, sweetie, she said, beginning to kiss him again, sliding her hand down his stomach. I'll show you how much I love you.

"I mean it, Lily!" Bobby said, jerking away from her and bolting upright, clutching the covers to his chest. "I don't know what's going on with you, but I feel really terrible."

Lily hesitated. Took a deep breath. Obviously, she wasn't going to get anywhere with Bobby by continuing to plow directly through his insecurities and questions. But how *was* she going to get through to him? Her customary tactic for connecting with him when nothing she said would make him understand was to have sex with him. To communicate with his body instead of his mind.

He was usually so pleased—make that pleased and shocked—by this maneuver that he fell right into line and was instantly willing to do anything she wanted, whether that meant listening sympathetically as she complained about his mother or watching the boys so she could spend an entire Saturday helping Sarah buy an outfit for her sister's wedding.

But clearly, sex wasn't going to work this time. This time, Lily was going to have to shock her husband into compliance another way.

And then suddenly, she saw the situation between the two of them as clearly as if she were an angel hovering near the ceiling, the Guardian Angel of Beleaguered Married Couples with Children, on a mission to make Lily and Bobby happy again. There was Lily, succeeding in acting a tiny bit more like a man. And there was Bobby, responding by acting a tiny bit more like a woman.

Lily couldn't help it: She started laughing. And once she started, she found she couldn't stop. She fell back on the bed, laughing and laughing, until Bobby finally eased back down beside her, wrapping himself around her to muffle her giggles, whispering, *"Sssssh!* You're going to wake the kids." That didn't really make her stop laughing, but he kept holding her anyway, and before long she felt him grow hard against her leg, the rocking of her laughter apparently succeeding where her earlier efforts, both physical and verbal, had failed.

He kissed her then, and she kissed him back. They kissed some more. Kissing, as she had discovered the night before, was definitely an art that was ripe for revival. Kissing progressed to love-making, soft and sweet but no less passionate than it had been in the van. And this time, Bobby definitely found his satisfaction, though he gallantly stayed with her until she was finished too.

Afterward, they lay wrapped in each other's arms.

"Why were you laughing before?" Bobby finally asked her.

"Oh," she said, trying to think of how to answer. Then she decided to simply tell him the truth. "For New Year's, I decided to try acting more like a man."

He pulled away from her and studied her face, trying to decide, it seemed, whether she was serious.

"Why would you do such a thing?" he finally asked.

Why, indeed? It wasn't that she saw his life, or the lives of other men she knew, as being better than hers. It wasn't really that she wanted to trade places in their marriage, to be the breadwinner like Alex Rosen's wife, for example, while Bobby stayed home with the kids.

"I wanted to be happier," she said finally. "Not just me. Us."

"So, did it work?"

"I'm happier," she said, beginning to laugh again. "But you're acting more like a girl."

Almost immediately, she realized her mistake. There was such a thing as being open, and then there was such a thing as hurling the truth at someone so brutally it came bouncing back and hit you in the face. Bobby looked so stricken she was afraid for a moment that *he* might hit her.

"I thought I was being nice to you," he said, "and you call that acting like a *girl?*"

"Well," she said, trying to stall so she could think, "what's so bad about being a girl?"

"You may want to spend the next year acting like a guy," Bobby said, sitting up fully now, dropping his legs over the side of the bed and pulling on his boxers, "but I don't want to spend mine acting like a girl. That is in no way my resolution. Got it?"

"Got it," Lily said miserably. But she couldn't help herself from wanting to keep pushing the subject. She *had* been happier the past few days, not just with Bobby, but on her own too. She didn't want to give that up.

"I loved the sex," she said. "Didn't you love the sex?"

"Yes," Bobby conceded.

"And it made me feel terrific that you did so much with the kids."

Bobby frowned. "I like being with the kids. But I don't want you to treat me like your *maid.*"

"OK, but I don't want you to treat me like *your* maid either!" Lily exploded. "That's what this is all about! I want us to be equals again."

"I don't want to be the girl," Bobby said stubbornly.

"I don't want you to be the girl either," Lily said, feeling as if it might finally be safe to slide her hand downward again. "In fact, I *very* much don't want you to be the girl."

She felt him begin to spring to life and found herself, even on the heels of their argument, getting excited again. She ran a hand over Bobby's muscled arm and felt strong. Felt his confident lips on hers and believed in herself.

She could act more like a guy, she thought, as he moved down to embrace her again. Or more like a girl. Or simply more like herself—whatever brought them closer together.

PAMELA REDMOND SATRAN is the author of the novels *Babes in Captivity* and *The Man I Should Have Married*. She is also coauthor of the bestselling *Beyond Jennifer and Jason* series of baby-naming books and a frequent contributor to such magazines as *Glamour, Parenting, Good Housekeeping* and *Bon Appetit*. She believes New Year's Eve should be celebrated on the night before Labor Day.

Expecting a Call

DIANE STINGLEY

"It's no big deal. He said he'd call 'sometime next week,' and it's only Monday."

That's what Rachel told herself when she got home Monday night, after she played back her messages and discovered that Todd hadn't called.

In fact, Rachel reminded herself, she'd checked her machine mainly to see if Marayah and Shanna had called, not Todd. It was *only* Monday after all, four more days until New Year's Eve. Well, three actually, since Monday was pretty much over and you couldn't really count Friday since New Year's Eve was *on* Friday.

And it was probably better that he hadn't called, now that Rachel thought about it some more. She'd had a long, stressful day at work, catching up on the days she'd missed going home for Christmas the week before. Todd was probably as wiped out as she was. He could still be at work trying to catch up from however much time *he'd* missed over Christmas. Although, Rachel thought to herself, strictly speaking the holidays weren't over, since there was still New Year's Eve and New Year's Day to get through.

Not "get through" she reminded herself. Rachel took great pride in that no matter how hectic things got, she never let the holidays get her down or stress her out the way some people did. Even if Todd *never* called, she fully intended to enjoy the party she was going to on New Year's Eve.

Not that he wasn't ever going to call. Rachel supposed there was always that possibility, and she should be prepared for it. Rachel was a great believer in being prepared for things. Because things happen. Todd could have an emergency of some kind. A close friend or relative of his could get sick or have a horrible accident . . . she was being ridiculous, morbid even, and she told herself to knock it off. Todd had looked thrilled when she'd asked him to go to the party, and it was *only Monday.*

The more Rachel thought about it, the more it made sense that he was probably still at work, putting in a long night catching up from last week and trying to get ahead of the game for this week too, since his office would be closing early on Friday for New Year's Eve. Which Rachel should probably have done, maybe stayed another hour or two. But just on the off chance that Todd might have called, she'd let that one report go until tomorrow. Not that she was *blaming* Todd. It had been her decision.

Rachel thumbed through her mail while she listened to her

messages a second time. She'd sort of beeped past Marayah's and Shanna's messages to see if there was one from Todd. She'd call both of them back tonight, which would take a little time as both she and her friends took a perverse pride in how completely dysfunctional their families were. Rachel (as she was sure her friends did) slightly exaggerated her stories for comic effect. Most of the people she knew pictured her relatives in North Carolina as far more Southern than they actually were.

So Rachel made some tuna salad and changed into her most comfortable jeans before settling in for an entertaining evening of rehashing with her friends every humorous and embarrassing detail of her trip home for the holidays. And during both conversations mentioned in passing that she had a date for their friend Bill's New Year's Eve party.

"It's no big deal," she told Marayah during her first phone call, and Shanna during her second. "Not even a date, really."

"Uh-huh," both her friends replied.

"Really. It's just someone I met casually right before I went home for Christmas. And he didn't have a date for New Year's either, so I asked him to Bill's party."

Rachel and Shanna and Marayah all firmly believed that a woman should take the initiative with a man if an opportunity presented itself. It's just that none of them had ever gotten up the nerve to actually do it, not right out. They flirted, sent signals, made their interest clear, used body language; but had never had the nerve to ask a man out.

"Way to go," Shanna said.

"Good for you," Marayah said.

"It's really no big deal," Rachel repeated during both conversations. "I just wanted someone to go to the party with. I don't think he's even my type."

After talking to Rachel, both Shanna and Marayah concluded that she must really like this Todd guy if she'd found the nerve to ask him out. But actually, the opposite was true. The very fact that Todd wasn't someone she was really interested in had made it possible for Rachel to ask him to be her date for Bill's New Year's Eve party. If he'd said no, it might have been a little embarrassing at the moment, but it wouldn't have been any big deal.

Not that going to Bill's party by herself would have been awful. Most of her friends would be there, and people were bringing people, and a lot of them were coming on their own. Midnight was a bad moment, but you could get through it if you had to, and she wouldn't be the only one there without a date.

Besides, if you counted all the New Year's Eve parties Rachel had attended, starting with her first one when she was sixteen, this would only be the second New Year's Eve party out of ten for which she hadn't had a date. It was a pretty good track record. And Jake wouldn't be there. After the horrible way they'd ended, that would have been really awful and uncomfortable. Thank God he'd been transferred and lived three states away. But enough about Jake. Jake was *ancient* history.

When Rachel got home Tuesday night, there was still no message from Todd. She felt really angry for a few seconds. Would it kill him to take five minutes out of his busy life and leave her a message to confirm their date? Rachel was surprised at her flash of anger. It wasn't as if Todd was anything to her, not really.

Besides, guys always called at the last minute. They didn't sit around agonizing about the arrangements for a date the way women did. You know that, Rachel. Quit obsessing. As far as Todd's concerned, he's going to pick you up sometime on Friday and go to a party, and for him that's just one more item on his "to-do" list. He could still call tonight, or tomorrow, or Thursday.

Rachel decided to take herself shopping for some new shoes and earrings to wear to the New Year's Eve party. And maybe a choker to go with the earrings and offset the neckline of the dress. Something fun, a little more flamboyant than she normally wore. She wouldn't go overboard and get a whole new outfit. Her date with Todd, if you could even call it a date, wasn't worth that kind of expense. Her black dress would do just fine.

Wednesday was frantic at work. Everyone was still playing catch-up from the week before, two big projects were gearing up for the new quarter, and time was crunched more than usual since the office was closing at one on Friday so people could get out early for New Year's Eve. By the time she got home it was after nine, and Rachel was exhausted. She kicked off her shoes and debated having a glass of wine before checking her messages.

Then she thought better of it. The best thing to do would be to give Todd a quick call back, make their arrangements, and then have something to eat and collapse into bed. She'd crawl under the covers with her new book and read for an hour or two and get a good night's sleep.

Rachel played back her messages. She had three. One from Bill, who always called everyone a few days before his parties. One from Shanna, who had decided to give Chris another chance, so she'd be bringing him to the party. Rachel shook her head. Chris was such bad news; but there was no point in trying to tell Shanna that.

And one from Rachel's mom saying she'd found a sweater Rachel had left behind from her visit home and that she'd mail it to her in the next day or two.

Rachel had managed to put *it* out of her mind for most of the day, it being the whole "Todd thing" as she now found herself referring to it. She couldn't believe he'd turned into such a thing in her life. An intrusion. A situation. Just by doing nothing, by *not* calling.

What was it with guys and calling back? The way they always put it off, you'd think a phone call was some sort of major undertaking. Why keep someone dangling for days? Why not just take five minutes and call a person? It had been eight days now. She'd asked him to the party on Tuesday, the day before she'd flown home for Christmas.

Why couldn't a guy say, "I'll call you Tuesday night"? Why did it always have to be vague, like "in a few days" or "sometime next week"? God forbid they might have to interrupt their Tuesday-night schedule for five whole minutes.

"Sorry, guys, you'll have to deal me out this hand. I have to *make a phone call.*"

As if it were climbing Mount Everest or something.

They just didn't get it.

"What's the big deal?" Todd would ask if he could see how annoyed she was getting. "Why do women always blow everything out of proportion? Hadn't he told her he'd call sometime next week? Was the week over yet? So what was she getting so irritated about? Women!" She should have gotten his number too, just in case. But she'd been in a hurry, and he'd seemed so thrilled that she'd asked him. It never occurred to her that he wouldn't call.

Rachel decided that the whole Todd thing was turning into a complete waste of energy. Rachel didn't believe in wasting her energy. Life was too short. And it wasn't as if standing there getting angry at Todd was going to change the situation.

Rachel left work late again on Thursday. She'd had a hard time concentrating, especially as the afternoon wore on. Todd had now become lodged inside the chattering part of her brain, where normally she'd find herself thinking about what she needed to pick up at the grocery store. Or if her mom had mailed her sweater yet. Or could she go another couple of hundred miles without an oil change. But in place of all that there was only one topic, one subject, one never-ending theme rolling around and around in her brain: When was Todd going to call?

What made it especially irritating—besides the waste of energy—was how monumental this stupid phone call had become, from a person who was absolutely nothing to her. A reasonably nice guy (or so he'd *seemed*) who didn't have plans for New Year's Eve. Period. Someone to take to the party. Someone who would do. But now he suddenly had all this power over her, simply because he hadn't called.

Driving home from work on Thursday, Rachel would feel completely calm for a minute or so, knowing that *of course* when she got home there would be a message from Todd, and she'd feel completely ridiculous for wasting all this time and energy. She'd call him back, and they'd make their plans, and she'd wonder what in the world had made her get so upset.

And then, just as Rachel felt herself relax, she'd wonder how awful it was going to feel if she got home and he *hadn't* called. And it would feel awful. Because it was so . . . she didn't even have the exact words for what was so awful about it. Maybe it was the waiting. The inability to do anything about it.

That's why they do it! Rachel suddenly thought to herself. The power of it. Just by simply not calling when he says he will, a man gives himself all the power. If he'd called me on Monday, it would have been no big deal. But now it's huge.

And then she was furious. Who in the hell did he, Todd what's his name, think he was not to have the common courtesy to call her? If he'd changed his mind or gotten a better offer, if he'd met someone and fallen madly in love, all he had to do was call her and say he couldn't go to the party. She could live with that. It was the *not* calling that was driving her crazy.

"Rachel," she told herself, "you are being ridiculous. I now no longer officially care whether or not Todd calls. As a matter of fact, even if he does call at this point, I'm going to tell him that I'd rather go to the party by myself. I was going to go by myself before, and showing up with a jerk like Todd would probably be worse than going by myself. So whether or not Todd calls has absolutely no importance whatsoever. Hell, I might even turn my ringer off and get to bed early tonight and finish my book."

Rachel felt much better, as if a huge weight had been removed. She'd been giving Todd a power he didn't actually possess, but that was all over now.

At 7:38 Rachel opened her front door and walked into her apartment. She set down her purse, humming to herself, and carefully checked all her mail. Then she went into the bedroom and put on her favorite old pajamas and her favorite old terry-cloth robe. After that she went into the kitchen and made herself a cup of hot tea and threw a chicken breast in the broiler. It would take about ten minutes to cook on the first side, so she might as well check her messages.

Shanna and Marayah had probably called to find out what time she and Todd would be showing up at Bill's. She wasn't going to tell them he'd never called. She'd tell them something had come up and he couldn't go. Even laugh if off. "Guess he got a better offer. Can't say I blame him. It's not like the sparks were flying with us." She didn't want them spending the whole party hovering over her and feeling sorry for her, giving each other those pitying looks when they thought she wouldn't notice. And thinking, "Poor Rachel. First Jake leaves, and now *this*."

Because not calling was the ultimate put-down. It was worse, much worse, than calling to cancel. Rachel hadn't ever gone through the no-callback before. Not like this. Some guy she met at a party or out at a bar with friends, someone you casually exchanged phone numbers with, yeah, sometimes they didn't call. That went with the territory.

This was different. This was someone whom she'd actually made plans with. And it wasn't as if she'd given Todd her number. If that had been the case, she might be able to understand and accept that maybe she'd read more into the conversation than had been there. But he'd asked for it. Said he'd love to go to the party and asked for her number so he could call her *sometime next week.*

Rachel was starting to get pissed again, and she didn't want to be pissed again. Not at Todd, who meant nothing to her. Absolutely nothing.

In fact, if he had gone to the party, she would probably have regretted it. Because he really wasn't all that hot. Okay looks. Okay personality. And it never failed that when you were with some guy you didn't really want to be with, you met someone really great. And then it got all awkward because you didn't want to hurt the feelings of the guy you were with. But you had to find some way to let the great guy know you were interested.

Of course, now that Todd wasn't going, there probably wouldn't even be anyone halfway interesting there and . . . Rachel had to get Todd out of her mind. He was turning into one of those horrible songs from a commercial that you keep hearing even though you hate the song. And the more you try *not* to hear it, the more you do.

She'd call Shanna and Marayah. That's what she'd do. Get her mind off things, have a few laughs, and then turn in early with her book.

Rachel walked over to her phone. No messages. Not that she was checking or anything. Not that she even *wanted* Todd to call at this point. But that big, red, flashing zero was hard to miss when you were reaching down to pick up the phone to call your—

And just then, just as she was reaching down to pick it up, the phone rang. Rachel jumped back and froze. The phone rang again. Dammit. How many times had she asked Jake to please call the phone company and order caller ID? Ten times? Twenty? He'd insisted that the phone be in his name (such a control freak; how had she *ever* lived with him?), and then had the nerve to say that if caller ID was so important to her, she should take care of it herself. Even though she'd asked and he'd agreed that when he ordered the phone service, he'd be sure to include it in their package of services.

And now that he was gone, the holidays were here, and she hadn't had a spare minute to change the name on the account, let alone upgrade the service. It would serve Jake right if she just kept racking up long-distance charges for the next month, then sent him the bill, since it was still in his name. Not that she would ever do something like that, but he'd deserve it if she did.

The phone rang a third time. One more ring and the machine would click on. Yes. That's what she would do. Let the machine click on. If it was Shanna or Marayah or someone she actually wanted to talk to, she could always pick up. But if it was Todd, then . . . well . . . he'd better start right in with a damn good explanation before she'd even *think* about picking up the phone.

The phone rang a fourth time and the machine clicked on. Rachel waited for her message to play through, holding her breath and telling herself that it needed to be a hell of an explanation, and even then she still might not—

"Hello?" she heard. "Rachel? Are you there? It's your mother."

And at that moment, listening to her mother, too demoralized to pick up the phone, Rachel knew, truly knew for the first time, that Todd wasn't ever going to call.

She listened as her mom explained that she'd FedEx'd the sweater Rachel had left behind at Christmas. Rachel rolled her eyes as her mother went into a long-winded explanation about how even though she'd mailed it three-day express, the sweater wouldn't really arrive at Rachel's in three days. FedEx didn't count the weekend, and they were taking New Year's Eve off as their New Year's holiday since New Year's Day fell on a Saturday this year. So really, it would be more like six days. Which meant it wouldn't actually get to her doorstep until Wednesday, which was almost a week, but what can you do? And the prices they charge! For three-day delivery that is really six, but apparently that was the best they could offer.

Rachel groaned, feeling her exasperation mount. Couldn't her mom ever leave a simple message? Did she always have to go into these monologues? There really wasn't anything Rachel could do about the sorry state of mail delivery, and companies taking holidays and saying it was three-day delivery when it was really six. Was she supposed to call her congressman? Get a law enacted that FedEx could never again, no matter what the circumstances, take six days to deliver a package?

Was any of this her personal responsibility? Had she even asked her mom to mail the sweater? Next time she went to visit her family she'd take one outfit, so that when she left there would be no possibility of leaving any articles of clothing behind and putting her poor mother through the ordeal of dealing with FedEx.

After her mom finally finished her message, Rachel slammed her forefinger down on the machine and hit the erase button. She knew her anger was completely misplaced, that her mom was only trying to be helpful and wasn't the real villain here. The real villain was, of course, Todd.

Rachel plopped down on the couch intending to call Shanna and Marayah, but sat there fuming instead. She had no desire to call them and talk about the stupid party that she now had no interest in going to anyway. Maybe she'd call them in the morning when she would hopefully be in a better mood.

Because right now, in spite of all her good intentions and pep talks, Rachel was extremely pissed off. And what really pissed her off was that she didn't think Todd was *worthy* of her anger, but she couldn't seem to get past it. Rachel was counting to ten for the third time, taking deep breaths, when a hideously loud and obnoxious sound suddenly erupted inside her apartment. Damn it all to hell. Her smoke alarm was going off.

Rachel looked around, wondering what in the world could be making her alarm go off, when she spotted smoke billowing out her oven door. The chicken! Damn, damn, damn. She'd forgotten all about it. Rachel leaped off the couch and ran to the oven, opened the door, grabbed an oven mitt, and pulled out the chicken breast, which was now completely ruined.

"Damn it all to hell!" she shouted, tears forming in her eyes as she threw the chicken into the sink. Feeling as if the alarm was slicing right through the middle of her head, Rachel tore off the oven mitt and went to open the living room windows, her eyes stinging from the smoke.

As she flung her front door open to let more smoke out, Rachel saw some of her neighbors peering out their front doors.

"I wondered where that was coming from," the guy from across the hall called out. "Everything okay?"

"It's fine," Rachel told him with a forced smile. "There's no fire. Just a lot of smoke. I left the oven in the chicken, I mean, the chicken in the oven too long."

"Are you all right?" her neighbor on the other side asked, and Rachel realized how she must look standing there in her old robe, with her fake smile and tears running down her cheeks, leaving tiny tracks in the mixture of smoke and sweat and grime she could feel caked on her skin.

"Yeah," she said, forcing a laugh. "It's just the smoke. Sorry for the noise. I'll take the batteries out of my alarm until it all clears out."

Rachel walked back inside her apartment, feeling absolutely furious and mortified and cursing Todd with every fiber of her being.

After dismantling her alarm, cleaning up the mess, clearing out the smoke, reinstalling her alarm, and cursing the day Todd had been born, Rachel found some leftover lasagna in the back of her refrigerator to have for dinner and topped it off with some chocolate-fudge-chunk ice cream before going into bed. She was pretty sure this had been one of the worst days of her life.

Even though she was exhausted, Rachel had to read for over an hour before her body began to relax enough for her to try to fall asleep. Every time she turned a page of her book, and her attention had a second to wander off, she'd see Todd's face, his barely-average-in-the-looks-department face. Really, calling it average was being kind. And then she'd hear Todd's voice, the exact tone and inflection of each word as he said, "Sounds great. I'll give you a call sometime next week."

But finally Rachel drifted off into a restless sleep, tossing and turning and having bad, angry dreams.

At 2:30 a.m., just as she'd turned over and gone back to sleep after waking up from one of her dreams, Rachel was awakened by someone calling her name. She opened her eyes and turned on the lamp next to her bed. Standing there, a few inches away, was a pale figure who looked remarkably like one of her old college professors—Ms. Amberton—who taught Psychology 101.

"Hello, Rachel," the figure said in an amused voice.

"Ms. Amberton?" Rachel asked, rubbing her eyes.

"Yes, Rachel, it's me."

"I must be dreaming."

"Honestly, Rachel, if you'd paid more attention in class, you'd remember that no one in a dream ever says, 'I must be dreaming.' "

"I paid attention in class," Rachel said defensively, then shook her head. Why was she defending herself to a . . . what exactly was it she was defending herself to? A ghost? Rachel didn't believe in ghosts.

"Yes, Rachel," Ms. Amberton said, sounding amused again, "I am a ghost. I'm the Ghost of New Year's Eve Past. One of the many ghosts you carry around with you. That's how I'm able to read your mind, which is the next question you were going to ask me."

"Stop doing that!" Rachel ordered. She'd always hated the thought of someone being able to read her mind and, as a child, had found the idea that God knew all her thoughts a horrifying idea.

"Why do you hate the idea so much?"

"Because it's an invasion of my privacy. My thoughts are . . ." Rachel shook her head. "This is ridiculous. I can't believe I'm sitting here defending myself in my own dream."

"That *would* be ridiculous, and psychologically speaking not very likely, but that isn't what's happening here."

"Yes, it is. This is lasagna and ice cream, and burned chicken, and smoke alarms, and a long day at work, and four stupid days of waiting for stupid Todd to call. Now go away. I'm going back to sleep."

Rachel closed her eyes for a few seconds, then opened them back up again. Ms. Amberton sat there staring at her with a pleased smile.

"I can't sleep with you staring at me like that."

"Your avoidance techniques are impressive, Rachel, but they simply aren't going to work."

"I'm not talking to you anymore," Rachel said, determined, and rolled over on her other side so that Ms. Amberton would be out of sight. But before Rachel could close her eyes, she felt herself swept up out of bed, and moments later she was standing outside her old college dormitory, where a huge party was taking place. Ms. Amberton stood by her side.

"What is this?" Rachel asked.

"It's your college dorm," Ms. Amberton told her, "which you already knew. And as you find all of this very uncomfortable, I think you should stop wasting time with questions you know the answer to. Because we're not leaving until you see what I brought you here to see."

"I'm not going anywhere dressed like this," Rachel said, looking down at her old pajamas.

"No one can see you. You know, for such a smart girl you can be very dense at times."

"Why are you being so mean to me?"

"You never paid attention in class."

"I did so!" Rachel said, offended.

"Name and define Freud's three divisions of psychic energy."

"What?"

"Never mind."

"Look, I've had a really bad day and this is like the last thing I need."

"You think I'm enjoying myself? Just follow me and then you can get back to sleep."

"Fine."

Rachel followed Ms. Amberton up the steps to her old college dormitory. People were lounging on the steps, hanging out of windows, and the music was blasting so loud Rachel was getting a pounding headache. But she stayed right behind Mrs. Amberton, figuring it was the only way to make the nightmare come to an end.

They walked down the hallway of her old dormitory, and Rachel felt a shiver of dread. Her dorm room was two doors away, and her memories of living there were mostly good. But she had a sinking feeling Ms. Amberton wasn't here to show her something good. As they drew near her room, the door opened, and she saw a younger version of herself come out the door, laughing hysterically. Behind Rachel's younger self was her college roommate, Lynn, who was laughing even more hysterically.

"Do you know what you're looking at?" Ms. Amberton asked.

"Well . . . it's me in college with my roommate, Lynn, and we're having some kind of party."

"It's the last day of finals, first semester of your sophomore year."

"Wait a minute," Rachel said. "If you're the Ghost of New Year's Eve Past, shouldn't this be New Year's Eve?"

"Bravo. At least you paid attention in your literature classes. And you're right, it should be. But you always went home for the holidays when you were in college, and you always had to spend New Year's Eve with your family since they saw so little of you."

"What do you expect? I was away at college."

"You might want to work on those defensive tendencies of yours, Rachel. I wasn't accusing you of anything. In answer to your earlier question, what we're about to witness happened a couple of weeks before New Year's Eve. That's close enough. I'm precise, not anal-retentive. Are you with me so far?"

"I guess."

"Your generation's ability to communicate verbally is pitiful. Anyway, on with our business. It's the last day of finals, you're at a party in your dorm, and you and Lynn are laughing so hard you can barely stand up. And it's not just because of the beer. Which maybe if you'd had a little less of, you might have done better in class."

"Hey, I carried a three point six average when I was in college."

"Could have been a three point eight," Ms. Amberton sniffed. "Do you remember what you and Lynn found so hilarious on the last day of finals during the first semester of your sophomore year?"

"I don't know." Rachel shrugged. "A lot of things were funny that night."

"I bet. Let's just follow them and see, shall we?"

"Whatever."

"Please don't use that expression around me. I consider it the death of civilized conversation."

"Whate—fine."

Rachel and Ms. Amberton trailed along behind the younger Rachel and her best friend, Lynn.

"God," Lynn said, barely able to speak. "What a dork. I don't know how you kept a straight face."

The younger Rachel contorted her face into a goofy expression. "Uh, Rachel," she said, in a mimicking voice, "do ya think I could have a dance?"

Rachel and Lynn stopped, both of them holding their stomachs they were laughing so hard.

"And then," Lynn sputtered, "when you said you would, but you suddenly remembered a final you forgot to take, God, I thought I was going to die."

"That's pretty funny, isn't it, Rachel?" Ms. Amberton asked. "Do you remember that kid's name? The one you humiliated in public?"

"I was a kid, too," Rachel said weakly. "I felt bad about it later. I had a lot to drink that night."

"His name was Peter Woods. He's really . . . what's that word you all use now? Hot? Yes, that's it. He's really hot now. *Much* better looking than Todd. More successful too. Does something with microchips."

Rachel winced at the mention of Todd.

"And he's got a good life," Ms. Amberton went on after a moment. "But you know what's funny? Oh, not as funny as you and Lynn were, but funny nonetheless. You probably haven't given him a thought in years. But Peter Woods has never forgotten you."

Rachel looked down at the ground.

"Do you know what he did after he left the party? Would you care to know?"

"No! I mean, please, Ms. Amberton, I've always felt bad about that. I'm not lying. I even thought about apologizing when I came back after the holidays, but I didn't know what to say."

Ms. Amberton simply stared at her for a moment, and then Rachel found herself standing outside the college library. Ms. Amberton tapped her on the shoulder and pointed. Peter Woods sat on one of the planters, hunched over as if he were trying to shrink into himself and disappear.

Ms. Amberton leaned closer to Rachel. "He wishes he'd never had all those beers. That's what gave him the courage to come over and ask you to dance. But now he's sober and he's sick to his stomach and he feels like he wants to die. Do you know what it's like to have someone you care about laugh at you?"

Rachel shivered. "I'm sorry," she whispered.

"He can't hear you. No matter how loudly you talk."

"What do you want me to—"

And then it was gone, all of it. The college and Peter and Mrs. Amberton. And Rachel was sitting in her bed in a cold sweat, feeling sick and guilty, and vowed she'd never again eat leftover lasagna before going to bed. She wondered what *had* ever become of Peter Woods. She hoped he *was* hot and had a great life, and that he never gave her another thought and had completely forgotten her name.

Rachel got up and took an antacid, returned to bed and turned off the light, and after tossing and turning for a long time, eventually drifted back into a restless sleep.

At 3:45 a.m. Rachel was awakened a second time to the sound of someone calling her name. She sat up and turned on the light. Standing next to her bed was the postal carrier for her apartment building, a tough-looking, middle-aged woman whom Rachel had always found slightly intimidating.

"What are you doing here?" Rachel asked impatiently, too tired and annoyed at the moment to feel intimidated. She wasn't particularly startled to see her postal carrier standing in her bedroom, the way she had been with Ms. Amberton. Now she was simply irritated. She figured it had some tie-in to the message her mom had left regarding the inefficiency of modern mail delivery. She remembered *that* much from Psychology 101, how the day's events get tied into your dreams. And these had to be dreams, no matter what Ms. Amberton claimed. But they were really starting to get on her nerves. Maybe she should have taken *two* antacids.

"Hey, it wasn't my idea, blondie," the postal carrier shot back.

"My name is Rachel."

"My name's Elaine, and the quicker we get this show on the road, the quicker I can get back to sleep. I've got to do my route tomorrow, unlike you yuppie types who all get the afternoon off."

"I'm not a yuppie."

"Man. Lighten up. Amberton warned me you were the easily offended type, getting all defensive over innocent remarks."

"I'm not defensive!"

"Whatever."

"For your information, Ms. Amberton *hates* that expression."

"And I hate the way she acts so snooty all the time. But live and let live, that's what I always say. So here's the deal. I'm the Ghost of New Year's Eve Present."

"But New Year's Eve isn't until tomorrow."

"Boy, that Amberton sure had you pegged. She told me you'd say that. It's close enough, all right? Now up and Adam. We're going to take a little trip, show you a little something, and call it a night. I've got the new Lands' End catalog to haul around tomorrow and it's going to whip my ass."

Before Rachel could finish wondering why all the ghosts in her dreams were so rude to her, she found herself standing outside an apartment building with Elaine by her side.

"Where are we?" Rachel asked.

"We're going to see your favorite person," Elaine replied.

"My favorite person?"

"Mr. No Call?"

Rachel felt a sinking feeling in the pit of her stomach. "You don't mean—"

And just like that Rachel and Elaine were inside Todd's living room. Rachel looked on, horrified and embarrassed, as Todd dealt cards to three other men sitting at his dining room table.

"Yep," Elaine said. "There's Todd playing poker with some of his buddies. They all decided to take tomorrow off and start celebrating early. And they're having a very interesting conversation. Let's listen in. You'll get a kick out of it."

"I don't want to."

"And I don't want to haul around your mail tomorrow, either. I want to sleep in and have someone bring me breakfast in bed. And after I've eaten my waffle and taken a long, hot shower, I'd like Ed McMahon to ring my doorbell and tell me I've won the American Publishers' sweepstakes. But those weren't the cards we were dealt. No pun intended."

Elaine snickered.

"I really don't want to," Rachel insisted.

"Sorry, hon, you don't really have a choice."

"I can leave."

"Sorry, hon, you really can't."

And it was true. No matter how hard Rachel struggled—and she struggled as hard as she possibly could, since Todd's apartment was the last place on earth she wanted to be—she couldn't move her body.

"I thought you were going with that what's her name, Rachel, you met at that seminar we went to?" one of Todd's buddies asked. "She was pretty hot."

Todd shrugged his shoulders. "Not half as hot as she thought she was, but not bad."

"That stupid, son of a—" Rachel sputtered. "Where does he get off—"

"*Shhh!*" Elaine hissed at her. "Just listen."

"So?" one of Todd's buddies asked. "What happened?"

"She seemed okay, you know? And I thought it was cool that she asked me to go to a party with her. But then she gave me this smile after she wrote down her number, like she'd just done me the biggest favor of my life."

"What an asshole!" Rachel declared. "I was smiling because it was the first time I'd ever had the nerve to ask a guy out! I was feeling good, so I gave him a smile. That's all it—"

"*Shhh!*" Elaine ordered.

"And that's when I knew," Todd continued. "Uh-oh, buddy. High-maintenance chick. We better rethink this. First off, since she thinks she's doing me the favor, if I so much as make one little move at the party, I'm going to get the 'Todd, I thought you understood we were just going to the party as friends' line.'"

"Hey, bud, just 'cause she's the one you show up with doesn't mean she's the one you have to leave with," said one of Todd's poker buddies with a leer.

"Yeah, well, this one was the type to latch onto me all night, if you know what I mean. Like it's okay if they spend all night talking to some other guy, but God help you if you even say hello to another woman."

"How'd she take it when you flaked out on her?"

"I didn't bother calling," Todd said casually, throwing some chips onto the table. "Ante up, guys."

"That's cold, buddy."

"I didn't feel up to the drama. And I didn't want to make something up. It was easier this way. Why go through all that for nothing?"

The other men nodded in agreement and tossed their chips onto the table.

"I'm done with high-maintenance chicks," Todd added. "I think I'm going to hit Kim's party tomorrow night. I heard Theresa might show up."

"Theresa's not bad," one of the men said. "I'm going to raise you five."

"I fold," Todd said. "Anyone need another beer?"

Rachel watched Todd stand up and felt her cheeks flushing from anger and mortification.

"Think he's got a point?" Elaine asked, poking her in the ribs.

"No! I did *not* think I was doing him the biggest favor of his life."

"Then why are you blushing?"

"I am *not* blushing."

"Whatever."

And then Rachel was sitting in her bed, with the light on, and there was no Elaine, and no Todd, and no poker game, only a feeling of complete humiliation. She sat there for a moment or two, her cheeks burning, and suddenly it all made sense. Rachel even laughed for a second.

God, she was being so ridiculous. Of all the stupid things. What she was doing now, or what her subconscious was doing now, was taking the whole Todd thing and blowing it all out of proportion. Dragging up old issues and bad memories, and anything and everything she had to feel guilty or insecure about. Everyone carries baggage around inside her head that stress can trigger and turn into something bigger than it really is. That much Rachel *did* remember from Psychology 101. She had so paid attention in class, Ms. Amberton.

These dreams were nothing more than the result of her getting obsessed about Todd's stupid phone call, and then the smoke alarm going off, and topping it all off by eating spicy food and chocolate-fudge-chunk ice cream before going to bed.

Rachel was going to get out of bed, take some Tylenol PM, do some deep breathing, and go back to sleep. And tomorrow, when she got off work, she was going to pamper herself. Have a good workout and take a long, hot bath and give herself a facial and a manicure. And she was going to go to that New Year's Eve party tomorrow night and wear her new jewelry and shoes and have the best time she'd ever had. And she was never, ever, ever, going to give Todd another thought.

At 4:15 a.m. Rachel was awakened a third time by someone calling her name.

"For the love of God!" she muttered as she sat up and turned on her light.

Standing next to her bed was someone she didn't recognize at all. A thin, bitter woman who appeared to be in her midforties, holding a drink in one hand and a cigarette in the other.

"Who in the hell are you?" Rachel asked.

"My name's Tasha Mason," the woman said wearily. "I'm the Ghost of New Year's Eve Future."

"Great. Do you mind putting out that cigarette? I hate the smell."

"Tough luck."

Rachel sighed. "I don't suppose I have any say so in any of this, do I?"

Tasha shook her head, flicking an ash into Rachel's potted plant. "Nope."

"So where am I going this time? And how many more of you are going to show up tonight?"

"I'm the last. I don't suppose you have any Scotch around here, do you?"

"I've got some wine."

"Never mind. I need to cut back anyway."

"Well?" Rachel asked. "Shouldn't we get going?"

"I'm in no rush. I've got nowhere to be. Might as well spend New Year's Eve with you. Which, actually, I do. About three of them. And, God, are they depressing."

"What do you mean? Why would we spend New Year's Eve together?"

"We're best friends. For a while. United in our bitterness and despair. And our hatred of men. And our disappointment in our ungrateful children. Blah, blah, blah. Eventually I go on the wagon, join AA, and we drift apart. I don't know what finally became of you. I just know about this next part. The future. You're in the middle of a horrible menopause, by the way, probably because you're so angry and disappointed and depressed. At least that's my opinion for what it's worth."

Rachel put her pillow over her head. "I'm putting my foot down this time. I am not participating. Do you hear me? Go away. I absolutely refuse to participate in this anymore. I'm sorry about Peter Woods. I'm sorry I wasn't madly in love with Todd. I'm sorry for every rotten thing I've ever done. But I'm not going to beat myself up anymore. Get out! Now! Get out!"

"You always were one for the melodramatics."

Rachel's pillow disappeared. Her bedroom disappeared. And now she was standing in a living room looking at Tasha Mason and a hideous, horrible, angry, bitter version of herself as a woman in her late forties.

She and Tasha were sitting on a couch, half-drunk, smoking cigarettes and watching Dick Clark's New Year's Eve special.

"This can't be me," Rachel stated firmly. "I would never smoke."

"Life does funny things to people, sometimes. They find themselves doing things they never thought they would. Now shut up and learn something."

"Just once before this night is over I'd like to get a *nice* ghost," Rachel muttered.

"I can't believe he's still doing these things," Tasha said to the future Rachel as they both watched Dick Clark introduce another band.

"I know," the future Rachel replied. "He's got to be what, eighty?"

"Doesn't look a day over forty. Men get all the breaks."

They each took a long drag off their cigarettes.

"What do you hear from your attorney?" Tasha asked.

"The son of a bitch is still stonewalling," the future Rachel replied. "Do you know Don actually had the nerve to claim that his practice *lost* money last year?"

"Jeez, how stupid does he think you are?"

"I think he really does think I'm stupid. Which is such a joke. If his father hadn't sold him his practice when he retired, Don would probably still be working in some clinic. To say nothing of all the marketing advice I gave him. I'm not stupid. I know he's got money hidden all over the place."

"Offshore accounts. That's what they all do."

"My attorney is killer. We'll get the bastard. I'm going to have another. You need one?"

"I always need one."

Rachel watched her older self stand up unsteadily and walk slowly and carefully over to the wet bar. And watching her, she somehow knew in her gut that it was true. It was all true. That what she was seeing was whom she would turn into.

"What happened to me?" she whispered.

"You don't have to whisper," Tasha said loudly. "What is this? Your third time around? Let me repeat, no one can see you or hear you."

"What happened to me?" Rachel asked again.

"I think you should listen a little bit more before I even begin to answer that."

"So," the older Rachel said as she stumbled back to the couch, "what should we toast to?"

She handed Tasha her drink and slowly eased herself down on the couch.

Tasha snorted. "Where do I begin? To my beloved ex-husband? My wonderful children who never call except when they need money? My glorious life? I know, let's toast Dick Clark. The only person whose been there for me every single New Year's Eve."

"To Dick Clark," the older Rachel repeated, and she and Tasha tapped their glasses together.

"Wait. Here it comes," Tasha said.

She and the older Rachel watched as Dick Clark counted down the last ten seconds of the year. The ball landed, and Times Square exploded with noise and confetti. And the two women sat there, completely silent, watching the celebration with empty expressions.

"What happened to me?" Rachel asked again as the two women each silently lit up another cigarette.

"What happens to a lot of people," Tasha answered. "You married for the wrong reasons. You weren't a mean person, but you weren't exactly a real nice person. Life caught up with you. It has a way of doing that. You thought you were owed something, but nobody is. You thought your life was guaranteed to turn out a certain way, but it never is. You thought you were special, but you weren't. Not any more so than anyone else.

"And then, every New Year's Eve, you'd think that somehow this year was going to be different. Only it never was. You kept thinking that January first was a magical day, but it isn't. It's just a day like any other day. And every year you got more and more disappointed that life hadn't turned out the way you'd planned. Which, by the way, it almost never does. And your plan was awfully vague. Great career. Great marriage. Great kids. Like you just press a button and there they are.

"And you didn't do the things you needed to do as a young woman to make getting older work out for you. You were always trying to play catch-up until one day it was too late. You couldn't catch up anymore."

"Like what?" Rachel pleaded. "What things didn't I do?"

"I guess to put it in simple terms, you never developed any character. And in the end, that's what gets you through. Character. You get that, kid, you'll be okay. Even if you end up with the wrong man or the job falls through. I finally got some about two years after this little scene. But it's a real bitch trying to develop some character when you're forty-eight.

"In your own bitter, pathetic way, you were a good friend. So take my advice. Don't waste any more time, time you can't ever get back. Do it now. Get some character. It'll go a lot easier on you. Oh, and be nice. Have a little heart. It pays off in the end."

Rachel's alarm went off at six-thirty on the morning of New Year's Eve. It took her a few moments to get her bearings, and when she did, she felt completely depressed. The last thing she remembered was that horrible vision she'd had of herself as a woman in her forties, a vision that even in the light of day still felt real.

Rachel shivered. What was the point of working and struggling if that was how she was going to end up? She might as well just pull the covers over her head and stay in bed for the rest of her life. It would be better to be dead than to be that woman.

"Do it now, kid," she heard Tasha say. "It'll go a lot easier on you."

Rachel sat up. But she wasn't that woman. That was twenty-two years from now. God, in twenty-two years, if she started now, right now, she could be the complete opposite of that woman. She could be . . . Rachel sat there for a minute and realized that other than in choosing a career, she'd never really thought about what she wanted to be. She'd thought about what she wanted to accomplish, what goals she wanted to achieve, what she hoped to have. But never, exactly, about what she wanted to be.

She didn't want to be the person she'd been during the past week; that much she knew. She didn't want to be the person she'd seen herself becoming in twenty years; she knew that for sure. So what *did* she want to be?

At first the words sounded a little silly to her. Wise. Generous. Kind. Forgiving. Strong. They made her sound like some kind of struggling saint or Mother Teresa wannabe.

But they were real words; they had to apply to somebody. Why not her? Why couldn't she be wise and generous and kind and forgiving and strong? And while she was at it, maybe a little less defensive and not so quick to take offense.

Things happen. Todd happened. Worse things than Todd would happen, things she'd have no control over. But who she was, that was something she could have control over. And she could start by saying it out loud, to herself and her friends, that Todd not calling her was in actuality, *no big deal.*

But first she'd have to get out of bed.

• • •

At nine o'clock that evening, Shanna and Marayah were getting a little worried that Rachel still hadn't arrived at the party.

"I know she acted like it was no big deal when I talked to her this morning, but I think she was really upset that Todd never called her back," Shanna said.

"What a jerk. That is like the worst, not calling."

"I know. What is the deal with that?"

"Beats me. I would never do that to somebody. Even if he was the biggest asshole in the world, I would have the courtesy to call him back if I said I would."

"I can't believe how calm she acted about the whole thing."

"Me either. Did she give you that line about how she was glad it happened because she actually learned a lot about herself from the experience?"

"She was just covering. You know Rachel. The more she acts like something isn't a big deal, the bigger deal it actually is. I wonder if we should call her and make sure she's okay?"

"Let's give her a few more minutes."

At nine-thirty, just as Shanna and Marayah were about to give her a call, Rachel walked in the door.

"Happy New Year, guys!" she shouted to the crowd.

"Happy New Year!" the crowd shouted back, getting a little tired of it at this point, but what are you going to do?

"You look great!" Shanna told Rachel, giving her a hug.

"Yeah," Marayah agreed, "you really do. Are those new shoes?"

"Yeah. I got them for the party. Can you guys come help me? I've got some stuff in the car."

Shanna and Marayah gave each other a worried look as they

followed Rachel out to her car. They weren't falling for her act; they knew how hard it was for her to admit when she was feeling hurt or depressed. But she was being so manic about it this time, that's what had them worried. It's one thing to pretend something isn't any big deal. It's another to act as if you were on top of the world. They each took a silent vow to stay with her as much as they could during the party. At least Jake wasn't going to be there.

"I've got all kinds of stuff here," Rachel told them as she opened her trunk. "Lasagna, and Greek salad, and stuffed mushrooms, and crab cakes."

"God, what did you do?" Marayah asked. "Spend all afternoon cooking?"

"Yep. I got off work early. Oh, and I made some of those meringue cookies you like so much, Shanna."

"Wow. Thanks."

"Hey, what are friends for?"

"Rachel?" Marayah asked hesitantly. "Are you okay?"

"I am so great."

Shanna and Marayah glanced at each other.

"Really?" Shanna asked. "Because you don't have to put on an act for us."

"Oh, I'm not. Do you know we're all getting old?"

Shanna and Marayah looked at each other knowingly. Rachel was talking about getting old; it was even worse than they'd thought.

"Speak for yourself!" Shanna joked nervously.

"No, I don't mean that in a bad way. It's just . . . we're all going to be forty one day. And fifty and sixty and seventy, as bizarre as that seems. And if I want to be cool when I'm forty, I have to start working on it now. So that's my new plan, my New Year's resolution."

"That's, uh, a good plan," Marayah said uncomfortably.

"For one thing, I'm going to start taking the time to thank people. Like my college professors. I took them totally for granted, but they taught me a lot. I'm going to send them all a thank-you letter. And my postal carrier. You guys know how many catalogs I order. I've never even thought about how heavy they must be to lug around. I'm going to leave her a plate of cookies in my mailbox with a little note thanking her for all her hard work.

"And my mom. She went to all this trouble to mail my sweater back to me, and I never even called to thank her."

Marayah put her arm around Rachel.

"Sweetie, just let yourself feel bad. I know it's New Year's Eve, but you can have a shitty one. We'll sit next to you and let you bitch and get it out of your system. We'll lose Shanna here for a while now that Chris is back in the picture, the whole midnight-kiss thing, but pretending like this is just going to make it worse. I think you really liked this guy and—"

"No, I really—"

"Rachel, we *know* you. You're still dealing with your breakup from Jake. And now this Todd asshole. So just let yourself feel lousy. Get drunk. Make an idiot out of yourself. I'll drive you home. Okay?"

Rachel laughed.

"You are such a good friend. You both are. But I'm dealing with the Jake thing and Todd was a learning experience. I'm fine, I really am. But thanks for being so concerned. Let's get this stuff inside."

Shanna and Marayah picked up the rest of the trays of food and followed Rachel back into Bill's house.

"I'm really worried about her," Shanna mouthed silently to Marayah.

"Me too," Marayah mouthed back.

But once they'd helped Rachel get her trays of food organized, Shanna got preoccupied with Chris and a certain redhead he seemed to be paying a little bit too much attention to, and Marayah started talking to some guy she'd met at Bill's Halloween party.

Rachel dished out her food and gave recipes to people who asked and refilled people's drinks and made sure she talked to anyone who didn't seem to be having a good time. The last thing on her mind was meeting someone.

Which is exactly why (the universe is nothing if not consistent) at the stroke of midnight, while couples kissed and singles hugged or hid out in the bathroom or kitchen or pretended to be mesmerized by the ball dropping in Times Square on TV, Rachel met someone. An attractive someone named Jim Hudson, who was smiling at her and came over a short time later to introduce himself.

"I wanted to tell you that your lasagna is some of the best I've ever had."

"Thanks."

"You don't believe me."

"I'm not sure. Either my cooking has improved or you don't get out enough."

Jim laughed (which won Rachel over a little) and offered to get her another drink.

"I'm good," Rachel told him.

"Oh. In that case, I guess I'm just wasting my time."

Rachel laughed, feeling herself relaxing, thinking as Jim smiled at her that he had the kind of face that grows more attractive over time. They got through the awkward, initial small talk, discovered some mutual interests, and had a pretty good first conversation.

When the party started breaking up two hours later, Jim asked Rachel if he could call her sometime.

"Sure," Rachel said. "How about Wednesday night at ten-thirty?"

"I beg your pardon?" Jim asked as Rachel reached into her purse for a pen and a piece of paper.

"Do you have plans for next Wednesday night at ten-thirty?"

"Uh, I don't think so—"

"Good. Here's my number." Rachel handed him the piece of paper she'd written it down on. "If you want to call, I'll be home on Wednesday night at ten-thirty. And if I'm not, I'll have a really good reason. Because sometimes, you know, things happen. But if you leave a message, I promise I'll get back to you the next day."

And then Rachel smiled, said she'd enjoyed talking to him,

wished him a happy New Year, gathered up her food trays, said her good-byes to everyone else, put on her coat, and went home.

DIANE STINGLEY lives in North Carolina. Her first novel, *Dress You Up in My Love,* was published by Downtown Press in December, 2003. Her second novel, *I'm With Cupid,* will be released by Downtown Press in February, 2004.

The Luckiest People

LIBBY STREET

 A sharp blast of frosty air wafts over my bare shoulder, and I'm suddenly standing in the painfully bright produce section of a deserted, but very well-kept, grocery store. Great pyramids of fruit rise up from white metal bases toward low-hanging fluorescent strips above. Innocuous Muzak ricochets off the sterile linoleum floors and envelops the aisles in a sort of bland brassy cocoon. I turn left and follow the smell of summer melons to a stand of cantaloupes. They're so fat and ripe I half expect them to burst open and blossom like popcorn. I lean over and inhale deeply—warm and refreshing, with just a hint of . . . camphor?

I step away from the melons and turn my attention to another of the massive produce stands. Piled high, in perfect symmetry, are thousands of bars of soap. They're oval in shape and individually wrapped in pale blue tissue paper, making the whole collection look like a mound of tiny pillows. I step closer and am overwhelmed by the crisp, tangy aroma of camphor and menthol. Each bar has a shield-shaped label, attached with a swath of canary yellow ribbon. The labels read: "Dom Pérignon."

It strikes me as odd that the distinguished French winery would venture into the personal hygiene market when, out of nowhere, one of the nearby melons begins ringing—a high-pitched electronic whimper. It goes in rhythmic spurts, exactly in time with the insipidly spiritless version of Prince's "Raspberry Beret" blaring over the loudspeakers. I approach the ringing melon and reach out to touch it when something occurs to me. . . .

I think I may be dreaming.

I force my eyes to open. The left does just fine, parting to reveal the blurry but familiar view of my minuscule bedroom. The right eye, however, seems to be crusted over with something. Oh, last night's mascara and eyeliner must have fused. Why is it that if you cry with this stuff on, it glides effortlessly down your face in inky streams, but if you sleep in it, you wake up a Cyclops? One of the great mysteries of life.

With my one functioning eye, I spot the phone on the bedside table. It continues to whine its annoying chorus, which, when filtered through my throbbing head, is the aural equivalent of being stabbed repeatedly with a spork—not deadly, but *ouch*.

I instantly recognize the phone number on the caller ID; it's Ellen. It's also nine-thirty in the morning on New Year's Day. I've known Ellen since junior high and I don't think she's ever called me this early.

I reach over and grab the phone, groaning with the effort. For some reason every muscle in my body seems to be stiff and sore.

"What's wrong? Are you okay? Did something happen last night?" I ask as fast as my cotton mouth will move.

"Relax. Nothing's wrong. I had a great time last night."

I heave a sigh of relief and then feel my head begin to pound. "Do you know what time it is?" I grumble into the receiver. Disregarding every makeup-removal tip I've ever learned, I begin to chip away at the matted black clumps on my right eye.

"Yeah," she replies in her raspiest hangover voice, "I just wanted to find out what happened."

"What are you talking about?"

"Last night . . . the party. I caught a glimpse of you at like nine-thirty, but you disappeared before I could find you again. And then at, like, twelve-oh-five you left a message on my voice mail."

"I did?"

"Yeah."

"Uh . . . what did I say?"

"Something like, 'I'm fine. I'm safe. I'll talk to you tomorrow.' "

"Seriously?" I ask her, perplexed. I reach back into the dark and murky areas of my mind, digging frantically for some memory that relates to this event. How can I not remember that? What is wrong with my head? I can remember the party. It was huge, elegant, glittering, and fuzzy—very, very fuzzy. Everything about last night is out of focus, like I'm looking through a thick pane of etched glass.

"Ruby?" Ellen poses, concerned. She says something else, but the sounds of Manhattan, just two floors below, drown out her voice. The noises are so close . . .

I sit up in bed—too quickly—all the blood rushes out of my head and dizziness takes over. A gust of cool air stings my back.

I turn to ascertain the source of the draft.

The window over my bed is open. Freshly fallen snow creeps in onto the windowsill. That's strange; why is my window open?

I cradle the phone between my ear and shoulder and slowly muscle the window closed.

"Ruby? Are you there? Ruby?" Ellen's tone now borders on real anxiety.

"I'm here. Sorry. My window was open. I can't remember—" As I turn back around, a powerful tension squeezes my chest, and I gasp reflexively from shock.

There is a man in my bed. Sleeping. There is a man sleeping. In. My. Bed!

He looks familiar, not from last night but from . . . somewhere. High school? Work? Some distant relative? Oh, God, that better not be it. No, that can't be it. I can picture him wearing a bulletproof vest, a shotgun in his hand. Oh . . .

With what little calm I can rally, I whisper into the phone, "Ellen, I can't talk right now, there's a movie star in my bed."

"What?" she screams "You're joking! Who? Who is it?"

"Would you be quiet!" Oh, God, no wonder I'm cold. "Ellen, I'm naked. I'm *naked* and there's a movie star in my bed."

Ellen, giggling more out of uneasiness than insensitivity—I hope—pulls herself together long enough to ask, "Is he naked, too?"

I take a deep breath and gingerly lift the corner of my rose-covered duvet and peek under the covers. Oh, shit. "Naked," I tell her.

"Naked?" she repeats.

"Isn't that what I said?" I bite back, exasperated.

The words *I am not a slut* begin to pound repeatedly between my ears, as though I were being made to write the phrase a thousand times on a blackboard.

"Who is he?" she asks with the eagerness of a Page Six gossip hound.

Instinctively I crane my head to get a better look at him. He's lying on his side, facing away from me. His hair is dark and wavy; it's a stylish and expensive haircut that's about three weeks past needing to be trimmed back into shape. His face is perfectly proportioned, with a strong jawline and soft, high cheekbones that are accentuated by a hint of morning stubble. His arms are chiseled, but not huge. The warm golden tan of his skin is interrupted only by a sprinkling of freckles cascading over his shoulders and onto his back. A palm-sized tattoo on his left shoulder blade reads *"Humanum est errare, sic eunt fata hominum."*

So here, naked in bed with a stranger, my high school Latin finally pays off: "To err is human, thus go the destinies of men." I think I like this guy—whoever he is. I guess that's a good thing since, it would seem, I've done all sorts of dirty and indecent things with him. Oh, God. I *am* a slut. I'm nothing but a filthy brazen hussy.

"Ruby? Are you with me?" Ellen tries again.

"I'm here," I whisper.

"What. Is. His. Name?" she asks, as though I were a child.

The harsh, bitter, disgusting reality of my situation hits me like a wrecking ball. "I can't remember."

"Oh . . . *shit.*"

"I'm a slut, Ellen. I'm a big giant . . . floozy."

"You are not a floozy," she says, chuckling.

Yes, I am. *Now* I am. For twenty-six years (well, nine if you only count the years I've been sexually active) I've made it my mission to wait till the third date, the fifth date, the *seventh* date—and now this. My stomach jumps, leaving me feeling hollow and woozy, the same feeling you get after that first big drop on an insanely high roller coaster. Only now, instead of physically falling, it's my self-respect that's suddenly taken a dive. I want to take a shower and scrub off the shame. I want to get out of this bed and leap out the window, but I feel terribly exposed, everything's all out in the open. He could wake up and see me here—in the nude. But then, it wouldn't be the first time, would it? Oh, God. I think I'm going to be sick.

"I could lock myself in the bathroom, maybe he'll wake up and tiptoe out at some point," I say, blindly patting the floor in the search for any shred of clothing to put on. "Isn't that what these guys do?" Ellen is the only person I know who has slept with someone like this guy—someone hot enough to actually set things on fire.

She laughs. "You watch too many movies."

"Sure I do. I watch so many movies that I can't identify the naked actor in my bed."

"Right. You may have a point there."

I feel something cottony and raise my hand up—boxers. I instinctively drop them and wipe my hand on the duvet. As I contemplate digging out the kitchen wipes that are guaranteed to kill 99.99% of household germs, it occurs to me that all the bits that go in that pair of boxers were, at some point last night, considerably closer to me than the boxers just were to my hands. I am just . . . dirty, in every sense of the word.

I draw the comforter up over my chest as Ellen starts, "I'm sure he told you his name, yeah? Don't you think?"

"I hope so." I take a deep breath to calm myself, fill my empty insides with air. "I'd like to think that I wouldn't hop into bed with someone whose name I didn't know. But then, I don't normally hop into bed with people in the *first place!* Damn! This is why I hate champagne."

Champagne doesn't produce a normal buzz. It's not like any other alcoholic beverage. Beer and liquor may get you loaded, but they never produce the disastrous false sense of invincibility that champagne does. A champagne high is something completely different; it makes you feel lighter than air, as though anything were possible. I think that's why it's become the New Year's drink of choice. After a few glasses of bubbly, a weight-loss plan of twenty pounds in four weeks seems entirely realistic. After a few more glasses, success in the weight-loss venture is not only realistic, but somehow fated by a higher power. Obviously, last night, champagne worked its despicable black magic and made me believe I am one of those women who can handle a one-night stand.

"What do I do, Ellen? What the hell do I do?"

"First thing, calm down. This is not the end of the world. Second, figure out his name."

"I told you, I don't *remember* his name!" Oh, no. I said that too loudly.

The mystery man stirs. I go rigid as a statue and hold my breath. He rolls over on his back with a sigh, then quickly drops back into a deep sleep. His amazingly defined chest settles into a gentle rhythm of rise and fall.

I allow myself to exhale—quietly.

Naked or not, I have to get out of this bed.

I carefully peel back the covers and am instantly assailed by the temperature of the room—something akin to that of an industrial meat locker. My skin becomes a blanket of goose bumps; every move I make results in an unpleasant prickling sensation. Slowly, and with great effort not to jiggle the mattress, I slide myself off the bed and onto the floor. Part of me wants to bolt for the living room and lock myself in the coat closet, but maybe if I sit here and stare at him, his name will come to me. Please, please let it come to me.

I twist my body around and quietly slither into the chair that's squished between my dresser and my nightstand. The chair that, by a horrible twist of fate, I cleaned off yesterday. Were this any normal morning the chair would be buried in semidirty clothes that I could slip on; as it is, all I have is a freshly laundered hand towel.

It's small, but, on the bright side, it's also "snuggly soft." I hold it over my chest.

"Are you sure he's a movie star?" asks Ellen.

"Yes," I whisper in response, "I can picture him in some sort of uniform. And sort of lounging on a sofa looking very . . . well lit. Something tells me I'm not remembering those things from last night." I think someone walking around a posh brownstone in a bulletproof vest, brandishing a loaded weapon, would make an impression even I couldn't forget.

"Okay," says Ellen in her take-charge voice. "Describe him to me."

I stare at him, sleeping peacefully. He looks like someone I might be interested in, someone I'd like to get to know. Of course, that'll never happen now. Now I'm just that easy chick he banged on New Year's. This is just the situation I've been trying to avoid. Men have no respect for women who jump into bed with them. Right? As stupid and hypocritical as that is—it's a fact of life.

"He's in his mid- to late twenties, with thick, wavy brown hair. Amazing skin. Long eyelashes. He's . . . gorgeous." Why did I do this? Why couldn't I just give him my phone number like any normal, decent nonslut?

"What color are his eyes?"

"Well, now, they're closed. Aren't they?"

"Ah, sleeping. Gotcha." She lets out a huff. "How about this: Can you remember any of his movies?"

"Uh . . ." I rub my temples in an attempt to massage some tiny detail out of my useless, aching brain. "There's one where they blow shit up. You know, cops or Army or something. Colin Farrell and—"

"You're in bed with Colin Farrell?" she shouts.

"I'm not in bed anymore—"

"But it *is* Colin Farrell?" she asks, her voice cracking with excitement.

"No. This . . . guy," I say—wincing at the fact that I've just referred to the naked man in my bed as "this guy"—"was in a movie *with* Colin Farrell . . . I think."

I get all my celebrity news from *People* magazine, which means that I can pick Adam Sandler's dog out of a lineup, or tell you what the *Survivor* castaways did with their winnings, but randomly identify specific actors and their movies? Not unless they've dated J. Lo.

"Colin Farrell . . . good. That's a good start." I hear the faint clicking of fingers on a keyboard as Ellen thoughtfully mumbles to herself. Finally she says, "Tell me if any of these sound familiar. Olivier?"

"No."

"Brian?"

"No."

"Stan?"

"No. Uh . . . well. Ssss-tan. No."

"All right." She goes silent. I hear a few more clicks, "How about Gabriel, Mike, Ron, or Angelo?"

"No. No. No, and no. This is not helping," I reply, losing what little hope I had that she would have the answer. "What are you doing?"

"Searching the Internet Movie Database. You got any better ideas?"

"Do they have a search matrix where you can plug in hair color, approximate height and weight?"

"I don't think so."

"Right." I sigh, trying to force my mind to focus. His name has to be up there somewhere. One tiny little neuron holds the key. "His name is something sort of common, but sort of uncommon at the same time. Old-fashioned, maybe? Or . . . oh, I don't know."

"All right, let's try this. Does he have pants?" asks Ellen carefully. "I mean, somewhere in your apartment?"

Pants? Oh, wallet!

"You're a genius!" Why didn't I think of that?

I let go of the hand towel and carefully slide myself back onto the floor. A recently purchased jute rug, which was meant to cushion my feet from the cold parquet floor, now digs into my knees and the palms of my hands. I press the phone between my ear and my shoulder and begin crawling over the rough—but "extremely durable and easy to clean"—carpet toward a heap that I believe is a pair of black trousers.

Two short catlike movements later and my hand lands on something flat and smooth. I lift the square object into the one grayish-blue stream of light coming from my bedroom's dingy window. Oh, thank God, a Trojan wrapper.

"At least I'm a *safe* floozy," I mumble with a sigh.

"What?"

"I found a . . . wrapper." I don't know why, but the word *condom* seems absolutely filthy to me just now.

"He's a *rapper?*"

"No! The, uh . . . Trojans I keep in my nightstand in case of emergency . . . I found an empty wrapper."

"Oh. How long have they been there? Could they still be good? Those things expire, you know."

"Come on, it hasn't been that long since I had . . . an emergency." Oh, no. Has it? I inspect the wrapper carefully and finally find the expiration date—six months from now. A wave of relief washes over me. Amazingly, the wave takes a hint of my disgust for myself with it.

I toss the wrapper back on the floor and, resuming my stealthy progress toward the pants, stumble upon a button-down shirt in my path. I quickly slip it on.

Oh, it's his. It smells like expensive . . . manliness. I draw up the collar and take a big whiff. God, he smells good. Or smell*ed* good.

"He's got good taste in cologne," I mutter to Ellen. "Can you search for that?"

"No."

"Damn." I sidle up to the black heap, while keeping one eye on the man in my bed. "I made it."

I pat down the top of the pants. He doesn't seem to have a wallet. Furtively I reach into the back pocket.

Ellen pipes up suddenly, "You'd better be quick about it. You don't want him waking up and seeing you digging in his pants like something out of *Pretty Woman.*"

Oh, crap. My life has just been compared to a movie about prostitutes.

I pick up the pace and dig through all the pockets as fast as I can. I pull out a wad of stuff from the right front pocket.

I inspect, "Two house keys on a Tiffany key ring. Forty-eight dollars and . . . sixteen cents. One Metro Card. And a receipt for . . . Tic Tacs."

"That's it? No ID? Nothing?"

"Nothing," I say, defeated. "God, Ellen, he could be anyone. He could be an ax murderer, or a drug addict, or a . . . a . . . Scientologist."

Who is this person?

More important, who am I? Who am I to do something this reckless, and dangerous, and stupid? Am I that easy to seduce? Am I that *easy?* I'm usually so careful about these things. I don't have random lust-filled sexual liaisons. I have awkward, mechanical sex with men who learn their moves from soft-core porn! How could I do something this impulsive and crazy and then, of all things, forget his name? It's beyond idiotic.

With a huff, I replace the wad of cash and receipts and arrange the pants back into a heap.

As I move away on my hands and knees, and sidestep to navigate around a pair of men's socks, I catch a glimpse of myself in the full-length mirror that I keep propped by my bedroom door. For a split second I'm paralyzed with fear. My brain, not knowing how to process the information it's getting from my eyes, concludes that the person in the mirror is an intruder—a strange, slutty woman dressed in a man's tuxedo shirt, who's broken into my apartment. A few seconds pass before all the pieces come together and I realize that the slutty stranger is me.

My eyes are encircled in flaky gray, my mousy-brown hair is a rat's nest, the man's tuxedo shirt I'm in hangs off me, exposing one shoulder and half of a bare breast. I am disgusting. I am repulsive. I am the prototype for a *Maxim* layout.

"What did I do? Why?" I whine, on the brink of tears, rubbing vigorously at the gray patches under my eyes.

Turning away from the mirror, I back myself against the wall opposite my bed and curl my knees up under my chin, trying to make myself smaller, and, I hope, undetectable, to the person sleeping peacefully in my bed. I try and remain perfectly still, partly to keep from awakening the sleeping giant, but also because every muscle ache is a reminder of my foolishness and last night's . . . exercise.

"Aw, Ruby," Ellen says consolingly, "you really don't remember anything about last night?"

"I remember the beginning. But the important parts are . . . hazy."

"Okay, what's the last thing you remember?" She says it like, "So, your life has gone missing. Where's the last place you saw it?"

"I'm searching for memories, Ellie, not keys."

"At least give it a try," she replies softly.

With great strain I try to force memories out of the darkness, like kicking up silt from a muddy lake-bed. I stir things up in the hope that something useful will float to the surface.

All I get are little flashes.

I'm laughing at something he's said, we're both in the back of a car—passing Bloomingdale's.

In my apartment, the living room, he's kissing my neck. He stops, looks at me and smiles.

"His eyes are brown, Ellie."

"Really? Anything else?"

He's got his back to the wardrobe in my bedroom, I'm standing in the doorway—taking my shirt off . . .

Okay, I don't want to know any more of this. "I can't . . . uh . . ."

"Fine, that's all right," Ellen replies sweetly. "How about you start from the beginning instead."

Good, sure. *Getting* dressed I can remember . . . and doesn't make me feel like vomiting.

I put on a black silk button-down blouse, dark slim-fitting jeans, and the highest heels I own (roughly two and a half inches).

After I dressed, I went to Ellen's apartment, where she promptly made me take off my blouse, and all but physically forced me to wear one of her designer tops instead. It was made of some wispy fabric that made me utter the cringe-worthy phrase "But I'll catch a cold in that." (This is, of course, second only to the phrase "It's all fun and games till someone loses an eye" on the cringe-worthy scale.) Ellen then told me to put on a pair of her four-inch stilettos, to which I responded, "It's all fun and games till someone loses an eye."

Ellen has always helped me out in this area, but lately it's been more like a mission for her. She thinks I'm turning into an "old ninny." She has yet to define "old ninny" to my satisfaction, but I gather it has something to do with not feeling sexy and only dating bores. And, I have to admit, the last few men I've dated have been a little drab and staid. It's no small surprise, though, when you consider that I meet most of the men I date through work. The art and antiques racket isn't exactly brimming with fiery young sexys. But Ellen insists that if I *feel* sexy, sexy men will be drawn to me—no matter where I meet them—so she's been dressing me up like a sex kitten every so often. Because I trust her expertise, and don't mind being treated as a life-size Barbie, I let her have her fun.

Ellen is one of those women you see all over Manhattan who are *subtly* stunning. I'm not talking about the wannabes who match their handbag to their shoes and still go for biweekly blowouts. I'm talking about the ones who hold their seven-hundred-dollar handbags as though they were bought on sale at Macy's for $27.50. The ones who know how to break in a brand-new pair of jeans so that they look like a favorite old pair—that just happens to be in a cutting-edge fit. They mix designer with designer vintage and always appear to have thrown on "any old thing," and yet still manage to vaunt an air of elegance. But don't let them fool you. The look takes styling and practice. Looking as good as Ellen does is an art mastered by years of observation and study, by years of dedication to little else. I'm not saying she's shallow or anything, just madly, passionately in love with fashion. Fashion is her boyfriend, and she is one hundred percent committed.

Fashion and I are not on such good terms. For me, fashion is the foxy next-door neighbor who would be a dreamy boyfriend if he would only talk to me when we pass in the hall, instead of just nodding. Fashion is something in magazines. I wear clothes—practical, durable, marginally stylish *clothes*. Then again, I don't have Ellen's resources. She gets half her wardrobe from the designer she works for, and the other half from the six-figure income the designer pays her. All *I* get from work is dusty.

In any event, normally I would have refused the four-inch stilettos on the basis of safety. However, last night I was feeling a little . . . gutsy. Though I didn't admit it to Ellen, I have been feeling more than a bit like a stuffy, middle-aged prude lately. My job is so cerebral, and requires so much formality and so little personality; I think some of it has seeped into my life outside of work. I've become . . . boring. It's that comfortable, tranquilized sort of boring that you ease into over time, where life becomes habit and things like taking a cab instead of the subway and staying up late to watch Conan seem adventuresome.

So last night I looked forward to shedding the "old ninny," if only for a few hours. I wanted to be someone new, a girl who flirts, and pouts, and plays the field. I wanted to be a sultry sex kitten who, unlike me, doesn't think too much, or analyze too much, or get nervous around men. I used New Year's Eve as an excuse to walk on the wild side—I donned the breezy, cold-inducing, five-hundred-dollar wisp of cloth and sequins—*and* I wore the stilettos.

Ellen was overjoyed.

"I will convert you yet, Ruby!" Ellen laughed while zipping up her body-skimming dress. "Somewhere under that tweed-loving exterior lies the cold, dead heart of a fashionista."

"Aw, you say the nicest things," I replied sarcastically.

As Ellen fluttered into the bathroom, I scrutinized myself in her bedroom mirror. I tried to "own" the outfit, as Ellen has so often chided me to do. The top hung perfectly off my neck in halter fashion, and grazed my back in just the right places. The airiness of the material disguised the two extra pounds that have attached themselves to my midriff since Thanksgiving (thanks to my grandma's famous holiday *pound* cake). I felt . . . beautiful in it, almost glamorous.

I couldn't help testing out my sexy facial expressions. As I've never really had any "sexy" expressions, I used what I'd seen Ellen do when she has her game on. I tried to replicate her bedroom eyes and deeply intense gaze. But, while she looks like a come-hither vixen, I look mentally challenged. Huh.

"What time is it?" I called to her.

"Don't worry, the party doesn't start until eight." As she returned to the room, she poked me in the back and demanded, "Stand up straight, slouch-monkey."

"Slouch-monkey?" Now, *that* is sexy.

"You're tall. Get over it. Squishing your shoulders down doesn't make you look any shorter, it only makes you look like you're suffering from premature osteoporosis. For me, add 'stand up straight' to your resolutions."

"Can't do it. My only New Year's resolution this year is this: I will make no New Year's resolutions."

She eyed me askance, apparently not appreciating my clever verbal Möbius strip.

I explained, "New Year's resolutions never actually start the year off well. They only expand the opportunities for self-loathing when you find yourself alone on Valentine's Day. I mean, seriously, have you ever actually completed any resolutions?"

"Every year."

"You're kidding."

She shook her head no.

"What were they last year?" I challenged.

"Take fewer cabs, tip better, and get TiVo."

She was totally serious. "You're crazy."

"What?" She smiled, "Those are resolutions."

"That's like saying, 'I resolve to have more money, get better service at the salon, and never miss an episode of *Coupling.*'"

"And?" she asked with a devilish grin.

"They're not really resolutions if they're *easy.*"

"Says who?"

Sensing that the conversation was making a beeline for "Is not!"/"Is too!" territory, I turned back to the mirror and changed the subject. "Who's giving this party again?"

"Gavin and Ken Kleinman."

"Are they *married* married?"

"They got first-class tickets on a flight to San Francisco, but didn't get there in time."

"But Gavin changed his name?"

"Ken."

"Got it."

"Don't worry, you don't need to know their life story. There will be dozens of other guests, and a bevy of cute cater-waiters, to distract them."

As Ellen applied a thin veil of Issey Miyake perfume to us both, I tried my best not just to *seem* blithe and seductive but to actually *be* it.

I was almost to "owning" it when Ellen pointed to my mouth. "You've got a little lipstick on your teeth."

Not so much sex kitten, then, as sex-kitten impersonator— not how you're supposed to feel when going to a colossal annual New Year's Eve bash that has been featured on the *Vanity Fair* party page.

As a guest at a party like this, you have certain responsibilities: Always look as fabulous as you possibly can, come prepared with witty responses and dazzling stories, and of course, a seasoned guest will *always* arrive fashionably late. Thus, at eight-thirty, after Ellen expertly applied a razor-thin band of eyeliner to my upper lids, we draped ourselves in two of her most divine cashmere wraps and headed off to the party.

Twelve blocks, and two cases of frostbite later . . . we approached the entrance of Gavin and Ken's magnificent brownstone. It was like something out of a movie. The windows were clouded over with condensation, the moist warmth of mass small talk bumping up against cold glass. The light and music from inside were diffused by the foggy glaze and gave the whole place an air of mystery.

"You ready?" asked Ellen.

"Yep." I made an effort to stand up straight and exhaled with my lips together trying to make them look pouty. (I read somewhere that models do that at photo shoots.)

My attempt at looking sultry earned me a look from Ellen that said, "Are you okay? You look funny." I just smiled and nodded my head at the door.

Ellen knocked and presented her invite to the butler (yes, I said *butler*). He welcomed us in, took our wraps, and we folded into the mass of humanity lingering on and around cushy down-filled sofas of obscene proportions and giant Jonathan Alder vases overflowing with exotic orchids. The walls were bathed in earthy tones of chocolate, dark almond, and caramel that made the whole place feel as cozy and luxurious as the inside of a fur coat—or a Mars bar.

I surveyed beyond the priceless furniture and accessories and noted the many wealthy, young, and hip partygoers. I expected nothing less, as Ken and Gavin, though renowned for their high-profile work in public relations, are better known simply for being rich and fabulous.

The music filling the space was pitch perfect for the mood and the crowd, a classic Parliament tune gave way to Earth, Wind & Fire just as a duo of waiters approached with champagne and hors d'oeuvres. A slender guy, who couldn't have been more than nineteen, proffered a silver tray dotted with a variety of bite-sized meats. He said, "They're Atkins-approved. Zero carbs."

Why is it, exactly, that everything these days has to be approved by Atkins? I don't object to people going on Atkins or anything, but for those of us *not* on the diet, "Atkins friendly" hors d'oeuvres are just calorie bombs, teeny little fat grenades that distribute their flabby shrapnel throughout the body, causing one's thighs to explode. Ironically, at Gavin and Ken's, none of the apparent Atkins aficionados seemed to mind that they were swilling down their mini-meats with seven trillion carbs in Moët & Chandon.

I grabbed a flute of champagne and said a polite, "No, thank you" to the Atkins-wielding waiter. Soon after, Ellen scurried off to talk to some women from her office.

Instead of following her like the lost puppy I felt like, I decided instead to wander around the house and calculate the approximate net worth of our hosts by assessing the value of their belongings.

As I walked through the house, I noticed that I wasn't the only person doing some appraisal. I was getting looked at—by men—lots of them. They scanned my face and all the way down to my spiky heels. They smiled at me and watched my progress through the room. I could feel their eyes on my bare back. It was . . . exhilarating.

After touring the dining room (converted to a dance floor for the occasion), and the library (stocked with careworn volumes that looked to have been purchased in bulk by an interior designer), I made my way toward the back terrace. Through the wide French doors I could see that Ken and Gavin had rented outdoor space heaters to take the chill off the smokers, several clusters of whom were already out there. Delicate paper lanterns crisscrossed overhead from one side of the yard to the other, giving the place a sense of enchantment.

As I reached for the door handle, an arm came out of nowhere and pulled the door open for me. The first thing I saw was a tuxedo shirt, complete with a line of ruffles. Through the flimsy white fabric I could see the faint red outline of a ringer T-shirt underneath. It read "Stop Plate Tectonics Now!" I smiled instinctively and looked to the guy's face. Instantly he struck me as beautiful and also somehow . . . familiar.

I walked through the door and smiled at him, said "Thanks."

He smiled back, and then ushered another man out behind me before walking out himself.

I pretended to admire the wood fencing and paper lanterns, and inspected the guy some more. He had on black wool pants, red Converse Chucks, and through his tuxedo shirt I could read the back of the tee underneath. It said, "Citizens for a Stationary Planet". That was it—done. I am a complete sucker for good-looking nerds.

I imagined that the stack of magazines under his bed was equal parts *Playboy* and *National Geographic.* I saw him playing Xbox before beginning his shift at the helm of a high-powered radio telescope. I pictured him perusing the latest *Spiderman* comic book after giving a lecture on the untapped potential of inert space gas as an alternative fuel.

I tried to ignore the little voice in my head that said, *You don't go out with guys like that, you date men who look good in suits and are uncomfortable in knitwear. You date men who keep their apartments tidy and collect things like stocks and golf balls. You date men with plywood personalities and a medicine cabinet full of Rogaine.*

Suddenly the little voice in my head went silent, drowned-out by the sound of tiny bubbles—the Don Ho classic, that is.

"Makes me feel happy. . . . Makes me feel fine. . . ."

The tingling warmth of the champagne spread over me, making my limbs a little lighter than normal. It felt like the bubbles were actually gurgling through my veins and lifting me up. I felt no nervousness about flirting, it seemed the only logical thing to do.

Unfortunately, the nerdy stunner had his back toward me. He was chatting with a thirty-something man who so oozed up-to-the-nanosecond Euro-trash chic that he almost *had* to be a poseur.

I casually sauntered across the patio and "accidentally" wandered into their line of sight. I desperately wished I had a handkerchief, or some other Victorian accessory, to drop and need assistance in retrieving. In the end, though, it just took a bit of waiting. After a few minutes his eyes landed on me, and I gave him a warm smile that was meant to say, "Hi there, Handsome. I'm *super* sexy and fun. I am carefree and sowing my wild oats. I will admire your scientific exploits and won't make you burn your collection of *Star Wars* action figures."

Then, just as the meaning of my smile was beginning to sink in (his eyes were saying, "Yeah, you don't look crazy"), I was violently attacked and thoughtlessly ripped from a perfectly respectable flirtation . . . by my boss.

Dr. Boyd Whalley (Ph.D.) has the sort of facile eccentricity that only a certain kind of all-male British boarding school can imbue—he is a caricature of the person he could have been. Had his childhood tutors not themselves been schooled in eighteenth-century child-rearing techniques, Dr. Whalley might have turned out to be a very interesting, even dashing, sort of a person. As it is, though, he is often pompously verbose and has such a quirky personality that, depending on your perspective, he comes across as either scathingly brilliant or like he's suffering from a profound mental disability.

Dr. Whalley announced himself with an earsplitting, champagne-laced, "Ruby, my dear!"

"Dr. Whalley, how are you?"

He inspected me quizzically and said in his prim British accent, "Strange to see you out of the office."

"Yes." I swear he thinks I sleep in the little cupboard under the coffee machine.

He smoothed back his graying locks and lit up a cigarillo. *I* tried to think of a decent escape plan before he could trap me in conversation. The proximity of the delicious Nerdy Guy, not to mention the need for a raise, blocked all rational thought.

Dr. Whalley asked, "Are you a friend of Ken and Gavin?" *Gavin* came out *Gav'n*.

"Not exactly, I—"

"Yes, I'm not what you would call a friend, either. Perhaps, friend*ly*. I inspected their Rodin, you know. I imagine they have it squirreled away up there. In the love nest. Not quite as valuable as they'd hoped, frankly. I think they'd wanted a villa in Cannes out of it. Quite an eccentric pair, wouldn't you say?"

I could only nod and mumble. I cursed not really being the confident, worldly-wise girl I was dressed as. *That* girl would have known exactly how to extricate herself from pointless conversation with her socially awkward boss.

He continued, "Did you ever manage to nail down the provenance of that little Buddha?"

"Not yet, I—"

"Must do some digging in the Frick records, I think."

Must . . . flee . . . "Well, Dr. Whalley"—I waved my empty glass—"I think I need a refill." I moved toward the French doors. "It was nice to—"

"Ah, yes. More champagne. One moment." He unceremoniously dropped his slim, brown cigarillo on the ground and darted ahead of me. He opened the door partway and leaned inside the house, waving his hand at someone in the library. Much to my dismay, a waiter appeared with a tray of drinks.

Whalley returned in no time . . . with the *entire* tray.

"That should hold us for a while," he said with a smile.

As I looked up from the tray, I noticed the Nerdy Guy eyeing me, and the tray, and Dr. *Freaking* Whalley. Nerdy Guy chuckled a bit, and I stared back at him, and shrugged my shoulders a little, as if to say, "I am not with Dr. Stuffy-Pants. Dr. Stuffy-Pants is my boss and I can't insult him by bolting. I would much rather be hanging out with you—even if you are consorting with pretentious imitation Euro-trash. I am easygoing and vivacious . . . and would adore your *Lord of the Rings* commemorative coin collection."

Dr. Whalley handed me a glass and took a big opening swig of his own. "How were your holidays, Ruby?" He always drops the end of my name so it comes out *Rube-eh*. "Where did you run off to? *Minny-Sota? Mary-land? Mont-gomery?*"

"Maine. My family lives in Maine."

"Right, yes. Of course. The lobsters. Is that what you have for the holiday? Lobsters?"

"No. We have turkey."

"Ah! Fresh . . . free-range . . . shot that morning, no doubt."

"Butterball, by the pound," I said. Then, noticing Whalley's attention had drifted, I added matter-of-factly, "But we prepared it while wearing ten-gallon hats, smoking Marlboros, and toting shotguns." No point in upsetting his notions—I do believe that, owing to his antiquated upbringing, Dr. Whalley still thinks of the greater continental U.S. as Britain's savage and rebellious colony.

Whalley, who had drifted deep into his own thoughts, mumbled, "Mmmm, of course."

"I mean, what's an American holiday without firearms?" I added casually, taking a sip of champagne.

"Yes, quite right," Whalley responded thoughtlessly.

Gorgeous, sparkly-eyed Nerdy Guy heard the last bit of the conversation and actually laughed out loud. Luckily, Dr. Whalley didn't seem to notice. I, meanwhile, guzzled down the last of my second glass of champagne.

Whalley emerged from introspective reverie and chirruped, "Years ago my parents and I went on safari. The guide, an Australian fellow, shot and eviscerated the game *himself* every evening. Remarkable."

"Yes, I can imagine."

"Have you ever been? Africa?"

"No, can't say that I have. But I always thought—"

"Amazing place, that. We were in Kenya. Quite wild and untamed."

Yes, I know. I thought to myself. And you've told me this fifteen times, each time when slightly sauced. Dr. Whalley, when feeling charming and clever, is a decent conversationalist, but with an undetermined amount of complementary champagne in him, he is really pretty insipid.

I could feel my life ticking away, slowly . . . and painfully. I felt guilty for not being more animated, or understanding of Dr. Whalley, but at the same time—it was New Year's Eve and I'm an American. We're hedonists, damn it! We don't have civilized conversations on holidays! We flirt and dance and make asses of ourselves. When we're pretending to be sex kittens, we don't talk to our bosses, we pose, and swish our hair and . . . other girly *things*.

The Euro-chic Poseur moved off inside and left Nerdy Guy all alone—watching me.

I tried to flirt silently. I stared back at him with a look that said, "I am trapped here. Otherwise, you would be free to talk to me. I am more wild and sex-kittenish than this conversation. I am fascinated by space gases."

I drained my third glass of champagne as Dr. Whalley blubbered incoherently about Dante and the Renaissance masters. And then the Nerdy Guy began to move—toward us.

I held my breath and tried to keep myself steady. I felt the champagne really kicking in, and I couldn't tell if it was the patio or my legs that were feeling wobbly.

Nerdy Guy positioned himself between me and Dr. Whalley, extending a hand to him. Whalley, a bit thrown off by the sudden, and somewhat bold, interruption, slowly shook the man's hand.

Nerdy Guy spoke, "Dr. Wharbley . . ."

"Whalley," I whispered.

"Whalley," Nerdy Guy repeated, "I've been wanting to speak to you. I'm in the market for some . . ."

"Art," I whispered on cue.

"Art," he continued. "Do you think I should take the plunge?"

Dr. Whalley, stunned and flattered by the question, began what was sure to be a long and detailed assessment. As soon as he began speaking, Nerdy Guy turned his head and whispered to me, "Now's your chance. Make a run for it."

"Ruby?" Ellen asks, "Ruby, babe, you there?"

"Yeah, I'm here."

"And they say chivalry is dead. Anyone who would voluntarily put up with a tipsy Whalley is . . . special. Definitely not an ax murderer."

"Maybe he's a very *charming* ax murderer," I reply cynically.

"He sounds gorgeous, and witty, and smart—"

"How do you know he's smart?"

"Ruby, his tattoos are in *Latin.*"

"If he even knows what it means. I heard that Britney Spears got a tattoo of a Chinese symbol that she thought meant 'mysterious.' It actually means 'strange.' What if he meant for it to say *hunc tu caveto?*"

"What does that mean?"

"Beware of this man," I moan.

"Listen to me. This guy sounds fantastic. Things like this just don't happen!" Ellen's voice is getting high-pitched and excited. Like a Chihuahua. "Sweet, adorable actors who speak dead romance languages don't just drop in your lap. It's fate!"

I almost wish he wasn't so *sweet*. If he were a dumb, inarticulate jerk, it would make the disappointment of losing him to the "Miss Right Now Effect" a lot easier to bear. Why, oh, why did I have to ruin his good opinion of me by going to bed with him?

"I am such an idiot!"

"Quit moaning!" she shrills.

"Fine. So how did I get from batting my eyelashes to taking my pants off? Did you see anything? Do you know who I'm talking about?"

"I couldn't have seen him, because if I had you'd be on the opposite side of this conversation," she jokes.

As though he senses he's being discussed, the stranger in my bed rolls over and lets out a loud sigh. As he exhales, his lips flutter out to a pout. They look full, and soft, and . . . inviting.

Oh, God. Oh, my good God. As quietly as I possibly can, I whisper, "Ellie, I'm disgusting. There is a naked movie star in my bed and I want him to kiss me. I'm one of those girls who will do anything to go to bed with a celebrity, aren't I?"

"Yes, Ruby. You are the sex-crazed fan of an actor whose movies you don't know and whose name you can't remember."

"Are you mocking me?"

"Yes."

"Look, he could wake up any second now, and I have no idea . . . I'm having a difficult time here—"

"I know you are, hon. So let's get back to the problem. After he saved you from Whalley, you walked back into the house. Do you remember anything else?"

"I had to go to the bathroom—all that champagne."

• • •

Well, it was the champagne and a sudden and extreme urge to fix my hair, touch up my makeup, and sober myself so that I could find him again and thank him for sacrificing himself to Whalley. Unfortunately, the downstairs powder room was decidedly occupied. I pounded on the door and heard wails of muffled moaning and giggling. Rather than wait out the . . . fun going on inside, I decided to hoof it up the stairs and seek out another bathroom. Apparently, three million other people had the same idea. The narrow hallway was crammed with well-dressed women. They lined the walls in loose little packs, and clung to the railing that headed up the second set of stairs to the third floor.

Had they all seen the Nerdy Guy? Were they all going to primp in the hopes of getting to talk to him? These were the things running through my mind at the time, and I had quite a while to ponder. When I took my place in line, the time was 9:35. When I reached the bathroom, it was 9:55.

Panic was beginning to set in: What if he'd already moved on to some other party? What if some gorgeous supermodel or the stunning *Real World* cast member who was rumored to be downstairs had already snapped him up? What if Dr. Whalley had finally succeeded in boring someone to death?

I did what I waited in line to do, powdered and glossed as quickly as humanly possible, and did my best to focus. Taking slow deep breaths, I tried to clear the champagne fog that was beginning to form in my brain. I told myself not to trip on my high heels, not to babble incessantly, not to lose control of my limbs in any way, shape, or form. I practiced walking by pacing back and forth across the bathroom floor, and only had to steady myself with the towel bar once. I repeated little mantras: "Be sexy. Be charming. Be *sober.*" Really, the hardest thing about getting drunk is pretending to be sober. It takes so much concentration. Coincidentally, concentration is the second thing that alcohol impairs. (The first thing it impairs is the ability to resist karaoke.)

The instant I opened the door a gaggle of women squeezed past me and, in closing the door behind them, knocked me out into the hall. I turned sideways and crept slowly through the throng of people. In an ill-conceived but noble attempt to keep myself from toppling over, I stared at my feet. I managed to side-step two misplaced champagne glasses and narrowly escaped an attack by a long flowing skirt, but, at about the halfway mark, a sharp pain stung my bare back—a scraping sensation from my shoulder to my spine. Without thinking, I moved away from it and careened toward the other side of the hall and smashed chest first into someone. I looked behind me to see a massive diamond ring being carelessly whipped about by a slim-fingered, highly intoxicated socialite. Her hands flapped to and fro as she admonished her friend for "not going to Aspen until February."

"I was just assaulted by a piece of jewelry," I said to no one in particular. I turned back and faced the person I'd inadvertently tackled, and my heart jumped straight out of my chest—my nose was halfway between *Plate* and *Tectonics*.

"Hey," he said warmly, like I was an old friend.

"Hi," I replied dumbly, not knowing what else to say. "You escaped."

"I *am* known as the Houdini of cocktail party chitchat," he said, flirting with reckless abandon.

I flirted right back, "Oh, really?"

"No"—he smiled—"but I have a great deal of experience with one-sided conversations."

"Talk to yourself a lot, do you?"

"Well . . . yes, as a matter-of-fact." He chuckled. "But I also have a slightly senile grandmother."

"Ah, I see."

"But Whalley was more of a challenge—he doesn't think he's Eleanor Roosevelt."

"Oh, I'm sorry. I should have told you . . . he thinks he's *normal.*"

He laughed, "Yeah, it was a bit touch and go there for a while."

"Well, I appreciate the effort. Thank you."

"You're welcome."

We both went silent. He looked me squarely in the eye, almost inquisitively—as if asking me some silent question. He let his gaze drift down my neck to my bare shoulders and back to my eyes again.

There was something electric about the way he looked at me. It liquefied my insides. The only thing I can think to compare it to is a high-school crush—like freshman year, and a well-built senior who oozed mystery and danger. It was the same sort of overwhelming attraction, a desire so intense that it's palpable. As a teenager, it's the newness of the feelings as much as the feelings themselves that make a crush so all-consuming. It's the freshness

of dreamy anticipation that gives the crush its power to invigor-
ate. And in that moment, with me looking at him, him looking
at me—I wanted him with the same pure desire of a freshman-
year crush. It made my heart leap, and all my little nerve endings
flutter with the question *What will become of this?*

We continued to stare at each other, goofy smiles plastered on
our faces, as the party broke through "dignified" and transitioned
into the "fun-for-drunks" portion of the evening. People appeared in the hallway wearing gold-embossed paper hats and
bearing the evil cousins of the shiny "Happy New Year!" hat—
the plastic horn and tin noisemaker. There should really be some
sort of regulation on those things. Store clerks should be required
to ask, "Are you going to be drinking and noisemaking this
evening? Or just noisemaking?"

I spoke first, "Do you want to . . . uh . . ." and sort of pointed
down the stairs.

He offered instantly, "They have a roof." A hint of pink rose
up his cheeks as he continued, "Well, obviously they have a roof,
I mean they have a *deck* on the roof."

The sensible, non–sex-kitten part of me thought, *Not without
my can of mace, mister,* but the new me thought something entirely different. The new part of me had felt his warmth and
smelled his deep musky smell and been completely floored by his
easy demeanor, his charm and wit.

The new part of me spoke: "Perfect."

"One second," he said. "Don't move."

He wove in and out of the crowd and darted down the steps. In
moments he returned with a half-empty bottle of Dom Pérignon.

Then he took my hand and guided me up two flights of stairs, the noise and the people thinning the higher we went.

When we ran out of staircase, he stopped suddenly, let go of my hand, and darted into a room.

A few seconds later he came out with a heavy wool blanket.

"Impressive," I said. "You a thief?"

"*Much* worse," he replied. "I'm an actor."

He guided me farther down the hall, and opened another door. An icy blast smacked me in the face; it made my eyes water and my muscles stiffen. He quickly draped the blanket around us both and ushered me out onto the roof deck. We slid ourselves across the icy floor to a wooden bench with a staggering view of the city lights.

"So that's it?" Ellen asks, disappointed. "That's all you remember?"

"No . . . well, I don't know. . . ." There are those stupid flashes of me taking my clothes off—which now, miraculously enough, seem slightly less horrifying. "He seems . . . *seemed*," I correct myself, "pretty decent, right?"

"Yes, Ruby, but that isn't really the point, is it? You still don't know his name." True, but for some reason I don't feel nearly as slutty. "Come on, what else? What did you talk about?"

"Uh . . ." I grasp on to anything that pops in my head. "He's going to Prague this summer to film a movie!" I say triumphantly.

"Good, excellent!" I hear her typing away again.

Several minutes pass and she grumbles, "So far I've found

about seven movies being filmed in Prague this summer—and those are just the ones in English."

"Shit." Okay, must think. He has to have told me his name. I could not have been seduced by a man whose name I didn't know. I don't care how drunk I was, I *had* to have thought of that.

"Anything else?"

"We were up there for a while, just sitting and talking. He made me laugh. I don't know. We drank more champagne . . . um . . ."

"Ruby, it's, like, *ten o'clock* in the morning. I don't care what you were up to last night, the man is going to wake up soon."

What can I do, damn it? This is where things get fuzzy. . . .

The roof was silent, except for the distant thumping of bass from the party below, I tried to keep the conversation going by being seductive. All the while I staved off the nervous dork within by downing more champagne. I wanted to be charming, and alluring, and not care whether or not he liked me, but I couldn't. I turned into a big blubbering mess.

At one point I asked him, "What got you into acting?"

He smiled sheepishly and replied, "In interviews I always say *Raging Bull*"—he tipped his head thoughtfully, looked at me— "but I think I can tell you the truth. *If* you promise never to tell another soul so long as you live."

I made a crossing motion over my left breast—and nearly ripped off my gauzy top in the process. Thank God, he didn't seem to notice.

He leaned in toward me, brushing my hair away from my face

with a flick of the wrist, grazing my bare shoulder as he did. He touched his cheek to mine.

I barely heard what he said, not because he was whispering, but because the sensation of his breath on my neck was all my tiny, ridiculous, champagne-impaired mind could process at the time. All I could think was . . . *New Year's Resolution Number Two: Kiss this man.*

He said, "It was *The Neverending Story.*" His lips grazed my earlobe as he pulled away.

I took a deep breath and tried to clear the images of his lips on mine that had suddenly flooded my mind. I wanted to keep it casual, as though I hadn't been completely seduced by his proximity. So, in a cataclysmic display of idiocy, I responded to his heartfelt confession with "Ah, yes, Atreyu! Reluctant hero of Fantasia, relentlessly pursued by the terrible *Nothing.* All his efforts thwarted by that gutless wonder Bastien."

The second it was out of my mouth I felt like a complete ass. He laughed—a soft, friendly, easy laugh—but it didn't help. I was sure I'd blown it.

When, two seconds later, he looked at his watch, I was *positive* that I'd blown it. I thought he was going to get up and walk away and find some girl who really was as poised and sexy as she appeared to be. But instead, he pulled a small box from his pants pocket, gingerly shook something out, and popped it in his mouth . . . Tic Tacs.

The low thumping of bass below us faded to complete silence. The whole city was hushed. I pointed to his hand and asked, "May I?"

He looked surprised that I'd noticed, and said an anxious, "Sure," before handing me the tiny plastic box.

I popped one in my mouth and crunched it, racking my brain for something to say. Just then the silence around us broke, and the deep hum of distant human voices rose up to the rooftop.

He looked at his watch again, then showed it to me. The digital readout blinked: *12:00:27*.

"Happy New Year," he said quietly.

"Happy New Year," I returned.

He leaned in toward me slowly, then hesitated. So I leaned in to meet him. We had a long, slow, perfect New Year's kiss that made me tingle—and drop the Tic Tacs.

I thought to myself as he kissed me, *Things like this only happen to the luckiest people. When they happen you have to grab on with both hands and let yourself go along for the ride. Even if it's fleeting, it'll be worth it.* As he pulled me closer to him, I felt the timid and boring part of me acquiesce. A giddiness, wholly removed from champagne and moonlight, swept over me.

I grinned at him. "Your nose is cold. Do you want to go back to my place?"

"Sure."

I patted around on the bench for my purse, then stopped suddenly as something occurred to me. "I'm Ruby, by the way."

"Hi, Ruby. I'm—"

"What? His name is what?!" Ellen demands—loudly.

"It's gone. Oh, God! He told me and it's gone. Gone. Totally in-one-ear-and-out-the-other gone. I was too busy trying to remember when I last shaved my legs to let it sink in. It's gone, Ellie." My heart begins pounding so hard that I can hear the *thump-thump* of it in my eardrums. "It starts with an *S* . . . I think. Sam . . . Steve . . . Stuart . . . S-uh . . . S-uh—"

"Simon?" Ellen asks optimistically.

"No," I huff. "Seriously, it's gone."

Though I no longer believe I'm a complete slut (only slightly and temporarily trampy), I do know for certain that I am the single stupidest girl *ever*. I have stumbled across a man who doesn't seem to care that I'm a bumbling dork, who continued to think I was sexy even after I said the words "reluctant hero of Fantasia" . . . and I can't remember his name.

Maybe my luck has run out. Maybe all I'm meant to have with him is one night. I can live with that. Well, I can live with myself for doing it in the first place, but I wish I could at least have a *chance* at a few more nights. (A couple of days wouldn't kill me, either.) But if he wakes up and I have to call him "Hey, you—Naked Man," I'm not going to have a snowball's chance in hell.

"I cannot believe this," I whisper to Ellen. "One of the sweetest, hottest men on the planet is in my . . . wait a second."

"What?" Ellen asks.

"Hottest men . . . holy shit! Hottest bachelors . . . *that's* why he looked so familiar. I don't know that I've even seen his movies. . . . Why didn't I think of this before?"

I untangle my limbs and crawl back to the bedside while Ellen continues to repeat, "What?" and yammer incoherently.

As quickly and quietly as I can, I flip through the stacks of old magazines under my bedside table. "I knew there was a reason I kept all these things. I'm like that little girl from *Signs*. . . ."

It has to be here somewhere!

I move on to the piles under my bed.

December . . . October . . . February . . .

Crap! Where's summer? Where are the summer issues?

Finally! June 28!

I free the slim volume from a thick bundle of outdated papers and magazines—one of last year's *People* magazines, the "Fifty Hottest Bachelors" issue.

I open the magazine to the feature section and calmly flip through the pages. "Come on, *People* magazine. Do me this one favor and I'll renew my subscription every time you send me one of those little reminders. I'll subscribe for three years at a time, if you want."

I hit page 74 and let out a great sigh of relief—a very flattering picture of the man who's in my bed. Fully clothed, of course, but it's definitely him. I let out a little *yip* of excitement as I read the words "high date-ability," "single," "deeply intelligent," "credits *Raging Bull* with inspiring him to become an actor."

Ellen pleads, "Say something, Ruby, before I come through this phone line and—"

"*People*. Page 74. June . . . last year . . ."

The bedsprings above me groan with restless tossing and turning.

I sputter into the phone, "Got to go, Ellie. Thank you. Love you. Call you later."

She says, "Wha—" as I click the phone off and shove it under the bed with the magazines.

I whip off the white tuxedo shirt and toss it back across the room, then gingerly creep back into bed and under the covers. Before I have time to fall into pretend sleep, he wakes fully.

He beams at me sleepily, props himself up on one elbow and looks down at me. "Good morning, Ruby."

I take a deep breath and exhale with a grin. "Good morning, Seth."

He leans over and kisses my cheek. "What do you want for breakfast? I'm making."

✳ ✳ ✳

LIBBY STREET is the pseudonym for the writing team of Sarah Bushweller and Emily S. Morris.

Sarah and Emily met on Liberty Drive in Dover, Delaware, at the age of four and have been best friends ever since. They began writing together via email and telephone—just trying to make each other laugh.

Their first novel, *My Perfect Manhattan* will be published in 2005.

Like what you just read?

Then don't miss these other great books from Downtown Press!

**Scottish Girls
About Town**
Jenny Colgan, Isla Dewar,
Muriel Gray, et al.

Calling Romeo
Alexandra Potter

Game Over
Adele Parks

Pink Slip Party
Cara Lockwood

**Shout Down
the Moon**
Lisa Tucker

Maneater
Gigi Levangie Grazer

Clearing the Aisle
Karen Schwartz

Liner Notes
Emily Franklin

My Lurid Past
Lauren Henderson

**Dress You Up
in My Love**
Diane Stingley

He's Got to Go
Sheila O'Flanagan

**Irish Girls
About Town**
Maeve Binchy, Marian Keyes,
Cathy Kelly, et al.

**The Man I Should
Have Married**
Pamela Redmond Satran

**Getting Over
Jack Wagner**
Elise Juska

The Song Reader
Lisa Tucker

The Heat Seekers
Zane

I Do (But I Don't)
Cara Lockwood

**Why Girls
Are Weird**
Pamela Ribon

Larger Than Life
Adele Parks

Eliot's Banana
Heather Swain

**How to Pee
Standing Up**
Anna Skinner

Look for them wherever books are sold or visit us online at www.downtownpress.com.

down
tOwn
press

Great storytelling just got a new address.

PUBLISHED BY POCKET BOOKS

10403

Be the Next Downtown Girl

Contest Rules

1) ENTRY REQUIREMENTS:

Register to enter the contest on www.simonsaysthespot.com. Enter by submitting your story as specified below.

2) CONTEST ELIGIBILITY:

This contest is open to nonprofessional writers who are legal residents of the United States and Canada (excluding Quebec) over the age of 18 as of December 7, 2004. Entrant must not have published any more than two short stories on a professional basis or in paid professional venues. Employees (or relatives of employees living in the same household) of Simon & Schuster, VIACOM, or any of their affiliates are not eligible. This contest is void in Puerto Rico, Quebec, and wherever prohibited or restricted by law.

3) FORMAT:

Entries must not be more than 7,500 words long and must not have been previously published. Entries must be typed or printed by word processor, double spaced, on one side of noncorrasable paper. Do not justify right-side margins. Along with a cover letter, the author's name, address, email address, and phone number must appear on the first page of the entry. The author's name, the story title, and the page number should appear on every page. Electronic submissions will be accepted and must be sent to downtowngirl@simonandschuster.com. All electronic submissions must be sent as an attachment in a Microsoft Word document. All entries must be original and the sole work of the Entrant and the sole property of the Entrant.

All submissions must be in English. Entries are void if they are in whole or in part illegible, incomplete, or damaged or if they do not conform to any of the requirements specified herein. Sponsor reserves the right, in its absolute and sole discretion, to reject any entries for any reason, including but not limited to based on sexual content, vulgarity, and/or promotion of violence.

4) ADDRESS:

Entries submitted by mail must be postmarked by July 31, 2005 and sent to:

Be The Next Downtown Girl
Author Search

Downtown Press Editorial Department
Pocket Books
1230 Sixth Avenue, 13th floor
New York, NY 10020

Or Emailed By July 31, 2005
at 11:59 PM EST as a
Microsoft Word document to:

downtowngirl@simonandschuster.com

Each entry may be submitted only once. Please retain a copy of your submission. You may submit more than one story, but each submission must be mailed or emailed, as applicable, separately. Entries must be received by July 31, 2005. Not responsible for lost, late, stolen, illegible, mutilated, postage due, garbled, or misdirected mail/entries.

5) PRIZES:

One Grand Prize winner will receive:

Simon & Schuster's Downtown Press Publishing Contract for Publication of Winning Entry in a future Downtown Press Anthology, Five Hundred U.S. Dollars ($500.00), and

Downtown Press Library
(20 books valued at $260.00)

Grand Prize winner must sign the Publishing contract which contains additional terms and conditions in order to be published in the anthology.

Ten Second Prize winners will receive:

A Downtown Press Collection
(10 books valued at $130.00)

No contestant can win more than one prize.

6) STORY THEME

We are not restricting stories to any specific topic, however they should embody what all of our Downtown Press authors encompass—they should be smart, savvy, sexy stories that any Downtown Girl can relate to. We all know what uptown girls are like, but girls of the new millennium prefer the Downtown Scene. That's where it happens. The music, the shopping, the sex, the dating, the heartbreak, the family squabbles, the marriage, and the divorce. You name it. Downtown Girls have done it. Twice. We encourage you to register for the contest at www.simonsaysthespot.com in order to receive our monthly emails and updates from our authors and read about our titles on www.downtownpress.com to give you a better idea of what types of books we publish.

7) JUDGING:

Submissions will be judged on the equally weighted criteria of (a) basis of writing ability and (b) the originality of the story (which can be set in any time frame or location). Judging will take place on or about October 1, 2005. The judges will include a freelance editor, the editor of the future Anthology, and 5 employees of Sponsor. The decisions of the judges shall be final.

8) NOTIFICATION:

The winners will be notified by mail or phone on or about October 1, 2005. The Grand Prize Winner must sign the publishing contract in order to be awarded the prize. All federal, local, and state taxes are the responsibility of the winner. A list of the winners will be available after October 20, 2005 on:

http://www.downtownpress.com

http://www.simonsaysthespot.com

The winners' list can also be obtained by sending a stamped self-addressed envelope to:

Be The Next Downtown Girl
Author Search
Downtown Press Editorial Department
Pocket Books
1230 Sixth Avenue, 13th floor
New York, NY 10020

9) PUBLICITY:

Each Winner grants to Sponsor the right to use his or her name, likeness, and entry for any advertising, promotion, and publicity purposes without further compensation to or permission from such winner, except where prohibited by law.

10) INTERNET:

If for any reason this Contest is not capable of running as planned due to an infection by a computer virus, bugs, tampering, unauthorized intervention, fraud, technical failures, or any other causes beyond the control of the Sponsor which corrupt or affect the administration, security, fairness, integrity, or proper conduct of this Contest, the Sponsor reserves the right in its sole discretion, to disqualify any individual who tampers with the entry process, and to cancel, terminate, modify, or suspend the Contest. The Sponsor assumes no responsibility for any error, omission, interruption, deletion, defect, delay in operation or transmission, communications line failure, theft or destruction or unauthorized access to, or alteration of, entries. The Sponsor is not responsible for any problems or technical malfunctions of any telephone network or telephone lines, computer on-line systems, servers, or providers, computer equipment, software, failure of any email or entry to be received by the Sponsor due to technical problems, human error or traffic congestion on the Internet or at any website, or any combination thereof, including any injury or damage to participant's or any other person's computer relating to or resulting from participating in this Contest or downloading any materials in this Contest. CAUTION: ANY ATTEMPT TO DELIBERATELY DAMAGE ANY WEBSITE OR UNDERMINE THE LEGITIMATE OPERATION OF THE CONTEST IS A VIOLATION OF CRIMINAL AND CIVIL LAWS AND SHOULD SUCH AN ATTEMPT BE MADE, THE SPONSOR RESERVES THE RIGHT TO SEEK DAMAGES OR OTHER REMEDIES FROM ANY SUCH PERSON(S) RESPONSIBLE FOR THE ATTEMPT TO THE FULLEST EXTENT PERMITTED BY LAW. In the event of a dispute as to the identity or eligibility of a winner based on an email address, the winning entry will be declared made by the "Authorized Account Holder" of the email address submitted at time of entry. "Authorized Account Holder" is defined as the natural person 18 years of age or older who is assigned to an email address by an Internet access provider, online service provider, or other organization (e.g., business, education institution, etc.) that is responsible for assigning email addresses for the domain associated with the submitted email address. Use of automated devices are not valid for entry.

11) LEGAL Information:

All submissions become sole property of Sponsor and will not be acknowledged or returned. By submitting an entry, all entrants grant Sponsor the absolute and unconditional right and authority to copy, edit, publish, promote, broadcast, or otherwise use, in whole or in part, their entries, in perpetuity, in any manner without further permission, notice or compensation. Entries that contain copyrighted material must include a release from the copyright holder. Prizes are nontransferable. No substitutions or cash redemptions, except by Sponsor in the event of prize unavailability. Sponsor reserves the right at its sole discretion to not publish the winning entry for any reason whatsoever.

In the event that there is an insufficient number of entries received that meet the minimum standards determined by the judges, all prizes will not be awarded. Void in Quebec, Puerto Rico, and wherever prohibited or restricted by law. Winners will be required to complete and return an affidavit of eligibility and a liability/publicity release, within 15 days of winning notification, or an alternate winner will be selected. In the event any winner is considered a minor in his/her state of residence, such winner's parent/legal guardian will be required to sign and return all necessary paperwork.

By entering, entrants release the judges and Sponsor, and its parent company, subsidiaries, affiliates, divisions, advertising, production, and promotion agencies from any and all liability for any loss, harm, damages, costs, or expenses, including without limitation property damages, personal injury, and/or death arising out of participation in this contest, the acceptance, possession, use or misuse of any prize, claims based on publicity rights, defamation or invasion of privacy, merchandise delivery, or the violation of any intellectual property rights, including but not limited to copyright infringement and/or trademark infringement.

Sponsor:
Pocket Books,
an imprint of Simon & Schuster, Inc.
1230 Avenue of the Americas,
New York, NY 10020